T0160319

RESET BOOKS

LUNAR ATTRACTIONS

Lunar

Attractions

CLARK BLAISE

BIBLIOASIS

FIRST EDITION

Library and Archives Canada Cataloguing in Publication

Blaise, Clark, 1940–, author
     Lunar attractions / Clark Blaise.

Reprint. Originally published: Garden City, N.Y. :
Doubleday; Toronto : Doubleday Canada, 1979.

Issued in print and electronic formats.
ISBN 978-1-77196-001-4 (pbk.).—ISBN 978-1-77196-002-1 (epub)

     I. Title.

PS8553.L34L8   2014   C813'.54   C2014-904562-X
C2014-904563-8

Readied for the Press by Dan Wells
Cover and text design by Gordon Robertson

Biblioasis acknowledges the ongoing financial support of the Government
of Canada through the Canada Council for the Arts, Canadian Heritage,
the Canada Book Fund; and the Government of Ontario through the
Ontario Arts Council.

PRINTED AND BOUND IN CANADA

MIX
Paper from
responsible sources
FSC® C004071

To the memory of
Murray Stuart Davis

PART 1

He stands at the rear of the rowboat casting toward a green rubbery beach of lily pads thirty feet away. The sun is low: watermelon pink as it hangs behind the cypress. The sky is a pale, scratched green, verging to peach; it is never blue in my memories of Florida. Trees are black and skies are white or purple, when not an unearthly pastel. The lake that day was glossy olive and thick as molten glass. We were anchored over submerged grasses, each stalk spotted with snails and larvae, the whole growth dense with bluegill. My hand had been in the warm brown water so long that the air itself seemed thin and cold. I could imagine myself breathing in that water. Birds could rise from the grass and mosquitoes hum through the water to settle on my hand and bite it. Nothing would surprise me. It seemed impossible that every cast did not produce a fish.

Then the grasses lurched, pushed apart by an urgent underwater current, and in the middle of a bald spot over the sandy floor I saw a tiny alligator, motionless but for the mild twitching of its tail. Like a lizard near a light bulb, it lay glued to the water, snapping at tadpoles with a shudder of its body as they twisted by.

Suddenly the boat shivered.

"Hey, hey, sonny boy!" My father's call was nearly a song. "Look at this!" The tip of the pole was doubled, and the line sliced the water like fine wire. I reached for the net; then I froze. He couldn't see it (he would never see it), and I have never completely rid it from my memory; it is the chord my imagination obsessively plays. Rising behind him nearly as tall and thick as a tree trunk, hung for just an instant the gnarled, stony tail of a full grown alligator. Then the tail impacted the water, smashing its surface with a sonic boom. I was blinded and pushed backward by an airborne wave of water. My father, in the luckiest fall of his life, was knocked forward over the middle seat and on top of me. Had he slipped backward he would have been lost. Like most habitual fishermen I have known, my father could not swim a stroke.

He still held the rod, and the line still cut the water in spasms that practically hummed. He was on his knees, face glistening, shirt plastered to his back. We were sloshing in six inches of water. "What in the Jesus hell?" he muttered. He'd skinned his knees, and the boat was rocking madly. I could smell the layers of tobacco, coffee, and toothpaste on his breath, and I saw too much white in his eyes. Nothing is more terrifying to a child than sensing the fear of his invincible father.

It was up to me to save us. In my own panic I thought the giant alligator and whatever was on the line were somehow related. Maddened mother and threatened cub, like grizzlies. I reached for the small knife he kept for snagged hooks. He was still too shocked and too slow to stop me. We were dead anyway, I thought: the gator must have been just under us. I snapped the fishline with a touch of the blade. My father was over me in an instant shouting, "Good God, *no, no!*" and beating the metal handle of the now-limp rod against the side of the boat. He beat the rod until he snapped it, and then he threw the stump, reel and all, over the lily pads toward the shore. In his rage he nearly fell overboard. His face was the darkest red I'd ever seen. His anger, for the moment, was directed at the water and sky, but he had seen me cut the line.

I held the lantern as he rowed back to the boat-landing deep in the cove near our cottage. A few stars were out by then, the full moon blazed like a spotlight, and I could feel shadows under us as we rowed home in our normal silence. The gator had been after my hand. That's what had caused the sudden parting of the grass. And the grass itself now seemed carnivorous, the brown spots little mouths full of piranha teeth. My father refused to believe what I had seen. Fishing was his purest love. For him, boat-sized alligators in the water he had to trust would mean the end of everything. He believed instead in something larger: a landlocked tarpon, a marlin; his imagination was as wild as mine. He'd buy new equipment, stronger line, and he'd be out again next Sunday. Only, he'd be there alone. He'd never take me with him again.

The shadow and the silence never lifted. A picture of my mind, age five.

We were Yankees. At least my parents were (I'd been born in Florida), but "Yankee" didn't cover it all. They were aliens. I didn't know for years where they had come from or why they had left. The accent that people detected in my parents I regarded as proof of superiority. "Don't nobody there speak English?" the telephone operators used to demand whenever my mother tried to call; I did the official calling in our house. My father used a different language when he added up figures, and I hated those incomprehensible syllables not because they embarrassed me, but because they injected some new barrier between us. I listened to enough Northern radio to know it was Floridians who had the accents—they who'd never seen snow or heard proper English firsthand. Of course, neither had I.

My parents were different in other ways. They were much older than other parents. I often thought they were too old to be parents at all. When my mother registered me for first grade, the teacher assessed her and asked if perhaps "*Missus* Greenwood"—the mother, not the grandmother, she meant, was out working. My mother was in her middle forties. In rural Florida back in the 1940s, a lot of first-grade mothers were little more than teenagers; missing some teeth, perhaps, chubby and stringy-haired, but as unwrinkled as their children. Haggard grandmothers were still giving birth with the result that the school was a nest of siblings and even more complicated relations. ("He your brother, Billy?" "No, ma'm. He's my uncle." *That*, said my mother, is your poor white trash.) I was an only child, a freak. Fathers of other first-graders were coarse and sunburned pop-eyed boys with bulging Adam's apples, florid with tattoos. Most had served in the recent war. My father was already greying; he'd narrowly missed serving in the first one. I was proud of my parents for being different if only because it meant I had to be different, too.

The school was a three-room wooden structure at the end of a long bus ride. The schoolyard was shiny with town-kids' bikes, and the steps were clotted with the discarded shoes of country kids who rode the bus. Except for mine. Under my mother's guidance, her reading to me, my drawing and the crayons she kept me in, I'd spent my first five years rehearsing for school. *Finally* I thought, *I'm getting my ups. My* desk. *My* books and pencils. The smell of new crayons and of just-sharpened pencils was the cleanest, most expectant smell I knew.

By some fluke, I am only partially right-handed. The smaller and—I like to think—finer things, like writing, brushing, eating, playing ping-pong and dealing cards, I do left-handed. In grosser activities like batting and throwing, I am right-handed. The inconsistencies are finely drawn. I write on paper left-handed and on blackboards right-handed. I draw with the left hand but paint with the right. What it means I'll never know. Perhaps that the awareness of such confusion is enough. Consistent people had no such awareness, no such pain from a hundred small confusions. "You'll never be able to play the violin," my mother said, and the judgment cut me, though neither of us had intended that I try. Golf and tennis, equally remote, were also out. For fifteen years I would have given serious thought to any good offer for my pushy right arm (never the left) that kept me from being a "southpaw." I would have given anything to be one, and even forced myself, over the years, into a passable short-range imitation. Eventually I realized that impurity was my sign.

That first hot September morning, we were each handed half a sheet of oatmeal-coloured paper, divided by four thick, crudely inked blue lines, and were told to copy the A's and B's the teacher had written on the blackboard. I turned the paper so I could write left-handed and turned myself so that I could write without a hook. The teacher, a heavy bespectacled woman in a shiny black dress, made her way down the aisles offering small words of encouragement, showing the boys how to hold their pencils and tapping their legs with a metal ruler until they tucked their feet under their desks. I had already filled two rows and was well ahead of my seatmate, whose pencil kept wobbling and falling from his fingers.

The boys didn't seem to mind the raps of the ruler; they were used to much worse. Parents often beat their children in public or in their front yards. You would see them, the child with his shirt off, holding on to a dining-room chair while one of those hairy tattooed young men lit into him, like a pitcher with a sneaky windup, exploding the strap instead of a fastball. My mother would turn me away, then hide her own eyes. She would also close her eyes at fight scenes in movies and leave the theatre altogether whenever horses were involved. She was a vegetarian and had a framed letter from George Bernard Shaw on the bedroom wall. All this made me a shy, sensitive, arrogant little boy. The teacher was over me now, a stout woman in a black satin dress, reeking of sweat and powder, coffee and tobacco. Florida heat, my mother said, drove everything to the surface. Without looking at my work, she flicked me on the elbow with the ruler. I tried to ignore it, but she persisted. They weren't gentle taps; they were sharp little whacks delivered by a disciplined wrist. I'd never been struck, nor even rebuked, by anyone but my father. But here on the first morning of school, I'd somehow become a problem, a case. And I didn't know *why*. The whole class had stopped writing in order to watch. "Don't tell me you don't know why I'm standing here. I can wait a whole lot longer than you can." She brought the metal ruler down across my knuckles, and the pencil leaped from my hand as my fingers sprung open.

I looked at her face for the first time, and it was the sudden revelation of her not-quite-human rage that made me burst into loud bawling. She'd taken her glasses off, and she was one of those piggish women whom glasses alone transformed into a kind of refinement. Without them she looked like an axe-murderess. She hooked her foot under mine, which was a few inches out in the aisle, and kicked it back under the desk. Then she pinched the flesh of my left arm and lifted it like something speared, showing that it, too, was out over the aisle. My throat was swollen and sealed, more from shock than tears. I wanted to reach out and strike something; ball up the oily banana-filled lunch sack of Lester Pilkington, my seat-mate, and with my good right arm heave it against the blackboard. I wanted to shout back: *I'm left-handed, how can I write without sticking my elbow out? How can I do that without pushing my leg out for balance?* But my voice was employed for crying.

"Pick your pencil up, David."

As I bent she administered (as I sensed she would) the final swat. The class was chanting for more and that was when she turned and brought the ruler down, flat and hard and with a rifle-loudness, on the nearest desktop. The silence was theatrical. Even I stopped crying.

"Left-handedness is not permitted," she announced. "It is spoiled and spiteful behaviour. And it is feel-thy. You-all will drag your hands across the page and everything'll get smeared." She demonstrated on the blackboard, smudging everything her left hand lumbered over. Watching her with the chalk in her left hand, the fat of her left arm jiggling, I *did* feel it was awkward and obscene. "See?" she said, showing us the chalk dust on her hand. "You-all will wallow like pigs in your writing. Now if we wrote up and down like the Chinese, or right to left like the Jews (the class snickered at such presumptions), no one would care. But we don't. In America we don't. Anybody can learn to write the right way if he tries. Four of you-all tried it with your left hands today, and three of you-all have done changed. Only one thinks he's too good, and I've warmed his hand and his britches and now he's fixin' to start again. Let's see if he commences with his left hand."

I looked down at my rows of perfect A's and B's. I tried to hold the pencil in my right hand but—like Lester Pilkington's—it oozed from my fingers. My right hand didn't respond. I squeezed tighter and pressed harder till the pencil point snapped and the paper shredded. I was sweating and my paper was smeared. I was in a panic. But still I believed in a higher purpose: the teacher had seen I was better than Lester. She was doing this to even it out. I was an earnest believer in fair play.

"All right, that's enough," she said, not unkindly. "Take new paper and try again. Write this sentence." She went to the board, and I followed to get the paper from her desk.

I AM LEFT-HANDED, she wrote on the board. "Do you know what this means?" I was able to guess most of it; the words seemed to have a voice all their own. I liked the look of LEFT in capitals: all straight, clean lines.

"The rest of you-all write this."

WE ARE RIGHT-HANDED. She told them what it meant, and they cheered.

"David, there is something else I want you to write." By now I was attacking my unique description with a virtuoso neatness. I had shrunk the letters to ant-sized squiggles, hardly thicker than the blue lines themselves.

"This," she said, "put this under your first line. David only."

PLEASE FORGIVE ME.

I am not an injustice-collector. I bear few grudges and none that I know of from the years I'm recalling. The teacher was right to single me out. I knew I was different; the rules for me had to be harder. It's that I'm beginning to realize how ready I was even then for all that followed. The simplest tasks were turned to torture. Under my scrutiny, obvious unities would decompose, and I would be forced to reconstruct them from my own limitless ego. I saw those first cheap scraps of war-surplus paper as deserts, the crude blue lines as canals. I tried to get interested in the textbooks and newspapers but got stuck on the pictures. Looked at closely, they were only dots. Seeing only dots, I refused to assume anything larger. I counted all the flesh-coloured points on the pink cheeks of "Tom," our reader's six-year-old hero, as he romped with his yellow-haired twin sister, "Peg." Tom was composed of three hundred dots of flesh on his face, legs, and arms, and several hundred more to denote his clothing. They romped through dots of grass. When I announced this instead of reading my paragraph, the teacher stood me in the corner.

But you see, I could well have said, *if they are only dots, who's to say that we're not, too*? Why, I wanted to know but never asked, did no one else see these things? Or—seeing them— not speak up? What was the secret of not caring? Right-handedness? Things that I noticed and considered important, from alligators to coloured dots, were either inspired, obvious, or crazy. At various times, I have been all three.

(Many years later, my friends in high school began "The First Church of Christ Solipsist," and I learned for the first time—this being far away from central Florida—that there'd always been a few of us around; we who thought we knew everything and missed nothing, for we alone had created it. Most of life was a distressing figment of our imagination. But those high-school friends had been encouraged and channelled early into special classes. In my first five years of Florida schools, I learned like a magician to be faster and slyer, and to guard my perceptions with my life. Everything I saw and imagined I saw, I stuffed back into the folds of my brain. I had a private world. Stars burned and buzzards wheeled under the ceiling of my scalp. Anonymous faces pressed against the lobes of my brain. I was like the fabled salt-machine that fell overboard and kept churning, eventually filling the seas. So was I one of the densely populated, generating a world.

Please forgive me.

In those days, my parents were to me not people, not personalities, but contending principles in the universe. There was something right about my father in Florida, but not my mother. He'd sought America and the sun. He was dark and outgoing, a salesman; he had a talent for blending in. But my mother was a tall, pale woman, marked by Europe, education, and her strong belief in order, justice, and simple decency— qualities she found missing in America, especially the South. She was a woman of many gifts who had survived by suppressing most of them. When my father was "on the road" selling furniture, she found herself with no society and no library, and an uncordial child who preferred the solitude of the atlas, the radio, and a Coke.

And so she yielded to her obsession for order and cleanliness, in Florida a futile and full-time occupation. Because nature had so ill-equipped her for Southern life—even fifteen minutes hanging the wash could give her a burn—she would rise at six to have it out by seven, the last hour of tolerable sun and temperature. And there it would flap dry as chalk after the first half hour until the sun went down and it was again safe, for her to retrieve it. She was a light sleeper. The shudder of the refrigerator, sirens on the distant highway, the roar of the wind in the oak and cypress, would waken her from sleep. My churning in a bed and grinding of my teeth would keep her awake.

Warm climates are noisy climates; they create oblivious characters who can sleep anywhere in any weather. My father never woke up on his own in his life. In my childhood I thought of sleeping without an alarm clock as a kind of selfishness, making someone else sacrifice her own sleep to cajole and finally muscle him from bed. Cosmic injustice alone explained his invulnerabilities, He could sleep through anything, eat everything, and char comfortably in the sun. He'd never known insomnia, bullies, allergies, or fat; he was even immune to insect bites. One mosquito in a room could suck me dry in a night, and every bite was a week in disappearing. Yet I have watched my father (let me say it now: I have watched my father like no son has ever watched his father) sit patiently in a boat while mosquitoes formed grey bouffants over our beads, driving me to mad gestures of handclapping, and not one would settle on any part of him. "Shh," he would say, "the fish."

(In those years I felt myself on special terms with "Mac," the ninety-eight-pound weakling of the Charles Atlas ads. My father looked like Charles Atlas, and I was fast closing in on ninety-eight pounds, though I was only nine years old. And "Grace," Mac's fickle girlfriend who deserts him for the muscular, unnamed sand-kicker, seemed an all-too-believable sort of girl. The three of them were forces of nature, stars of our longest-running morality play, directed by the unaging god in the leopard-skin trunks. Their actions conformed precisely to my vision of the world, except for the final retribution. My father was a sand-kicker. My mother, it seemed to me, would have been happier with a skinny Mac. For me there would be no day of reckoning, no "Wham! Take *that*, you bully!" The workings of grace in the physical realm were unjust. It was a realm I'd been excluded from; one to be distrusted, envied, and avoided.

I would say now that cosmic *justice* alone explained my father's invulnerabilities. Impressive as they were, they were never as strong as mine. I would say now that my father was not a natural sand-kicker. He was a built-up Mac who'd gone through all the book-kicking tantrums of self-hatred and through the furies of self-improvement long before my mother found him. And I would say that I was far from excluded from the physical. My envy and my clumsiness and my madness brought me closer, closer in passion, closer to flesh than my father ever dreamed of.)

Even as a child I could explain my failings, my "Mac"-ness. I'd always craved facts. I'd always respected the minute variations in every classification. Fish guides, bird guides, atlases, insect books, and star charts all fascinated me in my first ten years. I was helpless before those lists. I stayed in bed one entire summer attempting to memorize them all. And they helped me understand. *Birds.* No morality in nature accounted for catbirds or that putrid meat was sweet to vultures or that some birds killed while others sang and sipped nectar. I'd once seen a goose in the town park pluck a little puppy from a child and hold it under water till it drowned. Painted buntings that we fed were related to the buzzards we'd seen on the highway, tearing the flesh of spattered dogs. But where was my place in the human classification? I was neither bunting nor fish hawk (if anything, my emblem was the squat, bewhiskered whippoorwill whose croupy, unbirdlike cries punctured the night). Even a class of Florida schoolboys had its eaglets, owlets, sparrows, and starlings. And just as a hawk is disposed to bully, so was I congenitally oppressed. I had feathers, and I could fly, but I wasn't one of them.

Like catbirds and mockingbirds, and other subverters of the natural order, my mother and I came to the battle strangely equipped. We tolerated things very well. Though our bodies welted and reddened, and both of us sneezed on dry days from dust and on moist days from mildew, we somehow adapted. Most irritations we could turn to advantage. Never having trusted our bodies, we ignored small discomforts.

But on rainy Sundays that kept my father inside, he could only sit at the kitchen table drumming his fingers. On cold winter days, he'd come down with coughs and chills. If my mother was out shopping for a few hours, he would come to me with a pack of cards and beg for a few hands of gin rummy. He could not bear idleness or being alone; he never cared for newspapers or radio unless someone, even silently, kept him company. Nights were a horror to him (they were my element, young whippoorwill that I was); if he failed to fall asleep almost immediately (he was accustomed, as a travelling salesman, to yielding only when the car was veering too often into the opposite lane), all the lights would go on, he'd take medicine and ask for food or a drink. Depending on the hour, he'd want to call his friends, or he'd go out to the car and take out his order books and swatches of material, ask for the checkbook and go through the balances. I would sit with him far into the night listening to those incomprehensible syllables as he added: *unh, duh, twa, cat, sank, sis, set, wit, nuff, dis*—it sounded like pig Latin spoken by the Bowery Boys—*cat doors, cans, says*; how I hated him when he could retreat from me like that, when he seemed without even knowing it to have climbed to an impregnable niche that for all my searching I couldn't find.

The gift my mother possessed, the trick of her survival, was the gift of prophecy. It had come on her suddenly in her twenties when she'd left home and had been working in those interminable German cities of her youth: Leipzig, Dresden, Weimar, Prague. Those names, unlike my father's foreign words, were easy on my tongue and all of them fed my visions of stone facades, cobble stones, and trolleycars. She was a natural storyteller. She understood the play of precise unexpected detail upon a larger mystery. She understood surprise and suspense, and the role of character. The vivid bit-players in her stories at first seemed to overwhelm the pale figure of herself. Yet by the end the point of the story would always be hers—and hers alone—to have told. She had begun by reading tea leaves at a party in Dresden simply because she was from England and thought to have an intimacy with the spirits of tea. And the first time out the leaves had suggested to her something very simple and she said quite innocently, "You're thinking of your dog." But the shape behind the dog suggested a man's hat and she added, "No, not just your dog. A *man's* dog. And the man wears a bowler hat. Could he be an Englishman?" And to my mother's surprise the girl surrendered a piece of paper on which she'd jotted as a test, *Mann und Hund*. She was thinking of her father's dog, she said, not an Englishman. But the funny (and ultimately frightening) thing was that the girl ran away and married an Englishman a few weeks later. The Englishman had yet to be. She tried again, "seeing" purses, skis, and keyrings in the leaves ("it was never what I *saw*, really," she told me, "it was what I heard"). And within weeks she had a reputation. She concentrated on love-lives and businesses— the simple things that people kept secret. She was seeing the future more and more plainly and saying "you will" instead of "you are." She was getting voices on the street from people she passed. She wanted to stop them and say, "You're making a mistake. *Don't go.*" Soon, she felt, she would do it, and then she'd be crazy. She was going mad with pressure from other people's lives.

"*And then, and then. . .*" I would press, because of all the gifts, clairvoyance seemed to me the most regal. She'd gone far beyond my talent for seeing dots. She too was densely populated but the opposite of me. She had not created these people—they were real and she was frail. She might be crushed, but she would never explode. Such power to me would have been irresistible; how I would have used it!

Instead, she grew frightened of the voices. Even friends were now avoiding her. Whatever the power was, it improved with exercise. It was like a catbird's egg; something alien in her brain. She'd welcomed it and fed it, but it knew no gratitude. It consumed everything. She could feel a strangeness entering her face. Her eyes seemed larger and darker-ringed, her voice lowered, she bought strange bracelets and found herself more frequently among Jews and gypsies. She became vegetarian. And so she stopped the tea-readings, laughed off her successes and moved back to London, then on to Canada a few years later. She never read another cup. The voice deserted her and she did not regret having sent it away. It was as though for a month or two she'd been lifted from her sparrow's nest and given hawklike talons and the equipment to soar. Then she'd renounced the bid of some extraordinary self—perhaps an alien self—to take her over.

Misguided, I thought.

Not that she ever convinced me the power had totally vanished. She could tolerate her loneliness too well for that. I suspect that like me she was never alone. She was always hearing the voices, always playing back the film in which she had starred, however reluctantly. She'd been frightened by its appearance and she still feared its return, like a bout of madness or a fatal disease once arrested. But she also worshipped it; for in one month the voice had destroyed her faith in reason, in free will, even in chance. It was a god's voice. It had allowed her a certain surrender to fate and had stamped her with a deep cynicism that only her good manners kept disguised. Fatalism was her accommodation. It might have been the only thing impersonal enough to explain the peculiar marriage she had made and the bizarre places it had taken her.

A boy with a radio, magazines, and a retentive mind could learn quite a bit about the world, even as it filtered into central Florida between 1946 and 1950. Radio brought daily baseball from random northern stadiums, Arthur Godfrey and Don McNeill, Louella Parsons and Hedda Hopper, Toots Shor and "Grand Central Station," along with all the evening comedies, mysteries, and melodramas that have now become part of a collective nostalgia. Those daytime shows from exotic places—even Chicago and Miami Beach were exotic for me—were like invitations to adult parties. *"Here at the* *Stork Club tonight I'm sitting at the table of Humphrey Bogart and his lovely wife, Lauren Bacall. She's known as Betty to her many friends, by the way, so if I say 'Betty,' don't start accusing Bogie of carrying on. . . ."* And I would lie on my cot repeating "Betty. Betty Bacall. Betty Bogart. Remember that." I could hear the tinkle of their ice, last night at the Stork Club; I raised my Coke to Betty and Bogie, to the familiar metallic flip and flinty whirr of a cigarette lighter, and I joined the smooth, empty patter of celebrities being famous. Pearl divers in Yap were less exotic to me than a table at the Stork Club. "Toots Shor": the very name sent a chill through me when I was eight or nine. It meant that somewhere people never slept. Somewhere—call it Manhattan—people were happy, powerful, and recognized. My skull had more levels than the Empire State Building. It was high enough to house Toots Shor, Vic Raschi, Betty Bogart, and Hedda and Louella, all in the box-seat section of my brain. From the most anonymous corner of forties America, I craved for celebrity. Had I been born on the Lower East Side eighty years ago, I would have driven myself to perform, *to be somebody.* But in Florida, surrounded by an almost unevolved sullenness of nature, my craving for recognition was crossed with a monumental timidity. The things that I was not yet ready for, like Manhattan, were safely separated from the Lester Pilkingtons, mosquitoes, and the Florida sand-kickers that made my life miserable. The antipodes of my fantasies were set very early, and they lived for years in unreconcilable opposition. It took thirty years to plot new points between Florida buzzards and Manhattan storks, and to force some sort of continuity between them.

I would leave our cottage on dry summer afternoons in my eighth year and do some digging. ("Cottage" is the only word we have, though its seasonal connotations are all wrong. Picture a cinderblock rectangle with a flat, leaking roof, a screened-in porch, pump fixtures, and an added-on, quasi-indoor "flush commode." The shower was outside, intended only as a foot-washer. My father had added three walls of glass bricks—those emblems of forties elegance—to make it a proper stall.) The land around the cottage was mainly sand, under a layer of coppery pine needles. Water could be struck anywhere about eight inches underground. Our cottage was on fairly secure "higher" ground, and raised on additional cinderblocks, but we were surrounded by large lakes that rose during the rainy season to come nearly within our sight. The forest behind us would stand a foot deep in flood water and I have walked in those woods a week later, holding my nose from the smell of rotting fish, as bluejays pecked out the eyes of bleached, ant-torn bream. One reason I used to hate Arthur Godfrey's broadcasts from Miami Beach was his expropriation of the term "Florida"—*me!*—for his fifty-foot stretch of Dade County air conditioning. I would scream into the radio, "Miami Beach isn't Florida! Quit saying it is, you liar!" We could have been living in Topeka for all the ocean meant to us.

I would take a small shovel and go down to the lakefront where the sand turned to muck and the air smelled of earthworms. There were a few buildings nearby: a boat-rental office, some Yankees' deserted fishing camps with boarded windows and punched-in screen doors, and some shacks of the white migrant families who made the seasonal moss-picking and pecan-picking circuits of Florida and south Georgia. The lake was low after weeks of summer drought. The water was warm and soupy with a permanent green scum on top, frothy collars along the shore, and gaseous belches wobbling from the bottom.

I would dig in the purple-black muck, turning over spadefuls of that sour, infertile paste. It looked like the richest compost in the world: it was black and moist enough to quicken the pulse of any Yankee gardener. But this is Florida, Arthur Godfrey (I might have said then): our powdery grey sand may grow watermelon, celery, and lemons as big as grapefruit, but this stuff, rich as it looks, smells like an outhouse and kills everything it touches. It had, therefore, a fascination for me. My passion for digging was like all my passions, born in the nightsoil of my imagination, in a dream of escaping this world.

My part of Florida (now known as Disney World) was a crust of sand over a spring-fed ocean. North of us was Silver Springs, where glass-bottomed boats revealed it all: caves from which the water issued, limestone basins that held the sea in place, giant turtles and catfish that wallowed in its lower layers, bream and minnows that darted about the surface. I sometimes thought of us, at night, floating on county-sized hummocks, like the islands of ice that bumped along the Arctic coasts. Stamp your feet too hard and you might fall through.

I would go home just as the sun was setting. My arms would be black below the elbow, my body grey and crusty wherever I had swatted mosquitoes or brushed my hair back. I would leave a dozen holes half-filled with brown, foamy water. In the morning when I returned, the holes would have vanished like sand castles before a tide. This, in my round-about logic, I took as proof that there was intelligent life down there, setting up barriers to keep me out. I wanted to tear away the soil, to have my private peephole on Silver Springs. I wanted to live down there.

I used to like combing out my father's hair. I would stand behind him as he read the paper or dozed in a reclining chair, and I would lose myself in the job, innocent of the strange act I was performing. It was only digging, escaping. I stood close enough to smell the Vitalis and to see the fine white hairs running counter to the darker ones on top, like grasses under water. He was not growing bald from the top; rather, his hair had retreated in two wide bays as his parting and fore-head spread. Like other dark men who wore their hair slicked down—Latin generals and movie villains—there was something violent and glamorous in the way he was aging. Mild men shed hair from the crown and ended up with monkish fringes. I knew I would be like that.

He would read the paper as I combed. I was obsessed by hair-partings, even by burning one into my scalp like a yard-marker on a football field. I could imagine defining something so perfectly *now*, as a child, that I would never have to worry about it for the rest of my life. My father had chosen the precise degree on his skull's reluctant circumference for just the perfect parting. Not like the vain, balding men who parted their hair just above their ear-rims. His part was per-fectly centred; you could have counted the hairs on either side of the part and they would have come out the same.

I'd seen pictures of him at thirty, long before he'd met my mother, when his hair was dark and parted with forelocks falling, Rudy Vallee style. His hair at forty-seven might still have been wavy, but none revealed themselves; he'd bullied his hair with Vitalis for too many years. I would take his rat-tail comb and smooth the hair down over his forehead as he read, and suddenly his hair would be almost white, like the underbelly fur of some dark animal. There were thousands more white hairs than brown ones, mashed under that crust of Vitalis. They could afford to be patient, I thought; they knew they would win in the end. On Sundays when he didn't shave, a frost of dead white covered his face. His chest hairs were white, only the nipples brown and nubby. His neck and back were hairless, cool and smooth as a baby's. He used talcum, making the bathroom floor treacherous after each of his showers.

He'd been an athlete. He had a boxer's neck, seventeen-and-a-half inches. "That's so I can take it on the chin," he told me once, meaning "life" as much as fists, then he'd slipped his wide, mashed hands around my scrawny neck, no wider than a wrist, and said, "Turkey-neck." He'd rapped my chest. "And pigeon-chested." Pigeon-toed, too, if he'd noticed, and I waddled like a penguin. He'd boxed in Golden Gloves, been a winner in two countries under different names, in all the sub-lightweight divisions. He'd turned professional, but quit, he said, after getting knocked out for the first time. He had no scars. "*Visible* scars," my mother would say. She despised boxing; she left the house on nights of Joe Louis fights when my father and his salesmen-friends—and me, unobtrusively— would sit around the radio under a yellow porch light as Don Dunphy reported from ringside at Madison Square Garden, and beers were downed in central Florida.

So he had a fighter's neck, a barrel chest, and long arms; short legs were his only defect. He had two curious growths: warts at the tip of each nipple. Nipples bothered me in the first place (we had no business with nipples at all), and I wondered if the size of nipples had anything to do with one's masculinity. If so, I was in trouble. Stripped, most boys showed concave little welts, hardly more than vaccination marks, while mine were pink and puffy, borne on the tip of a roll of fat. I used to pinch and fan them with spit to make them shrink and pucker whenever I swam or was forced to strip for gym. Stripping was a special horror; boys in central Florida gathered for the sight of the only circumcision they—or I—had ever seen.

I used to worry about my father's little warts—like drippings on a sand castle. Did they hurt him? Did they rub? Once I even touched them, and he gave my wrist a vicious wrench. To continue: a slablike mole on the side of his navel, like a hardened excrescence. I assumed for many years that nature meant for something to come out of, or go into, so prominent a depression, and from the smells of the moist, rancid cotton fluff I extracted from my own, I knew it would be a foul bit of knowledge once it came. Of other parts between his navel and kneecap, I have no knowledge. We were a circumspect family, very formal with each other. I remember only one occasion of quasi-nudity. I was climbing the stairs in a duplex we inhabited—I was in junior high, then. The bathroom stood at the top of the stairs. My naked father was standing, propped against the lavatory, shaving before the mirror, buttocks to the open door. And between his legs, halfway to the knees, something incredibly thick and dark was hanging. Before he could hear me, I quickly turned and went back downstairs and slammed the front door. But I investigated a few minutes later; the mirror was still steamed, the floor slick with talcum, and a bath towel was dangling like a bird's wrung neck over the lip of the basin. It probably was a towel I'd seen, slumped between his legs.

His legs held the greatest fascination. Legs go first in salesmen as well as athletes. Years of roadwork, followed by more years of standing around in stores that would fire you if they caught you leaning, let alone sitting down. Veins pop to the surface and stay. The veins of his calves and even his shins were pencil-thick and congested, aimless as rivers that had lost their mission. There were permanent raw creases (like my mother's red glasses-pit on the sides of her nose) where for years his black silk stockings had cut across his shins. Where he bought black silk in Florida I'll never know, but he owned nothing else; each pair of the same unforgiving stretch and tightness, kept unwrinkled by a garter belt that clamped over rubber nodules at the bottom of his boxer shorts. And what I'd thought of as the permanent stain of black silk wasn't a stain at all. It was a fine weave of minuscule purple veins, finer than a net, fine as linen mesh, advancing up his legs from farther down. He had huge white kneecaps, and bulging ankles, and the ankles made me turn away. The ankles were the focus of all his troubles. They were permanently swollen, a jumble of veins like a ball of purple worms.

I haven't spoken of the face. I cannot remember the face as it was then though I would know his smell, his shoulders, ears, nipples, and ankles anywhere. I can draw a map of the veins on his hands but the face surprised me freshly every time. His eyes were green, nose Roman, face as round as a ball. The pattern of deep pores on his nose and forehead was like something plucked. Yet his skin was clear, like pigskin or fine leather, like the whorls and knots that nature puts in wood. He had gifted teeth: straight, white, never corrected, never a cavity. They were precisely even, like a set of baby teeth that had never fallen out. I had my mother's teeth, breaking through in many sizes, angles, and colours.

I don't mean to insult my mother by not recalling more, but she was not quite so remarkable. At least, not as many people thought so. I think of her as a waterbird growing progressively white; I think of her having long, narrow feet and long legs that flared at the thigh. I think of a long, thin neck that with age and sun grew loose and darkened, and of a forceful, dominant nose and grey eyes that looked permanently penetrating, or startled. I think of a woman of enormous patience, whose simplest gestures were binding and decisive.

I was ashamed of my body even as a very young child. I was a proud child, even arrogant about things I knew, but I have spent more hours in the deepest shame than I have even in modest satisfaction. I have a small frame—tiny hands, small feet, a wrist half my mother's size—but fat has always been attracted to me. Between the fat and my bones I imagined an indistinct network of limp muscles and tiny blood vessels, effective enough for registering pain and a pulse, but little more. I never had the satisfaction of feeling a ball of muscle in my biceps or what was called an "abdominal wall," or tracing wide blood vessels up my arms or feeling resistance from anything clenched. I had headaches from the first grade, suffered my first hay-fever attack when I was five and first asthma when I was seven. My feet were more spongy than supportive. If I walked more than a few blocks a day, I'd have to tape metal arch supports around my feet in order to sleep that night. It seemed that Nature herself had studied the strengths of my parents and decided that the race, unless pinched back, was genetically poised for a major mutation. And so, the comic misprint of my genetic code. I'd been given enough handicaps, from cowlicks to flat feet, to turn me envious (and observant) of everyone else's beauty. I found beauty where no one before except artists and fetishists had looked. I admired hair-partings, high arches, showy veins on the arms and backs of hands. I used to admire the rippling of my father's forearm muscles—like piano wires responding to the idlest touch—as he lightly tapped a single finger. It seemed unfair that he had so much help from his body—a bicep that loomed like a softball in merely lifting a cigarette. While I envied them all, the only children I ever trusted turned out to be, inevitably, left-handed or hay-fever sufferers. We would meet each other in the height of hay-fever season (the first week of school when everyone was trying to make a good impression), carrying our balled-up hankies, rubbing our watery eyes, sneezing in sets of eight or ten, then collapsing on desktops or against cool lockers. "Crybaby, crybaby," the unthinking, the right-handed ones would tease. I've never met a hay-fever sufferer I didn't like. It makes for a finer person.

Once my father came home from "the road" with a present for me—a grey, string-tied box with "Wilson" on the outside. Inside were boxing gloves. "Oh no, you don't," my mother cried, lifting them like something dead and rotting, then balling up the tissue paper and stuffing the gloves back into the box. "You will never do this to my son."

"Why don't you ask the boy for once?" They were glaring at each other as though I, the "son" and "boy" of their dialogue, were a thousand miles away. It gave me time to take the gloves out again and to slip them on. Cool inside, they bolstered my wrist like a shaft of steel.

"See?"

"David—give them back this instant!"

I held my hands out, laces up. I meant for them to decide, for my father to lace them or my mother to tear them off. I hoped I would wear them. It would be something different, and in my way I've always been a sensation seeker. Both of them grabbed but my father got there first and simply flicked away my mother's fingers. By his standards it was not a violent act. Her fingers had been shooed away like flies, but she held them as though they'd been burned. From the look on her face I knew something important had happened. One of those moments full of adult significance that happen to be played out on the physical scale of childhood. My mother retreated to the doorway, holding the tips of one hand up near her cheek. She stared without sparing a blink.

My father was on his knees and he remained on his knees a foot and a half away from me, his face as round and grinning as a harvest moon. "Take off your shirt," he instructed, and he peeled his off as well. We were nearly the same height, I at seven, he on his knees; I soft and white with a roll of fat across my chest and stomach, he with white chest hair thick enough to comb and the dark nubby nipples of a man in his prime. "Hit me," he ordered, laying a wide yellow fingernail on his chin. "Hard as you can, on the button. Come on."

I had to close my eyes, not from squeamishness, but for the windup to my blow. It was to be an uppercut straight from every Western I'd ever seen, the kind that sends a villain over the bar into a stack of whisky bottles. But when I opened my eyes I was on the floor and my armpit pained from the force of nonconnection.

"Never like that. Straight, always straight."

My mother had come a step closer.

"Again. Line me up, straighten your arm, aim for my nose."

"Your nose? Really?" And suddenly I realized I'd always wanted to punch my father on the nose.

I lined it up, gauging the distance, and let my right hand—the jabbing hand—fly. This time I was watching; he simply leaned back, far enough for my glove to miss, and this time he gave me a loud, gentle slap on my sweating side.

"Again." And this time I didn't aim; I let fly from an angle and he dodged his head the other way, getting in a slap on my ear as I lunged past. He was grinning in a way that showed no teeth. It was not a grin. A grimace, perhaps, and mocking. He was treating me (I realized with horror) as an adversary. He was even showing a certain respect. And I was reminded suddenly of those schoolyard challenges I always fell for ("Hey, Greenwood—let's see who can hit the lightest—you go first!" Okay. "Hey! That's pretty good—I hardly felt it. Now my turn." And I would watch the eyes-closed, tongue-out windup, the clever imitation of a roundhouse punch, and I would wonder how he could stop himself in time to deliver a blow even lighter than my tap. And of course he never intended to. I'd be down on the ground with my breath gone, and he'd be jumping around me, holding his knuckles. "Guess you win, Greenwood. You sure can hit light. Congrat-ulations!") What had I gotten into with my father? Was I to be given five of my most punishing lunges in order to stand still for five—or even one—of his? Was that what my mother had tried to save me from?

My father was forbidden by law—he'd told me once—to ever use his fists. They were lethal weapons. I lunged again, and then swung with the left and right simultaneously—he leaned, ducked, and swerved so quickly that a link of hair fell forward over one eye. At least I'd done that. Jarring his hair loose was respectable damage. "Knocked your hair down, Daddy!" I shouted, "T.K.O.!" But he butted my front teeth with the heel of his hand.

"Keep your mouth shut when you're boxing. It's a good way to get hurt." But I was hurt. I was flaying and my arms were numb with frustration and the pent-up screams of rage and humiliation. His face was still as round as the moon, but for all the leather I could lay on it, just as far away. I couldn't hear anything outside of the roaring in my ears, the slaps and nudges of his open hand. I was getting closer to him all the time, if only my arms and breath held out.

Then came my mother's piercing scream—"*Staap!*"—and I saw her body coming, skirts out like blankets, as she threw herself on top of me. "This is slaughter—I won't allow it. *Slaughter, slaughter!*" she cried, and each time she shouted *slaughter*, her leg flicked out at my father's face. He fell backward and she kicked again; she had one arm around my shoulders, pulling me tight against her as she kicked. I wanted to crawl under her dress and disappear, but my boxing gloves betrayed me; they were as wide and heavy as the room itself. Nowhere to crawl with gloves like that. My mother quit kicking, and then I heard and felt my father's hand fall once across her cheek. I tore at the knots on my gloves with my teeth, but my lips were burning and my teeth were sore. I couldn't unburden myself of the things that had brought my parents to blows.

In the end, my mother won. I had won as well—that was the talent for survival we both possessed. My father left the cottage by slamming the wooden door and forcing the screen door off its hinges, and left the yard in a muffled whirr-r of sand that pattered through the screens and sifted onto the sofa. "Look at you!" (She was sobbing now, worse than I had been.) "Just look at what he did!" She wet her handkerchief and wiped my lips and cheeks. My body was slick with sweat, and she pointed out the red patches that would be bruises by morning. Her handkerchief was a dull pink. "You're not a fighter, precious," she kept saying, holding me and swabbing my body with rubbing alcohol. Her cheek was blooming, purple at the edges. "It is immoral. Immoral. But most of all," she said, laying her hands on my shoulders and getting down on her knees to comb my hair, "most of all it is immoral to turn a higher person into something lower."

"I hit him first," I said.

She brushed this aside. I wanted to end it before she came out with something I didn't want to hear. I didn't want to hear anything critical. "You had no choice, darling. He started it, the fighting. Always him. You are not the type, and he can't understand that." She said all this in a flat voice that reminded me of her prophecies, a voice literally from a different world. "David"—and she gave me a shake that rattled me in all the places that would be bruises by morning—"the boys who start fights with you—they are like Goliath. But you are David. They'll grow up fighting. They'll kill themselves fighting. Let them! Pity them! They'll never understand. They'll go to their graves not understanding." She was talking of my father, I knew.

Later she said, "You'll never be like him. He tries to love you, in his way. But don't let him drag you down to his level. *This—these gloves*—this is all he knows. He had no chance—he used what God gave him and it brought him here. You must use *this*"—her fingers brushed my hair and gently buffed it out of my eyes—"to get away from here and to get away from these people."

She then unlaced the gloves, things that lay like cement blocks on my hands. I would suffocate, I felt, if I had them on for another second. "Fighting only makes it worse for people like . . . us," she said.

When she took them off, my hands were cool with sweat, numb and light, wondrously separate from my body. She put the gloves back in the grey box and carried it all—crushed box, gloves, and stuffing—out in the dark to be burned.

I suppose this is how we grow up: by learning that even implacable principles are in contention. One day the world is fixed forever, without cause, effect, or mitigation. We respond naïvely and mythically: clusters of stars tell obvious stories (only a cynic could doubt the design in Orion's Belt); seasons arrive and depart by grace alone; disease and death are bestowed as punishments. Miniature people inhabit our radios, and everything in the world, living and dead, possesses a soul. Then suddenly the spontaneity deserts us. We embrace new authorities—books and teachers, movies and friends— we become transmitters. We learn of light-years and vacuum tubes, sound waves and psychology. We push back the borders of permissible innocence.

For most, it is a welcome transition. Most kids are good learners. But for the few who still remember the underground lakes, creatures uncovered in a casual dig, the mossy filigree of your father's greying hair, who still feel a shiver with the bell and the words, "*The Gillette Cavalcade of Sports is on the air!*" or when your mother begins a story, "*In Prague, the gypsies once . . .* "; who still leave the small town's only theatre in love with Debra Paget, Margaret O'Brien, or Diana Lynn, who can still project themselves with appropriate sweats and chills from third-grade geography books to the rat-infested wharves of Manaus, the pushcarts of old Delancey Street, or the salt-flats of Tobago, the change becomes too much, body and mind rebel. I went, I think, mad.

And I think now, had it not been for that molten core of Debra Paget, Toots Shor, and Arthur Godfrey, the teletyped reconstructions of baseball games in the class-D towns we lived in—my eccentric orbit around a vulgar gravity—I might have sailed on into deeper space, dark sides of unknown moons, until something truly alien captured me for good.

As I grew into childhood, the atlas became the prime book of my life. It was my mother's 1920 British atlas, a detailed evocation of a vanished world, precisely the thing to move me deeply. The World that Was became for me the World that Could Have Been. I memorized the member-states of the League of Nations, the lists of prime ministers, kings, and governors-general, all by then defunct, exiled, or dead. I traced out the continents and their infinite divisions: all their princely states, empires and caliphates. There were still "unexplored regions" on every continent but Europe—sandy patches marked *Arabia Deserta*, blank areas marked *Tundra*, or simply, *Unclaimed*. Fuzzy green or pink patches everywhere, where rivers, mountains, settlements, and boundaries simply vanished. My mother had been young in an ancient world.

The anchors in her atlas were the German and English cities that I knew for sure had once existed, simply because she'd been there and told me stories about them. And others, as I asked her. What were they like? I wanted to know, to make them live for me. She remembered train stations, views from the *Dampfer*, outings to Oostende, tapestries in Bruges and Ghent.

Her family was split into an English and a German branch. She'd spent her first eight summers with cousins on the Rhine and still called some things by their German names (*Strassenbahnen* and *Eisenbahnen*) even when riding them in England and America. She told me of gypsies in Prague, of cakes bought in *Konditorei* and eaten in gardens under a benevolent Hapsburg sky . . . and then I would go back to my screened-in Florida bedroom and copy out the Baltic littoral, the Danube valley, the Alps, the British Isles, scattering the maps with constellations of dots, some of them first magnitude and some of them faint, and ask her to put city names to all that she could. And she couldn't. Budapest, Brno, Gstaad, Zürich—how I loved to wield my sharpened pencil in my precise handwriting through the vowelless contortions of slavic V's and misplaced J's Köbenhavn, Aix-la-Chapelle, 'sGravenhage: cities could begin with apostrophes; capital letters could stand up and stretch in the middle of words, and every letter came equipped with mysterious dots, tents, accents, and slashes. There were *worlds* out there, outside of Florida and our ugly predictable English. Hieroglyphics had never died. I drew Florida maps with private spellings of familiar cities: 'dJäjxsønvijl, mjHàMij, tâMPajh, and asked my mother to guess what they were. And she couldn't.

I memorized everything. I respected anything that confirmed uniqueness, peculiarness. I cultivated a fondness for any place unjustly ignored. I memorized populations as diligently as capitals, even if half the noses counted in 1920 had not survived till 1949. It was 1949 that was unreal to me. I asked my mother to quiz me on capitals, but she, who had travelled, was hopeless. Europe was an experience she'd long absorbed, a tapestry in which a thread or two was hers alone. Who needed to know how many threads there were and what they were called? And now the tapestry was folded away, dead art bringing no light, no pleasure, and she was in America by accident and unvoiced protest. It was my father, a vagrant born on the rim of America who'd pierced it first on skis, who had the same piety for maps, the same urge to transcend his origins, the same naïve trust in facts that I did. For us there was an equation between road maps and reality, road maps and freedom. He was in Florida because that was where the roads had led him and finally given out. The end of the sock. And I was here because I was a child and it was my condition (though not my fate—that I knew for certain) to be a Florida boy, locked in a room with his maps and *National Geographics*, listening to network radio, plotting his escape.

I took my father's typewriter and began copying in helpless imitation the names and populations of the "Important Cities of the World" listed in the 1920 gazetteer. No town in Florida, I noted with satisfaction, existed. And when it was complete after ten closely typed pages, I memorized it. Every human counted in every city in the world with over one hundred thousand people.

And still I wasn't satisfied. The various states had always bored me, too long familiar in their shapes. But I saw that if I reconstructed them county-by-county, their sad inevitability was somehow redeemed. I could relive history, pushing west from Boston to the Berkshires, pushing south from Jacksonville, north from New Orleans. I could stop history whenever I liked, and suddenly there was no "Massachusetts," no "Florida"—at least not the pixie-slipper or gun-shape that I'd inherited. Cities were like spiders curled in their web, with the smaller, irregular counties clinging to them and the larger, more regular parcels flung far away. Like those boxy Western states, as though no one who lived that far away was worth much intricacy; just a few convenient notches, like Nebraska's and Utah's, amateurish carpentry to make a tighter fit. Boundaries *should* be ragged and unpredictable things, like Europe's, where every line meant that an army sometime in history had run out of steam.

I took to painting my maps in bright watercolours and plastered the walls with Tiffany blobs of partial states, leaving the familiar outline only a shadow, like the hint of a full moon in a quarter-moon's brilliant crescent. Then I ignored them altogether; I let the inner pressure of adjacent counties establish new states of long, narrow, north-south counties (I could *feel* the mountain ridges forcing those stretched-out shapes) and others of square, quilted patches. I created a United States of three hundred states, another of twelve. And after I'd done them all, dozens of times a day, county-by-county, then done states of my own from existing counties, I found that I knew all the counties as automatically as I knew the states, which led me to memorize the county seats, which left me with nothing more the atlas could teach me.

But now I was only beginning. I started with familiar continents or with the outlines of ancient empires, and I carved them into new divisions. I was the Voice of History, decreeing that the Saracens, the Carthaginians, the Austro-Hungarians, the great lost causes of the past, should have another chance, or should triumph. Then I abandoned the familiar continents altogether. I created counties of my own: oceans, rivers, and mountains of my own; developed their own cities and coastal towns, networks of road and rail; drew for hours with ruler and hard pencil the city maps, down to the measliest public park and square, naming every street and river and mountain in languages of my own invention, all of which employed bushels of diacritical marks. Gradually these new maps replaced the old, the "real" ones, on my walls and in my affections. I could prop my chin in hand and stare into those cities of my own invention, hear the rumble of their *Strassenbahnen*, see their cafés and *Konditorei* swell with Sunday crowds, and see the picnickers on the river banks. And then I would watch them run for cover as enemy bombers suddenly strafed them, blowing craters in the streets, scattering their limbs to the wind. That was also me, dropping a fountain pen on my creation from a few inches above my elaborate chart.

Back then it seemed inevitable that I would be a mapmaker, a geographer ("Geopolitics is the coming discipline," my mother once told me, citing one of those inspirational "Why Your Son Should Be A _____" columns sponsored by a public-spirited insurance firm and published every week in the *Saturday Evening Post*). For years I accepted that calling and geared all my occasional reading to that end: geography, geology, archaeology, or perhaps city planning. What I didn't realize until much later was that the maps and cities and the anonymous crowds I had set in motion had nothing to do with a precocious cartographical gift. All those thousands of lustrous facts were messages from something inside me. My words began as copies of something verifiable, and I tinkered within the milder restraint of alternate reality, and then finally I abandoned the known world for an invented reality entirely my own. On my private planet I was Royal Cartographer, Air Marshal, Pope, President, master linguist, anonymous citizen, and mass murderer. My maps were only accidentally maps; the atlas was the only book I had to build on. What they really were were chapters in an inner fury I couldn't yet control. Those maps, like my designs of fantasy fish and my resurrection of anything extinct, were never an indication of a scientific nature—quite the opposite. My mind was a partial vacuum which would suck into itself (and spew out, transformed) anything that made the slightest systematic sense. It was not reasoning—I possess only the feeblest powers of induction. Those maps were this book, in a voice that was about to bury itself and not surface again for thirty years.

Into this perfectly insulated, perfectly self-sufficient world I had made, my mother one night lobbed a mortar shell. In five more months, I would have a brother or a sister. We would move from the woods into town. My father would quit the road and try opening a store. We would all try to become something more resembling a family. My mother's concern was only with me: could I adjust, did I know how much noise babies made, what demands they placed on a mother, especially one (I learned for the first time) who was forty-eight years old and who had already had four miscarriages?

Despite being an only child, I burned with the desire for a sister. A brother might well be a hawk, the proper inheritor of my parents' gifts and not their contradictions, who, even with a ten-year handicap, would assert his mastery at a mortifyingly early age. I could imagine a sister, however, so perfectly in tune with me that we wouldn't have to speak. This sister never had a face or flesh or even a name though it was understood that like all sisters in books and movies she would have a casual if not spectacular beauty. She was a presence, conveniently twinned to me, since I would refuse to endure the long sentence of her mute babyhood. She was always with me, asking my advice, showing me her drawings. I allowed her to be superior to me in schoolwork. Teachers praised her but only tolerated my erratic performances. It was she who assured them that I was doing my work and that I was in fact superior to her in every way. And despite her perfect manners, gentle ways, and pleasant appearance (I could not have tolerated a sister as fat and loathsome as myself), she too had no friends. She had me.

Part of my mother's prenatal preparations included a set of examinations for me. The four miscarriages from so healthy a mother indicated perhaps some genetic quirk. Why had I survived, the doctor wondered, and so I was taken to the University Hospital in Gainesville for blood samples, and then tested for metabolism, intelligence, glands, and muscle tone. Bones, brain, kidneys, heart, lungs, and urinary tract. Parasites, too. All children from the deep woods were assumed to have intestinal worms—even careful, blobular ones like me.

Those days of testing were the first public humiliation of David Greenwood. The hospital was run like an induction centre, and the intern looked at me as a drill sergeant might.

"My God," the first doctor exclaimed, "ten years old and a hundred and twenty pounds!" We didn't have scales at home since my parents had not gained a pound in thirty years. "Do a sit-up," he demanded, and I couldn't. They took blood ("smallest, deepest veins I've ever seen!") and metabolism readings. I breathed into rubber balloons, surrendered small pipettes, then large cylinders of my turgid brown blood, drank sweet concoctions, yielded urine, defecated neatly into polished bowls, ran up stairs, tried lifting weights, and took batteries of intelligence tests, too many of which were spatial and mathematical. I liked the older, kindlier doctors; the interns were blond and hulking, with lab coats that barely stretched across their chests and shoulders. If I had a terror in my life, it was of being judged by brutally healthy men who would laugh at all my inventions. They shook their heads over me, telling my mother they didn't see no way I'd get into the army when my time came, less'n I shaped up fast.

It was decided that theoretically I had no business having been born, or surviving. Something recessive in those two splendid constitutions would doom any child to my fate or worse. Low calcium intake ("Good thing he don't try any athletics. Probably break a bone every time out"); lack of muscle tone ("Jell-O"); a slow intelligence ("Don't be fooled by all this *stuff* he knows," the psychologist told my mother. "He takes it all in but he doesn't control it. It controls him. It's what we call wise idiocy. The institutions are full of inmates who can rattle off facts, like that all day long. But when they eat, they don't know the difference between a knife and a fork."); thyroid deficiency ("Basal metabolism minus thirty-five . . . it's a wonder he can get out of bed in the morning. Or does he?"); obesity; flat feet; allergies. The only normal thing they could say about me was that I was loaded with intestinal worms, for which, they were glad to say, a remedy existed. They gave me other pills: thyroid extract and calcium, cleaning their drawers of samples they seemed to have little faith in. "Try them—maybe they'll help," they said. "Come back in a month."

I had a feeling on that drive back down from Gainesville with my father driving and my mother sitting beside me in the back, her arm over my shoulder, that she saw in me the embodiment of the Voice she'd suppressed in Germany: I was some kind of genetic dead-end that she was stuck with (*Only a mother could love that one*, I'd heard one hulk laugh to another. They'd assumed after the first battery of tests that I was "trainable" but not capable of processing normal speech). The thought that another one just like me was now inside her, waiting to assert less "trainable" demands, was too much to bear. She'd been sent to the hospital for reassurance and been given a death warrant. The fault was in her (it would not be like her to blame anyone else), which meant, in the world she came from, the fault was in her life. She'd been too old. She should never have married. The same expert medical opinion, I was pleased to know, had absolved me from any guilt or responsibility for the fat I was swimming in, for my midday torpor, my weekend sleeps. So far as I was concerned, I was a brain kept alive in some brine solution. I lived only there, inside the cranial vault with my sister and my maps. Thank God.

My father looked over his shoulder and called back, "What's all this talk about worms? How did he get worms *there*, of all places?"

"It's this place," my mother said.

"People get worms from uncooked meat."

"In civilized places, people get worms from uncooked meat. Here they get worms from the soil, from the water, from . . . everything."

"He eats too goddamned much. That's why he's so fat."

I was staring straight ahead, lining up the white lines with the hood ornament and the St. Christopher statue on the dash. My father didn't go to any church, but he kept the statue, just like his other salesmen friends.

"Children in Africa and India and Florida are frequently infested with intestinal parasites," my mother went on in a weary institutional accent. "One shouldn't be ashamed or seek to re-examine one's life just because one's child is infested with worms. You heard what the doctor said—let me get it just right—*'jes' pull down his p-jays at night and train a flashlight on his cheeks. When they come out to lay their eggs, jes' hit 'em with this-here cream and pow! they go up like a minefield.'*"

"And pow!" I repeated, looking up to her, smiling. I felt her arm twitch around me, and I thought she was playing a joke on my father. But then I saw her mouth and throat working; the rest of her face had broken into a mask of the sheerest terror, and tears were running in broad torrents down her cheeks. I thought of her then as a little girl whose father had won her an enormous stuffed animal at a shooting gallery. I was that stuffed animal, sitting quietly beside her, rolling with our fancy new car, defending myself against the judgments of the interns, communing with my twin, unborn sister, comparing in my mind the new life in my mother's stomach and the teeming worms in mine.

Perhaps the pregnancy and the worms were the evidence I was waiting for: there *were* things in the world—physical things I had not suspected or foreseen—that could invade my life. That other world crashed in on me that summer of 1950 when I turned nine. We rented a frame house on an unpaved street a mile out of town—I would be able to bicycle to school in September—there was to be an extra room for the baby (the "boy" my father kept saying, as though drawing a distinction between it and what he already had).

One Sunday morning in June I bicycled to the bus station to pick up the fat Orlando paper, and I remember standing in line while bundles of papers were unclipped, waiting my turn behind an unaccountably large, Sunday-best crowd, all of whom were buzzing over the headline. "It's *war!*" I heard them say, and then I read: N. KOREAN REDS INVADE SOUTH. TRUMAN IN EMERGENCY MEETING. I could barely bicycle home for fear of ambush, grenades, waves of tanks and bombers that might waylay me. The only South I knew was the one I was living in and I felt myself a fat, insignificant Paul Revere shouting out "WAR! WAR!" all the way down the Dixie Highway to whatever corner church crowds were emptying, praying only that I would be spared long enough to reach home and be allowed to die with my parents.

Perhaps it was the pregnancy (and the thought that he might finally have a proper heir) that caused my father, that midcentury summer of the move and the war to take the first big gamble of his business life. Ever since coming to the States he'd worked for other people selling furniture "on the floor" or "on the road," covering the South for seven or eight small factories. Now, with some friends, he intended to open a store.

All his friends were men just like him: they lived on the road and talked only of cars and speed traps, hotels, sports, and the twice-yearly "markets" in High Point and Chicago. Words like "road," "floor," "territory," and "traffic" (which meant people, not cars) were for me furniture-words, part of a safe, protected world that we alone had entry to, related to other darker, more secretive words like *schlep* and *schlock* and *kitsch* and *schmatta* and *schvartze*; slushy, insulting words from that part of the furniture world my father and his friends all were fleeing, a world with a single ugly name: *borax*. If anyone had asked me, I would have related those words to my father's other secret language; it took me years to learn that the easiest language I ever mastered were codewords in a fluid subterranean world, a universal language spoken by the handsome swarthy friends of my father with their flashy, hell-raising names (Vince, Tony, Lou, and Nick), as well as by the balder men with baggy eyes who no longer travelled (Morrie, Julius, Harvey, and Irving).

I knew the men by their cars and accessories: Chryslers and Caddies, by the white plastic Jesus on the dash ("I don't care if it rains or freezes / Long as I got my plastic Jesus" schoolkids crooned), the soft, pitted pigskin sleeves on their steering wheels with the amber plastic knob screwed onto the side; they handled those bulky cars with just two fingers on the knob. Their left arms were darker than wood from their daily two-fingered drives across the South. They had the same magnetic trays for cigarettes, quarters, toll tickets, and gas receipts, and their backseats were always piled with thick cases of upholstery swatches. I knew those cars and those men. They were interchangeable, and their dirty stories about Negroes and women were interchangeable. ("Ah, Lou"— they'd say to my father before starting a story—"your kid is listening . . . it's okay?" And my father would shrug.) They all had picture books, bought in New Orleans or Baltimore, that were passed around when the wives left the room. They'd been in the war—all but my father—and had the stories and tattoos to prove it. They sang a lot after beers in their childhood languages, as did my father, the best singer of the group.

They were a breed: salesmen. They were the only adults I knew. I was fascinated by them and liked to hang around them without being obtrusive. I learned to mix drinks and to keep a few inches of Coke and ginger ale for myself. I gorged on bowls of chips and peanuts and managed, when we drove over to the coastal towns where most of them lived, to slip away from the oppressive company of "the girls" (meaning wives) and from the incessant bicycle-riding of all the "Little Tonys" and "Vince, Jrs." to get into the breezeways and gamerooms where the men were drinking and telling stories and playing the shuffleboard and pinball machines they'd picked up "for a song" from friendly cops or friendly bars. I'd sit there with a Coke, keeping to the darker corners, reading the fake plaques and dirty fake degrees they loved to hang up, the smutty sayings in ornate script, the nude pinups and the rows of framed black-and-white snaps from the Chicago markets where the men would dress in dark suits and pose at restaurants with grinning women, as though even the Tonys and Vinces of central Florida plugged into the Stork Club circuit once a year. My father was in those pictures, wearing suits he never wore at home, arms around men and women I'd never met.

They were salesmen; they had special gifts I would never have: they could talk their way out of traffic tickets, talk their way into stores that didn't want their lines, get waitresses to sit with them while they ate or wait for them after work. They could play ten kinds of poker, sort out a gin-rummy hand within three or four discards, and talk about thousands of miles of state and national highways as though they were streets in a town they'd never left. They were all, in some attractive but frightening and perhaps untrustworthy way . . . performers. I had to like them; I wanted them to like me. When they were together in a single room, the noise could be deafening; yet each of them alone was as silent and sullen as my father. It was my mother, normally a talkative, alert, and observant woman, who clammed up on those Sunday afternoons out on the lawns with the girls.

The men were inside planning. A store was the thing—no more travelling.

I was coming alive in new ways that summer. The pills must have helped; I was awake more hours of the day. On Sundays we would drive over to Daytona Beach and I'd be allowed to steer the car, sitting on my father's lap as we speeded down the sandy beach. The sand was like glass and my mother would say, "Not too fast—the boy might panic." In those years, my compassion, like my fear, was universal. I felt sorry for tires on scalding concrete, sorry for the engine's labours in all that heat, sorry for the chrome and metal, baking helplessly. I imagined the engine filling its lungs with fresh sea breezes. I could rest my arm anywhere without burning it. Sitting high on my father's lap, feeling that powerful car yield to my gentlest command, I felt myself grown up and immortal.

One night the radio news told of the death of George Bernard Shaw. It was the first death to hit me; his signed photo had always hung over my mother's bed; it was the first thing she packed whenever we moved. I sat on her bed, staring at the photo: *he'd been alive, all these years*! Until today. I'd thought of him as a relative. Hearing his name on the radio, "the greatest playwright since Shakespeare," was like hearing my own name—an impossibility. "Whatever are you crying about, dear?" my mother asked me, seeing me on her bed holding Shaw's portrait in my lap. "He was very old, over ninety. Now cheer up; go outside and play."

I went to my maps instead, and for the first time, they failed to come alive. I couldn't hear the crowds, I couldn't pronounce the words I'd labelled them with. The maps were too much of my inner world, and I couldn't justify even to myself what they stood for, what *good* they were. That had been the question the doctor had asked me in Gainesville: "David—what good is it knowing the population of Belém? And the capital of Mozambique? Why, I haven't even heard of those places!" When I couldn't answer and began to blush with shame, he'd patted my shoulder, taken a puff on his pipe, and assured me it was all right, though I knew it wasn't. Eventually I took all of my maps down from the walls and tried to rid my mind of the useless statistics, the endless names that I'd been storing in my skull.

There was a ditch behind our new house; being summer, the ditch was nearly dry. It didn't seem promising for my obsessions with Silver Springs, but at least it was damp, soapy, and septic. The kids in the neighbourhood said that during the rains it sometimes flooded and then was filled with snapping turtles, snakes, and gators. That was enough for me to try digging one last time.

I started with a trowel about six feet from the centre of the ditch, hoping to divert some of its moisture into a patch of garden I'd begun. I'd planted radishes and watermelon: one for speed, and the other for spectacle. The first few mucky feet went easily enough; what water there was had little choice but to follow. The powdery sand was moist a few inches down; moist and warm, and finally sludgy a foot below that. By the time I got to my garden, I was digging down past my elbow, where the pillbox bugs curled into balls and several worms pulled back, lightened of half their bodies. The sluggish drain-water was slowly fanning out behind me; it just might reach my garden, where it would die.

It was then that I saw it. Or at first, saw something halfway down my pit, where the sand turned from grey to brown and from warm to cool. A vast black rubbery thing like an underground cable or pipe. It was coated with sand, but shiny black where a few drops of water had washed it off. The surface was curved; I imagined the whole circle would be eight or nine inches in diameter. Which meant, if flesh, it was at least a boa constrictor. But I didn't think it was living in any animal sense—roots to absent trees were always possible—I thought I'd struck a cable.

Underground cables where there was only partial electrification and no buried wires meant to me in 1950, wartime, that I'd uncovered something I wasn't supposed to know about. I was easily embarrassed by hearing things and seeing things that I wasn't supposed to know about. So there I sat, trowel in hand, arms brown to the elbow in scummy groundwater, blushing over having uncovered secret equipment: German, Japanese, ours, or Russian. And afraid that if I touched it with metal or my hand, I might be electrocuted. Already, I imagined, a red light was flashing in a secret hideout, and some shaved-headed Russian or slant-eyed Korean had noticed the break. Within minutes, a secret agent would come driving casually down our dusty street, stop in front of our house, look around back, and seeing only me, say into his disguised radio, "*It's only a kid. Capitalist swine—I'll take care of him.*" And he would come genially to where I was sitting. I'd seen the movies, heard the radio dramas, read the Hardy Boys. "*What's up, sonny? My, my, looks like you've been digging for treasure. Found something, did you? Ah-hah, looks like you and me'll take a little ride. . . .*"

Shivering now, looking overhead for MIGs or helicopters, I basted the black cable in a trowelful of water. The sand washed away. It was smooth, black, and rubbery. Carefully as an archaeologist, I dug out the earth around it. When I'd followed its length for perhaps a foot and uncovered its other side and washed it. I knew I didn't have a cable or a root. Nothing dead reflected light the way that thing did. It could have been a body, a freshly planted Negro, or at least his arm. A fine finlike spine grew along the top, but not like any fish's I'd ever seen. (No, not like fishes on *this* planet, a voice sounded from deep inside me, but Venus has oceans.) *They* had planted it and were waiting for a signal. There was no time to waste. I risked the destruction of my planet if I didn't act. I saw a vision of myself on the cover of *Time*: "Saviour Greenwood."

I prayed an instant, then plunged the tip of the trowel into that fin-headed monster. It squirmed, flipped, wriggled itself out of its muddy nest and slid into the scummy water that was now flooding the hole, and I could hear it grinding as well as splashing, and I plunged again and again until I could see the white of its backbone and the dark blood welling over it. I pushed into its soft red meat until the bone snapped and my trowel slid free, and two pieces floated to the top.

I must have lived longer with the fear of retribution— alien retribution—than any child in America. I let my garden die rather than return to the ditch behind the house. I came to believe, in time, that anything pursued to its origins or its conclusions, arrived at madness. I couldn't tell a soul what I had seen or what I had done. I lived in terror of the egg-and-tomato man, a swarthy foreigner whom no one trusted ("a gypsy," my mother said, to which I appended *masquerading* as a gypsy, which seemed a new low in deviousness); I feared every stranger and every friend of my parents.

And worst of all, I feared my parents. The thing had been buried in our yard—who but my parents had put it there? I looked for fine fin traces in my father's hair and along his arms. And what was it, really, that my mother was growing in her stomach? What was it, really, that had been planted in mine? "So silent, dear," she would say, pulling me to her.

"Is it because I'm pregnant? You know you'll always be special."

"*I know*," I wanted to say, but finally "*Was I adopted?*" was what I asked, my first words in a week.

My mother let out a cry of anguish and pulled me so hungrily to her mouth that I thought she would devour me. "*Never, never*, think that," she cried. "I nearly died having you."

Oh, fine, I thought; I ask for reassurance, and this is what I get. And then I'd been circumcised—probably the first ever attempted in that rural Florida hospital. "And when I brought you home from the hospital, dearest, your father nearly hugged the life out of you."

I was sorry I'd brought it up. The world was a relentless place, and things were fated to happen to me, I decided ferociously.

The final weeks of waiting were unreal to me. My father was home all day now—I'd not yet been told that he'd quit the road—his presence was something none of us were used to. He'd decided to open a showroom. When he wasn't at the banks or out scouting properties, he was in the living room hunched over the typewriter sending out letters to all the stores he'd once sold to, and to all the factories he'd once represented. "Contacts" another furniture word.

And despite all appearances, I was a backwoods boy; moving into town was like bursting out of a jungle onto the asphalt rubble of Miami Beach. The air, the light, the sense I'd developed of myself and of my parents, had all been nurtured without a society, deep in the woods. Now we had neighbours. Kids played baseball in the open field across the road, and we all bicycled till the sun went down. (I can still hear their voices: "You comin' out again after dinner?" and it means to me now that I once participated; for a few months I had a bike and friends and it must have been a good and endless summer.)

For my mother, everything was geared to the birth. My mother persisted in guessing that I'd have a brother, thinking that a brother would be my preference. Someone to teach how to throw and catch, to fish, to quiz me on capitals. I didn't want anything like that; I didn't want to master or compete. I wanted something precisely like me, yet utterly different. A brother could only be a travesty.

With three months to go and the summer ending, my mother was in maternity clothes. That embarrassed her—she was nearly grey by now—and her ample bone structure made her look slovenly, not pregnant. I could see her when she thought she was alone, giving herself sharp slaps on the side, lifting her stomach in both hands while closing her eyes and letting out long, quivering breaths. And I could hear my sister inside, apologizing, as clearly as I had heard those turtles and fishes underground, as perfectly as every inanimate object in the world spoke to me of its heat, its anger, and its pain.

She would come into my bedroom with a flashlight as I pretended to sleep. I could hear that same remorseful breathing as she set the flashlight down and peeled down my pajama bottoms, and I could feel the cool oily salve she spread. I could imagine my parasites there on my rectum, flopping and flashing like sardines in a fisherman's net. I could almost hear the hiss of their expiration as the ointment spread, mowed down like Japs on Iwo Jima.

Though my mother suffered from the heat, hay fever, and the agonies of a very late pregnancy, she remained competent—even cheerful—throughout. "You'd think this year at least they'd spare me hay fever," she laughed, as we sat at the kitchen table, wet hankies balled in our hands.

"Will she—it—the baby—have hay fever, too?" I asked, knowing full well that she already did, and my mother answered no, she didn't think so. This baby would be perfect. My father, after all, counted for something in these decisions, and he'd been spared hay fever and every other defect. I feared my father's reaction. I could imagine my mother holding a baby, changing her, feeding her; it was my father I couldn't imagine with her. I had a nightmare of him waking up in the night—in the sullen fog he was always in for an hour after waking—and crashing into the nursery, lifting the baby and dropping her on the floor in order to quiet her. I could feel her suffering, her mature mind locked in a baby's helpless body, and with a loud scream I awoke from the nightmare, only to find my mother, flashlight in hand, working on my parasites. "I'm sorry," she said. "Go back to sleep. I'm almost finished." And I told her my dream—the clear vision I'd had of the baby broken like a doll at my father's feet. She cleaned me, then washed her own hands. Then she sat on the bed with me, hands on my shoulders, trying to pull me close, though I resisted.

"You don't understand your father like I do," she said. "He's very anxious for this baby."

"Only if it's a boy," I said. "If it's a strong boy who doesn't disappoint him."

She looked down—I'd hurt her, I knew, and was glad—she untied, then reknotted my drawstring.

"David, let me tell you this. When I brought you home from the hospital, I was worried, too. Not that he'd *ever, ever* intentionally harm you, but that he wouldn't know what to do, and so would ignore you. And you were so good, so quiet—you only slept and lay in your crib. You were the best baby the nurses had ever seen. But as soon as the nurse and I came through the door, he took you from me, and he kissed you. He didn't take his lips off your cheek from the door, through the hall and all the way back to your room. And then he laid you in the crib, and when I got there, he was holding onto both corners of the crib and the crib was shaking. I thought something terrible had happened, and for a minute I panicked. He was crying, David. I've never seen him cry like that before or since. He was on his knees crying like his heart was broken. I looked in the crib expecting I don't know what, but you were sound asleep under your blue blanket. And through his crying I could only make out, '*God, he's so beautiful, and I've hurt him. I've hurt him.*' Oh, I tore the cover off and picked you up, and what do you think I saw? A little red bruise on your cheek—a million burst little blood vessels like a strawberry where he'd kissed you. It disappeared completely within a week. But that's the kind of father your father is."

Perhaps I was like my father in this way, too; my passion—even my love—had no outlet. It led back to myself, and it still leads me to fall on my knees and shake the crib or the desk, to pound my fist a hundred times a day in a fit of sudden anger, remorse, or embarrassment. The only child is inevitably a monster: all that love dammed up inside him, all those adult eyes assessing him, and with nothing *in his scale* to return it to. Like a queen bee, he possesses some instinct to assure himself, even murderously, of supremacy. He exercises a sterilizing influence, destroying whatever will or potential there had been to create more like him. With a profound insidiousness,

I had made myself the fulfillment of all my mother's expectations: I was mild, obedient, and despite what the interns said, intelligent; as unlikely as a lamb of causing injury or offense. And I knew I was so profound a disappointment—or perhaps only a mystery—to my father that he too must have abandoned the notion of fatherhood after seeing what his errant sowing had produced.

And then suddenly, all the planning—the packed bag, the crib and curtains—were nothing but fire drills before the conflagration. One Saturday morning in September I heard loud metallic thumps coming from the laundry shed in back of the house, and I found my mother, bent double, holding onto the laundry tub. A wrinkled bedsheet that had been put through the wringer lay stiffly coiled on the floor, and from that alone—her face was pale, but not registering pain—I knew something frightening had happened. If she could walk—or bend—she would never have let a clean sheet drop. "Call Daddy," she said, and I could hear in her voice what she had tried to hide: pain, fear, a final summoning of strength before passing out. "I can't . . . move," she said apologetically, looking down at her feet, and then I saw that her legs were flowing with blood. Blood had covered her shoes and now was spilling on the concrete. I ran from the shed and called the operator as I had seen so many times in the movies, shouted the address and the need for an ambulance. When I got back to the shed she had slumped further to the tubs, like a fighter who is fatally beaten but whose overconditioning will not permit him to fall.

"Bring . . . blanket, sweetheart," she said. "Mommy's cold."

She explained to the stretcher-bearers—thinking perhaps they were doctors, or that they cared—that in the night and early in the morning she had noticed a furious kicking, then suddenly, as she began the wash, she'd felt a limp heaviness, accompanied not by labour pains but by a burning weight, like molten metal.

I knew from movies that childbirth was painful and sometimes fatal, but my mother, I decided, was not the type to die. You could always tell in war movies and Westerns which of the minor characters were bound to die. My mother never admitted pain, never took medicine; it would be bad plotting—too obvious—to let her die. I had faith that life respected the same rules, that she was safe because of what, in essence, she stood for—no matter what adversity she was facing. Neighbours, attracted by the ambulance, drove me to the hospital.

I had been in the waiting room three hours, pacing in the proper movie manner, when my father finally arrived, a suddenly smaller and older man, as he and a nurse ran my way. He left two of his salesmen friends at the reception desk. From the way they were dressed, I could see they'd been out, perhaps with bankers, discussing business. And it was from the nurse's running and the way she held one hand on my father's arm as they entered the waiting room that I knew something was going wrong. The whole mood was wrong; we weren't supposed to feel this anxiety. It was planned to be a happy time for my father and me—in that bag we'd packed, there was a Thermos bottle, and my father and I were going to drink coffee together as we waited it out. And nurses were supposed to humour us, scold the fathers mildly but indulge their silliness. And fathers were supposed to be boyish, with a rim of pajama showing under their pants cuff, cigarettes burning in both hands. But my father was in his best black business suit and starched white Arrow Darts shirt, and suddenly I remembered something my mother had told me that same night she'd sat on my bed: "*It's very dangerous, what I'm doing. But you're too lonely, precious. I'm too old to be having a baby. If something goes wrong, remember how much I loved you. Remember that your father loves you no matter how he shows it. . . .*" I had blocked that until now, and I also remembered my mother's hatred of Catholics and their hospitals;

that they'd save the baby and not the mother, especially if she weren't a Catholic. The whole moral question was up to me; for my father, I knew, had been a Catholic—which meant, in a pinch, that he would always give in to them.

"Save my mother," I told the nurse.

She squinted at me and then shouted out to the reception desk, "Who told this boy?" The nurse on duty, chatting with my father's friends, merely shrugged.

"Nothing's going to happen to her," my father said, reaching to shake my shoulder, which I avoided. Then he turned to the nurse and his face appeared stricken. "*Is* she . . . I mean . . ."

"Dr. Chandler is very good," she replied.

My father grabbed the nurse roughly around her shoulders and began to rock her. "What are you saying?"

"Really, Mr. Greenwood, you should take your little boy out of here." His friends were waved over, but they stopped at the door, too shy to enter. "Your wife is hemorrhaging, Mr. Greenwood. If it stops in time, she is in no danger. If not— then Dr. Chandler is there. But this is not the place to go into it. The only thing to do is wait. Now please let me go."

My father loosened his tie with an idle, clawing gesture; his eyes were red, unseeing. He took the nearest chair and slumped in it like a man twice his weight. Then he fell forward, head nearly on his knees, and I heard those high-pitched, wheezing sobs that my mother had described, and I decided to stay.

And so we settled into a parody of the Hollywood waiting room: my father and his friends sticking cigarettes in their mouths maybe thirty times a minute, and I, strangely controlled, reading through a tattered pile of *Life* and *Saturday Evening Post*, hearing (I thought) the slap of rubber gloves on a baby's bottom, moans, a woman's screams, fevered consultations; hearing my own sister's voice calling to me that she was coming, she was here; hearing my mother's voice, implanted in my head like that mystery voice of her own leaf-reading youth: *If you can hear me, dear, you are not to worry. I have gone, but I have left you a sister. Look after her . . .* and as I tried to slap that voice out of my ear, I heard other voices: "This is Louella Parsons from Hollywood. Well, it's a sister for David Greenwood, but his mother, I'm sorry to report, died in the delivery room. . . ." *Slap.* "The Gillette Cavalcade of Sports is on the air! Today, direct from the delivery room of All-Souls Hospital in Hartley, Florida . . ." *Slap.* "This is Toots Shor. Last night in Florida . . ." *Slap, slap, slap.*

"*Are you crazy? What the hell are you doing?*" My father was over me, shaking me as I swatted the side of my head as though to empty it of water, and he shook me till his friends came over and pulled him off.

But in swatting my head, in seeing the panic in my father's eyes at the kind of deranged scene I was making, I had made the final connection. The creature I had killed behind the house in the ditch was not a Korean spy smuggled ashore and sequestered for an eventual rendezvous; nor was it any kind of conventional alien being. The creature had been my sister, lying in the ground like a seed. And somehow in my love, my impatient love, I had unearthed her prematurely (like a child discovering his unwrapped Christmas presents in their secret hiding place), and I had killed her as surely as if I had cut my mother open with a trowel.

It was anticlimactic when the nurse finally came out. I looked for blood on her smock but there was none, merely the curls of her hair plastered to her forehead to show the strain. She had a new expression on her face, one that is now covered by a comic cliché: *I have some good news and some bad news.* I caught that double focus, but misinterpreted its terms. I thought my mother had died; that my sister and I would be farmed out to ancient, unknown relatives in England or Canada; or worse, that we would remain here in Florida with my father, a man incapable of surviving an hour alone, a man who could not cook, clean, or even wash the dishes. And so my thoughts as I prepared to hear of the death of my mother were on my own future, the injustice and inconvenience of fate.

The nurse stood by the swinging doors, expecting my father to rush toward her for the news. But he didn't even see her; he had turned to the wall, sick and coughing, holding the coffee in his shaking hands. She walked over to him, putting a hand on his shoulder, and stooped to speak softly in his ear. After a few seconds, when it seemed from her gestures that she'd said the same thing many times, he began to nod. He stood and straightened his tie and took his rattail comb from his inner suit-pocket. Two careful swipes of the comb and every brown and silver hair was perfectly restored: his parting glistened with oil and sweat. Then the nurse came to me, still disapproving of my presence, and her words were cold. "Your mother has had a very serious operation," she said. "She lost a lot of blood, but now the bleeding's stopped. I'm taking your father in to see her now. You stay here and be good, hear?"

During the next hour, the magazines on my lap, and with a new expectant father pacing the ward in the proper manner, I had more than enough time to reflect on life, death, and fate; on the suddenness of a dream's collapse. There would be no sister. The woman who had been "picking up the baby's room" that morning and then "doing a small wash" could be dying in a hospital four hours later. The sister who in some mythical future had been my age, dangling her feet with me in a warm Florida lake, had just died without the dignity of having been born. She had been the realest thing in my life; no one in my family had occupied my thoughts, fantasies, and vivid dreams like her. Nothing ever would, I vowed; it would be my way of keeping faith.

I was boarded with neighbours for the next ten days while my father moved into a motel and my mother recovered.

When we finally moved back to the house, the "nursery" was dismantled, and the room became an office with two card tables spread with papers, weighted down with hunks of stone and my father's cigarette roller. My mother had aged in some definitive way. She had entered the hospital young for her age. When she came out, she merely looked her age, but she started looking it overnight. She was quieter. She spoke less to everyone but would hug me to her when I least expected it. I learned to stay a few feet away, for the hugs confused and frightened me. They were impulsive and inarticulate, like something from my father. I could feel the strain in her arms, the pounding in her neck, and I was afraid that all her stitching would give way. "I should have died, David," she said once, holding me as she sat at the kitchen table. And I stood beside her. "They told me I had died. I *died*—do you understand?"

The statement filled me with a wondrous sense of adventure. Of course I understood it. I had spent most of my ten years between life—the sweaty, sunshiny experience that I imagined most of my classmates knew—and a long lunar night that I alone inhabited, and that anyone else, I was sure, would call death.

"There won't ever be another baby," she said another time. "I'm sorry . . . I'm too old."

"That's all right."

"The baby died, you know. That's what caused the miscarriage. She—or he . . . *it*, let's say, had something . . . wrong. It wouldn't have lived."

"That's all right. I'm glad you're here."

She hugged me all the tighter. "Was it a girl?" I asked, trying to make it sound casual, though my throat had clamped shut.

"No, not a girl. An *it*—just think of it as a mistake. I didn't see it and I didn't want to. I can't have normal babies, darling. I had you and you nearly died, and I've tried to have five others I couldn't carry as long as you, or as long as this one.

Who knows the purpose of it—why did I come back to life? For what? Why did I have you and not the others?"

Another time she said, "I think it must be because you're very special. That's why I was saved."

"I'm not thinking any more about it," she said one last time. "It's all over. Thank God it's all over."

In the years to come my father would open stores, display rooms, warehouses, and outlets every year or two—a passion for building, not maintaining. He was too much the salesman to also be a manager: at the first good offer he would sell; at the first reversal, dump it. I had the almost physical sense— never more acute than in the deep South in the last years of the forties and the early fifties—of our lifting ourselves up from the mire into something cooler and drier and finally more healthy. The lines between everything were sharply drawn in the South; social mobility was not climbing a ladder, it was walking a cable over a windswept chasm. And Southern failure was the most horrible, most permanent kind. It tolerated no comebacks. My father loved risk; he was a salesman, and a healthy commission was all that he asked for. He wouldn't have known what to do with retirement plans, Blue Cross, and life insurance; he resented Social Security because he knew he would never retire to collect a penny. A salesman, like a plumber, always had work, and he knew he'd be working till the day he died. Insecurity was a reasonable bail for release from winter and the dead end of being French in Canada. I didn't know that till later.

Nor did I know when we inspected the site of our first store what forces in the universe we had tapped, what slightly disreputable relationships between furniture and fraud, furniture and shabbiness, we had unleashed. It was a great game at the beginning. We had three property options: to build a cinderblock bunker at the edge of town, slap neon trim around it, clear a parking lot in front, and be the owner. Or we could lease some deserted wartime barracks at the edge of an abandoned airfield which we could never own, but which, for the cost of renovation, would provide roomy facilities on a long-term lease for practically nothing. Or we could rent a cinderblock structure already standing, recently a roadside tavern called "Bunky's Hide-Away," now deserted. Unlike the first two options, we could take possession in about a month, and the landlord would remodel

I wonder what might have happened had we chosen to build, or to lease the airport—options favoured by my mother and me respectively. She was always farsighted, willing to sacrifice now for benefits later, and especially to pay any price for the privilege of being boss. The bonus would be the opportunity to design it herself, for it to be something unique in her Southern experience—clean and new and uncorrupted by prior contact with Florida. And for me the raised, peeling barracks with their rotting ladders, the interiors scurrying with lizards and still hung with wartime pinups and yellowed calendars, and the immense grounds with its mysterious asphalt runways meandering into the forest seemed to be life's sacred equivalent of all my map-fed fantasies. I would take my bike from the barracks parking lot, and, gathering speed, arms flat out like a plane, make for the walls of cypress that sealed the farther end. The runways ended in giant banks of sand, oil drums, and rusty rolls of steel mesh that powdered at my touch. Perhaps the war had ended before something grand could be built, or perhaps the jungle had struck back in the five years since. But the thought that for just a signature and the will to remodel we could rent the jungle and have a purchase on history struck me as something heroic and Brazilian, like a landing strip on the Amazon. I begged for my private empire of roads, water, buildings, and jungle. I should have known that any course that seemed so obviously preferable would be overlooked. In the end, my father made the proper business decision. He would pay rent, which was deductible anyway, and take over the remodelled tavern just out of town.

Doubtless the decision was guided by business logic. There was, admittedly, something pretentious in my scheming and something ambitious in my mother's, but I think we were also guided by different associations than my father. I cared nothing for furniture and my mother thought of Bauhaus and studio design. But for my father there was a connection between bars—and nothing is lower, dirtier, or dingier than a Southern roadside tavern—and furniture. They were the places that he and his friends would stop in for a cooling beer before putting another two hundred miles on the speedometer and earning a good night's sleep. Taverns were in trade—another furniture word—after all; military airports weren't. He felt secure with rents and leases and someone else to set things right. There was something in him that chose, time and time again, places like "Bunky's Hide-Away" to convert into furniture stores. I came to think of furniture as a temporary plateau in a building's slow decline. After a restaurant came a bar, after a bar a furniture store, and after us, a used-car lot.

And there was a final thread in the association that I failed to pick up until our last furniture store much, much later. And the thread leads from my father back to me. It was simply this: furniture had been an accident. What he really wanted was a club, a place where he could dress up every night in his black suit and starched Arrow Darts, gold ring and jewellery, and those black silk stockings pinned high with garters. A high-class place with glamorous customers, where he would glide soundlessly between the velvetized dining room and the sweltering kitchen, be the *bon vivant* out front sitting with the customers and sipping wine or perhaps a single scotch, and storming into the kitchen to chew out the help for any imperfection. He thirsted for glamour, like me; he looked like George Raft and aspired to the same life, to be a Mister Lucky, a Bogart in Casablanca, a Toots Shor in Manhattan, and a talent scout like Arthur Godfrey, an ambassador of God's country.

The building selected for the "outlet" was low and square, a socket of cinderblock in a scrub clearing two miles out of town on the state route to Palatka. "Wrong kind of traffic for a bar," the real-estate agent had told my father; too much family traffic, not enough truck farmers looking for a beer.

There is nothing more desolate than a boarded-up, deep-South roadside tavern in the humid, hurricane-breeding weeks of early October, and that was the week my father and his friends signed the papers. The place had not been swept or disinfected, and there were still some bags of torn-open potato chips on the little metal clamp-trees on the bar; empty beer bottles tipped on their sides, and others standing but crammed with cigarettes and full of some foul-smelling liquid. "Bunky's Hide-Away" neon tubing was still twisted in the window. The mirror behind the bar was studded with beer and whisky decals. The smell was like crawling into an empty, still-moist beer barrel, as though rancid beer had been used to swab the floors and varnish the tabletops. I vowed never to sip the flat remnants of beer after any more furniture parties. And since it had been a bar, set in a scorched patch of indifferently paved sand, every effort had been made to keep it dark. "A tomb," my mother said. Our clothes smelled of beer; our sweat afterward ran sweet, not salty.

We had some of my father's friends, the banker and real-estate agent with us; the friends were all enthusiastic. Salesmen are professional promoters, natural supporters of any cause. "Not bad, Lou," they told him now. "New fixtures, coupla coats of paint . . ."

"New tiles on the floor."

"Dark tiles, though, Lou. Kinda makes the wood stand out, you know?"

Lower the ceiling.

Bigger window out front.

Lots of lights. She'll need new wiring.

Take out the bar, but leave the mirror. It'll work, Lou.

Air conditioning, of course. She'll take three units at least.

Snap it up, Lou.

My attention had been drawn by a different sign, one that Palmetto Realties had pounded into the sand at the roadside. I'd always noticed those signs—they are universal—but it was the first time the offer had applied to us. It made me feel that goodness and charity still existed in the world, even in Florida.

FOR RENT. DESIRABLE PROPERTY
OWNER WILL REMODEL TO SUIT TENANT

It seemed like such a generous, friendly offer that we would be ungrateful to turn it down.

The "outlet" was to be a furniture display room, a service not open to the public, but to other manufacturers and retail buyers. The idea was for three or four salesmen, all tired of the road and in various stages of alcohol dependency, shot nerves, and marriage-neglect, to convince manufacturers to ship their goods to a single outlet, and for the potential buyers—hotels, motels, and of course retail furniture stores—to take a day's trip down from Jacksonville, or over from the Gulf, to see the goods actually in stock and not merely in the catalogue. Having the goods in stock would guarantee faster delivery. We would also insure for damages. We'd been reading that the scrublands south of Daytona were due for development and that even the Gulf Coast towns like Clearwater and Bradenton could be made habitable year-round; this was the chance, my father said, to get in on the ground floor. Like all of my father's schemes, it was risky, but a natural money-maker. For him, as manager, there would be twice the commission he'd have made on the road.

He was the perfect salesman; he had the salesman's perfect timing and the salesman's respect for facts—which is not to say truthfulness. Salesmanship is a performing art with customers as the audience, and of all the salesmen I've ever listened to, my father was the best. He could register utter conviction in any product, and he knew just when, after the hard-sell, to let the customer suddenly flounder in his uneasy freedom ("He's taken the hook, let him run with it"). He could always tell when a customer was susceptible to something slightly more expensive ("a step up") . . . never less.

He'd been trained in *borax*, the form of furniture salesmanship that treats the salesman even more contemptuously than he in turn treats the public; a system as dependent on commissions as waitressing is on tips, where salesmen are pitted against each other like fighting cocks. Until he went on the road, my father had never had a restaurant lunch and even now he ate furtively. Always the *borax* training, the *borax* anxiety, that while you're out for coffee and a sandwich, someone else is writing up sales. Or worse, that a pigeon you'd worked on for months, sweated blood over, would drop in for five minutes to leave off a check for the full amount—and someone else would write it up and pocket the full commission. Back in Montreal, before I was born, he'd sometimes threatened salesmen with a beating and thrown managers against the wall for stealing commissions, or condoning it. He'd resigned jobs in a moment's fury over the loss of fifty cents. But that was *borax*: everyone profited by being a shark; better mayhem than complacency. Salesmen were easy to find and jobs were everywhere for the talented. He could threaten a manager with his fists—those lethal weapons—be fired, and have a job and a raise ten minutes later. Or someone would speak to him of a better job ("more traffic") in another town, and he'd leave that day. My mother would pack, take a bus, and find an apartment in some new town a little farther from Canada, a little closer to permanent warmth. Eventually, in one of those warm little towns a long way from Canada, I'd been born.

The furniture salesman dreams of deliverance from *borax*, of opening a store of his own, or at least of enjoying the kingly dominion of the road where he can set his own hours and beat out the opposition by pushing himself harder, sleeping less, and making sure that no matter how he does it, he's parking in front of the town's biggest store by a quarter to nine. But the pace eventually kills them all: they grow violent, morose, and alcoholic. Eventually they all have little accidents, or sometimes one big one. The lucky ones, they say, get killed. The unlucky ones get injured and lose everything since they carry no insurance. The tragic ones don't get hurt at all. They run over a child and become pariahs, for there is always booze on a salesman's breath.

The salesman's timing had always been with him. Never to anticipate a customer, but knowing when to supply the needed reinforcement. And yet—and this is the reservation of his life, of many salesmen's lives—as a consumer he was more vulnerable than the poorest pigeon. I never understood in the years that I was dependent on my parents' reality why we and the friends we had, who supposedly knew so much, were always being stuck with broken appliances, "lemons," underwater property, bad marriages, bad bosses; why life, in the view of these muscular, tattooed, violent men, was such a series of inexplicable bad breaks.

My mother never had that timing. When customers fell silent, perhaps pondering their finances (the moment for inserting the *banderillo*: "*Shall I begin writing it up?*" or "*Remember, you only pay twenty percent down*"), my mother, anticipating their embarrassment or perhaps projecting one of her own, would withdraw the pick smoothly and painlessly. "Or perhaps you'd like to see something a little less expensive," she'd say, and they would nod gratefully. She wanted to sell nice things to good people and she wanted to make friends more than sales. She'd been an interior decorator and a designer in Europe and London and then Montreal; what she'd despised was *borax* and everything it stood for.

The only exciting part of the furniture business for me were its special codes, its secret language. "Son of a bitch gets a number and a half and still he *kvetches*," salesmen would say of dealers in larger cities; a "number" being a standard 50 percent markup, and a number and a half being reserved for French Provincial *kitsch*, velvet chairs, and lacquered Chinese dressers.

My father's world was always "under a number"—a *boraxy* 47 percent—and like all men in the trade he carried a little wheel in his pocket to figure out any markup on the spot, though he never really needed it. He could figure out 47 percent of any number in his head. We would walk into stores in strange towns and I would memorize—since I had the freak memory—the retail prices off the various tickets, and once we were back in the car he'd ask, "Okay—the breakfront. What's he selling it for?"

"Two forty-nine ninety-five," I'd say. His face would pass through several shades of red before his lips thinned and he spat out, "The bastard's only taking forty-four percent markup unless he got a special deal. I can't give a deal like that. Somebody's underselling me, and I'm going to find out who." And now, with his own showrooms, he could set his own prices; he could undersell any travelling salesmen.

And so I was trained early in the art of comparison-shopping; entering stores and reading the tags, trusting it all to my wise-idiot memory, and to spilling it to my father who waited in the nearest parking lot. I felt like a scout, a spy. My father was the Lone Ranger and I wanted to call him *kemo-sabe*.

"Are you *sure*? Ethan Allen eighty-two-inch triple dresser? Mirror, with spindles? What code did they use?"

That was my special knack in *borax* houses: cracking the codes on the back of tickets, parachuting behind enemy lines and getting out. A fat little kid—who'd ever guess what I was doing? Because the cardinal rule in *borax* is never to lose a customer. No one enters a *borax* house for the goods or the atmosphere; salesmen attack like jackals and sitting is discouraged. But the ticketed prices are only try-fors; *borax* is like an Oriental bazaar, only the customer hasn't been told. On the back of the ticket there would usually be some letters. AooI, for example. The salesman has only to look on the back of a $34.95 lamp to see AooI and to know he can make a spot reduction. "Look, take it as-is, and I'll give it to you for, ah, twenty-nine ninety-five." He knows because of the code—any ten-letter word that doesn't repeat a letter. My father's code was WASHINGTOL, a favourite *borax* code all down the East Coast. I grew as adept at reading those letters as my father was at figuring 47 percent.

And I used to play making up codes; a lot of names in the gazetteer had the requisite ten unrepeated letters. CALIFORNIA came close; CALIFORNYE was good. One day by accident I discovered another, a word that I didn't understand but had been hearing for years. I submitted it at a Sunday party just before the opening of the store, proud of having made my contribution: a new code for a new store. "That's not funny," my father said, balling the paper in his pocket. My word checked out in every way: BANKRUPTCY.

My faith was restored by the renovation of "Bunky's Hide-Away" (now "Greenwood Displays")—also my older suspicions about the veneer of surfaces. Booths and tables were removed, the ceilings lowered, and spotlights placed in their recessed sockets of soundproofing. The smell of wet plaster, new wood, and asphalt cement gradually mingled with— then overcame—the fumes of stale beer, secret urine, and cigarettes. The transformation from a place of dark, rancid anonymity into something bright and guiltless—how easy it was! How superficial? It was terrifying. And then the arrival of the first batch of furniture from the smaller manufacturers, a sofa and two chairs in nubby terrycloth: "Tango Red" ("Niggerlip Red" said one of my father's friends as he helped uncrate it); chairs in chartreuse and electric blue. My mother winced.

In mid-November, Greenwood Displays was finally opened, with a smorgasbord for the press and dealers. We'd received enough consignments from various Georgia and North Carolina manufacturers to make for an impressively filled display room. The bar had been removed, and a smaller, portable one brought in for the day. And that was where my father stood, greeting the reporters from a dozen weeklies and dailies in a six-county area. We had a barman that day, recruited from a country club, and a candy-blond "hostess" to take drink orders. I'd been certain that no one would show, and of course I was wrong. All the buyers from north-Florida department stores came or sent representatives; the furniture trade magazine sent a photographer, and the local paper sent their women's page editor. We offered furniture-food: chopped liver, corned beef, dill pickles, ordered from Jacksonville and sent down with a friend. I went around before the people arrived, peeling the union stickers off the crusts of rye, and snipping off the cellophane casings around the sliced meat. And I helped myself; I might be on pills, but I was still a fat little kid.

The building filled up; like on Halloween night, the arrivals were steady, and the parking lot was jammed. It was a furniture gathering: loud, smoky, arms around shoulders, flashbulbs popping; we'd have photos for our gameroom, too, if we'd had a gameroom.

"Hey! Damn comfortable!" That was my father, pulling a buyer down onto the sofa with him, both sloshing their scotches on the Tango Red, and laughing loudly. The buyer agreed it was damned comfortable, though neither looked comfortable despite their grins. My father didn't dare lean back, for then his feet wouldn't quite reach the floor. Fortunately perhaps, the seat pitched him forward rather violently.

"Damn comfortable! Come on, all of you, try it for Chrissakes! They're gonna love it!" Even I could imagine that set, Tango Red, lime, or electric blue, making its way into motel and hotel rooms across north Florida. Was it really that easy? Were customers really blind when they looked at furniture? Was it just my privileged position of being (for once) on the selling side that made me see its faults?

The society reporter, looking cold in a sundress, trying to control a cigarette, a glass, and a thick pastrami sandwich oozing with juice and mustard, sat daintily on the edge of a chair and smiled bravely at the men, asking my father the likely retail price of what she was sitting on and the place of its manufacture. I admired her juggling, first disposing of the cigarette, butting it in a discarded paper cup, then the gradual sinking into the slope of the chair until she realized that it was not going to be a comfortable experience. She forced herself to sit straight, at considerable agony over the long haul. She asked my father more questions and I could hear him, in five minutes, tell her more of his own travels and long experience in furniture than I had heard from him in a lifetime. She extracted a notebook from her handbag, put on rhinestone-rimmed glasses that hung from a silver chain around her neck, and began to write. I roamed around the serving table, snitching crusts of rye and swabbing them in the pools of succulent fat and mustard. Tall green bottles of Canada Dry were out, and a case of Coke to mix with rum was under the portable bar, buckets of ice, bottles of mustard with knives in the top, bottles of brown booze, and a barman with tattooed hands. I could tell he loathed me.

I was embarrassed for us all, as though we'd staged a terrible play and invited powerful critics to judge it; we'd sold tickets to an expectant audience and were somehow flubbing our lines. I could feel my father's strain as he called out across the room, "Jerry, Jerry Forza—come on over here you son of a bitch! I haven't seen you since Chicago!"

And Forza shouted back, "Lou Greenwood, you canny old bastard—where'd you get pastrami in Florida, huh?" I stood there and looked for my mother, who had by now joined my father, the lady reporter, and a couple of buyers in the lurid ensemble at the centre of the floor. I could feel an embarrassment welling up, an embarrassment all the more acute because this time we were the perpetrators and not the victims. I felt such sorrow for my parents, for my father's brave front (never more pathetic than when his grin was spreading across his face, and his voice was cracked from so much forceful, desperate insincerity). I felt from my mother's hushed noddings and her own unsipped ginger ale as she leaned against the unyielding chair that she longed to be able to shout out, "The show is cancelled—refunds at the box office!" I swabbed new bread, avoiding the scorn of the bartender, and guzzled leftovers from bottles of Coke, soda water and flat ginger ale, then gradually made my way over to my parents. I could make out the thread of a dozen conversations going on about me, and I longed to stop and answer the questions they were asking each other—the one thing I knew was the name and location of every factory. And I knew, because I found salesmen transparent, that in the forms of their enthusiasm and reassurances, their promises to place a few orders, they were lying.

"Eight-way hand-tied," my father was saying (standing now by the red sofa and lifting off the cushions, pushing his hands into the frame itself; my mother held the missing cushion tightly on her lap). And the woman reporter mumbled, "Hmm, eight-way," and a buyer repeated, "Hand-tied?"

"*Eight*-way. *Hand*-tied." My father was puffing from the strain.

"Tied—by hand," said my mother.

"That's a very interesting shade of red," noted the woman reporter, whose name, I'd managed to hear, was Margaret Montgomery. It matched her lipstick.

"We're introducing it. Something with flair," said my mother, as though picking up a cue. She was a flairless woman, and red, I knew, made her especially uncomfortable. She didn't own anything red, chartreuse, or, as she called it, Butcher Blue. She was a pastel woman. If it wasn't a "restful hue," then it wasn't for her. I thought of her life as a retreat from an undisclosed torment, something so exhausting that it left her without a moment's peace. But my father liked flair, vibrant things.

"What'll it sell for, Lou?" asked one of the buyers, pointing to the sofa.

"Ah-hah, I thought you'd never ask. The whole suite"— (pronounced *sweet*, and the Pavlovian associations have lasted to this day)—"will retail for about two, two-fifty."

"That's fifty more than you told me," said Margaret Montgomery.

"Hell, I said that? Okay, two hundred. No, two twenty-five. Looks like I just lost twenty-five dollars, and I haven't even sold it yet." He tried to turn it into a joke, but I'd caught the skepticism in her voice. I'd never heard anyone doubt my father; my ears were burning.

"One hundred and fifteen dollars wholesale for the suite. Hundred and five for bulk orders. That's a promise—I hope you're writing that down, miss," he said, still smiling. He was into his act—salesmanship, spontaneous misrepresentation, but what made it art was his passion and belief.

Unit costs, he was explaining. All the jargon of bulk orders. "Look, I know there's not a store between Atlanta and Miami that takes even twenty units at a time. So the big boys won't give you a break, right? But Lou Greenwood, he'll treat you right. You don't have to be putting up a hotel in Miami Beach before coming to Lou Greenwood for a break. *You* might not buy twenty, but I'm taking twenty or more and I'm getting the discount, and then I'm splitting it with you. Fifty-fifty. I'll sell you one, I'll sell you ten—you get a break either way. I've got twenty stores signed right now to exclusive contracts to buy only from me"—(but that's a *lie*, I thought. Only last night you were saying *if only* I could sign these bastards to exclusive contracts)—"I've got builders as far south as Cocoa Beach coming up next week. If you all come in with me, I can order a hundred units at a time—a thousand—and I'll pass the savings on. That's how Greenwood does business."

You could feel the heat radiating from the Tango Red sofa. And not from the people, just the colour. Maybe it had been a wartime colour, something developed by the Signal Corps for landing markers. It was the colour of my father's mind; dazzling but untextured. You wanted to turn away from its intensity, but you could feel it beating down on you even with your eyes closed. It was a solid colour: unwavering, but shallow.

Under it were eight-way hand-tied springs, which sounded good, but could jab your eye out if you got too close. And in my mind and my mother's mind was the need for those restful, watery hues, soothing to contemplate, but deep and treacherous, ready to suck you in.

"I'm covering the so-called human-interest angle—what there is of it, Mr. Greenwood," Margaret Montgomery said, after the furniture men had gotten their information. "I mean, why would a man who's done as many fascinating things as you have want to come here? That's the story."

She had a Northern accent. Her rhinestone glasses seemed to age her twenty years; she was like a business woman in the movies—bustling and efficient and not very pretty in her office—until suddenly she takes off her glasses or lets down her hair. And then you see she's really very young and pretty and her voice loses that sharp, cynical edge. When Margaret Montgomery said "human interest," she took off her glasses and closed her notebook, and she sat forward with her elbows propped on her knees and her hands out flat, under her chin.

"I mean, why would a man who's travelled all over the world and been the buyer of the biggest furniture store in New York City want to open a place here, of all places?"

What? I nearly blurted, and I could see my mother stretch forward before easing back again in her chair. Her eyes seemed to shut longer than necessary between blinks. My father, a world traveller? My father in New York? His voice dropped to a confidential whisper: "I never said I travelled. We can't help where we're born. My wife is English. I'm French. I left as soon as I could—the wars, they were terrible, you know. I saw the second one coming; I was here before it broke out. But leave me out of it—we came here for health reasons. My wife has been seriously ill. She needed the climate. I opened this place up because it's more satisfying to have even a small place of my own than to work for the biggest store in New York. But I have the experience, see, of selling to hotels. Waldorf-Astoria—you've heard of it?"

She didn't answer, but smiled.

"Then you know."

It was all too fast for me, I was still back savouring the main course—New York—with the French dessert yet to come. Margaret Montgomery put her rhinestone glasses back on and glanced at her notes. "Mr. Greenwood, where exactly were you born?"

I saw a chance to help him out of his obvious embarrassment; I sensed the woman was out to trap him, but she couldn't touch me.

"Mont—" I started.

"Who?" and she looked down to her notes again before looking up at me, as though the notes and not her eyes were the irrefutable source of all authority.

"Montpelier," said my father. "A section of Paris."

"David—this isn't for you," my mother said.

"Mr. Greenwood, that's not what you said earlier."

"I'm an American now—that's what counts. These people down here—they might not like it if they knew I was a foreigner, understand? Write what I told you. Boston, did I say?"

She turned to me, taking off her glasses and staring at me, like a teacher. She was dark-haired and blue-eyed; pale-skinned, and her lips were now a faded Tango Red. Faded, it wasn't so bad a colour. Her voice was very deep, like a radio actress who played unlikable characters. She had the weak "R's" not of a Southerner, but of a New Yorker. She was dangerous. She was not a friend.

"David, did you ever live in New York where your daddy was the buyer of a big furniture store?"

I could feel the responsibility for the future of the store. I was on a witness stand; I could hear her thoughts: *Think before you answer, David. You're under oath.* It took each of us a long second or two to frame our answers. Then the three of us spoke at once:

"That was before he was born," my father started.

"Why question the boy? He's very high-strung—" said my mother, only louder.

"Yes," I cried, loudest of all, and for a moment I could see it, a Manhattan monument to furniture somewhere between the Empire State, the Waldorf-Astoria, Grand Central, and the Stork Club, in that general neighbourhood.

"Fine," she said.

"Why not go outside and play, son?" my father suggested.

"David—go out. This doesn't concern you."

"And David," asked Margaret Montgomery, "what do you think of the furniture your daddy is selling here?"

I had to think of something quotable; her pencil was sharp and tapping the paper. "I don't think this kind of red would go good in Florida. It's too hot. And that blue—it isn't a restful blue, is it? It's kind of a nervous blue, don't you think?" I looked to my mother for confirmation; "nervous blue" had been her contribution to a late-hour argument I'd overheard. Her face was whiter than normal; my father's darker. But the reporter threw her head back and laughed like a man, until her body was racked with coughing. The salesmen who had heard me, and others who were attracted by the laughter, picked it up. ("Well, I got me a nigger outlet in Atlanta might can move it.") *There*, I thought, *selling isn't too hard.* Just be honest with the customers (as my mother always said) and you'll never go wrong. I'd brought everyone to their feet with a single sentence.

"You won't write that down, will you," said my father. It was not a question.

"I think it's *charming*. Plus the fact it's my sentiment exactly."

"Miss—" he reached out for her writing hand, but didn't quite catch it. It was as though he'd started with the intention of crushing it, then changed tactics at the last moment. "Miss, what are you drinking?"

"What I'm drinking is ginger ale. What I'd like is a gin and tonic."

"Gin—we don't have gin."

"I know. Bourbon and scotch, rum and Coke."

"David go back to the office now. That's the last warning you're going to get."

Slowly I stood, but didn't move. "Look, Mr. Greenwood," she was saying. "I know I can do you some good, and I don't have any reason not to. But I'm not going to do as much good as you seem to think I should. So let me get a story out of these frolics, and—"

"This is a showing, and a showing is a damn serious piece of business. This is the first dealer's showing in all of north

Florida, understand?" His hand lay nearly across her arm; I doubt if she could have lifted it if she'd wanted to.

"I'm sure it is—for you. Just don't make it so damn serious for me, or I'll show you exactly how powerful I can be. And I might tell people what I really think—you wouldn't like that, now, would you?"

"I told you, forget what he said. He's spoiled—*I said get out of here*—and sometimes, you can see, he's slow. He's—I don't know, not always right. He doesn't know what he's saying. We've had him looked at by the best people in the state. He can't help it, but by God I'm warning you. If you hold him up to ridicule in your paper, I'll sue. What kind of paper takes advantage of a crippled child?" I'd never heard the tone of righteous indignation from my father; it was a chord I didn't suspect he could play. Perhaps he'd been improvising, but it worked: I could see her bowing her head.

"Get lost," he snarled, slapping out at me and just missing.

I wanted to move. I wanted to run just as when I'd discovered my mother in the laundry shed. But it was as though the floor were the sheerest ice, and I had no traction. The reporter also put her hand on my arm. "You won't lay a hand on this boy, of course." She winked at me, then smiled maliciously. A group of buyers, attracted by the tone of voice were clustered around. "I might tell the truth about this ghastly chair. How would you like to be known as the man who turned the clock back fifty years? What have you got against the twentieth century, Mr. Greenwood?'

My father slumped so low, I wanted to comfort him. He'd worried all that morning about what he should wear, trying on suits and jackets and various combinations of Arrow Darts with sober ties, open-neck sports shirts with palm-tree patterns, and finally he'd chosen a dark, Florida-winter suit that looked wet or varnished. That would show that he meant business, but he'd also worn an Arthur Godfrey grey-and-red silk shirt to show he was a man of his times and place.

The trouble was, he didn't have anything between snappy George Raft suits and something that even Harry Truman might have thought twice about. And somehow, I felt, she'd spotted the flaw, caught him in his vanity where he thought he was safe. And so that's why I suddenly found myself crying—for my father—who wouldn't have been hurt so badly if be hadn't worn his dark, shiny suit and hadn't expected quite so confidently to be treated like a VIP. He had more faces than I did—I had only one—and it was heartbreaking, when you have so many, to have chosen badly.

(I'd always pitied people through the clothes they wore; even the bullies in school I could imagine standing cold and naked in their bedrooms the very morning of a day they would later beat me up, shouting, "What should I wear, Mommy? I have to beat up this fat kid after school," and when *Life* showed pictures of dead gangsters slumped in their barber's chair, I'd think, *he didn't know, did he, when he took the shirt out of the wrapper that morning it would end up soaked in blood before the day was over.* . . . And many years later, when Kennedy was assassinated, the full weight of the event hit me only when I saw the blood-stained striped shirt with the ragged bullet-tear. *Jackie*, I could hear him shouting from the hotel bedroom as she put on her pink suit in the bathroom, *what should I wear? The white, the blue, or the striped?* I always chose my clothes as though they might appear as "Exhibit A" in some posthumous melodrama; loss and poignance and tragedy could reach me only on the plainest level.

And it was like that in school, as I read the captions in our history books and compared them to the pictures. The pictures moved me. I hungered for those old photos, evidence of a past reality I'd been cheated of. "MODERN LOS ANGELES" the caption would say, but the picture told a different prewar story, with high, black boxy cars and men in dark suits wearing flat straw hats. It was silent-movie Los Angeles, and the anger I felt in the disparity between photo and caption would make the picture come alive for me. I would frequently caption scenes of everyday life, like this one in November 1950, with my father in his dark suit, surrounded by curious salesmen and with two women—one young, attractive, and smiling—and the other older and retreating with a sofa cushion on her lap. It was like a still from a movie that I wouldn't want to see. It would be called "SOMETHING HE COULDN'T SELL."

Did others ever feel it—the stiffness, the embarrassing awkwardness that passed for life? I would stare at the pictures in my school books, unable to turn the page because of the drama that was unravelling in my brain. "MODERN FARM FAMILY ENJOYING RURAL ELECTRIFICATION" said the self-satisfied caption, and there would be the heartwarming scene from a staged farm living room: Dad smoking a pipe, dressed in tweeds and a sweater, reading a paper, Mom knitting, Dog, Boy, and Girl kneeling before the enormous radio. *But they aren't modern*, I would think (not stopping to add, they're not farmers, either). Judging from their hair and clothes, the size of the radio, it couldn't be later than 1936. This is 1950. Those kids were my age then; they're grown up now and married, and that radio is junk, and maybe Dad got killed in the war. Or maybe even Boy, dead on Iwo Jima. I'd only met one man who smoked a pipe: the psychiatrist in Gainesville. I wanted to cry for such unacknowledged passing of time and to scream for such smug duplicity passed off as education; I was only ten but it stabbed me, and made my head echo like a great empty room. I couldn't turn those pages, for the same reason I couldn't leave the atlas and old magazines: *you don't know what's coming*, I would breathe over their picture. Anzio, Iwo Jima, the Bulge mean nothing to you. You can still stop Hitler. No wonder you smile and knit and smoke a pipe. I never felt more alone than knowing that in all the classroom including the teacher I was the only one to notice the age of the picture, or noticing, care.)

"Mr. Greenwood, I'll level with you," I heard the reporter say, and my father hunched closer to listen. They dropped their voices; their faces were alternately tense and relaxed. My mother and I picked up some discarded cups, then stood by the door as buyers started leaving. We made sure they each had order pads from the boxes of "Greenwood Displays" stationery that had arrived the night before. Then my mother went back to the Tango Red, and I went to the office in the back. I couldn't overhear, but I'd always been able to read faces, not lips; I didn't always know what people meant, but I never failed to understand the effect they were having. And what I saw on my father's face was something entirely new—and frightening.

The office, which contained only an old card table and folding chair plus a new filing cabinet, was in the old storeroom of the tavern, where the crates of beer had been stacked. The air conditioning didn't penetrate; it would always smell of stale beer. On the table my father had scattered dozens of papers weighted down by ashtrays banked with the butts of his machine-rolled cigarettes. There was, as well, a secondhand adding machine, the best toy ever devised for a child like me. I used it for totalling imaginary baseball statistics—how many years of improbable productivity, in home runs, pitching victories, or stolen bases would it take me to surpass Ruth, Young, or Cobb. But today I wasn't interested in baseball or in making any noise. Today I was just minutes away from making the most upsetting and most inevitable discovery of my childhood.

Under the unifiled papers and envelopes I saw a copy of the store lease—I was attracted to the revenue stamp pasted over a map of Florida—and though I was under the strictest orders not to touch a thing on my father's desk, I was confident that I could read it and return it half-hidden to its pile as stealthily as a spy. I was so certain of what I would see there—the name of the store, our names (it being the first time we had ever done anything official-looking, the first time we'd ever had legal "party of the first part" status) that for a long time I read over the lease and saw our names, Louis and Eleanor Greenwood, Greenwood's (Furniture) Displays. I had almost put it back with a feeling of reassurance—perhaps I had mistaken that look on my father's face, perhaps the buyers had really been impressed and not laughing at him—when I read the lease a second time. Something had registered—the most important thing. Greenwood's Displays appeared several times, but our name—my father's name, Lou Greenwood—hadn't appeared even once.

I looked behind me, for suddenly I felt a presence in the room, but it was empty. I was a spy, and I had discovered something incriminating—it was always at that moment in the spy and private-eye movies that the hero is discovered. There were many names, the most frequently appearing one being something so foreign I couldn't pronounce it. It looked like the names I'd written on my maps. If the strange thing I'd uncovered in the ditch behind our house had a name, it might be this: Louis-Nöel Boisvert. "S" and "V" together sounded Russian. I wanted to scream, but the reporter was still there, and I caught myself with an even more awful revelation. "Boisvert" was the *right* name; he was my father. Those words he used in counting were Russian; those stories my mother told me about "Germany" were really about the camps in Russia I'd read about in *Reader's Digest*, places where their top agents were trained in replica American towns to learn American ways. The whole store was a front; my parents were spies. I was adopted, and the reporter had to be told.

And who would believe me? My mother had made me afraid of Southern police, and J. Edgar Hoover was too far away. I thought of those movies I'd never liked before, the ones in which a woman is made to think she's crazy, due to the evil plotting of a husband and another woman. It would be even easier to do that to a child, to make a child look crazy. I could see myself an unconvincing imitation of a child, going to the authorities and claiming I was both adopted and living with spies, or maybe even—I had fallen through to another level—*aliens*. Of course: my mother had telepathic powers, and my father had uncanny strength. That creature I'd found in the ditch meant *something*, and sooner or later, they'd look for it, find out it was dead and who had killed it, and then I'd be a goner. Perhaps the pregnancy had been a hoax, a way of legitimizing the creature's existence in our family. All of this must have flashed through my mind in a matter of a very few seconds, for I was still in the folding chair, afraid to move, cold with sweat, when the front door closed and the reporter left. I felt I had only one place to go—out the window into the parking lot, and into town as fast as I could go.

I was too late to catch the reporter, but I ran faster and farther that day than I ever have in my life; I was tireless, running on the kind of terror and promise of heroism that drove the messengers of ancient Greece. I was afraid only that *they* were after me, that some advanced machine disguised as the Greenwood Displays panel truck would bear down on me, swerve once onto the shoulder, and crush my message before I could save the world. My mother—my "mother," I corrected myself—with her special sensitivity would of course know where I was; I only hoped I could reach a sanctuary before they caught me.

All this happened in half an hour. I had gone from dutiful son, a bit smart-alecky perhaps, but on his best behaviour, to a maddened guilt- and hate-ridden monster, who, if police had been present, would have turned his parents in as spies, kidnappers, and perhaps even aliens. For it had said *Louis-Noël-Boisvert, Alien*, on the lease. My mind was full of those Hardy Boys adventures; wherein Frank and Joe, catching the clue of a bobbing light on the water, a mysterious antenna, an attic light on when people should be sleeping, are able to break up a Nazi spy ring, detect U-boat landings, and thwart the poisoners of reservoirs. My head was bursting with images of recent war movies; I clutched them like medals, and then I started singing with the fervour of a Christian martyr all the songs I'd learned in school: "The Marine Corps Hymn," "Anchors Aweigh," "Semper Paratus," "Off We Go, into the Wild Blue Yonder" . . . and I remembered an offhand remark of my mother's from years before: *Eight years old, and the music they teach him in this bloody country are war songs. . . . No wonder, Lou, no wonder. . ."*

My father had said, *"So what? That's the way things are here."*

At the time, I'd agreed with her—there was something strange about a class of eight-year-olds learning for weeks on end that *it's hi, hi, hee, in the field artillery.* Now I saw it for what it was: another clue to her alienness.

I had been running along the gravel shoulder of the state road with the only thought in mind being to get to town, find the newspaper office, and spill my story to the woman reporter. It seemed I'd been running for hours—perhaps it was only twenty minutes, but I could not remember a time in my life, suddenly, in which I had not been running in terror. I knew the road well, but not from this perspective. I was beside a long-deserted tract of that same sour muck I'd dug in by the lake. It was a wet, black, scooped-out desert, with a few splints of dead cypress stuck in it like toothpicks. I'd gone nearly two miles, and suddenly my lungs and legs were burning; I ducked into the shrubs at the side of the road and scrambled down the embankment, out of view of the road. I got as close to the slough as I could bear, then stretched out.

The whole saucer-shaped field was humming with dragonflies and mosquitoes. Finicky white herons walked the surface like generals in dress uniforms, thrusting their beaks occasionally into the mud. The dead cypress poles supported all manner of birdlife, from buzzards on top, woodpeckers in the middle, to kingfishers perched on the knees a few feet above the top of the grass. The smell was faintly of cooking gas and human waste, but mainly a totality of every potential putrefaction in nature that I'd never thought of defining. It could have been the end of the world.

My legs were trembling and aching. The dead trees seemed to dance in front of me, the numbers of waterbirds multiplied, and the buzzards overhead, a permanent feature of Florida skies, were defining a circle directly over my head. I was afraid to close my eyes for fear they would take it as a sign and drop on me in a second. I did not want to die that way, eaten alive by vultures. And so I stood and let myself slide down the embankment to the edge of the bog. I could see a grey, doglike shape moving across the mud and into a patch of tall grass. There was something patchy in his fur, sloping in his hindquarters, that made me realize he wasn't tame, not even once-tame and gone wild. He loped too easily, head low to the ground; he was wild.

I could imagine an alien city under that saucer of foul mud, something intricately connected to our store, and the ditch behind our house. At night, this same peat bog glowed with purple lights from the spontaneous combustion of natural gases. But maybe, I thought now, they were the exhaust fumes of giant generators. The creature approaching me as I took my first step onto the mud was their watchdog, something strangely doglike, a good disguise. Everything was making sense: the fact that my parents didn't look, act, or sound like other parents; that I wasn't like other kids; that the doctors and all the others had had such strange and special names for me that I was "one for the book" wherever I went.

There were other dogs now, following their grey leader, and they had lifted their heads, sniffing in my direction. I was well out on the bog, halfway to the first dead tree. Each step I took was getting softer, and soon I would come to puddles that lay permanently on top. The dogs were fanning out, following the drier edges of the bog.

The mosquitoes were so loud that I didn't hear the sirens. And the first crack of a rifle was dry and remote. But a dog yelped, jumped high, and then keeled over. And a second. And the dogs disappeared. I turned and saw two state patrolmen squatting in the bushes where I had been resting, rifles still drawn. My parents were standing behind them.

I turned slowly, putting my hands behind my head, the way they did it in war movies. I closed my eyes and waited for them to shoot.

There is much I realize now about that episode. I had gone mad; paranoid schizophrenia, fed from the radio, papers, movies, and comics, and triggered by the loss of my name. There were logical explanations, and they were laid out to my mother by the same Gainesville psychiatrist who'd tested me earlier. "Why, of course my husband changed his name," I heard her say to the doctor, to whom in private I confessed what I'd seen in the office that had driven me out the window. "His name is no more 'Greenwood' than mine is Harry Truman. But it *means* green wood. *Bwa-vair*. He just never got around to changing it officially."

"That can still set a sensitive child off," I heard him say. "A name's a pretty big thing, when you come to think of it."

My mother tried in her own way to explain things to me, but I was like a patient in convulsions whenever she approached. They put me under blankets, despite the heat, and I shivered. I trusted the doctor, the first man I'd seen who smoked a pipe; I showed him my maps, my sketches, I let him quiz me on capitals and populations. We talked about the thing I'd dug up. ("Those are not rare, David, believe me. It's only an old mudfish sleeping away the dry season deep down in his mudpack. A living fossil, lungs and all—nothing else, believe me.") I talked to him about Silver Springs, about the death of George Bernard Shaw. "You mustn't feel connected to every death, David," he said. "It's only a natural thing."

But I couldn't admit to him about my sister. I denied that I'd been upset when they told me "it" had died. I felt I didn't look good in that story.

He brought me my father's passport. Louis-Noël Boisvert, b. Beauce, Québec. It was an old green passport, stamped only once for entry at Highgate Springs, Vermont, in 1939. His picture was the Rudy Vallee shot, forelocks flopping. "We wanted you to be American," he said. "No good, being a Boisvert in that place."

"We were at war, you see," my mother said. "America wasn't."

I asked to see her passport. It was also green, but well used. Double-headed eagle stamps, their claws containing swastikas. Entry stamps for the Deutsches Reich, police stamps for France and Switzerland, Poland, Czechoslovakia, and Hungary. "All gone now," she said. "Everything swallowed up." I learned for the first time where she'd been born—London—and her maiden name—Eleanor Woods. The German branch was also Woods (in German, Wald); she'd lost first cousins on both sides of the Somme. Her father, a staff officer, had been gassed, evacuated, and advised to get out of England altogether. South Africa had been his first choice, then Australia. Papers were late in coming, and they'd chosen Canada. But Eleanor had despised Regina, staying only long enough to finish college. Her parents died, and she took off to Europe for training. Then she'd worked in London until she realized she wasn't any more English than she was European, or Canadian. So she picked Montreal as a compromise, she told me now; not as deadly dull as the rest of Canada, not as snobbish as London, not as frightening as Germany. Or the States, she added.

"The rest you know."

The time always comes for parents of an only child to realize they have raised a monster—that they are, in a sense, *his* children. They had shown me their passports and confessed their lies. Not lies, just lives. My father had entered legally but had fallen behind in his annual alien-reporting. Finally he'd dropped all pretense, had become Lou Greenwood in the remotest corner of America, and established a new personality. He'd paid the lawyer to fix it on the lease, just in case anyone wanted to raise a claim. And so I understood at least the structure of a small deception; the flesh of it was yet to come.

If the human is an organism, he must preserve, in some psychological state, at least, the distinctive stages of a creature's development. I had been a larva, some hideous squirming thing living just under the surface; I'd had a crisis, the extent of which I was still too young to grasp, and now I was becoming a pupa, something chitinous and inert. I always saw myself very clearly as an animal, and a particularly lowly one at that.

I met the woman reporter Margaret Montgomery several times that winter in her house, where my father often dropped me off. After a few visits, I came to like her and to find her less frightening. She didn't wear rhinestone glasses at home. She was a funny, smart, and bitter woman, and she hated Florida as much as my mother did, and hated it in ways that I understood.

She had a daughter a year older than I, but no husband. The girl, whose name was Beatrice—called Bea, pronounced in two syllables—was nothing like the mother: blond, taller than I, and freckled. She seemed always to be dressed for a party; in pink dresses, black patent purse and pumps, and a small gold wristwatch. She wore the same clothes to school, where she was one grade ahead of me: a tall, isolated little girl who never acknowledged me there; but in her house she would treat me with a rare honesty, even intimacy.

She was one of those children for whom adolescence was approaching in patches; her nose was already as long and stately as an adult's; her teeth were also long, white, and straight, but still seemed overendowed for her mouth. I thought of her as a British princess. She never called me by my name, but rather, "Little Boy," and sometimes, "Curious Little Boy," as in "Curious Little Boy, what have you been doing since I last saw you?" And I, with my hunger to convert any tolerant child into a friend, and any different kind of girl into a sister, would take it all.

"Doing curious little things," I would say. It was a very private kind of friendship—a very appropriate one under the circumstances—which was the only way I could have handled it.

We spent our weekends in her back yard playing Monopoly. Monopoly lay on the outer reaches of my sociability, and somewhere near the rim of her maidenly reserve. Like me, she'd always lived with adults; we were both replicas of an ideal we carried, formed from books, movies, the air itself. In our Monopoly games, she would be banker, I deed-keeper. Perhaps she knew of my fondness for colour; what more beautiful game than Monopoly, the cool blue or fiery red tips of deeds! I always shuffled the deck. I liked to mix them up. She was hard to play with—I abandoned myself to the game, as always— but she did not. Girls and women were always doing that in serious games: getting up, counting objects in their purses, or simply staring beyond and through me. I thought of women as either easily distracted, or exquisitely gifted with a kind of psychic perfect pitch that responded to calls that men couldn't hear. My mother was like that, sitting at times with a deck of cards in her hand and rows of solitaire laid out, still as a statue. This girl, Bea, kept pacing around her yard, looking up to the second-floor bedrooms, carrying her purse as though she intended to leave me with the Monopoly board, and I would gaze at her with a kind of wonder. She bit her lower lip, rubbed her thighs, sighed, lifted hair from her eyes between two fingers; women's gestures. I didn't know why my father had driven me to this particular house or why he was staying back.

"Don't you think they're taking long enough? I mean, Monopoly can go on for days."

"Especially the way you play it."

"Oh, don't be smart, little boy. I want to go back inside. We've got television. But no, I've got to stay out here."

"It's your move."

She sighed, smoothed the grass before sitting, and we went around the board a few more times. Monopoly Anxiety: I knew how my father felt confronted with bills and the visits of a once-friendly banker. Sometimes Bea failed to notice that I'd landed on her property; this disconcerted me.

"Why don't you go in, then?"

She shot me the don't-you-know-anything? look; girls always knew something I didn't, or couldn't, know.

"Is your father divorced?"

"*No!*" I only knew it was a terrible word, as though he were a convict or Communist. It was such a terrible word that I couldn't say it; couldn't even say *divulge*, or *diverse*.

"*Please*, little boy, don't exasperate me. It's all right to be divorced. My mother's divorced. It only means your parents live away from each other. I get to spend the summers in New Jersey and the winters here." She anticipated my next question. "New Jersey is much better. All my friends are there. You're the only person I know in Florida—isn't that something?" She smiled briefly.

I thought I read something in that smile, something that made me say, and say very softly, "I'm glad."

"You're all right. You'd fit in in New Jersey. I don't think you belong here."

"You're like a sister," I said, trying to communicate all that the word meant to me, and failing. She winced.

"Anyway," she said, dismissing me and looking back to the house, "let's hope she gets tired of Florida and decides to move to California or something. Hey—you want to know something, little boy? I've been on the real Ventnor and real

Marvin Gardens—what do you think of that? These are all New Jersey places." Her fingers started walking down the expensive side of the board, disrupting houses and hotels. "My daddy takes me for real walks on the real Boardwalk, little boy. What do you think of that?"

I fanned the deeds out. They were real? I couldn't believe it; *everything* was real. I was given toys while other kids— no smarter, just luckier—were given the real things. Maps, leases, digs in the mud; even a Monopoly board, for some people, was a real city. I looked up to the big frame house and made out the shadow of my father passing a window, white shirt flashing behind the screen. "I guess he'll be down soon," I said.

It was a signal to begin packing up. We carefully counted our assets and cashed them in. I liked laying the money back in the drawers, then sorting the deeds back into groups. My father was standing at the doorway, motioning for me as I carried the box away.

"Little boy," Bea said, reaching out to stop me for just an instant, "strange little boy, I've been thinking of what you said back there. It's true, you know. I am your sister." Then she giggled, exposing those long adult teeth that were symbols, to me, of all her secret knowledge.

I would like to think that I understood her, and perhaps on my separate level, I had. But she had given me credit for more worldliness than I possessed. I mumbled something about being only a stepsister, and part-time at that.

"Silly little boy," she laughed, and tapped me lightly on the arm. Then she ran ahead, far in front of me, across the wide green lawn. In my imagination, she is still running, and my father is still standing in a doorway, a flash of white behind a screen.

Of the acts that conclude childhood, I have only a brief one to offer. It happened in Margaret Montgomery's kitchen on a cold, wet December afternoon when Bea and I were confined indoors. My father had dropped me there as he often did, then taken Bea's mother to her office, he said, on his way to the bank. Bea and I had started with cards—gin rummy, at which I excelled—then Monopoly (my nemesis), and finally turned to crayons and watercolours. She was precocious in a pictorial way, favouring horses and lighthouses, windy days, green fields, and white fences. I could copy things accurately, but needed a model.

In those months after my "hallucinations," as they were called, I'd turned to sketching and colouring, something my mother encouraged me in. She bought me the biggest box of Crayolas then on the market: sixteen, then twenty-four, and finally forty-eight crayons in boxes thicker than cigarette packs. Forty-eight colours nearly exhausted the inventions of crayon-science (four kinds of brown and half a dozen stops between azure and turquoise), and, given my mood on a particular day, my reaction to the whole forty-eight would be gratitude for the variety of the universe, or depression that there was not a colour among them that did not remind me of something disgusting: lipstick smudges on Chesterfield butts; the funny little furry balls that floated in our toilet, too small to flush; nervous blues, Tango Reds, bottle-green flies, bread mold.

Bea and I had spread the crayons on the kitchen table; forty-eight long new ones and her old shoebox full of wrapperless stubs. Bea's lighthouse was taking shape; I could never compete with that. I could do some birds, some fish, maps, and baseball pictures. Also Bugs Bunny and Captain Marvel, but those were all private pleasures. I'd be ashamed to admit to any of them.

It then occurred to me that a hundred crayons on a table-top formed a beautiful pattern, a dazzling accidental map far lovelier than any I'd done. I was happy enough just gazing at them, and gazing at Bea's long fingers with the painted nails as they hovered over colours, dropping old ones and plucking up new. "Why don't you draw something, you quiet little boy?" she asked.

I said only, "I'm thinking of something."

Perhaps I said it strangely; she stopped drawing and said, "Thinking of what, David?"

I started peeling off the paper of the new crayons, and then I broke them up. "Get a cookie sheet," I told her, "and turn on the oven." I sliced, chopped, and grated those forty-eight hues into a heap of colour, a thick, textured, multi-coloured pizza of wax, a Persian carpet. Six minutes in the oven, watched through the glass till the colours ran but didn't burn or bubble. Then I took it out and set it on the floor. We stood over it, walked around it, aware, I think, that something remarkable had just been created.

"What *is* it, David?" she asked, and I couldn't answer, for I was lost in its reds—the blood of my dead sister. I kept thinking—and the multifariousness of black; every colour was tending to black, but I had caught them before they yielded up their essential green, or blue. I saw in them the elusive shimmer of things still moist but dying—birds' wings, fishes' backs; I still remember it, it is—or was—a replica of my mind at the age of ten, a repository of facts and textures and colours. And as I stared, I grew frightened of it, as though I were staring at my own disembodied brain. A voice whispered to me, *this is crazy; you've done something crazy. You're loony, that's what.*

I asked Bea not to tell her mother what I had done. Then I lifted the mass with a spatula and put it in the sink. The running water brought out all the beauty, one last time. Then I smashed it like peanut brittle and threw it in the garbage.

I called my mother out at the store and told her I'd been at the movies. That was another of my father's codes. Then I sat in the living room with Bea Montgomery, watching television and waiting for my father to pick me up.

PART 2

I'll call the city Palestra. We arrived there the summer I turned thirteen, and we stayed till things fell apart. Palestra was the first real city I'd lived in and the first place in which I had felt at home. It is still all that I know of America—really know from work and sex and school—the rest was central Florida and what I've lived through less vividly since.

Palestra had engulfed three steep river valleys then extended itself through a series of suburbs and satellite cities, filling in every valley and level hilltop with townships and sprinkling the terraced hillsides with weathered frame houses, linked like Swiss chalets by painted staircases. It was strung out and cut up, condensed only in "the stadt," its ten-block downtown core. Otherwise it was a collection of orbiting clusters of separate jealous identities. In that first summer, I rode all eighty streetcar routes (they had been the city's first attraction; I'd thought streetcars—my mother's *Strassenbahnen*—had existed only in her stories of Leipzig and Dresden), and I committed their names and numbers to memory.

Being Floridian, I'd never seen sooty brick buildings or hills and valleys, and never had I seen black people riding buses and shopping in stores, handling merchandise that whites would later touch. It was all a wonder to me. I'd known only forties versions of New York—airborne shots sweeping uptown from the Battery—and thirties visions of small-town America, where simple people passed their lives rocking on porches behind picket fences.

(In those towns drugstores had soda fountains and boys dreamt of becoming soda jerks. They ganged up in club-houses to do good deeds. They paired off with dimpled girls then went off to war. The normal ones all returned. The dimpled girls were waiting. The boys went off to college and came back lawyers. They hung out their shingles and married the girls who'd waited. A new generation was born. *The agony I felt*! I ached for those Joan Leslies and Diana Lynns and June Allysons, those high-school sweaters with the single letter in the middle, those sodas, jalopies, and unclouded visions. And longing for them, suspecting it was my fate to be separated from them by being fat and Southern and having parents who'd come too late to America and spoke with accents, knowing that even our splendid rustic name of Greenwood was only an invention, I mixed my respect for Mickey Rooney, Jimmy Stewart, Ronald Reagan, and Fred MacMurray with a kind of guilty loathing.

Those perfect American lives terrorized me. I felt I had no right to them. They nagged at me like the nutrition charts that hung in classrooms, honoured like dictators' portraits. Wholesomeness eluded me. "Balanced" meant only gluttony, plates heaped with red and white meat and multicoloured vegetables, cereals, fruits, and everything the dairy industry could think of selling. If sensible diets were the norm—if Jimmy Stewart was the norm—then I was a reprobate. I might have been mentally and physically nothing but junk, but evidence seemed equally persuasive that too much wholesomeness did something to the brain.)

And of course I knew the South where towns were also small, and people rocked placidly on their porches. They boiled their vegetables brown and deep-fried everything else. And the lives they led were savage.

Palestra was an almost-northern city; Triple-A but not major league, one of those cities the road maps didn't know what to do with. We weren't over a million so PALESTRA wasn't spelled in compelling capitals and we just missed the yellow urban scab that signified inclusion in the Top Ten. We weren't even the state capital so we didn't have a star. We were only old and industrial and less important than we had been. The population had once topped a million but now had declined to six hundred thousand. As large cities went, it was a known bad risk. New investment was shy and the old wealth shipped its profits elsewhere. We weren't in disrepair, we were merely shabby.

Yet that cluttered past contained its riches; the *nouveaux riches* of the 1880s had willed us the artifacts of a more confident culture. We had opera houses, museums, galleries, and universities. The planetarium had a prewar Zeiss projector; the city zoo was practically a game park. The Palestra Symphony was considered the third-best in America—nothing Triple-A about it. Yet every decade the population declined, as though Palestra alone were fighting some secret and distant war that claimed only its most attractive and most ambitious leaders.

It was one of those cities in which a number of famous people had been born. Despite their later attachment to New York or Hollywood, I knew them as Palestrans, like me. In that first summer, I would encounter their names almost daily: *Palestra-born songstress . . . actor . . . composer . . . novelist . . . industrialist . . .* and because I identified so loyally with the city, I never forgot who they were. I would read their books and see their movies and honour their innovations in nickel-plating and flash-frozen foods. They were like distant relatives whose fame added lustre even to my name, should I wish to invoke them.

It was also a city in which a number of very strange people had died. European royalty, exiles, exotics-on-tour. Even in the fifties it retained a number of consulates, a few lodges of the Sons of Serbia, Estonia, and other defunct republics and chapters of benevolent societies that maintained graves and sponsored parades and picnics on obscure saints' and national days. Bizarre faiths and extinguished movements all endowed with perpetual trusts maintained their impish memorials. Nearly every outcast of the early twentieth century had found a tolerant podium first in Palestra. I accepted this as unremarkable, little suspecting that such openness to heresy and self-expression might have been one reason why so many famous people had come from Palestra.

It was a city very hard to like. You had to love it to stay there at all.

In other words, Palestra—cut up and stretched out, absurd and alien—was a perfect place for us to have come to. I took to Palestra fiercely; it contained everything that I could feel affection for. I memorized the locations of suburbs and their ethnic demarcations. I tried to make myself a native. I combed the city the way I had once studied every hair on my father's scalp, every mole and vein on his body. A sober little child, I overlooked the comedy that made Palestra a joke on the postcard circuit. The city had been founded by a sect of pious Germans as a kind of New Jerusalem. The patchwork of ten intersecting blocks that formed what was still called "the stadt" was named for Christian virtues. But now the virtues were merely words, many of them blasphemous, that we deliberately mispronounced. The avenues were *Intercourse, Salvation, Communion, Hope, Faith, Duty, Valour, Dignity, Compassion,* and *Judgment* (to help with the sequence, kids were taught a jingle: *India Sang, China Hopped, France Drank, Venice Dropped, Chicago Jumped*). The east-west streets were *Tolerance, Patience, Charity, Temperance, Good Works, Continence, Deliverance, First, Second,* and *Third.* (For that, it depended on one's age: children learned *The Poor Cold Turkey Got Wet; Chilled Drumsticks 1—2—3*; adolescents learned *The Preacher Can't Think; Girl's Wet Crotch Distracts, a-one. a-two, a-three.* There must have been other versions.) Nothing is more arbitrary than the street names we inherit, yet it usually takes a revolution to actually change them. No one in Palestra ever thought of changing the names, but we all learned indigenous ways of pronouncing them. Both "Dignity" and "Charity" were stressed on the second syllable to rhyme with "gritty," appropriate enough for the rows of Army-Navy surplus outlets and mysterious trading companies that had gathered down there. "Continence" I took as a geography reference; and "Hope," in my radio-fed little world, was only the name of a comedian. "Patience" was right for the rows of partially empty frame tenements and boarded-up movie theatres and marginal gas stations selling private brands. Patience Street seemed to be waiting for something and was doomed to disappointment.

My father had accepted a job as furniture buyer in a downtown department store called Seligman's. The store had been in decline since the depression, after a glorious nineteenth century in which the "Anna Z. Seligman Center" had been endowed, along with medical scholarships and hospital facilities. My father was fifty-three that year, silver-haired and anxious to "turn it around" after so many false starts in so many cities. We rented a house on Daley Ridge, named after Jas. T. Daley, founder of a canned foods empire. The same Jas. T. Daley, had endowed the museum and the library.

The advantage of the Ridge was that it did not automatically reveal one's income and origins. The Ridge was old enough and tolerant enough to contain a little bit of everything. It was not quite a suburb, which meant the trees were mature and the frame houses spacious (but all in need of new pipes and fixtures); the plumber's pickup parked under a chestnut or the City Parks crew sawing down an elm were integral parts of life on the Ridge in the early fifties. People on the Ridge were nearly all middle-aged, with kids my age or older.

The choice had been between renting something old and spacious on the Ridge ("Your coloured are starting to move in," the agent had warned us, "so I wouldn't recommend buying") or buying a tract house in the newly opened northern suburbs, one from a row of identical embryonic shells whose minute differentiation—in the colour of trim or the shape of glass panels on the front door—would appear only in the final days of its gestation. In the end, my mother deployed the fact that Ridge schools were considered the best in Palestra ("If you don't mind your Jews," the agent had advised, perilously, given our ambiguous name, my father's accent and dark good looks, and his position at Seligman's) to keep us with something cool, used, and spacious. But even after we'd moved in, we would tour those new houses every Sunday, admiring the built-in dishwashers, disposals and lazy Susans. The back yards looked out on rows of timber (and would continue to for the next several months); they all had small "Colonial Malls" a few minutes' drive away, with parking space for perhaps thirty cars. "Soulless," my mother declared, but my father had set his heart on building a house in the suburbs, someday.

(But it wasn't soulless—at least not yet. If my first thirteen years have any meaning, it is this: two worlds exist. One we create; it is ours alone, private and untranslatable. The other is always there; we do not control it. It has never changed; we can only discover it. There are gates to it everywhere, and sometimes the two worlds slide together. When the gates are shut, then it becomes without a soul.

I remember one deep-summer Sunday, walking out alone behind a tract house that my parents were looking at, to the edge of the clearing where the idle bulldozers were parked. The back yard was only a gully of skinned clay ending in a line of mature elders, oak, and laurel. The woods dipped sharply into a steep-sided ravine that smelled of encroaching septic tanks. But there in the remaining stand of woods, at the edge of a very small, stagnant pond not fifty yards from the bulldozers and the land they had skinned, stood a tarpaper shack. And in the knee-deep water beside the shack, three boys were jigging with long, sharpened sticks, bent over the water like Amazonian Indians. It was a scene from my remotest Florida childhood, when other blond boys wearing buttonless shirts and torn underpants had gigged frogs and scraped the mud for turtles. But this is "Verona Heights Development," I kept reminding myself. My neck grew prickly, the way it did in science-fiction movies, when you knew a hairy alien arm was about to reach out or an immense shadow about to fall. Suddenly one boy plunged his stick in the mud, shook it, and brought it up bent with a mud puppy, a gash of red running down its white stomach, and its frail limbs fluttering. The boys came whooping out of the water back to the shack, and a toothless old woman came out and grabbed the stick and slipped the creature off it. They disappeared inside.

I was sitting on a bulldozer looking down at the water, then back to that shell of a house, just to make sure that we were all in the same time and place. On my walk back across the naked clay, it occurred to me that within a year this grove of oak, laurel, and box elder would be gone, and the gully would be filled, and the shack would be a pile of rotting boards. And someone in a "Verona Heights Romeo Ranchette" would inherit a damp basement every spring. And if I had not climbed on a bulldozer one Sunday morning in the hills north of Palestra, none of this would be known, or believed.)

I was now walking in a city like the maps I'd drawn as a child. My imagination had always lived in a place like this, a willful, unnatural city where the roads followed improbable contours. My own creation drawn on the scale of one-to-one.

I absorbed the flow of streets. I could rule the streetcars from Daley Ridge to "the stadt" and the museums or walk down eight hundred wooden steps to the river below me. I could visit the Daley-Palestra Public library, an enormous grey fortress with a green copper roof and carved marble lions at the door and escape to their card catalogues, flipping through the thousands of entries until I'd find the grey, crumpled, ancient cards to books purchased sixty years before in the 1890s, when the aged authors were still alive. And never in the intervening sixty years had they been pulled or corrected. Perhaps the book was lost or had never been borrowed. My neck would prickle again as I held the card: *Björnholm, Axel L.* (1793–), *Songs of Modern Sweden*. And there I stood in 1953, my hands trembling at the statistical evidence of near-immortality that I was holding.

I rode my bike through the hearts of older neighbourhoods with their signs in other languages, and I would see, faintly painted on the taller brick buildings, faded advertisements from a vanished era: ISADORE ASH & SONS, IRONMONGERS, in script as dated as Gothic German and I would wonder: what is a monger? how long had Isadore Ash been dead? were his sons still here, or had they like everyone else gotten out? A sign like that or those of DYERS & SOAP-MAKERS would throw me back to those old *National Geographics* that still held me fascinated: city scenes of Model T's and sidewalks draped with telephone wires.

During rush hours, Palestra Street Transport still put some of its oldest trolleys back in service. Wooden-sided and cane-seated, they accommodated only a fraction of what the newer models did, especially since only a fraction of the public wanted to ride them. They had very few seats, but wide platforms for standing and many poles to lean against. Those streetcars were like rolling porches. People who stood could lay their parcels down and lean against a post to read their papers, and those who sat could really stretch. I would wait for those old ones, thinking somehow, as I rode through unfamiliar parts of the city, that I was commanding imaginary time as well as space.

Palestra was the New York City of the minor leagues, the largest city in America with a Triple-A team. This was at the tail end of an era, when cities had teams and not just franchises. Major-league baseball was northern and eastern, and in a pinch, mid-western, more a guild than a sport. The Palestra Braves had never been good; few Braves ever went on to stardom. Attendance averaged only a few hundred each night, and perhaps two thousand for a Sunday doubleheader. Perfect for me, a lover of anything vulgar yet still exclusive. I became a regular bleacherite that first summer; then, after the inevitable Saturday defeat, I'd change personalities and trudge across the small baseball parking lot to the giant green-roofed fortress of the Daley-Palestra Library and Natural History Museum, more impressive in every way than 'The Home of the Braves." The ball park, in fact, was constantly threatened with demolition; Palestra must have been the only city in America where the municipal sports facility lived in terror of an expansionist museum. And I must have been the only regular from the bleachers to have an emotional stake in both establishments.

In those years I had a well-developed appreciation for museums but a deep dark lust for baseball. And Triple-A baseball responded to my love. The Braves needed me and I could love only what was slightly imperfect. For a lover like me, a Saturday game in August, when Palestra, deep in the second division, played Syracuse, another starless squad going nowhere, was bound to be an intimate experience. After the third inning the box seats were opened to everyone. And I would sit silently with a hundred other boys—most of them on Legion teams, wearing their caps and cleated shoes and carrying their oiled and darkened gloves, but some like me: hopeless, moist-skinned cases with some deep desire that baseball quenched or projected. The hundred or so adults were regulars. Unemployed, girlfriends of the players, gamblers, American dreamers.

The joy of Triple-A baseball for a boy who'd seen nothing but Class D in central Florida was first of all its polish and competence. Ground balls were spectacularly fielded (Triple-A was the permanent home of slick-fielding, light-hitting Latins), fly balls were caught and pitchers found the plate. Back in Florida I'd been used to a dozen passed balls and to outfielders reeling under fly balls till in a daze they crumpled, holding their skulls for protection. That rarely happened even with the Braves and when the great teams like Rochester and Montreal—the Cardinals and Dodgers of the future—came in, I could visualize, like a distant mountain range, the outline of something inspiring. And there was beyond the security of competence, the magic catalyst of intimacy. We were close to the players and most of them were flattered by our attendance.

They were very young or very old. Tolerating the old—and in the minors anyone over twenty-five is old—was a special agony. We could feel the bad knees and sore arms and swinging guts of the old-timers who'd hung on in the majors during the war then been sent down never to resurface. I hated them. Their achievements were all dishonest. Their home runs and shutouts would get them nowhere. They had no dreams. The waste of setting records in anything short of the major leagues struck me as some kind of ultimate tragedy. I could picture our most successful pitcher, a thirty-six-year-old left-handed knuckle-baller, coming back to his Palestra apartment at midnight, saying, "I won again," and having his wife roll over and snarl, "So what?" I wanted to shout out to him he was wasting his time, but the painful thing was that obviously, like me, *he still cared*. It was tragic.

The special pleasure of Triple-A was the propinquity to promise, the closeness to talent that might prove itself just for once, unlimited. Always the possibility that next year would bring us not just a .300 or even a .400 hitter, but a .700; a forty-game winner, a superman. The stadium cliché—*Tomorrow's Stars Today*—was right. We were blessed with precognition. By the time our stars reached the major leagues they'd already be tamed, never as magnificent as in the diminished setting of our smudged lights, brown grass, and canny has-beens. We knew them all years before Mel Allen or *Sports Illustrated* "introduced" them to "America." It was a perspective that I treasured like all my other slants on America. From Florida I had studied the cities of the world and forced myself to know the Loop as well as Don McNeil, Los Angeles as well as Joe Friday, and of course to absorb the grid of magic called Manhattan and everything within it. Triple-A fed that passion. It was the last place where it was still possible to thrive on pure, raw talent.

(After the broadcasts I would wait for the interview with the "star" of the game—normally a Braves' opponent. In all of Palestra there might have been a hundred souls—all-night chefs and taxi-drivers—who stayed tuned after a defeat for the cloying modesty of the winning pitcher. But one night the star was a young outfielder named Enrique Hernandez and the interview exposed attitudes that were foreign and frightening and a dozen years ahead of their time. Enrique was eighteen and he spoke through an interpreter. His voice was high and melodious, nearly a whine; that's why the translation came as such a shock. He'd been signed on the soccer field. He hadn't played baseball except as a joke. But Enrique Hernandez was simply faster and stronger and better coordinated than anyone else on an island of fast, strong, coordinated boys. The scout had given him two thousand dollars to sign, more than he had ever seen. They'd taught him the game in a week, put him a month in Class D, then promoted him to A, then Triple-A. The only criticism one heard of Enrique Hernandez was that he was lazy. He made the game look too easy. There was an implicit contempt in all his actions—lobbing the ball to the infield behind the runner, taking good strikes and swinging at bad pitches, deliberately catching balls at his shoe tops or belt buckle—that outraged the fans and managers. He'd introduced insult and humiliation to the game of inches. True, he was hitting over .400, and sometimes from right field he'd throw out lazy runners at first base; but the sportswriters all said that if he'd model himself after Joe DiMaggio or Ted Williams, he'd be hitting .600. With his gifts, it was a sin not to. Just think what Stan Musial would do with a fraction of Enrique's natural talent. And so the shock was profound when the interpreter cleared his throat and said, "Who is this Ted Williams? Who is this Stan Musial? I am Enrique. Enrique is the greatest."

The announcer giggled. I snickered. I had the impression that Enrique must be grinning, too. No one could even *think* such things and mean them. "Well, that's very interesting, Enrique," said the announcer. "Very interesting. It's nice to see a cocky, confident kid in the league. Look, though. Six months ago you were still cutting cane down in Puerto Rico. Tonight you let one of our boys—one of our *slower* boys, I might add—get over to third base on you. You just lobbed it in to second, and he tore right over the bag and steamed in to third. Made you look bad, Enrique."

"*Me sooker heem!*" Enrique squealed angrily in English. "Me throw heem out at home next play. He *muy estúpido*. No run on Enrique."

Until that night I'd never heard the voice of naked confidence. It was frightening. I dared it only in my dreams, but Enrique controlled eighteen men like figments of his imagination. His interpreter went on, "Enrique say it take only a pitcher and Enrique to play your Palestra team. Everyone else, he can sit down." This brought tolerant chuckles from our announcer. Boys from the cane fields—they were all from the cane fields in those years—were supposed to be proud and colourful as well as moody and shy. But basically they were supposed to be grateful. I even wanted Enrique to admit he was joking. The announcer went on, "Well, some might call him arrogant, fans, but you've just heard what makes Enrique Hernandez one of the most exciting young ball players in the most exciting league in America." And I could hear that same young, black, high-pitched Spanish voice in the background laughing. "Ha!" it said. "Enrique the greatest. Nobody he play like Enrique."

Enrique Hernandez hit only eight home runs that half year in Triple-A. But in his rookie year in the majors, he hit thirty, and for the next fifteen years he averaged between thirty-five and forty a season. The statistics welded themselves to me as a principle from which I drew secret reassurance. For the truly gifted, the major leagues are *easier* than the minors. Triple-A, Palestra, adolescence—these are the sterner tests. There was, of course, a flaw in the argument, for Triple-A specialized in its own brand of successful slugger. Big fly-ball hitters who were the terrors of middle-sized parks. They'd go to spring training with a new major league club each year and make it through all the early cuts, then be back with us by the middle of June. It never mattered; they'd still hit their forty homers and win the title. What it meant was contradictory, but I forced a self-serving interpretation. It meant that *élan* and arrogance were the signs of a hidden genius. Consistently impressive results in the minor leagues pointed only to a consistent mediocrity.)

I had roamed the city for nearly two months without meeting any kids my age (at thirteen I was still waiting for the melting of baby-fat, the brewing of those endocrinal potions that would turn me from boy to man). The fat boys at the baseball games with their dull button eyes pushed into their ruddy cheeks were doomed to fat and were slow in every way. My fat, I liked to think, was thin-fat. Inside me was a skinny, precocious teenager ready to leap. I wondered where and how it would happen, this thing called adolescence. My life was a small gear meshed with an infinity of larger ones leading eventually to giant wheels turned by giant turbines labelled at times "girls" or "friendship" or simply "happiness." My little wheel would have to whirl a thousand times to make the giant wheel groan a notch.

One Saturday in late August, miserable with hay fever and reluctant for some reason to spend the whole afternoon in the open air at the ball park, I crossed the parking lots and entered the enormous museum and library complex. Usually I chose the library, for I loved the smell of old books. I felt at home wherever people were silent and polite. Those were hopeful signs for me, evidence that the virtues that were natural to me—self-control, curiosity, consideration—were still alive even in this year and this city. The library was the only place in the city that a thirteen-year-old could go to and be assured of respectful attention by an adult. Nevertheless, on this particular Saturday, I didn't go to the library. I turned left and walked down the corridor through the Marine Hall into the museum.

The giant rooms were dark and nearly empty. Emptiness was partially an illusion since the Dinosaur Hall tended to dwarf the onlookers and the theatrical darkness to obscure them. Only when noisy Cub Scout packs scuttled through was I aware of crowding. Young artists often brought sketch pads with them and spent a whole afternoon in front of the brontosaurus, copying just the feet. My favorites were more dramatic and less subtle. I preferred them stuffed or visualized in some less accurate way. *Water-Hole on the Veldt at Dusk*, with thirty predators, their prey, and carrion-eaters slurping in peace. Neutral benevolence, like a library—I wanted to believe it was possible. Others were less reassuring: a pride of lions with a zebra kill. A circle of musk-oxen arrayed against Arctic wolves. Everglades swamp-life ("hello, old friends," I thought, suddenly smelling that sour purple Florida muck I'd once dug in and feeling a wave of heat reaching up my pants leg). The stuffed displays were all very old and European. It was hard to imagine a young American taxidermist.

Most of the displays dated to the last century and had been done in the ateliers of England and Germany. (*Hannes Fischer, Berlin, 1883*, I read, as though it were a nameplate under a famous painting; obscure fame both interested and depressed me. Then I thought of my own long-dead Wald great-uncles, Hapsburg skies, and the strange, compelling beauty of people's obsessions.) I found myself staring at Hannes Fischer's most famous display, the one the museum thought highly enough of to put on its promotional postcards. Next time, I told myself, I'd bring a pencil and sketchbook. I stood in front of the glass case for several minutes, staring with the intensity I'd once been capable of with maps, until the displays were no longer dead for me and the glass no longer a barrier.

It was the most violent of all the displays. *Nubian Lion, Attacking Bedouin and Camel.* The lion seemed small for the damage it was inflicting. As one claw raked the camel's neck, the other had opened a gash on the Bedouin's leg just about the knee. His flintlock had jammed. He was reaching for a knife under his robes. He was a dark, fine-featured man. The camel was doomed. Its eyes were white with terror, and its neck was twisted fatally. And yet the gore alone did not explain the full horror for me. There was an almost-narrative element that kept me in front of it with my hands sweating. I, too, was that Bedouin.

Though everything was perfectly realistic—the robes and the flintlock were genuine eighteenth-century artifacts—the scene was anything but realistic. There was no sand at their feet, no mural behind them. It was closer to the quality of nightmare. I'd never associated lions with the desert (and the caption mentioned that the Nubian lion was now extinct); they seemed superfluous to its own vast malignancy, like the heaped-on hideousness of vultures, hyenas, and vampire bats. How did a lion lie in wait? Did it track, did it boil from the sands without warning? Did it bound over the dunes, counting on the raw improbability of its existence as the best protection? It was so small, like something anyone might be excused for dismissing. I could sweat with that Bedouin, for I, too, was thinking: *Look, Khalid, a lion—must be chasing an ibex. Oh, how strange, he's turning our way, Khalid. What can he be after? I'd better take out my rifle just in case. Fire a warning sh—damn! It's jammed. Could he be after us? Move, Khalid! By Allah's beard, he's attacking*—I must have been standing before the case in a dream, for when I finally pulled out of it, aware of smudges on the glass, a girl was standing next to me looking both at the case and at me.

"*Kitsch*," she sniffed. She was shorter than me with hair so black and a face so broad she looked at first Eskimo. Which, I told myself quickly, couldn't be. She was merely a clumpy girl my age with lifeless hair and large mouth and a nose that had never been babylike.

"Why *kitsch*?" I asked, glad to know the word from the furniture business. I'd never applied it to anything outside of Chinese chests and French Provincial bedroom suites.

She carried a spiral-binder sketchbook and she'd been up on the second floor sketching the Chinese pots and medieval church doors; things real artists sketched, and she was good. "Cluttered, for one thing," she said, apparently deciding that my use of a codeword at least merited a response. "Trying too hard to tell a story. I mean, 'Bedouin and Camel,' for God's sake—the Nubian lion should be the focus. Fischer's work was always like that. The idealized Bedouin comes straight out of German Romanticism. The Prussian barons all filled their hunting lodges with stuff like this—you know, of course, that's how we got it. Pre-Nazi pornography passed off here as an educational exhibit." Her voice was husky, like June Allyson's, the r's softened in ways that seemed foreign. I couldn't guess her age—anything from an unfortunate thirteen to a youthful thirty-five. No one had ever spoken to me with such assurance or had so assumed my ability to respond. And of course I couldn't. Everything she said seemed right. Or wrong; I didn't know what she was talking about. I was immediately ashamed of having liked it. Crude of me. I nodded.

"The *tableau vivant* as an art form is an abomination, don't you agree? Can you imagine anything more repulsive than stuffed animals? It's like mounting deer's heads. European decadence passed off as great art in provincial America."

Now *that* was something I could respond to. She was insulting Palestra. "What *do* you like, anyway?" I asked.

She flipped the pages of her sketchbook. "Nothing on this floor. Window-dressing with dead animals. Ugh."

"You must not be from here," I charged—triumphantly, I thought, until I saw her sneer, brief but unmistakable. I had just confirmed something that she thought despicable.

"I mean," I stumbled on, "people here don't travel very much. They haven't seen other things to compare . . ." I wanted to tell her why—if I had known myself—the lion and the Bedouin were not cluttered and why the excess appealed to me, but I was frightened of her. I doubted that my feelings mattered very much. And I was tongue-tied for another reason. It had taken my imagination about ten seconds to turn that squat Eskimo body into something gently molded. She was not fat; she was prematurely formed. Her pituitary had done its work. It took a few more minutes to work on her face; to overcome my astonishment that a child's fat cheeks, child's braces, child's pudgy fingers could accompany such a mind. It took a few more seconds to accept that face and to discover its dimples, and then to like it. To prefer it to any girl's face I'd ever seen.

"Haven't I seen you at J.A.'s before?" she asked.

I wished fervently that she had. "Junior Achievement?" I asked, eager to the point of naked deception to establish some sort of contact. They were the people in high school who organized companies, sold stock, and made products. They frightened me; junior editions of the salesmen I'd been raised with.

"Are you kidding? God!"

"What, then?"

"Christ."

"Tell me. Junior something, right?"

She looked me over carefully. She was on the verge of telling me and I wanted to whisper: *you can trust me*. But then she snapped her sketchbook shut and looked straight ahead at the lion and the Bedouin. Her face was grim, deeply insulted. Then she looked beyond the glass case, out to the Cretaceous Hall with its fifty-foot murals of dinosaur life. There was a group of teenagers milling in the hall, some with sketchbooks, and all of them, for an August Saturday, as oddly dressed and as oddly shaped as we were. Many of them carried handkerchiefs against their hay fever.

"J.A. is through there," she said, pointing to where several of the boys had gathered before a camouflaged door in a tyrannosaurus's claw. They started to go inside and now the girl I'd been talking to ran like a little girl to catch them.

"What's J.A.?" I shouted back to her in a voice that echoed, but she didn't turn. "Take me, too!" But still she didn't turn and now the giant rooms were empty and silent. The door had closed without a seam and without a knob.

The guards now were beginning to stand. It was five o'clock on a Saturday afternoon and except for the group I'd almost joined, visitors had to leave. The guards who finally came to me and motioned me away from the prize exhibit must have thought I was crazy, shouting, "What did I say? What did I say?" into an empty corridor.

Daley Ridge Junior High School was attached to the senior high, the whole yellow-brick complex occupying two full city blocks with yet a third for playing fields, tennis courts, and a parking lot. Though "The Ridge" as an address had lost some of its lustre, the schools were still the best and they would remain the best long after The Ridge had deteriorated noticeably. Later generations came for the schools alone; parents sacrificed equity for the sake of education. The second generation of students in the once-exclusive suburbs were better than the founding generation had ever been.

And so we rented a frame house on one of the last streets within the school district of Daley Ridge. The street wasn't "typically Ridge," being younger and blue-collar. All were white, and none were Jews, and most had come north in the same piecemeal fashion we had, though none from as far south as Florida. My father wasn't happy with the address. As a downtown executive he was expected to put on a better show. My mother didn't care for the neighbours but she was only a block away from a direct bus to the art galleries and museums and the downtown shopping. For me, already an adept with street transport and most of what the city had to offer, the residence made little difference. Where I slept and ate was unreal to me; I didn't live anywhere but in my own imagination. Maps, baseball, and a stamp collection. My parents, who had been my world for twelve years, were about to bow out. I felt that first summer as I had once on my father's lap at Daytona, steering a powerful convertible as he manipulated the pedals: invincible.

School came round again. I was in the third of twelve sections of the eighth grade, and fully half the boys in the class seemed from their bulk, their careful clothes, and well-combed hair, their wadded-up handkerchiefs, possible allies if not friends. Gone were the childish smells of paste, crayons, and sharpened pencils. The classrooms of Ridge Junior High smelled of old textbooks, the aroma of issues long settled, like the reading rooms of the public library. Here the twenties architecture with the unscarred fifties desks and fluorescent lighting seemed to say: *We've given you the best.*

We expect the best from you. No nutrition charts; only rolled-up maps, a flag, and portraits of Lincoln and Washington. The glass cabinets in the hall contained athletic trophies as well as last year's Honour Roll: Highest (five A's), High (three or four A's, one or two B's) and Regular (one or two A's, three or-four B's). There were ten on last year's Highest Honour Roll from the seventh (now eighth) grade: Allen, Carpenter, Duivyibuis, Posner, Melnick, Feigelman, Stewart, Soberman, Williams, and Silkin. Six were boys—my competitors.

Every room had a public-address system—for giving announcements and (the joke went) for secret monitoring of classes at random. The school never fully quieted down. There were always students in the halls looking purposeful, groups of students on the playing fields practising formations; students were always walking out of class by some complicated system of prearrangement. This was my first experience of a northern school, the first time I'd not sat all day in the same desk in the same room with my fellow whites, taught everything by the same old woman. Suddenly we had black students, male teachers, and five minutes to hustle between classes.

I was not going to stand out; I could see that. On that first day I overheard enough conversations to know that up here, at least, the girl in the museum had been no freak. My classmates were carrying thick library books, and they would retire with them to corners of the cafeteria while munching on a sweet roll. Are you Soberman? I wondered. Duivyl-buis? Stewart? Allen? Melnick? I could make out the names on those thick books. Names that had drifted into my consciousness, then right back out again as adult and forbidden: *War and Peace, The Red and the Black, The Brothers Karamazov.* I had avoided such books not out of laziness, but out of superstition. They were part of an adult world as much as bars or stories of Fatty Arbuckle were, and I would be allowed to understand them not gradually, but only after an initiation that would be years in coming and then finally automatic.

No one had told me that it was time to try them. Now I was afraid it was too late—like diving, or ice skating—to start.

In the first few days of school we were asked to sign up for activities. Since I enjoyed being officious, I chose usher squad. Also, I suspected I looked less like an onion in slacks and sports coat. Of all the nonathletic activities, ushering was the only one not to depend on talent, popularity, or reckless self-exposure. Ushering also carried benefits: early dismissal on assembly days, free movie admission, and the thing I truly desired—entry into a backstage world. We would arrive in the auditorium in time to watch orchestras rehearse, and we were introduced to guest speakers—some of them locally famous people—when they were still alone on the stage rehearsing. And once their voices changed, ushers were chosen for P.A. work in the high school, working the consoles, taping the assemblies, and reading the announcements to every room. It was celebrity.

The first event was "The Blackthorne Show." Blackthorne was a mentalist, mind-reader and hypnotist who advertised a further speciality: the ability to transfer his gifts to selected members of the audience. *Dr. Blackthorne will release the same powers in you!* the posters read.

The posters of Blackthorne scattered about the school showed a dark-haired man with a black, pencil-thin moustache, dressed in black tie and cape. The real Blackthorne, whom the ushers met while arranging chairs on the stage, was a small, straight, white-haired man well over retirement age, wearing a grey jersey with hood and pockets—the kind that boxers did roadwork in—and dark slacks. He seemed quite fit but for a grave, ruddy face topped with the wiry now-white hair that had been his professional glory. The posters had shown lustrous, waxen hair, slick as a coat of lacquer. But the different posters that he brought with him and had us put at the corners of the stage were of an intermediate phase of his career, necessitating a shock of greying hair, sometimes plastered and dyed, sometimes teased and whitened, to vary the effect from diabolical to distinguished. The moustache too had waxed and waned through several moltings. In the early pictures, it had seemed painted on, a villainous version of Groucho Marx's. He'd settled this time, however, on a bushy-haired, mad-scientist image, allowing varying shades of grey and even streaks of stark white to work their way up nearly to the twin partings. Between the partings, however, he'd elected to go all-black and then slicked it down; the effect managed to be both sinister and pathetic. He looked like the kind of old man that boys instinctively avoid.

I'd expected an accent, but Dr. Blackthorne spoke in a reedy mid-Atlantic voice, one that barely carried over the orchestra pit from the front row where he was sitting. I worried for him; I knew so well, it seemed, about well-dressed professionals down on their luck, about people who deserved bright lights and sophisticated audiences and who had to perform a sleazy number in the glare of a junior high school auditorium before five hundred unawed skeptics. We'd arranged the chairs, and now all of us (there were ten ushers, sleek as porpoises in suits and watered-down hair) were standing embarrassedly by the chairs, wishing we weren't implicitly a part of what was about to happen.

"You," he said, and though he didn't point, I knew he meant me. "Come down here."

I took a seat three away, which seemed plenty close. His cheeks had been powdered; the skin was raw and beaded underneath, having been asked too many times to appear pink and youthful. There were flakes of lipstick wedged in the wrinkles around his mouth. He gripped the bottom of his jersey and peeled it off; he was wearing a formal shirt and cummerbund underneath. His hair was like a helmet, nothing disturbed. He took out a small mirror and barber's combination comb-and-scissors and flicked it through his moustache.

"Well, David, how do you like Palestra?" he asked, still looking in his mirror, talking out of the side of his mouth. When he trimmed his eyebrows, a white powder sifted to his lap. I was still Southern enough to answer, "Very much, sir," more from shock than politeness.

"More going on here than in Florida, I suppose."

"Yes, sir."

"Father happy at Seligman's?"

"Yes, sir."

"I'll tell you something about Seligman's. Within a year, they'll be out of business. That's not mind-reading. You can tell your father in case he doesn't know." He put away his mirror and scissors and turned to me. "I've done you a little favor, and now I want you to do one for me. Want to be in my show?'

"Doing what?"

"Doing what you're told." He didn't smile, but got up and stood in front of me. He threw his head back and worked his thumb under his collar, grunted, and sealed it with a gold stud. My father went through the same agony every morning, sealing his starched Arrow Darts, then working in the wire collar-stay behind the tie. He'd never been able to find shirts sufficiently tight around the waist and sufficiently wide around the collar to accommodate his ex-boxer's neck. The compromise (as with Blackthorne) was simply to suffer, to stuff the neck flesh into the unyielding collar, rather than to wear a larger shirt that might possibly bunch around the belt. Blackthorne, too, had been a physical man.

"Were you ever a boxer?" I asked, putting off the answer to his earlier question. He seemed surprised and a little displeased, judging from the frown and the arching of one darkened eyebrow. I could almost read his thoughts: *I ask the questions around here, sonny,* and he was a man who repressed his anger only by visible effort. "I was never a *boxer,* no," he said, pronouncing the word disdainfully, as though referring to the breed of dog. "But I was a gymnast, many years ago." He was holding onto the ends of a black tie which he'd just worked under his collar, when suddenly he rolled his eyes back, elevated his chin, and executed two crisp backward flips ending precisely on the spot he had begun with his hands still at his collar clutching the tie, which he nonchalantly proceeded to knot. My fellow ushers on the stage seemed not to have seen the demonstration, and within seconds, I wondered myself if I had only imagined it. Blackthorne's voice now took on a deeper register, and when he called out to the boys on the stage and to the lightning crew high above us, he had no difficulty making himself heard.

"How long before we start?"

"Ten minutes," I said.

"Very well . . . I will call for fifteen volunteers from the audience, and you will be one, right?" I nodded. He put on his black jacket, crumpled up his jersey, and threw it up onstage. "In my duffel, please," he called to the boys, all of whom scrambled to comply.

Once the auditorium filled, Blackthorne was transformed. His tinny voice had disappeared but retained a mocking, metallic quality. His face at a distance was firm, pink, and glowing. He controlled the five hundred in the dark and the fifteen of us on the lighted stage like some masterful animal-tamer. "

I'm getting a message for a Paul. Paul . . . happy? No, I get images of happiness. *Gay.* Paul Gay? *Wait*—there's more. Lord. Gaylord! Paul Gaylord—stand up." And one of the deep-voiced, raw-boned ninth-graders stood, blinking exaggeratedly, falsely shy and secretly pleased. "I have a message for you, Paul. It is from a girl." The audience roared, Paul bowed his head, and a meek "Oh, yeah?" filtered up to the stage.

"I get the same of a tree—a girl with a tree's name—do you know such a girl?" There were giggles from up on the stage, and a tall, blond girl covered her face.

"I might," said Paul Gaylord.

"I see I've got the names right," said Blackthorne, holding his temples and closing his eyes. "Now for the message. It's about Friday, right? You and this girl are supposed to be going out on Friday—isn't that right?"

"I ain't sayin'."

"But she has a message for you, a very important message that she doesn't know how to deliver. She's asking me to deliver it now."

A chant started up, with loud, deep-voiced laughter that meant something dirty.

"Oh, yeah? What's this big message supposed to say?"

"Oh, that wouldn't be gentlemanly of me to say. But I'll tell you this much: what she will tell you is the truth. Girls don't tell the truth very often, you know, so pay attention to her. That's all." Blackthorne held a stern pose for about ten seconds, then smiled, concentrated, and delivered another message. Paul Gaylord was left scratching his head and shrugging his shoulders in every stage-gesture of mock innocence, arrogance, and manly indifference.

Blackthorne performed many such feats, most of them more specific and less philosophical than Paul Gaylord's message, but the Gaylord episode stuck in my mind because it seemed to me (without ever having had a date and with a complete ignorance of sex), that some desperately important *sexual* message was being communicated. It was so important that Blackthorne was willing to "fail" to be impressive in front of his audience. *She's pregnant*, I thought, though I didn't even know how pregnancy occurred. Such a conclusion was so far from any speculation I had ever made that it struck me as a partial miracle, wrought by the magic of the stage.

The highlight of his act was his special "deep hypnosis" of a subject and the temporary transfer of his magical powers to him. "I understand there is a new student on the stage, one who knows no one in the school—is that true, David Greenwood? Come forward, please."

I stood, nodded, and approached.

"Now, David, I am going to place you in a deep trance. You will be perfectly safe. And while you are in the trance, you will *be me*. No, don't worry, not physically. (Laughter) Now I will place my hands on your head. You will close your eyes and count backward with me, and when we reach four, you will be asleep. Agreed?"

The moment his hand grasped my temples, I felt something cold and metallic like a ring work its way through my hair, settling finally on the skin behind my ear. "Eight . . . seven . . . " I was not feeling sleepy, but I did feel a buzzing in my left ear, the one facing away from the stage.

"Four!"

I was never more awake. But I believed I must be asleep; either that or I was the type who couldn't be hypnotized, in which case, my brief minute of glory would be snuffed out.

"Now, so that he cannot see, I will place a hood over his head—after passing it around to our other volunteers so they can check it." Five or six of the others tried it on and confirmed their blindness, and passed it back. Blackthorne then slowly eased it over my head. A grey fog descended, which I expected to gradually darken into total blackness. But it did not. *I must be asleep*, I thought. *I do have Blackthorne's powers. I can see perfectly yet I can feel that something black is over me! They don't know I can see—it's like being invisible.* My ear was roaring with static every time that Blackthorne moved.

"Now, David, can you see?" He was standing ten feet in front of me, hands outstretched. He raised three fingers. "How many fingers am I holding up?"

Say two came a woman's voice bursting into my ear. and I blurted out "Two!" so suddenly and loudly that I jumped. I was terrified, he'd split me in two.

The audience laughed. "Fine," said Blackthorne. "Now, David—I am going to give you the power that the poets, the scientists, the prophets have all dreamed about. '*O, wad the pow'r the giftie gie us, to see ourselves as others see us*' You understand? You are going to leave your body, David Greenwood. Your eyes and ears are going to travel to mine, and your brain will settle in mine. Or should I say my eyes and ears and my brain are going to settle behind your black mask." He slapped his hand and held up four fingers. "*Now*! How many fingers am I holding up, David?" He held up four.

Say four.

"Four!"

Light applause rippled from the audience. "No, no, ladies and gentlemen, boys and girls, not yet. That could have been luck. Or a little trick, right? No, no, we must have something harder." Two teachers wheeled a blackboard onto the stage then turned it away from me toward the audience. "David, I am writing something on this board. Tell the boys and girls what it says." The audience started laughing and applauding.

"Silence, please. David—what have I written?"

The woman's voice whispered in my ear. It said: *Mr. Wilson got a parking ticket this morning.*

Mr. Wilson was the principal. I could see him in the front row, pumping his right arm up twice and smiling. I repeated the sentence. Now the ripples turned to waves of sustained applause, which Blackthorne cut short.

"David—do you know the names of anyone onstage?"

"No, I don't."

"Yes, you do, David. You know their names and homerooms."

The whispered voice came in. *The first one is Laura Fisher. Seven-three. The second is Irving Melnick. Eight-two.* Irving Melnick was a name I was grateful for; one of the Highest Honour Rollers and one of the lunchroom chess players: a spare, bespectacled boy who was in history and a study hall with me. His hands would tremble as he laid out endless rows of solitaire with a pack of miniature cards. He'd seemed like potential friend-material, but I'd not known how to meet him. The voice in my ear kept crackling; it was difficult to keep up with it. *Denise Tozzle, nine-four.* Tozzle? Did I hear right? I couldn't afford to get a name only slightly wrong; by now I was Blackthorne's accomplice. "Denise . . . Denise. . ." I said, and *Driscoll,* came the correction. Then a Chuck, a Bonnie, and Wesley Duivylbuis, another Highest Honour student, whom adolescence had begun to ravage. Two Nancys, a Bonnie, a Dave, and a Murray. And a final girl, a tall blonde by the name of Laurel Zywotko. She was in my English class, and by virtue of her tight skirts and fuzzy sweaters, her swivel walk and a bosom that managed to be both pointed and mountainous, I had—like every boy—noticed her; she was, in fact, in the pure animal blandness with which she invited stares and seemed to return them, the reason I looked forward to English class. The trouble was that she rarely attended. *Laurel Zywotko,* came the whisper in my ear and I almost blurted out, *and she's pregnant and wants to tell Paul Gaylord about it.* But I only repeated the name in the same dull voice, smiling to myself under the black hood. She stepped forward and a few dozen whistles broke out from the audience.

My performance was not to end on the mere recital of a few names. I was asked to turn my back on the students and Blackthorne, and each of the volunteers was to whisper a secret into Blackthorne's ear. *He* was then to project it to me, a sensational feat of mental telepathy. I was terrified, having no way of seeing *who*—let alone *what*—was engaging Blackthorne's attention. I stared through my transparent hood out into the motley, cheering, half-standing, passionately believing crowd. Some of the front-row kids were giving me the finger. I could imagine them turning on me.

"Now, David, one student onstage has just whispered something to me. There is no way you can know who whispered it, or what the message was—am I right?" And I could picture him behind me, arms outstretched, for the students

in front of me were standing like spectators at the last minute of a close basketball game, roaring back, "*Right!*" And
the roaring continued so long that all I heard was "*Dermice
Tozzle jwana void dunno logger atcher school.*"

I must have shrugged my shoulders; it was pure terror
that had kept an amplified "What?" from escaping my lips.
Blackthorne suddenly shouted, "Please, the thought-transfer
requires absolute quiet." And the audience hushed immediately, as though that last-second rally had fallen short. I
longed for a thinner body, a deeper voice, not the bulbous
frogshape of my unmelted baby-fat; *then* I would be worthy
of their applause, bug or no bug in my ear. And they wouldn't
dare attack me if I made a mistake. I'd have been a hero.

One more time, came the woman's voice, clear at last.
*Denise Driscoll wants a certain boy to meet her by her locker
after school.* I repeated it. From giggles and moans of recognition in the audience, I was right. They were mine now,
and I could forget about the voice in my ear; like a child who
"drives," with his father doing all the work, I'd convinced
myself that the headful of messages I was now receiving were
all correct; I could be doing this without assistance. *Wesley
Duivylbuis is next*, came the voice, *and he is thinking of a certain postage stamp* . . . Then the voice broke off suddenly, the
way UN interpreters sometimes did; *nothing to worry about*, I
thought. And so I began, "Wesley Duivylbuis is thinking of . . .
of . . . *Wait*, the voice commanded. I was interested in
Duivylbuis, another study-hall chess player and reader of
heavy books, since I, too, was a stamp collector, a natural hobby
for an old mapmaker. The voice crackled again. *He is thinking
of a Scott . . . is that right, Scott? Catalogue number . . . A16 . . .
1938 . . . from what? Cay—Cayman Islands—is there such a
place?* And from under my hood I was nodding happily, ready
to deliver a brief geographical account if necessary. *Wait.* I
was picturing that beautiful set of stamps which I myself had
recently purchased from A. King Gordon, the stamp dealer

on Temperance Street. *Stop, it's a trick! Oh, dear.* The voice went dead; the audience fell silent.

"Ladies and gentlemen, boys and girls, please," announced Blackthorne. "The boy is under great strain, as am I—if I do not get full cooperation from my volunteers, I will waken him now from his trance."

He's deliberately withholding information from Blackthorne. He wants you to guess what's on the twopenny stamp without telling Blackthorne first.

"I'm not getting a clear picture. . . " I began.

That's good, very good.

I heard the first scattered boos from the audience. They changed my mind.

Don't say anything more. It's a trick. Let Blackthorne handle it.

Wesley Duivylbuis could have tripped me up on a thousand simple facts from the thick books he was always reading. But pride and suspiciousness led him to one of the few areas where I happened to be well fortified. I almost giggled under my hood. I sensed Blackthorne had pushed Duivylbuis aside and called for a more cooperative volunteer who was not out to prove something at the possibly harmful expense of a fellow student, but Duivylbuis had refused to move. His voice broke through the general confusion: "Let him read *my* mind! I'm thinking of it now. If he's so good, he can read me as well as he can read you!" *Yeah, yeah*, came the low rumble from the audience.

I turned to face Blackthorne and I could see he was furious and beginning to move toward me, waving his hands as though to wake me from the trance. "I am responsible for him while he is under the trance. He could be injured with your tricks. . . ." But then I took a slow, tentative step toward him, hands outstretched, and I too began to wave. The noise in my ear was deafening, picking up every movement of Blackthorne's, and amplifying. "Wait!" I shouted. "This boy is thinking of a stamp."

Stop, hissed the voice.

"Enough. I shall waken you," announced Blackthorne.

"Right so far," said Wesley Duivylbuis.

"I can see it. It is an old stamp . . . no, not *too* old. My age . . . 1940 . . . maybe a little earlier. From a very small place. Let me get this . . . Cay? Cayman Islands? Is there such a place?"

"Right!" came Wesley's voice, a freshly changed one that suddenly cracked with excitement. "So far."

"He is thinking of a particular stamp from that year and that little island," I said, trying to maintain the oracular tranced quality of voice that we've been trained to accept as hypnotized; though I found it hard not to laugh, not to give myself away in the manner of a child who has found so good a hiding place that only his laughing reveals it. But I saw that 1938 issue clearly: halfpenny, penny, one-and-a-half, two, all the way up to the ten-shilling value that I hadn't been able to afford. I owned the "short set," from the orange farthing up to the one-shilling brown, all with young King George VI in the corner and native scenes from those God-forsaken Caribbean islands occupying the centre. I'd bought them two Saturdays before from King Gordon, a man who normally didn't cater to young collectors but had tolerated and abetted my interest in British-American stamps. Ah, yes, Wesley Duivylbuis, I can see you also proceeding to the office of King Gordon, down the dark corridor of stippled glass doors, thinking yourself unique for knowing about stamps from places you'll never visit.

"You are thinking of a twopenny stamp. It has a number in a catalogue. Scott Catalogue—"

"Right!"

"Number . . . A . . . A . . . six. No! A-sixteen!"

"Right!"

"The colour of the stamp is deep violet."

"Right! And what's on the stamp? Just tell me what's on the stamp."

"On the stamp . . . " I pressed my hands to my temple. "Try harder, give me the picture. This is very hard. On the stamp . . . I see . . . palm trees . . ."

"Yes!"

"I see a man's head—a king's head—in the centre. And in the middle I see . . ."

"What?"

"I see . . . a turtle!"

"Fantastic. He's right!"

I could hear the cheers, deafening applause.

Duivylbuis was still shouting, "Amazing! Amazing!"

The audience was standing now to applaud, and Blackthorne took the opportunity to run over to me, lift off the hood, pluck out the microphone, and snap his fingers in my face. I allowed myself to return woozily and modestly to consciousness, and to accept the handshakes of Duivylbuis ("What'd I do?") and a couple of others. When the audience finally quieted down, Blackthorne came to me again and placed his hands on my temples and said, "You are now awake, David. And you will remember nothing—absolutely nothing (and here he jabbed his knuckles into the hinge of my jaw) of what you have done. You feel strangely rested and happy." Then he took my hand, like the tuxedoed M.C. at Madison Square Garden, and raised it high, clenched with his. The two of us took our bows, and then I retired to the line of volunteers behind him.

By then I had conveniently forgotten about the trick veil and the bug in my ear. I had a sudden horror that he had indeed put me to sleep at the beginning and forced me to undress and perform undignified acts onstage, while feeding me a waking-up fantasy of my divine omniscience. I checked my dark pants, found them properly creased, impeccable. So I *had* done it. I'd merely imagined a voice in my ear and a transparent veil; I had done it all myself. I had powers (fat little me) that my mother never dreamed of. A week in this school, and I was a star. I was standing between Irving Melnick and Wesley Duivylbuis, who'd parted ranks for me, a little respectfully. "Are you a stamp collector?" Wesley whispered and I frowned at the absurdity.

"No, why?"

"Fantastic."

"Yes, very impressive," said Irving Melnick in a high, gravelly voice that had done all the changing it was going to. "There's a trick to it somewhere, though."

"Trick to what? What did I do?"

"Obviously, if it wasn't a trick, this guy would be kept under lock and key by the FBI or something—he'd be too valuable. He wouldn't be performing for junior high school kids. But it was interesting."

And later, when I left the stage to perform my function as usher, I noticed the students were staring at me, some whispering, "How'd you do it?" and others risking a quick "What number am I thinking of?" Conversations all died as they filed around me.

As was customary, the ushers went backstage after the auditorium had emptied to give the official thanks. Blackthorne was back in his jersey, looking tired, but he managed to shake each hand and to remember every name. I was the last, and he didn't let go of my hand, but instead led me over to the wings. His face became flaming red, incensed, as he pulled me away from the group. "How's your jaw?" he asked, and I had to admit it still was sore where he'd jabbed me. "Well, you're lucky. That was a stupid little trick you and your pimply friend tried to pull. You're just lucky you pulled it off."

He told me he could have clipped me on the neck and I would be paralyzed for life. And he'd do it, coming up to me in a crowd when I least expected it, if I ever told anything to anyone about the way he worked. He walked me back to the rest of the ushers, his face a rosy pink, smiling broadly, his hand loosely pinching me around the neck.

Duivylbuis, Melnick, and I were in the same American history class, taught by the track and cross-country coach, Toby Church. He also taught Boys' Health, the only required course set by the state. Aside from the two courses, Mr. Church occupied himself exclusively with track and cross-country—duties that he performed impeccably. He was, in fact, a legend in high-school athletics; his picture had appeared in a small box in an early issue of *Sports Illustrated* when "a Church-coached team won its 150th consecutive meet." He was described in that same box as a "Lincoln scholar and history teacher," the first half of which he passionately believed. He was otherwise a modest man in his late forties with short blond hair turning to grey, flaring cheekbones ruddy with razor burn, and a dimpled chin usually ringed by smaller nicks. The only thing that Mr. Church had difficulty with was American history, which baffled him like a poorly laid-out cross-country course. Very rarely, in fifteen years of teaching, had he managed to lead the class beyond the full complexities of the Civil War. The reason for that was that he had read Sandburg's *Lincoln* and liked to augment the textbook with weeks of reading to us in his droning voice from Sandburg.

Wesley Duivylbuis was already crowding six foot, a blond boy with rather long, precisely combed hair. He belonged to Daley Ridge; there was even a Duivylbuis Park in the area, though Wesley never alluded to any personal connection. It was he who chose the passages for Bible-reading each morning. He also came to school in a Boy Scout uniform once a week (modestly storing the sash of extra badges in his locker). In gym, he cut a competent and compassionate figure in basketball or volleyball, often serving as captain and frequently not choosing me last. He had been handsome and would be handsome again, but now, incongruously, for one who lived and ate so temperately, his cheeks had sprouted pus. I would study those patterns as though they were constellations. Red giants, white dwarfs, mature yellows: I wondered if he, too, studied them with a view to pattern and design, to perhaps naming some of the permanent features. Such wanton disfigurement in so blameless a life implied some sort of guiding malice. But if this was the price one had to pay for puberty, I thought, even if it left me pocked and purple, I would gladly pay it.

Oh, thirteen is an ugly, awkward age!

Duivylbuis was bright, religious, patriotic, a Boy Scout, and even athletic, without "going out" for school sports or even following a team. The only contact between Wesley's world and my own was stamp collecting. And because of my triumphant mind-reading, I could not admit to him that I too collected stamps, also specializing in British America. In fact, fear of detection would cause me to approach King Gordon's office every Saturday morning cautiously, pressed against the wall and ready to duck in to a stairwell or men's room should I hear Wesley's voice from King Gordon's opened door. It was absolutely necessary that he believe I had read his mind, rather than having merely consulted my own.

And yet I insisted to myself that I was like Wesley Duivylbuis. At least, I thought so at thirteen, and I wanted him to know it. There were a few areas, of course, where Wesley was more intelligent, others where he was bizarre, and others in which I had no sympathy or understanding. I could forgive his lack of interest in the Palestra Braves (I felt it as a keen unworthiness in myself), but nothing in my background attracted me to community service, to religion, to summer camps, Boy Scouts, or after-school jobs. I blamed these lapses on the large family he came from—there were Duivylbuises on all the honour rolls from high school down to grade school, as though single-handedly they were out to prove the superiority of their gene-pool and way of life. His father, an important downtown executive, had refused to buy a television set. He and Wesley had designed, and then installed, the first set of seat belts in Palestra. Even at lunch Wesley showed himself a devotee of nutrition charts, despite their inefficacy against pimples. I took only a sweet roll and milk and saved the additional eighty cents a day that my mother gave me; these savings, plus a generous allowance, were spent at King Gordon's office every Saturday. And I did nothing for my allowance. Duivylbuis had an after-school paper route, a summer job at the Y-camp, and an all-purpose lawnmowing and snow-shovelling service. He, too, had an allowance, smaller than mine. The rest of his earnings were put in the bank for college. And I liked to think I was like him!

If Duivylbuis was an inspiring figure, then Irving Melnick was frightening. He was my height, but thin. He wore blue jeans, as did the criminal element in the high school, but his were never properly faded; and worse, they always had very wide turned-over cuffs. The high-schoolers wore their jeans on the rim of the hip; Irving wore his up around his navel. He looked terrible, of course, as anyone does in turned-over, high-waisted jeans. I never wore them for the same reason—the only ones wide enough for me were about eight inches too long (Levi Strauss having projected the proper height for my waist at about six-three).

It wasn't the clothes that made me shy of Irving; it was what I sensed was his madness. Insanity ("always close and often indistinguishable from genius," according to my first seven years of teachers and schoolbooks) seemed to hover around him, he of the trembling hands, facial tics, chess, solitaire, baffling responses, and open challenge to all authority.

(My introduction to him had been in the first gym class. The moment Irving came on the basketball court, the coach had blown the whistle. "*You*—why aren't you wearing your white gym socks?"

Irving stared down at his brown argyles. "How can I run in white socks?"

"What?"

"I said, how can I run in white socks? I'll look like a rabbi."

"A what?"

"I said, how can I run in white socks? I'll look like a rabbi."

"A what?"

"I don't wear white socks. I have a religious excuse."

I looked down at my own white socks, remembering, as I had changed into them, how light, how springy, how close-to-athletic they'd made me feel. White socks did that for me. This kid was crazy—what was a rabbi?

"Go take a shower and report to Mr. Wilson."

"Why should I take a shower? It's only nine in the morning."

"And when you get up there, he'll have a full report from me—including talking back."

"I don't believe this. You want me to take a shower and report to the principal because I'm wearing brown socks? I mean, isn't that irrational? I think we should talk about this because you've got a problem. Anyway, I gave up communal bathing when I was nine years old."

Irving embarrassed me; I was afraid we'd all have to do laps because of his irrational attachment to brown argyles. . .

"Do laps!" the coach commanded. "Twenty laps around the basketball court!" His voice was now a high-pitched scream.

Irving stared at the four corners of the Olympic-sized court and slowly shook his head. "No," he said, "if I thought it would help you any, I'd be happy to do it. But I don't think I can help you—you're being totally irrational."

"I'll show you what's irrational," the coach sputtered, his voice almost strangled with a glorious, pure hatred, his upper body trembling with rage, the most powerful hatred of an adult for a child that I had ever seen. He fired the basketball at Irving's head, a bullet pass that was intended to cave his face in. I could never have gotten my hands up in time, and surely the coach never thought Irving could. But those nervous, trembling hands were quick; they not only blocked the ball, but caught it.

Irving dribbled it twice then rolled it back. "Now what?" he asked. "Are we supposed to bounce it?"

It was that scorn of Irving for his subjects and his obvious contempt for his teachers that frightened me. In study halls he worked out chess problems and played out hands of solitaire with a pack of tiny cards. He carried a small chessboard with him, the pieces so tiny he needed tweezers to lift them, and he would sit in the lunchroom while waxed-paper balls were batted over his head and butter-daubed straw covers were shot past his ears, devising new chess problems and transcribing them into a notebook. He didn't comb his hair; he wore sweaters directly over his undershirt, despite the school dress code specifying "collars" for boys. Three silky black hairs lay curled on his chin, uncut. He was the complete antisocial high-school intellectual.

In those years (and especially in the Southern years that had preceded them), I always allied myself with the boys who dressed carefully, who combed their hair and manifested good manners, who looked clean and well cared-for. In the rural Southern schools I'd attended, we were always the minority, and the minority banded together for protection against the redneck sociopaths in every class. My friends were reliable; they didn't tear up books, steal bikes, or start fights; and if we walked or rode home together or sat with each other on the bus we could get through the day without violence. But by eighth grade, many boys had begun grooming themselves for different reasons—for girls, of course, a variable not yet admissible to my simple equation of contentment with TV, stamps, and baseball. Overnight my allies had become the uncombed, unkempt, surly, unattractive, and frankly embarrassing. It's a big lesson to learn.

If there are basic forms of exceptional minds, Wesley and Irving personified two of them. Wesley was like a surgeon; his workspace was clean, well lighted, and uncorroded. He tried to keep it that way. Ideas presented themselves neatly and were discussed like complicated diagnoses. Conclusions were reached reluctantly by instinct, preferably by induction and elimination. He kept an infuriatingly open mind; even in classroom discussions, he referred to the *theory* of the atom, the *theory* of electron excitability, the plays *attributed* to Shakespeare. If I called him on the phone, asking what he was doing, the answer came back, "Talking to you." I learned to ask, "What were you doing just before I called?" Of his performance on a test, "I trust it'll not be too disappointing"; of report-card projections, "They may permit me to return next year." Perhaps it was false modesty and some of it later hardened to affectation, but much of it was pathological secrecy, masquerading as scientific cautiousness. There seemed to be two things he did not question: revealed religion and the scientific method.

Of Irving, I had the impression of a vast, entangled intelligence, cleared for a moment to discuss a particular subject; but that subject always squirming, struggling to escape, or maybe return to the luxuriant undergrowth of his thinking. He proceeded not by logic but by analogy, sideways across vast areas of knowledge; it was necessary for him to know a great deal from many fields in order to synthesize even a small amount from any one. And both of them were intellectually at odds with their personalities. Wesley, kind and Christlike on the outside was also a skeptic, a believer who was bleakly cynical. And Irving, violently antisocial, hostile and aggressive, was also a passionate and uncritical observer of everything that went on around him.

I? I had no intellect, no personality.

One day at lunch I sat next to Irving and asked him how many games of solitaire he had played.

"Today?"

"Okay, today."

"Twenty-five. I'll do fifty more tonight."

"All together, then. How many?"

"This year I'll do 27,375 . . . I've done 22,810 this year so far."

"What do you mark down in that little book?"

"Results and probabilities. I can look at the first card that's turned over and predict within four or five cards how many I'll end up turning over."

"I hate to ask—but why?" I had always associated solitaire with my mother, profound loneliness, and suppressed feelings. Irving Melnick was lonely, but if anyone sought it, he did.

"To be the world's leading authority on this kind of solitaire," he said. "When my studies are done I'll write them up and send it to *Scientific American*."

I'd never heard of the magazine and the format of such an article was a little hard to visualize. He explained it—or tried to—as a matter of function and variables. There were pages of equations, some with Greek letters. He rephrased the familiar rules of solitaire in mathematical language that added mystery and dignity to the whole operation. Thirty-seven of the fifty-two cards were unknown at the beginning of every game; fifteen were eventually known, seven of those immediately by virtue of having been turned over. Known and unknown were bound to each other by certain "elegant" equations. Modern probability theory did not consider a ratio of 15:37 "disadvantageous."

"You mean your equations can tell you what *that* card is?" I asked, pointing to one still in the deck.

"Of course not. This isn't"—he sneered—"clairvoyance. It doesn't make any difference to the equation what its temporary value is. If the *same* cards remained in the *same* position for every game, *then* it would matter. My equations have to hold through twenty-five thousand temporary changes of value."

"I see." Which was, of course, a lie.

"Solitaire is really quite an elegant game. More than bridge or chess, I think, because one can never play against a perfectly logical opponent the way he does with solitaire. I find myself at times actually drifting off when I play solitaire, like listening to Bach or late Beethoven. Do you?"

"No, not really."

"What's *strange*, though, is this. When I started I averaged no more than ten or eleven cards "up" at the end of each exercise. Now I average over eighteen. That's the thing I'm trying to account for. Is it in the player or in the cards? Am I just more observant now, or am I cheating without even acknowledging it? If I can't account for that variable, then my work is useless."

I told him that I didn't really understand what he was talking about but that I had my fantasies, too, with maps and long chains of discordant geographical facts. He seemed interested, and I told him more. His nervous eyes scanned my face as though they were reading me. Finally he asked, "You mean just memorizing?" I had to admit, ashamedly, yes, just memorizing.

"I see," he said, going back to his cards.

The next time I talked to Irving, I tried to come prepared. I told him about an interesting girl I'd met in the museum with all sorts of talents and opinions. I didn't mention that he reminded me of her and that I believed all affinities must somehow converge. "She said she belongs to something called J.A. and it meets in the museum. Behind a door under the claw of a dinosaur."

He considered this a moment, as though weighing it for possible subtleties. "In my experience, anything that begins with a 'J' must be avoided. Religiously, so to speak."

I said I knew what he meant.

"It usually stands for Jewish."

I realized I didn't know what he meant.

"But in this case it means Junior Archaeologists. I know—I once got interested in archaeology, I'm ashamed to say. I was seven or eight—typical childish waste of time. You *work* very hard, they have you *schlepping* under the sun, but it's not *challenging*, you know? Can you imagine a greater idiocy than digging up *arrow*heads or something? I mean, if the Indians had ever *done* anything, okay. . . . Archaeologists say they're making contributions to history, and history contributes a few useless bits to sociology and economics and politics—but, God, it's a great chain of mediocrity." He took a breath; that high, gravelly voice had gone down a notch in the middle of his denunciations. "I mean, it's brilliant in a way, isn't it, putting an idiot like Coach Church in a *history* class—Boys' Health and American history—where else could you put him?"

I smiled, showing support but not encouragement.

"What do you think of him?" he asked.

"I don't know. He's a coach, not a real teacher."

I thought I read disappointment, perhaps exasperation, in a brief frown he shot me, but his speech, his ideas, came so rapidly that he had little time for gesture or anything mannered.

"That's the error, you see. That's what *they* want you to say. *Of course* he's a teacher; he performs the function of teacher and he occupies the space and salary of a teacher: *ergo* he's a teacher. *They* want you to say, 'Oh, for a coach he's not bad, and besides, look at all the fame he brings to the high school.' But finding a place for him as a teacher is what makes it possible for them to throw all that money away on sports. Now, if they got rid of him as a teacher, they couldn't justify his salary as a full-time coach. They'd get rid of him, we'd lose track meets, and soon we'd drop track. So you see how he's responsible for the lousy education we're getting?"

I nodded, more hesitantly than before. Teachers were always criticized—for their voices, their looks—but I'd never heard anyone criticize the whole system. And Daley Ridge had the best schools in the city—what did Irving want?

"Want to hear my idea?"

I nodded.

"Well, there's a history test next week, right? Church always gives 120-point tests—90 multiple-choice, so that his wife can grade them on a stencil. A great educational innovation. The others are fill-in-the-blank, completing a sentence in your own words. Or word. Now, all we do is copy out the test. I'm doing forty, others are doing ten. You can copy the last ten, okay?" I agreed to that. "Then I'm sending the whole test to my cousin, who is a history professor at Columbia. She said she'd take the test seriously and see how she scores. And we'll publish her results in *The Weekly Daley*. I'm betting that a Columbia professor can't score higher than a 'C' on one of Church's tests. It'll be interesting."

Amazing, I thought. I didn't understand the plan at all, but I was for anything that would enhance our academic reputation.

Church taught history like a coach. Each chapter and the test that concluded it was a meet for which we were trained, brought to a peak, then tested. He began each lecture by announcing the pages he intended to cover, and he would stay in his lane without fail. The year was 1953, and our U.S. history book was a genial reflection of its times. *The Story of Our Nation* was, in fact, highly readable, employing a muted first-person narrator called "Spirit of America" as an offstage voice, a kind of *Our Town*—like stage manager. He would enter at the beginning of each chapter and summarize the high points.

> Well, quite a few folks in the South didn't see it that way. They figured they had a pretty good life and slavery was just one part of it. They didn't mind if the folks up North didn't keep slaves. They just resented (*did not like*) so-called Abolitionists (a-bo-lish-unists) sticking their noses in where it didn't concern them. Least, that's how they looked at it. So you know how it is when members of a family or even neighbours get to squabbling. Pretty soon it gets out of hand, and that's what happened to Our Nation. We raised a real ruckus—sort of shows you when Americans set their minds on something, they go all out.

> What happened was the saddest story in our history, and it's the one I've got to tell you now. . . .

At the close of the Civil War, "Spirit" was a little older, battered and even bandaged (he'd been represented first as a child, and by the last pages of the book, which took us up to the founding of the UN, he'd not really aged that much. He had, however, sprouted a bar of distinguished premature grey at the temples and now he smoked a pipe, that benevolent, authoritative pipe smoked in every ad and comic strip by people we're supposed to trust). Coach Church often had trouble distinguishing "Spirit" from actual historical figures; instead of "what the Constitution says" it became "what Spirit tells us" and the coach enjoyed dropping his voice to the cadence of a Ben Grauer or Westbrook Van Voorhis while reading us "Spirit's" moving words. This was practice for the weeks in the spring when he would be reading us hundreds of pages of Sandburg's *Lincoln*.

(In those years, I used to worry about that bar of grey at the temple—could it be that America was getting old, or even middle-aged? "Spirit" was otherwise boyish-looking— was this a compromise struck with the literal-minded who'd naturally wondered about "Spirit's" eventual aging? Unlike Superman, "Spirit of America" showed a susceptibility to injury, nearly dying of the cold at Valley Forge, shrapnel at Gettysburg, gas in the Ardennes, and the vicious counterattack in the Bulge. Even now he was worried by the Communist Menace in the World, and even on our shores. Perhaps all that worry explained the grey, *or . . .* perhaps . . . the grey had been planted there by Communists; Communists, we'd been told, were active wherever books were written, published, sold, or taught. The most frightening show on television was "I Led Three Lives," and I worried myself sick that all the women Communists in it were exactly like my mother: vaguely foreign and outspoken, critical of the newspapers, suspicious of what the government said, and always feeling guilty about something the country was doing. My mother had admitted she would have voted for Stevenson instead of "that prime idiot"—if she'd been a citizen—and she doubted that the Rosenbergs were guilty. I asked myself how Irving was any different from the schoolteachers, union leaders, professors and lawyers that Herb Philbrick was always exposing. You knew they had to be Communists if they sounded a *little* smarter than anyone else. And weren't the *good* teachers in the school—the ones I liked—somehow *too* interesting, appealing *too much* to our minds and personalities? The students still talked about which teachers had voted for Stevenson the year before; there was something untrustworthy about them; they seemed too smart to be teachers. Ike was like Coach Church, as reliable as Herb Philbrick's grey-haired, pipe-smoking, crew-cut FBI contact, "Gerry." Always there when you needed him. If Irving succeeded in "exposing" the coach as a terrible teacher, was it in order to fulfill some Master Plan, to install a master spy in Daley Ridge Junior High? And I was guilty too; I had copied out ten questions and given them to Irving. And what kind of name was Melnick? It sounded Russian.)

In the following week, we had our first batch of examinations. History would obviously be my best subject—whatever I read seemed to stick with me—and I had the knack of all good students of being able to lift possible test questions from the general haze of fact and narrative. The test was much as Irving had described it; I copied ten questions for him and left early, thinking I'd gotten a perfect paper. I went to my locker and checked out a few doubtful answers with the text; I was right on all counts.

It didn't surprise me when the results were read to us two weeks later that Wesley Duivylbuis should get a 118 and a couple of girls get 112. The surprise was that Irving Melnick got a 79. The coach had come to class that day, his arms finally loaded with those long yellow sheets (happy day!) and announced that we were obviously a very bright class. Because today, for the first time in his fifteen years at Daley Ridge, someone had gotten a perfect score. And when he read, alphabetically, Duivylbus' 118, it had to mean that either Irving or I had gotten it. After a girl named Flaherty, the coach raised his head, took off his glasses and smiled. "Now comes the perfect paper." A girl named Fulton, Flaherty's alphabetical shadow for the past seven years, threw her hands over her face and squealed. My jaw dropped. "David Greenwood—one HUNDRED and *TWENTY*!" After me came Fulton, Gordon, and a Greenberg.

The spoils of perfection were quick in coming. A few jeers and a low whistle from the back ("he musta read the coach's mind"). Irving tapped me on the arm. "Very good," he said. "But not good enough." At that moment the coach read, and paused briefly, "Irving Melnick . . . I double-checked this, Irving, but there's no mistake. You just didn't study. Seventy-nine."

Irving broke into a wide grin and snapped his fingers. He hissed across the aisle, "You got 120 out of a possible 79, Greenwood. How'd you do it?"

Irving, too, was carrying important papers. The letter from his cousin had come along with her test results After class, Irving and I deposited it with the editor of *The Weekly Daley*, our junior-high paper. Irving knew him; through Irving's suggestion and sole effort, *The Weekly Daley* was probably the only junior-high paper in America with a weekly chess puzzle concocted by a student. Irving guessed correctly that they would be happy to publish his headline: COLUMBIA PROFESSOR BARELY PASSES JUNIOR HIGH HISTORY TEST! It was then that I learned that Dr. Sharon Freisilber, "a history professor at New York's prestigious Columbia University," had scored a 79 on a recent eighth-grade American history test in Mr. Church's class. Furthermore, she had administered the test to her American history students, and the median score was 81— approximately two points lower than Mr. Church's students.

"God! I knew we had a good school, but . . . wow!" The editor was overwhelmed.

"You might publish this, too," said Irving. "Cut out the names at the top and bottom. It's a letter from that professor."

About twenty minutes later, the P.A. system wheezed to life. It requested that Irving Melnick, David Greenwood, and Wesley Duivylbuis report immediately to Mr. Wilson's office. "Must be a brains convention," I heard someone mutter, and I carried a smile with me all the way down to the principal's office.

The vast majority of students passed through Ridge Junior and Senior High rarely seeing the principal, and certainly without ever meeting him in his office. There were three outer offices, all noisy, crowded and overlit. The registrar, assistant principal, and vice-principal intercepted student problems long before they reached Mr. Wilson's desk. But we were ushered straight through by Miss Geraldine Horwathy, the assistant principal. She was a tiny, intensely wrinkled woman who wore her hair in a glistening chestnut-coloured ponytail. It was the hair of a six-teen-year-old, and she bought all her dresses at the schoolgirls' counter; but the sweaters, frilly collars, and the wide bangs that covered her forehead could not entirely cover the few inches of flesh that contended with the world. It was beaded, sagging, and withered, her mouth defined by a convergence of wrinkles rather than the strokes of harsh pink she laid around it. She did not acknowledge us; merely stood as we entered and marched us directly into the principal's office. Mr. Wilson was on the phone and did not look up.

The room was carpeted and lit by a mellow table lamp with a sturdy marble base. Heavy drapes blocked the window. It was hard to believe we were still in the school and that it was eleven o'clock in the morning. Miss Horwathy motioned for us to take chairs, which Irving and I immediately did. She and Wesley Duivylbuis, who was in his Scout uniform that day, remained standing. Mr. Wilson, while talking, looked directly at us without registering a flicker of interest or rec-ognition.

Until that moment, I'd been bracing myself for a new round of congratulations. I could do no wrong in this school; as mind-reader and test-taker, I was batting a thousand. And now journalism—though my role had been small—I should have copied twenty more for Irving. But now I saw that something was wrong.

"Thanks, Jack," said Mr. Wilson, and hung up.

"Well, gentlemen. You must be Melnick. Much as guessed. Wesley—we had your brother here two years ago—a fine lad. You're Greenwood, then. The mind-reader."

I chuckled nervously.

"I wouldn't laugh if I were you. I assure you, you have nothing at all to laugh about."

Irving slumped in his chair, suggesting, ever so slightly, inattention. Wesley stood at ease with his legs apart, hands clasped behind his back. I didn't know which way to sit.

"Well?" he asked. "Explanations, please."

"Sir?" said Duivylbuis, clearly puzzled.

"About what?" I asked. Did he suspect me of cheating, the first perfect paper in fifteen years? Did he believe that I really had superpowers? Would I be forced to confess and maybe have Blackthorne paralyze me for life? I felt an aching in my throat.

Irving slumped ever so slightly and let out a long, insolent breath. Mr. Wilson leaned back in his swivel chair where light from his desk lamp barely reached. Odd shadows played over his face, chiselling out his chin and a firm lower lip, casting black shadows across his eyes and forehead. It was impossible to read any expression; the mouth was all that counted, and his nostrils served as dead, unblinking eyes.

"Are you telling me you don't know why you're here?" He seemed reasonable, almost amused, the way interrogators started in prison movies, before threatening other things.

"Greenwood—you're the mind-reader. Why are you here?"

My throat tightened one final notch; nothing but tears would now escape. But I was still too shocked to speak.

"Wesley?"

"One is generally called here for disciplinary reasons, sir."

"Irving?"

"Why don't you tell us?"

"I want to read you boys a letter that has just come into my possession. It was given by one of you—or more precisely, by two of you—to the editor of *The Weekly Daley* not twenty minutes ago." He cleared his throat and fumbled for glasses.

"'Dear Itzie' it begins. That's you, I imagine, isn't it, Irving? I'll go on:

> I appreciate the urgency of your request and hasten to comply. Actually I got so intrigued with the test that I had thirty more copies run off for *my* sophomore American history class. It's a classic of its type—congratulations.

> My own score, bearing in mind your instructions to answer with what I *knew* and not what I *thought it wanted* (a sobering distinction)—was 79, as graded from the marking key you call 'A Probable Perfect.' In other words, your teacher is probably right on 79 questions and wrong on 41.

How did you obtain a copy of this marking key, Irving?" the principal demanded.

"I made it up," said Irving.

"And gave it to Greenwood here?"

"No."

"We'll see. It's rather suspicious, isn't it, that the first perfect paper in fifteen years suddenly crops up on the same day a marking key is stolen?"

"Not stolen," said Irving through clenched teeth.

"I'll go on. This gets more interesting.

> One need not invoke the formulas of a certain 19th-century central European (the love of whom dare not speak its name)—

I think we can guess who this person is she's talking about, can't we, Irving?—

> —to call them 'wrong.' To be really precise, at least fifty of his ninety multiple-choice questions are unanswer-

able without a fifth choice: 'none of the above' or 'all of the above and then some.' It's depressing to know that even 'good' schools (whatever that means these days) are teaching such—"

and again Mr. Wilson broke off. "I will spare you the obscenities, since Miss Horwathy is in the room, but it's the level of language one might expect from such a per son, though it is still shocking, considering the exalted and influential position she holds,

—such horse *manure* (we'll call it). Incidentally, three of my students shocked me by getting 'perfect' papers according to the key. I have spoken with them and warned them they face severe penalties if their work doesn't improve.

Itz, I can't believe that even a teacher as stupid as you say this one is actually taught that 'Lee was a great general but: (Q.94) *he still put his pants on one leg at a time.'* Reminds me of that *shtunk*—

Is that the word, Irving, *shtunk*? I want to get it straight for the lawyers. What does it mean?"

"Means what it sounds like," said Irving. "In his case, it means Nazi."

I, too, knew the word; a furniture-word applied to most bosses and certain kinds of complaining customers.

"I see. If you don't wish to cooperate by translating the document, I'll get it translated myself. What is it, Russian?"

"Japanese," said Irving. "We're Japanese."

"I hope you're having a good time, Irving. Because I'm having a good time. And now we come to something very interesting in this letter.

Reminds me of that *shtunk* you drove out of teaching last year, hoisted on his own petard. 'If you look at the records, you'll find that most of the death-row prisoners in Southern jails are Negro and most of the prisoners in Hitler's jails were Jews, and I say where there's smoke there's fire....'

So it was you, Irving, who sent that cowardly letter to the *Star* last year behind Mr. Herrnbosch's back?"

Irving only smiled.

"Do you realize that man was forced to leave Palestra? A well-organized hate campaign drove him out of this school and out of this city? *He can never teach again*! Are you proud of that?"

"Yes."

"I think," said Mr. Wilson, folding his glasses and again leaning back, "that this is the saddest document I have read in my twenty-five years of administration."

"I agree, Mr. Wilson. Absolutely," said Geraldine Horwathy.

"You admit, Irving, that this letter from Professor Sharon Freisilber of Columbia University was addressed to you and pertains to information transmitted to her by you, and that further, on this date you submitted said document to the editor of *The Weekly Daley* to be published?"

"The letter is the property of the sender and may be disposed of by the receiver only with the sender's permission," said Irving.

"You may be interested to know, Irving, that I was just talking to Jack Stacey, who happens to be the legal counsel for the Palestra School Board. Your smug little pronouncement overlooks one crucial fact, and that is you are a minor and cannot assign such rights, and this is a school, and on these premises the principal exercises all parental authority. It may also interest you to know that test papers are school property and cannot be copied, transmitted, or caused to be reproduced without the school's permission."

"How interesting," said Irving.

"Oh, I think so. Do you realize the harm this letter could do if it were published?"

"I was thinking of the good it would do."

"No, Irving, this time we know who's behind it. You Won't have one of your cowardly little victories like you had with poor Don Herrnbosch. This time it would result in legal actions against you taken by Mr. Church. We, of course, would back him one hundred percent. Mr. Church has a case here for defamation of character and defamation of professional standing. Of course, you won't be standing alone—there's David Greenwood and Wesley Duivylbuis and doubtless a ring of others to stand with you, along with this, this"—he dropped Sharon Freisilber's letter as though it were something vile—"disgrace to the profession. I will communicate to her chairman, of course, indicating the legal actions to be taken against her. You see how wide a net you cast, Mr. Melnick."

Wesley Duivylbuis cleared his throat. "Begging your pardon, sir, but I am not a party to anything you've been talking about. I really don't know why you've called me here."

"Are you *absolutely* sure? I want to believe you, Wesley."

"You can believe him," said Irving. "He cannot tell a lie."

"Don't try my patience further. Wesley, on your word—your ha-ha, Boy Scout's oath—I'm exempting you from all I'm saying to these other two, and I apologize for any embarrassment I might have caused. Now, as I was saying—the school has registered a complaint of common theft against the three—sorry—*two* of you. So far as I'm concerned, it's the same as if you'd broken into the building on the weekend and stolen our athletic equipment. But this is far more serious than stealing a few basketballs. This is motivated by cold intellectual arrogance, and it strikes at the very heart of the educational process. This is a Communist tactic, Irving. Character assassination, engaging in a criminal conspiracy—a conspiracy of self-appointed intellectuals. Perhaps you're aware of the famous Loeb and Leopold case? I'm sorry, Wesley, to have dragged you into this, but I naturally assumed that anyone who got as high a grade as you must have done it—well, illegitimately. Please accept my congratulations on that outstanding 118 score. Perfect papers we will deal with later."

And with that, the tears that had been building simply burst forth in a long, low wail: I saw my whole life ruined, myself in jail for having copied ten questions, and worse, I saw my perfect paper—the first perfect paper in Daley Ridge history—being dismissed as a trick and used as evidence of my guilt. Oh, we were wrong, deeply, deeply wrong; I couldn't imagine a single complaint I had against Mr. Church or his teaching, and the letter from Irving's cousin seemed stuck-up and vicious.

"I wanted you to get an idea of the implications of your actions," said Mr. Wilson. "It seems to have gotten through to one of you, at least."

Irving stared at me, then said, "I don't believe this."

Wesley put a hand on my shoulder and told me to cheer up, it wasn't that bad.

Mr. Wilson leaned forward. "I want to be fair. Frankly"—and for the first time, Mr. Wilson allowed himself a slight smile—"I will admit that Toby Church is not an exciting history teacher. But—and let me emphasize this for all of you—if this school were somehow destroyed and I had to build a great high school from scratch, the first person I'd look for is Toby Church. If I had a million dollars to start a school of my own, Toby would be the first man I'd try to lure away. And why? Because in fifteen years here, he's turned out consistent champions of the highest order. He builds *men*, not . . . punks. What you've done—tried to do (and I don't mean you, Wesley)—to Toby Church is to stab him in the back. *Just like you did to Don Herrnbosch.* Because you lack the guts to confront him openly. But the reason I'm taking all this so calmly, boys, is because I know there is nothing any of you—or any group of you—can do to harm Toby Church in this school or in this community. I'm concerned for you. If I pick up the telephone and call the police, I can ruin your lives. If *this* gets published, I will be obliged to expel you. You will never get a high-school diploma. You will never go to college. Irving—do you honestly believe that a quote—unqualified idiot—unquote could lead this school through what is now one hundred and sixty-two consecutive track victories? Do you realize that eleven Daley Ridge seniors last year got track scholarships to leading universities? You didn't know that, did you?"

He let the revelation sink in a few minutes; the burden in my throat had lifted. A compromise was coming, something to grab on to. "Now, the records show that you are both intelligent boys—obviously not as intelligent as you think you are—but intelligent enough to perhaps even yet make a positive contribution to society. You've had your prank—that's all that it was, a prank, right?"

"I want Mr. Church to read that letter," said Irving, his voice a low, gravelly growl. "And I want him to know about his test."

"I'm afraid that's impossible, Irving. The letter and the test are school property. It would not be in the school's interest to inform Mr. Church of their existence."

He tore the papers into small pieces, then swept them into his ashtray.

I caught my breath at last; I could have laughed out loud. It was over. Irving scowled.

Finally, Wesley Duivylbuis spoke. "Mr. Wilson, in all fairness to Irving and to David and to the others you said were involved, I don't think it's right to ignore the problem. I got a 118 on the test, but I could just as easily have gotten an 80, like Irving. I wasn't answering anything but what I thought *he wanted*. Mr. Church is like you say, not a . . . stimulating teacher. I don't believe in attacking authority like they did, but I believe something should be discussed."

"Yes," said Mr. Wilson. "I agree. What is it, Irving?"

"You seem to think I'm protesting against authority," said Irving. "I'm not. I love authority. I'm protesting against incompetence and ignorance. This is an intellectual problem, not a discipline problem."

"Thank you, Irving. What's your solution, Wesley?"

"I think since it's only chance who gets who for history, and since Irving and David and maybe I, too, can't learn from Mr. Church, we should get transferred."

Mr. Wilson lay his hands on the desk and drummed his fingers, then spoke. "No. We're not talking about gum-chewing here. We can't ignore the seriousness of what happened by just shifting the blame around. I consider this far graver than pushing a teacher down the stairs. We're talking about a concerted attempt by a small band of self-styled *sympathizers* to attack one of the finest living Americans I have ever met, and an attempt to reduce his effectiveness in a critical educational area—American history—by ridicule and the propagation of contempt for all that he stands for. That's what worries me." And now he leaned forward, and his full, round pink face came into the light. If he'd had a gavel, he would have pounded his desk, for that's what he was doing: pronouncing sentence.

"And so, until further notice, I'm expelling you, Irving Melnick, from all classes at this school, effective immediately. For you, David Greenwood, for your admitted theft of test questions and admitted membership in a ring of conspirators, the grade of 'F' will be registered against your name on this test. I am being lenient because you are new here and this is your first offense."

He stood and walked around his desk to talk to each of us briefly before dismissing us. "Wesley. I'm impressed by your loyalty to your fellow students and your willingness to bring certain problems in a particular section of a particular class to my attention. Of course I will look into it." He shook Wesley's hand, then turned to me. "As you are new to our school, David, and are obviously not an instigator of the plot, I'll lift all those restrictions, including the failure of your so-called perfect paper, should you sign a statement renouncing all participation in future attacks upon teachers. I think such a statement would be particularly sincere if you would also tell me or Miss Horwathy the names of other students who participated in this action."

I promised I would think it over.

"Irving, you've been in trouble before, but we hoped you would gain judgment and intellectual maturity to control your obvious arrogance and disrespect. But you've gotten worse, if anything, and the time has come to indicate to you that there are rules that we do impose and that we will not permit to be broken. Now go and clean out your locker. I want you to go home and think about your actions. I am calling your mother in for a conference, and I pray that some formula can be worked out to enable you to stay in school. You have a contribution to make, I'm sure, and I refuse to believe that you're a lost cause."

Miss Horwathy followed us out, and she pulled me harshly by the elbow as we entered her office. She ground her knuckle into my arm and whispered, "I *told* you last time to keep your mouth shut, and you went ahead and almost ruined things. You just don't know how to stay out of trouble, and believe me, you're going to be in plenty of it if you keep up this way—mark my words."

Irving and I walked outside behind the school, where the cement walks overlooked the parking lot and various playing fields. "What'll happen to you?" I asked.

"He'll call my mother in and he'll try to frighten her and she'll giggle at him and tell him what a fine job he's doing. Then I'm afraid they'll force me back."

"What about your father?"

"Never knew him. Everything I am I owe to my mother."

We passed three robins perched on top of a chain fence; the outer ones flew off as we approached. Irving retraced his steps as soon as the two robins returned, and again the outer ones flew away. "Why is that, do you suppose? Is the middle robin smarter than the other two, or dumber, or what? Why doesn't he perceive the same danger?"

I told him I couldn't guess.

"Middle children in a family are supposed to be more secure than first or last children—did you know that? Ever think what might have happened if the old kings had passed their empires on to their *middle* sons? The first born is the absolute worst choice—out to erase his father's memory and all that."

I didn't see what that had to do with robins. I told him I was an only child.

"Duivylbuis was most impressive in there, wasn't he? Think it's the Boy Scout training? I joined the Cub Scouts once and forged my mother's signature in order to collect all the badges. I had so many badges and arrowheads, I looked like the Cub Scout catalogue. They got suspicious of me on a camping trip when I couldn't put up my tent and got scared of the dark."

I couldn't help but laugh.

"It's not fair about your perfect paper," he said. "Wilson wants names, but you can't give him any names because there aren't any. It was just me and you. I memorized a hundred and ten questions, and you memorized ten. I'll tell him that if you want."

I told him it was okay.

"Duivylbuis is a middle son, you know. I've never been able to figure out if he's exceptionally clever or exceptionally stupid. What *was* perfect on a test like that—what you got, what he got, or what I got? Maybe 118. It's the only 'A' now. All I know is Duivylbuis is someone I've gone to school with for eight years and I've never beaten. Except in chess."

We were looking down over the faculty parking lot, and Irving pointed out Mr. Wilson's blue station wagon, and Coach Church's green station wagon parked next to it. Last year he had kept a chart: who parked where, what happened to the cars—and eventually the teachers—with Stevenson stickers.

"You remember Blackthorne?" I said. "He did it all with microphones. Everything except the last thing about Wesley's stamps was relayed to me by Geraldine Horwathy. She just admitted it."

"I thought it was something like that."

"Don't tell Wesley."

"All the cars with Stevenson stickers used to park on the far side," said Irving. "Some of the kids from the high school went over to the parking lot one day and poured paint on every single one of them. I don't remember Mr. Wilson ever calling anyone into his office."

There was something I was close to asking him that day, but couldn't quite get up the nerve for.

The Rosenbergs were innocent, weren't they?

I was a manly child, never boyish. Not manly to look at or listen to, needless to say, and sixty years ago, a manly child who was clumsy, fat, and studious was likely to think himself not properly masculine. He was supposed to go through a phase of elongated boyishness called adolescence—growing out of his clothes month-by-month, raiding the refrigerator at all hours, playing records in the "rec" room, keeping secrets from his prying parents. A manly child without a boyish phase may even seem queer. Certainly he had no one to tell him he wasn't. He may even seem to himself, queer. After the twilight of childhood came the night, and then the darkest hour. I was almost fourteen, and my first year in junior high was nearly half over. I had no real friends yet, but had entered a cluster (Irving and Duivylbuis were two of them) of serious students with either deficient, irrelevant, or rampant hormones. It was a time of the wildest variance: boys were six foot two or barely five foot; some had chest hair and respectably hairy jowls; others of us still had high voices and the stuffed, cylindrical shapes of babyhood. It seemed for those months that my voice, relatively, was rising, my hips flaring, and shoulders pinching ever-narrower.

And so I would not seem a likely candidate for sexual attention, let alone gratification, from the sexiest girl in the school. And yet such are the disguises of the moonlit night; that a boy like me, churned in the nightsoil of suburbia, would discover more about sex than any of the double-dating, sunlit boys driven to movies by their fathers.

I had assumed when I began writing this proto-fiction, that the digging episodes of my childhood and the map fantasies were approaches to art, metaphors lying beyond me waiting to be claimed, named, and mastered. And my dream of a sister—was she not the guide, the artist's female-within, whom I loved and continued to love, more passionately than myself? Were not all my irrational attachments a love of her and of a nameless art? Did she not assume the shape of Diana Lynn, but just as frequently, of a Bedouin, a baseball player, or even a Nubian lion? It seemed so, in my childhood.

But when I think of that long, deep night of my thirteenth winter, with hormones seeping into my brain, if not my blood, altering its contours and deepening its cavities without the least modification of my blimpish body or piping voice, then art alone is insufficient. I might have been an artist at the age of nine, but at thirteen I was a rapist-*manqué* and if I still responded to the unformed and uninvented metaphors of time and space it was because they were approaches to the ultimate mystery: the body. The female body. It's pretension to call a love of painted shapes a prelude to fiction; I was seeking absolute power, absolute vengeance. Those maps were megalomaniacal fantasies, explorations of the unsettled provinces of my own and of others' bodies. I'd tried first to claim my father's, and he had slapped me down; I was always too "good" to ever try with my mother's. And so I created a sister and she died, and then I created maps. The mudfish, the worms in my stomach, they were real to me as projections of my body—my wretched, unresponsive body. I didn't take the equations far enough. The mudfish was my sister, and I killed her—yes! But my sister was my penis, and I wanted to chop it off—yes! In drawing maps and creating continents, I was reinventing and renaming myself; devoted, like "Mac" in those Charles Atlas ads, to my own brand of dynamic tension. I looked to those maps for confirmation the way narcissists look into mirrors, the way skinny teenagers lift weights.

Another thing I know—and I have learned it as I write—is that my kind of innocence, because it is so complicated, is the most dangerous, most corrupt kind of knowledge. We all "know" this, of course—what is propriety but the stench of repression? Rapists would not be rapists if they were not such prudes, the last Victorians. We've been liberated to look for real evil only in the realm of conspicuous piety. Only a "good" kid, only the best, could have gotten into the trouble I did.

I see us groping, a whole group of us. Some groping successfully at sock hops, movies, and bowling parties; some masturbating in their beds; some not even knowing yet how to do it (*soap it down, but be quick about it*); and then I see us in that profound dark, stumbling suddenly into such brightness that we are forever imprinted. An image comes to mind from John Hersey's *Hiroshima*, a book I read sometime in those high-school years, of a Japanese house painter doing his work high on a building's side several miles from Ground Zero of the first atomic blast. Though he was incinerated, the wall stood, and the brightness of the flash was sufficient to fix his shadow forever to the freshly painted surface. Most of us were like moles, stunned in that first sexual blast. I, too, was frozen in a single gesture, in the glare of Laurel Zywotko's blazing sexuality in the winter of 1954.

I'd had two previous encounters with her that first year. The first had been onstage with Blackthorne. She'd been the girl with the message for Paul Gaylord, the message being, I'd thought: *I'm pregnant*. She was the tall blond girl with the tight, fuzzy sweaters who caused pandemonium in the back of the room on the few days each week that she bothered to attend. In 1954 the ideal of sex was still the pinup: the clinging sweaters and tight skirts, the pasty, inviting lipstick, the slender ankle, all that overwrought and unavailable studio sexuality churned out for horny soldiers to venerate inside their footlockers. Sexy girls wore their hair very short that year and accented their ears with big round earrings; Laurel did that, too. At fourteen she was ripe for a GI tour with Bob Hope; *there* was the cure for all my sister-fantasies of platonic companionship; *there* for the eighth grade was Hollywood beauty on our terms. And since she was in my homeroom as well as my English class, I knew by 8:45 each morning if I was to endure a useless seven scratchy hours in my manly gabardines, or if later in the morning I'd have another hour of sneaking glances at Laurel Zywotko. Every glance at her excited me as though she were undressing behind a gauzy curtain. The gauze was her sweater.

The other occasion that somehow fused me to the fate of Laurel Zywotko was to be mine alone, an occasion of accident like all my discoveries. It was during a PTA open house in which parents were invited to meet our teachers and inspect our mid-year work. It was a winter evening, not severe, but zipped-up-jacket weather. Since my drawings were on the boards and my name near the top of every listing, it was to be a proud evening for me. Parents were not as universally young as they had been in Florida; my mother was not nearly as out of place there as she had been in the South. And so it was a happy, confident evening. My father hadn't come; Seligman's was staying open every evening (and Seligman's *was* failing; I'd kept Blackthorne's prediction to myself but I was enough of a salesman's son to know when my father wasn't drawing life from his work, when it was draining him).

"Oh, my goodness," I heard a loud, high-pitched voice, "Itzie's told me all about your boy." "Itzie," I remembered, was Irving, who naturally hadn't come. I'd never told my mother about his expulsion, nor about my "F." Despite my failure on the first test,

I'd gotten "A's" on everything else, and eventually been rewarded with an "A" in the course. Irving had taken a weeks' vacation, then returned unchanged. Mrs. Melnick was the size of a fat elf, even shorter than Geraldine Horwathy, with short black hair chopped just over her ears. She was dressed in a long skirt, black sweater, and a silver necklace that made her look strangely bohemian. The intention may have been to ridicule the suburban mothers, or she may simply have had no guidance.

"Melnick couldn't make it tonight," she told my mother, referring, I guessed, to Irving. "He got mad at me at dinner and told me to go entertain everybody without him." She giggled, then abruptly stopped. "Where's your husband?"

"Working tonight. He's furniture buyer at Seligman's." My mother was nearly a foot taller than Mrs. Melnick, and looking uneasy.

She wrinkled her nose at the mention of Seligman's. "It's going under, you know," she said, and kept her nose wrinkled like a comic actress holding a pose till the laughs died down.

"I beg your pardon?"

"Seligman's is broke. I know 'cause my brother, Morrie Freisilber—he's a lawyer for them. My mother used to take me to Seligman's to visit the Santa Claus man. I was so small, I could keep going till I was fourteen years old already."

"I see."

"And we weren't even, you know—"

"Santa is universal," said my mother.

Then Mrs. Melnick sat down; her gestures were as abrupt and dismissive as Irving's. She looked at my mother as though they'd never met.

"She's very strange," my mother said. "I hope her boy's a little smarter."

My mother and I were leaving the school, passing by the front steps where spruce trees framed the entrance and stone lions guarded the stairs. As we came round the trees, I heard the explosive sibilance of a girl's whispered "*stop!*", a deep-voiced laugh, and then a slap. But when we finally got to the lions, there was only Laurel Zywotko sitting alone on the ledge next to the lion, one arm over the lion's head, face down, sobbing. She wore white-and-brown shoes and white socks which flashed in the dark as she kicked them against the ledge. She had no coat or jacket, just one of her normal fuzzy sweaters; I wanted to lay my jacket over her shoulders. But when she saw me she lifted her face long enough to stare and smile. She'd just lit a cigarette, and she caressed her cheek with the hand that held it. It was the most sexual gesture I'd ever seen, the most riveting sexual moment of my life.

"Who *is* that?" my mother asked.

"Laurel," I said, the name trembling on my lips, the first time I'd dared pronounce it.

"A high-school girl?"

"No."

"A teacher?"

"No . . . my class."

"No—I don't believe it!"

With two words I had ceased to be a child in my mother's eyes. *My class*: I could as easily have shouted, *I'm no longer your little boy*. My mother walked on alone to the bus stop and I was left a few feet in front of Laurel, uncertain which way to move. She motioned to me with her finger.

I walked on numbed legs, out of breath from ten short steps.

"Hi," I said.

"Hi." She managed a brave smile; her thick lipstick was smeared. I wanted to say, *I didn't know you smoked*. Until then I didn't know anyone my age who smoked. Because it was Laurel, it was forgivable. But I knew I'd dislike having to defend it to my mother. The ledge with the carved lions jutted out at my shoulder-level; her brown-and-white shoes nearly danced on my stomach.

"What's the matter?" I could see she'd been crying. Her cheek was red. She took two drags on the cigarette, then flipped it into the bushes. She leaned over; we were close enough to kiss.

"He slapped me," she whispered, and her eyes darted to the bushes beside us. "My lousy brother, he slapped me." Then she sprang back, stately as a statue, and turned a profile to me as she lit another cigarette. I thought I heard rustling in the bushes, and for a moment I could have rushed in, determined to seize her brother by the throat and deliver Laurel Zywotko from his clutches. But she called down to me, her voice soft and serene: "You're nice—I don't think I've seen you in school. You come and see me sometime," and smiled.

"My name's David Greenwood," I said. "I'm new this year." After one long drag, she tossed the second cigarette into the bushes, stood, smoothed her skirt, rubbed her arms, and skipped back along the ledge to where it melted into the top steps, then went back inside the school.

I felt I'd grown six inches and aged five years. It was cruel to do that to a parent, but I could see that my mother didn't want to believe what she had seen, and it was more important for me to raise myself to Laurel's company than to spare my mother's feelings. "She smokes," my mother said. "She looks cheap. I hope you don't have anything to do with creatures like that."

"Oh, everyone smokes," I said.

"She's only thirteen and she's trying to act twenty-five. She'll come to grief."

I answered that I'd never noticed, particularly, how old she looked; most of the girls looked a lot older. But I wished she'd seen some of the boys in my class. Abboud, for instance, at thirteen with a spongy mat of chest hair and jowls that were darker than Vice-President Nixon's. We walked on to the bus stop in embarrassed silence, a properly teenaged scene that began for me only that night. I was finally a teenager, thanks to Laurel Zywotko.

I was being pulled in three directions at that moment and for the rest of the year. As a retarded physical specimen I wanted to return to simple childhood. And as a certified teenager of thirteen years and eight months, I wanted all the trappings: a fringe of dirty peach fuzz down my cheeks and on my upper lip and relief from the high-pitched voice I was still afflicted with (only two other boys in my class seemed as endocrinally deficient as I, and I lived in dread of the morning when a boy named Richie, two inches shorter than I and often taken for a fifth-grader, would suddenly rumble forth a sentence and add six inches overnight). And I was still attracted to my mother as a society-in-herself, all I would need as friend and companion, even as teacher. I wanted to tell her this, but red-hot tongs could not have forced it out that night. I mentioned instead that some boy had just slapped "that girl you saw, you know, what's-her-name, that Laurel."

"I don't doubt it a minute," she said. "Dressed like that, I could have slapped her myself. How does her mother let her go to school like that?"

"No mother," I said.

"Father, then."

"No father either."

That had been the story on Laurel, as related by her brother, Larry, a ninth-grade thug. Clear-skinned, blue-eyed and blond-haired (the long masses lovingly tended and plastered back in a ducktail), he wore black corduroy jackets with the collar up and shiny tight black slacks. A blue rattail comb always peeked from that hip pocket; it was never in there longer than thirty seconds without being extracted for a few quick flicks through the hair. Larry Zywotko flaunted his smoking with a Lucky pack always twisted in the sleeve of his tight white T-shirt, and between classes he would stick an unlit Lucky in his mouth and saunter coolly down the halls. He attended school even less frequently than his sister, and much of his day was spent in the boys' room, smoking by an open window, collecting a "crapper fee" from anyone unlucky enough to have to go during one of his custodial tours. Some girls found him attractive in that pouty, dangerous, James Dean way. He moved like a cat, carried a knife and used the foulest language of any boy in the school. And most of the foulness had to do with his sister. "That cunt," as he called her, "that whore" (all of which made her more of a desirable victim to me). I was immune to all of Larry's language and implications; I didn't have the slightest idea of what they actually meant. He implied they shared an apartment somewhere in the lower town and had wangled admission to Daley Ridge by fraud. There was an uncle-guardian involved, but he was always drunk. Larry let it be known that he was the real guardian—meaning owner—of his sister, that whatever—*whatever*, he repeated—he wanted "off" her, he got.

For a price, though, he wouldn't be greedy. He extracted money from boys he found eyeing his sister (not me, of course; recognizing me would have cheapened his merchandise). "That'll cost you a dollar," he'd say in the lunch line the next day. "She told me you was givin' her the eye." Or "She told me you tried asking her for a date, Romeo. That'll cost you five—next time see me first." We had to put our lunch dimes (only dimes) in the upper left-hand corner of our trays. This made it easy for Larry to walk down the line and scoop a dime or two (or maybe nine or ten) from every fifth or sixth tray, sometimes winking, sometimes flashing his sharklike smile. Most of his victims were boys a little like him, but not quite as tough.

That's why, when he came striding down the lunch line the next day, asking, "Which one of you assholes is David Greenwood?" in his thick dark boots, jacket open, shirt top unbuttoned with gold medals flashing, I quickly turned, trusting that no one knew and no one would tell. But a few seconds later the heaviest hand I'd ever felt came crashing down on my shoulder and spun me around. He scooped up all five dimes and said, "An advance. Bring ten tomorrow and every day this week." The boys next to me stared glassily ahead, happy to have been spared, but kids at the tables near the line stopped eating in order to get a load of Laurel's latest boyfriend. Larry dropped a crumpled piece of notebook paper on my tray, then looked me up and down and snickered. "Geez—she must be hard up." He flipped a Lucky into the corner of his mouth, fixed the curl in the middle of his forehead, and was off.

I stepped out of line. Dimeless, I had nowhere to go. I was about to throw away the paper when I noticed the writing. Uncrumpled, it read:

DEAR DAVID GREENWOOD

You were nice to stop last night. It was my brother who hit me. Give him $$ and he will go away for a week. I'm all alone at home. My address is:

Miss Laurel Zywotko
2516 Patience St. (upstairs) over Polish News.

Love, Laurel

Patience Street was at river-level, three hundred feet below the Ridge. One could drive down, taking switchbacks, or walk directly on wooden staircases that clung to the rockface. The ridges of Palestra were all connected with these wooden funiculars; there was something medieval about them, like immensely long ladders propped against the walls of an inhumanly high fortress.

Below us were the worst addresses in the city. Patience Street had slipped beyond being a slum; it was now boarded-over and deserted, an area where old storefronts and cinema halls served incongruous ends like paint-and-body shops, coal yards and truck depots. I had often gone over to the edge of Daley Ridge that first summer (there was a link-fence in Duivylbuis Park at the point where the land gave way and steps began), and watched the sunset over Palestra. We had a clear view of the river as it worked its way through three or four affluent ridges on its way to the downtown, and I'd once had a binding image of the whole area below us as an underground colony, an anthill, with the crust temporarily lifted off.

I was standing on the crust now, and a million years of geological processes had removed a few square miles below me as remorselessly as an open-pit mine. The city had bred itself in that pit; the traffic three hundred feet below and miles away was as small, deliberate and silent as insects. And now, in winter, I recalled one of the pleasures I'd indulged in since leaving Florida. In the hard-baked summer clay of Georgia and Carolina I had searched out anthills, and, working carefully with butter knives and spatulas, had cut wide circles in the clay several inches around the hole, pried gently, and often been able to lift the clay like a plate, exposing the tunnels and chambers beneath: the egg rooms, the cloud of ants surrounding the queen. And before they could scatter, I would drench the rooms in rubbing alcohol and then drop a lighted match. With an instantaneousness that gratified my own sense of random horror, the full ant society would be obliterated in a single Hiroshima-like cataclysm. I would not do it unless the full lid of clay pried off easily; I had to see the before-and-after. It was not eradication of ants that I sought, but confirmation of supremacy.

That is how I felt as I began my descent of those eight hundred steps to Patience Street: like a god becoming an ant.

Three hundred feet can make a lot of difference. On our clear winter mornings, a sluggish fog would hug the valley, condensing on cars and freezing them white. We'd have clean snow in their cold gritty rain. As I started down those stairs—as steeply banked as any football stadium—I held the rails with both hands, as though I were walking a rope-bridge. Few people attempted the climb; those who did were cleaning women, and black. When I reached the vacant lot on Patience Street where the stairs finally ended, my thighs were numb and my shins ached from the flexing of unused, braking muscles. If the Zywotkos walked these stairs every day they went to school, no wonder they were both such marvellous specimens. Or perhaps that explained why they came so rarely. If I visited regularly, I wondered what changes I would notice.

Innocence was my protection. Had I had any idea of what Larry Zywotko had been collecting money for, or what Laurel Zywotko was known for among those deep-voiced, T-shirted boys with unlit cigarettes dangling from their lips, I would have fled in terror. I thought only that Laurel, despite her "F" grades and her lurid sexuality, was a good girl underneath it all, forced into inglorious behaviour and unwholesome company by her evil brother. It even occurred to me, on that long descent into the pit of Palestra, that if she had no parents, she was still adoptable. Perhaps that's what she wanted: me as a brother. And so I was a happy little boy trudging my way down Patience Street, past a church (St. Sanislaus), boarded-up stores and a laundromat filled with manly Polish women.

Two-five-one-six Patience Street was in the middle of the block, an unpainted wooden building standing half-naked after demolition had scraped away everything on one side. The rubble had not been removed. There were no windows on the side now exposed; only the outline of radiators, lavatories and a staircase that had once existed.

There were two doors. One to the street-level *Polish-American News*, which featured yellowed, unfamiliar papers and dusty, sun-faded magazines in their steamed-up window; and the other, which opened on an unlit and unswept stairwell leading straight up at an exhausting angle. The stairwell was colder than the street; if anyone lived upstairs (there were no names), they might not have heat. It was impossible to connect either Zywotko with such a place.

I climbed. It got warmer. There were no decorations on the walls of the stairwell, no name on the door. The runners of hard grime along the walls, the stains around the door handle had to be Larry's doing exclusively.

I knocked but no one answered. I turned the handle and it opened. I was in the anthill now, in the queen's chamber. The room was small and littered, and the pattern of litter, like iron filings around the poles of a magnet, all pointed to the sofa. The fall of clothes—jeans, boots, panties, dresses, corduroy jackets, a camel's hair coat, shoes, pajamas and balls of dirty underwear—all radiated from the sofa. Then the camel's hair coat on the sofa twitched and dropped to the floor: Laurel Zywotko's head appeared, then a shoulder from under a thin blanket. The shoulder was bare—only the black bra strap appeared—and I wanted to flee. I was still at the door. I could still get out.

She had a distracted look—those bright blue eyes were wild, but unfocused. She was obviously awake but still in a dream; I wished there had been a buzzer outside, a way of easing into her presence.

"Larry said—" I began. She still didn't blink. I caught disapproval at the mention of his name.

"*You* said, remember? You gave me the note and told me to come." My explanation was dubious, even to myself; had I dreamed (*love, Laurel*) that note? Was this Laurel the same Laurel always so carefully dressed, so carefully made up? Was I actually alone with her, in her place where she went half-dressed? The whole trip downhill was only a numb and painful memory centred on my shins and knees. I was sleep-walking. I had no control over what I was doing and no reason for having done it in the first place. She too was in a trance; we were in separate dreams, trying to unite.

And then a strange thing happened. I could almost see it happen, starting from under the light blanket and reaching finally to her face. Her body turned, the legs raised and lowered as though she were pulling on slacks under the blanket. She hunched over, keeping the blanket bunched in front of her, and only then did her eyes clear and soften, and she smiled in my direction. Her voice was that same gentle whisper. "I remember," she said. "Let me make some coffee."

No one had ever offered me coffee; it emboldened me to take another step inside. "You're alone?" I asked.

"What do *you* think?" she smiled. "*We're* alone. Just throw your coat down . . ."She meant it literally; there were no chairs or tables that were not filled with clothes, plates, bottles and ashtrays. I dropped it on the floor, feeling giddy. Another first. And now she was sitting up, bare arms embracing her still-covered knees, keeping only the thin blanket between her breasts and legs. Her shoulders were the purest, most dazzling white or pink-white, I had ever seen. I was stunned; my feet wouldn't move. "Hand me my cigarettes," she said, pointing to a crumpled pack of Chesterfields just out of her reach. Larry's unopened pack of Luckies lay nearby. I took a step with the greatest difficulty, and when she took the pack from me, our fingers touched; she looked up and smiled. I had nowhere to sit, so I boldly sat on her couch. I could feel her toes slide out from under me.

"You're not here to do anything naughty to me, are you? 'Cause you've caught me in bed with nothing on. Just this—" She flicked her bra strap and I gave an involuntary shiver. "You'll have to be a good boy and not peek if you want me to make that coffee—" She said this in a voice that compelled an eager agreement, obviously inviting me to a game. Until that moment I'd not thought of any one but *me* as being in danger. In my fantasy, I had come on a mission of mercy; who knew what dragons in the form of her brother I'd be asked to slay? Her *situation* had attracted me more than her beauty; if she'd been as homely as the girl in the museum, I could have believed in myself as a saviour. I liked her better now without the sticky lipstick, just smoking quietly.

"Turn your head—I'm getting up."

I turned.

"Close your eyes."

I closed, but in a semblance of closing that focused everything, like through a keyhole. She reached over and picked up her brother's dirty shirt from the floor; wore it but didn't button. She wasn't wearing pants; only black panties to match the bra. The sofa lightened and she stood. My gaze was in line with the kitchen and when she entered it and stood by the stove, I was watching. She dropped the shirt. My eyes were wide open.

Laurel was taller than I, but slim, of course. The panties were too small and didn't quite cover the bottoms of her buttocks. My eyes couldn't take in her body all at once. There was so much I wanted to stop over, and hold. Her long, smooth white back distracted me from the legs. I could have stared at her shoulder blades, even her calves, her ankles, even her elbows, and especially the incredibly sharp upturned points of her bra that extended just beyond her upper arms (in the three-quarter view I had). I wanted to focus on everything simultaneously with the result that I was taking in nothing.

"I know you're peeking."

I wasn't embarrassed to confess. She turned to face me, leaning now against the door frame, one hand on her hip, shoulders slouching. So long as I live, that will remain for me an image frozen like the house painter in Hiroshima, of an unattainable, desirable beauty. "I'll bet you're hot now. Come get your coffee. I don't serve *any* man, not even you." *Man*! The light from the front window was full upon her. Her eyes were a fiery blue and her voice had lost its hoarseness but kept its rich, deep promise. "Let's see you strip down like me."

She unbuttoned my shirt as I held the coffee. I felt dwarfed by her; those pointed breasts nearly rubbed against my shoulders. Undressing—even before boys—always embarrassed me; this, somehow, wasn't so bad. While the scene was hardly natural, it seemed to me part of something much larger than mere undressing. It was an invitation to descend into the magma, to go down to the pit where different laws applied. And I was also profoundly democratic; if I expected to put my hands on every part of her, I knew I'd have to let her do the same to me.

"How do you feel?"

I wanted to say, "fine," but I muttered instead her word, "hot." My mouth was dry, my fingers cold and numb and 187 trembling. I sipped coffee. My shirt was unbuttoned and my belt undone. She stepped back and took an old bathrobe from the heap on the floor and put it on, belting it loosely and said, "*Miss Sadie Thompson*—you know her?" The robe was short, exposing most of her long legs, and now with another layer over her breasts, I was even more powerfully curious. She went to the radio and turned it to one of the "bad stations," a Negro station that played music that whites weren't supposed to listen to. "The pants," she said, "take them off." She was dancing now like Rita Hayworth, her long legs out, exposing a flash of black panty in the parting of the bathrobe, and if her hair had been long and the same colour, she would have looked like Rita Hayworth, whose image had been forever fixed for me by the pinup posters on the walls of the Florida barracks we never rented. My shiny gabardines dropped in a pile. My thick legs were red from the chafing walk in the cold, and my underwear bulged: that too did not embarrass.

"Good, good." She was swaying with the music, writhing about the room, dancing over the dirty clothes' piles, making me dizzy from keeping her in view. She pulled her panties down and I saw a flash of golden hair. She pulled them up again; she passed close enough for me to reach in to the robe and touch the satin softness of the black bra; she turned and pulled her panties down again and flipped the ends of the bathrobe over her gyrating hips; I could see more hair and strange new flesh and she backed toward me, finally back to the couch breathing hard. I was there, standing in front of her and she peeled my underwear off and put two cold hands along the shaft of my flushed and hurting penis. "Oh, a Jew," she said, rubbing its exposed head, circling its rim with her fingertips. "Come on," she said, lying back and motioning me to lie beside her, "take me. Put your hand here," and I let my cold, numb fingers slip under her panties into the matted hair. I had practically no hair to offer her and I felt bad about it, but I dug deeper, not knowing what to expect or what I should be doing. She was breathing hard and had bent her body in such a way as to present her face to my penis—*penis* was the only word for it I knew, though I guessed it changed its name at times like this—and she put her mouth on it and over it as I kept digging.

There was something tight down there, something in the moist hair like a leather thong, and I thought it must be a tendon, something painfully female that I had dug too deep for and mustn't disturb further. But by this time I couldn't explore further; my legs were folding and unfolding; my whole clumsy body was responding to the thrust of her head and I could hear her between strokes begging, "Take me, take me" (*where, where?* I thought desperately), and her voice was harsh now, uncontrolled. My hand was on that thong, and my fingers reached around to feel a knot; it couldn't be a growth—and when I tugged, she didn't cry. And then the thong came loose in my hand, and suddenly a thick, warm organ began to stir, it filled the palm of my hand, stiffening and growing thick and I realized I was holding an organ like my own, only larger; I realized this as a kind of pain matched by a kind of numbing pleasure flashed into my penis, and my hand now was sliding up and down on her . . . thing, what ever it was . . . the same way her mouth was on mine, catching the rim on every stroke, and I made sure I did the same with my fingertips until I felt her back begin to arch, her lips drive into my lap suddenly hard and her mouth fall off my penis as it began to pump for the first time, a clear fluid that could only have come *from her*, I thought—something she'd been trying to inject into me—though it felt it had come from me. "Now!" she shouted, suddenly standing and holding her organ in both hands triumphantly before me, a leather thong still resting around one end, and long ribbons of thick yellow fluid shot from her, first to the floor, then to my leg and finally across my chest; mine, too, had risen in a small plume, then settled again, matted in the old moisture of my lap. And in the process of standing before me, Laurel had taken off her bra. When I finally took it all in: penis, tiny concave nipples and the cruel, flushed face of Laurel Zywotko's transition to Larry, I knew I would not get out of that room as easily as I had entered.

He put his hands—she put her hands—on my shoulders and pulled my face to that wet matting, and I did what had been done to me until she lay on the floor squirming and once again she mildly erupted. I was not too excited, nor was I disgusted: I was detached and observant. I watched as we lay there on the floor. I saw two golf balls inside the cups of the black satin bra; I saw "F" papers in Laurel Zywotko's name; I saw silverfish in the worn matting that passed for a rug. I both knew and refused to know that Laurel Zywotko (*love, Laurel*) did not exist, had never existed, and that I had met a bigger dreamer than myself. I still believed in Laurel Zywotko though I found myself saying to that now-still body on the floor, eyes open, hands on penis, stomach glistening, "You know, you look just like your brother now."

I hadn't meant to humour her—I'd meant it, I think, in the spirit of madness to which I was also a party; I meant, in essence, there is no difference between us except degree of criminality, which meant degrees of boldness. Never could I have imagined such acting out; never could I have demanded such obedience from the rest of the world. She still lay on the floor. She, in the process of rising, him. So long as I addressed her as Laurel, she would lie there, I hoped, a smiling, loving girl reaching either for the bra or a T-shirt. Chesterfields or Luckies. I had dressed safely and was sweating by the door; Laurel's apartment must have been a hundred degrees, and I started shivering as soon as I opened the door. "What'll I say if I see Larry?" I asked, and she turned to me, now sitting on the floor and adjusting her bra. "Tell him I'm tired of all this shit. He either stays home or he stays out and never comes back. He thinks he's such a big man. Look—if he tries to collect money from you or anything, just tell him to fuck off, see?" I watched her tie her penis down with the leather strap, and then tie the loose ends around her waist. Then up with the panties. "Go downstairs, doll, and buy me a paper, okay? And a pack of Chesterfields." She picked up Larry's pack of Luckies and threw them down. "I don't know how he smokes those awful things. Ugh. Here, there's money in my purse."

I bought the paper but not the Chesterfields, and left it outside her door. And then I walked back up to the Ridge; 783 steps, to be exact, counting them numbly, doing penance. It was dark when I reached the top. A full moon burned above Duivylbuis Park; you could have read a paper by its light. I was still shivering and now my thighs were bloody from chafing during the two long walks. I stood back by the fence at Duivylbuis Park looking down into the moonlit magma of the streets by the river, convinced that I'd just been shown the secret parts of Daley Ridge's sexiest girl. And I walked home greatly relieved that we, the two sexes, were not so different after all. I imagined that the girls in school all wore different kinds of balls or rubber devices in their bras, which accounted for the different effects they gained. It was merely a social expectation that dictated the choice of sex; after a certain age, those who'd been told they were boys finally were given a suit and tie. Soon they were rewarded with the need to shave. And those who'd been raised to become women started stuffing their chest with rounded objects and wearing dresses and makeup. It was only primitive women, like the ones in *National Geographic*, who grew them naturally. And, I must have thought, with my fat and ever-pink nipples, too bad they hadn't decided I should be a girl. Probably I would have done better at that, and without too many props.

For the next few weeks, Laurel attended school more regularly than Larry, and Larry, when he did attend, never tried to collect anything from me. He was still collecting from others, however, who willingly or passively forked over. It was now well into winter, and I was involved in schoolwork, trying to keep up my grades in history and not to slip into B's in math and science. I was less fascinated by Laurel, and she never acknowledged me again. It was only when I remembered her by the kitchen door that she still excited me, though I no longer associated it with the girl in the fuzzy sweater.

After Christmas, Little Richie, the last holdout against adolescence, began to lose his soprano voice. His childhood melted away overnight, as I feared it would; he hadn't grown but suddenly he looked like a hardened jockey instead of a child, and that left only me, hormonally deficient.

"When?" I kept asking my mother, thinking that it was totally within her power. Why wouldn't she press the switch, give the pills, whatever it was that parents did? She was being perverse, like mothers who put their sons in dresses and curls because they'd wanted daughters. I was still a few inches shorter than she, still wearing my father's discarded white shirts, and still getting all my clothes from the humiliating "Husky" counter at Seligman's. (The only clothes I liked to get were shoes. In shoe stores the mirrors were set so low that my feet and ankles looked as lean as anyone else's.) *When* is it going to happen: the growing pains, the ravenous appetite, the razor blades (sharing with Dad the bathroom mirror), the double-dating, the springing out of the lean, precocious *me* from the pod of lard that encased me?

I was taken to a doctor who put me on amphetamines and some thyroid extracts. Suddenly I was energetic and hopeful and lost some weight. "The onset of secondary sexual characteristics," he intoned, "is determined by many factors. Heredity for one." (My father was boxing at sixteen. My heredity should have made me a superman.) "Body weight, for another," he scowled. He gave me a set of shots in the upper arm, and kinky black hairs sprouted there overnight; a small clump of misplaced pubic hairs. The injections helped. It was as though the ineffectual hormones had been circulating aimlessly, just waiting for a jolt of pace-setting maleness. The last resistance of childhood fell away; I began smelling gloriously foul under my arms and as I stealthily applied my father's "Fresh," I felt stubble. Underarm stubble. I examined my penis and found stubble again. It was not hard to imagine growing pains in the femur at night (nothing spectacular; every morning my Senior Citizen gabardines "broke" just over my shoes, as they always had). My wrists remained discreetly hidden under their cuffs. My classmates were in the weed stage, when cuff buttons popped after first wearing and every week, it seemed, pants cuffs had climbed again to sock tops. Their bodies resembled the frames of skyscrapers: nothing yet filled in, but the promise of something awesome was there, from the points of their sloping shoulders and the wide sails of their white shirts, to the nipped-in waists, hidden by shirttails. I still was watching, still admiring.

Then one day Laurel didn't attend and (as a trained observer in these things) neither did Larry. No one mentioned it for at least a week—Laurel's name was never called on the rolls anyway—it came so far at the end of the alphabet (with no

U's, V's and only one W to insulate it from all the S's) that kids usually snickered ". . . and Beetle Bomb" after the name of Devvie Weinberg. After a week of absence, however, our homeroom teacher asked if anyone had seen "Laurel" (like certain notorious actresses, she'd gone through the school with a single, entirely adequate name). No one had. "She's been out for a week," the teacher said. And on Monday when Laurel still had not come, I—the class monitor that week—was sent down to the nurse's office with my teacher's request for a tracer. The nurse looked up Laurel's health card, then Larry's. Officiously, I mentioned that they lived on Patience Street, but their files showed a respectable Ridge Boulevard address and phone. I shrugged and returned to class.

In the afternoon I was called from the class to Geraldine Horwathy's office. A secretary ushered me in; I found the vice-principal frail, stern and silent behind her desk. She glanced up silently and eloquently: *You again*, her eyes said. *Now look.* Two uniformed Palestra policemen, introduced as Lieutenant Shea and Patrolman Puchinski, nodded at me. "This is the boy you wanted," said Miss Horwathy. "You may talk here—I'll leave." See seemed to lower her head as she passed me, and to shake it slightly, a gesture of infinite disappointment.

Lieutenant Shea, the head of Juvenile Branch, was a small, precise man, fine-featured, his dark hair etched a bit with grey. His face belied the uniform; he belonged in grey flannel. His eyes were green, his skin a ghastly winter white. Puchinski reminded me of a wood-shop teacher, the burly, stubby-fingered kind who turned out to be fanatically devoted to intricate detail. His uniform buckled around each button and was stretched shinily across his chest. Shea was the obvious senior, but Puchinski generated the gut authority. Shea began by reading from a black notebook.

"David Greenwood, four-two-two Mohawk Drive, Daley Ridge?" I nodded. "There's nothing to be afraid of, just a slight irregularity we wanted you to help us with if you can."

He smiled and I nodded again, enthusiastically. "We're look-ing for a classmate of yours. A Miss Laurel Zywotko."

"Yes . . . " I said, most deliberately. "I know Miss Zywotko."

"I believe you know where she lives, is that right?"

"Ridge Boulevard, I think. The nurse—"

"—We know about the nurse's records. But you gave the nurse a different address, didn't you? You said"—he con-sulted his notebook again—"Patience Street, didn't you?"

"That was something I heard, I guess."

"Who'd you hear it from?"

"Guys talking, that's all."

"What do these guys say?"

"Just talk, you know." I shrugged the way one of the guys might shrug. "They talk about her and her brother."

He was busy writing; it made me feel important and use-ful. "I think we'd like to know what they say," he said. "Exactly. Some examples."

"Just things."

"I think you'd better tell us right now what kind of things. No beating about the bush."

"Well things like—'You been down to Patience Street yet?'—and about her and her brother living down there alone and all. And sometimes her brother—"

"What about her brother?"

"He used to brag. Just talk, you know how it is." They looked as though they'd suddenly made themselves pur-posely stupid; no, they didn't know how anything was. "You a friend of this brother, or something?" asked Puchinski. His voice was high; I could imagine a layer of fat or maybe mus-cle lying on his vocal cords. It was a high, clear, menacing voice. "What number on Patience Street?"

"I don't know."

"You want to tell us now or you want us to get it out of you down at Juvenile Hall?"

"Twenty-five something."

"David," said Shea, "we checked out the address on Ridge Boulevard this brother of hers gave at the beginning of the year. It's a phony."

"You afraid of this Larry, that it?" asked Puchinski. "He some kind of tough Polack, that it?" Shea and Puchinski had a good laugh. "Tell us now and we guarantee it your name won't get involved, unless, you know—"

"Unless what?'

"Unless you *are* involved."

"In what?"

"That's what we want to know. Look, you're shaking like a leaf. We get called in here to trace an absent student who gave a false address—now, believe me, that's pretty strange—and the first person we talk to tells us a brother and sister living alone together down in the slums and he's shaking like a leaf when he tells it—plus the fact he knows an address but he doesn't want to tell all of it."

"I don't know any address. I don't know anything about it."

"It? Who said anything about *it*? What is *it*?" Puchinski eased his weight on Miss Horwathy's desk, looking satisfied.

". . . About being in school. Or not being in school. Probably she's sick or something."

"And him? This Larry? He sick, too?"

"Probably they're both sick."

"He's lying, Lieutenant," said Puchinski. "Get him in the car and we can get it out of him. He's aching to tell us, but he don't want to do it in the principal's office."

"That it, son?"

"No."

"I thought so. Stan—go with him to his locker. Take any books you'll need, and your jacket. You're coming with us."

In the cruiser, I started parcelling out the truth, first to myself—how much *did* I know, really? How much *could* I tell, really?—and then I started parcelling it out to them, little by little. More than anything, I wanted to be indispensable, a

175

source of revelation; I enjoyed knowing more than they did and I wanted them to need me. I decided it was okay to suddenly remember the full address. I snapped my fingers and said, "Twenty-five sixteen! I just remembered."

"Come on," said Puchinski. "That's Saint Stash's Church. No one lives there."

"No," I said, "the church is up a block." He smiled, and Shea turned to him with a wink. But there was no smile for me. Puchinski turned from the front seat and reached back, balling up my jacket collar in his two thick fists. "From now on, you tell us what we want to know *as soon as* we ask it, understand? Don't make the lieutenant and me play games." He let go and pushed me back.

We started driving down the switchbacks to Patience Street, approaching from the downtown end, where two-five-one-six was still connected. I didn't recognize the building till we were parked in front.

"Twenty-five sixteen."

The Polish-American News was still open, and I suddenly realized that the old man inside might remember me, deeper-voiced or not. I hadn't been back to Patience Street since that afternoon, but gazing at the building now from the back of a police cruiser, I felt as though I had, almost as though I'd never left. From a police cruiser, everything seems smaller and shabbier than it does from the street. Twenty-five sixteen Patience Street seemed ready to topple over. I could smell Laurel Zywotko on my face and hands; if they'd had a police dog, he'd be pointing at me, for Laurel Zywotko was very, very close. I could feel that tightening in my crotch just thinking of her slouched against the doorway. *That* doorway, just ahead. In school everyone still talked about her, but I was the only one who really knew what complications went on under those sweaters and skirts.

"Okay, out."

I crossed Patience Street flanked by the policemen but feeling as though I were handcuffed. The same stairwell I had climbed two months earlier was still empty, but now littered with random broken bottles and old papers that had swirled in from the street. It looked more unoccupied than ever. I prayed that it was. The officers buzzed from below, discovering a bell I had missed. No answer. We began climbing, Shea a few steps ahead.

It was he who turned, halfway up. "Oh, Christ. You smell it?" he said, and when we joined him, Puchinski caught it, too. They were like dogs responding to a special whistle, alert to a different range of stimuli. I didn't smell a thing. "Stay with him," said Shea, "I'm going in." He took two more stairs and turned again.

"Cuff him."

The door was locked. I could smell something now, too sweet for gas, but just as penetrating. And something else: decaying meat. Shea kicked down the door and wrapped a handkerchief over his nose. Puchinski and I were handcuffed on the landing.

Fumes washed over us in waves, each wave more powerful for the few seconds of stale, untainted air before it.

"Here's one of them," Shea shouted from deep inside. "Murder. Five-six days old. Boy tied in a chair and strangled with a leather cord. Mutilated."

Then he came bursting out and took half a dozen stairs before dropping his hanky and gulping for breath. "There's a note on the body," he gasped. "Signed LZ. Talks about guys who know what to do to men who fuck their sisters and make them whores."

"Holy shit," said Puchinski.

"Says '*You won't find me so don't look. LZ.*'"

"Christ. It's going to be a big fucking case."

"The biggest man." It was hard to tell if Shea were smiling, or still winching from the smell. "Spells it H-O-R-S. I think a kid wrote it. Take *him* inside and get a preliminary identification," said Shea. Puchinski un-cuffed me and pushed me inside. The effect of the smell had been worse outside; inside, the hot dark cluttered room stank so strongly that the specific decaying odours were momentarily blocked. "There," said Puchinski, pointing. The kitchen chair was turned toward us, and in it, arms lashed behind him, sat the body of Larry Zywotko. But his face was purple-black, a bruise that had become his head. His shirt and pants-front were slashed open; all I could see was black. The floor beneath him was a single dull dry brown stain.

"That him?"

I nodded.

"Okay, get out. Wait on the steps."

Puchinski pulled out a hanky and went into the kitchen.

When he reappeared, he was holding his handkerchief over his mouth and nose and stumbled past us all the way to the street before stopping. Shea and I walked down. My legs were numb. This *has* to be a dream, I thought. *But it's gone on long enough.* Then, when I got to the sidewalk, it suddenly hit me. It wasn't Larry in the chair—it was Laurel! Someone had done that not knowing they were killing her, too. And then finally the odours of the death got to me, too, stronger in recollection than in actual fact, and I vomited in the gutter.

"Okay," I heard Shea say to Puchinski, "I'll get on the radio. Homicide will send a squad down to seal the place. Stay out of sight, but guard that place—no one enters till the crime lab comes. I'm running this kid in for more questioning. This is going to be a big case, and one fuckup now will be on your file for life."

Puchinski took up his position just inside the stairwell, and I walked back to the squad car with Shea. There was so much I wanted to ask; I was about to start when he suddenly grabbed my arm and twisted it behind me and marched me to the car. He opened the back door and pushed me onto the seat, face down. "Stay that way till I tell you to sit. Shut up till I tell you to talk." He got on the radio and spewed out the address, the code numbers and the request for a photographer and full lab. "Male, Caucasian, juvenile. Positive identification of Larry Zywotko—I'll spell that—ninth-grade student at Ridge Junior. Cause of death, I'd have to guess, strangulation. Leather thong around the neck, tied to a chair. Torture and mutilation indicated. Activate all files, known sex offenders." I could see him wiping his forehead with the back of his hand; he looked whiter than ever, sick. "Looks like a castration. Severe bleeding. My guess he's been dead five-six days. Stomach's blown open, corpse turning black, putrescent. Christ, what's left up there is turning to soup. Put out an APB for Laurel Zywotko, fourteen, sister of deceased. Implicated in a note found on the body. Photo probably available Ridge Junior. This is top priority, repeat, top priority. Bringing in one David Greenwood, that's Green-wood, for questioning. Officer Puchinski is remaining at the scene. Out." I could already hear, faintly at first, the crime-lab sirens.

Until that moment, I'd felt myself somehow privileged, a guide or a guest, and the cuffs had seemed part of the protection. Suddenly I began thinking like a suspect—would they take me into *Polish-American News*? Why had I gone down there and bought a paper that one day?—it nearly creased my brain with guilt—and for a moment I acknowledged the guilt. What *had* I been doing five or six days ago? I'd been going to movies nearly every evening, even school nights, or else I had gone to the museum or library—what kind of alibi is that?

Lieutenant Shea turned around. He motioned me to sit up.

"Okay, kid, now it's murder. I'm through fucking around with you. It started out nice and friendly, nice and slow when we thought it was truancy. But there's been a pattern to all your answers—you're guilty as hell about something. The vomiting was a good sign—I'll tell you, if you hadn't of vomited, you'd be in deep trouble now, deep trouble. But the pattern's still there—you're holding back. I want to know everything. I want to know who his friends were. I want to know *exactly* what they say about him and his sister. I want to know how come you knew this address." His radio was squawking with cries of distress and suspicion, agonies from streets I knew so well.

I wondered if I should volunteer that my parents were aliens, that Greenwood wasn't our name. But I began, "My name is David W. Greenwood and you have my address and I'm an eighth-grade student at Ridge Junior High. My father is the furniture buyer at Seligman's, and we just moved here in the summer. I learned this address from something Laurel said to me one night at a PTA open house. My mother was there and you can check it. She was crying outside, and she said her brother had slapped her. When I went over to her, she thanked me and said I should come to where she lived and visit her. The next day she passed me a note with the address."

"What did you do when you visited?"

"Nothing. I mean, I never went. I mean, I walked down here all the way and I got to this building, but I thought there must be some kind of mistake. I went into the newsstand there, but no one seemed to understand English, so I just bought a paper and walked away." (Hah, take *that*! I thought.)

We drove off, passing a number of squad cars with sirens and flashing lights. I put my head and cheek against the cool wet window and I soon realized I was shivering just as I had been that day in the apartment. And my throat was aching; it wanted to cry, but I couldn't let it. The terrible thing was I didn't know that I *hadn't* killed Larry Zywotko. I'd killed him in my fantasies and I *wanted* to kill him to save his sister, take her with me and move away. I'd wanted to *be* Larry, with a Laurel all to myself. *Had* I done it? Walked out at night like a zombie down the seven hundred and eighty-three steps and into that unlocked apartment? Strangled him? Strangled him with that leather thong she tied her penis with? Then it would have my fingerprints on it! But how could I have gotten him into a chair by myself; how could I have tied him? I had the will and the motive and maybe even the opportunity, *but I didn't have the strength*. I could bank on that. They would have to prove I was physically capable of overpowering Larry Zywotko, and thank God I was the mess I was.

Even at two in the afternoon, the Juvenile Hall was full of school-age kids, most of them black and older than I, all of them the type I would not follow into the boys' room. They recognized Shea as they waited on benches or slouched against the counters, aimlessly blowing smoke rings or snapping their chewing gum, breaking into arrogant grins and insolent half-salutes as he passed. "What say, Lieutenant?" and Shea walked past them, swatting some on the arm, snarling at others, calling most by name or "sport" or by a brief, appropriate insult. I felt like the bat boy, trying to shake a home-run-hitter's hand when all the team had gotten there first. I was royalty among skinny black car-thieves; I was taken into a private, frosted-glass cubicle that looked recently reclaimed from the amorphous rows of chairs, desks and benches. There were three such cubicles, all marked JUVENILE INTERROGATION. Shea's name was on the door.

He hung up his overcoat and took off his uniform jacket. He loosened his tie, dropped a ball-point pen and a cigarette pack on the bare tabletop, then pulled open the top drawer of the desk and extracted a tablet of official-looking yellow paper. He lit a cigarette, inhaling deeply and biting the smoke back as it began to come out. Then he jabbed the pen into writing position, jotted down the heading, and said, "All right. A stenographer'll be right in to take down everything, but I want to start with it right away."

"Okay." I was eager; I saw a chance to tell something I alone knew to someone important who had to listen. Like being taken inside a flying saucer and living to tell about it. Maybe I was smiling; I know my hands were trembling.

"Wipe that fucking smile off your face. You're in serious trouble, kid. I can lock you up right now." He punched the ball-point, forgetting that it was already in position; he punched it again and it jammed. I handed him mine.

"Here's a warning to you. I can hold you in cells as a material witness, and I will if you don't come clean. And you've seen the kind of company you'll have out there. They don't like rich white kids from the Ridge, and they especially won't like it if I tell them what happened to that boy. If they hear it was some fat queers got together and tied a boy up and cut his dick off before they strangled him—if they were to hear something like that, then we might find you hanging in the cell before morning came."

A stenographer came in—a sallow, diseased old man in a white shirt many sizes too large for him and baggy pants held up by suspenders, called, incongruously, "Rick." His face and his cheeks were the colour and nearly the texture of a peachstone. He seemed to me some sort of caricature, like a reject from a Dick Tracy strip. Shea fed him a set of facts— my name, age, point of apprehension, the information from the house that had already been given over the radio, and the fact of my "inadvertently" having given away the address. "We'll wrap it up this afternoon if we get lucky, Rick. Crime lab's there now. What'ya think, Rick? Think this fat little fag and maybe the girl together could have tied a fourteen-, fifteen-year-old up?"

"Looks to me anyone over ten years old could knock the shit out of him."

"We'll need to get his handwriting to match with the note." He took one of my school notebooks and handed it to Rick. "See that this gets down to the lab."

The insults didn't have their calculated effect on me because I'd never before heard such language. My father's cursing, rich and plentiful, was rarely in English, and when it was, it tended to be blasphemous translations from French, never anything sexual or scatological; and I'd lived in such isolation from normal children that I'd never learned the various catchwords of my generation. When Laurel had used the word "shit," I knew it meant unpleasant behaviour, nothing else. Thanks to Rick, I now guessed what it meant.

"How'd you do it, kid? Who'd you do it with? It'll go easier if you tell me everything now."

"I didn't do anything."

"Take it all down, Rick. We'll nail him on perjury, any little detail that doesn't check out—and with that I can hold him in cells for a week. Christ, that'll sweat the rest of it out of him, huh, Rick? A week down in juvenile detention with those animals?"

"More likely bleed it out of him," Rick observed.

"All right, I want names. How long did you know the deceased?"

"Larry?"

"I got all day, kid. Yes, Larry—and let me give you a tip. I know you're lying as soon as you start repeating the question. Try again."

"I never knew him. Only when I saw him at school and he would take money from people in lunch line."

"I didn't hear that."

"I didn't know him."

"Then how come your chin is shaking? Oh, they're going to love you downstairs. You better like to kiss nigger lips, 'cause there ain't nothing they like better than a fat white boy. Ain't that right, Rick?"

"Less'n it's a white girl."

"Why do you keep saying that?" I cried out. "I don't know what you're talking about and I don't know why you're trying to call me names or something. I didn't know Larry and I don't know the names of his friends or even if he had any friends. He used to take money from anyone he could. He used to spread stories about his sister and tell everyone he could get anything off her he wanted. And he tried to keep selling dates with her. There was a kid in ninth grade named Paul Gaylord, I remember. He once had a date or something with her—that came out in a mind-reading show at school."

"Okay, now, that's the cooperation I want. Paul Gaylord—we'll pick him up. This Larry ever take any money from you?"

"Sure. After that time I talked to her at the PTA open house. Next day he took money."

"And it made you mad, didn't it?'

"Sure."

"And there were a lot of people mad at Larry, weren't there?"

"Sure, I guess."

"And a lot of people who wanted to date his sister without having to pay for it, right?"

"Probably."

"And she'd probably like to date a lot of guys without Larry getting a cut, right? And you say she was putting out for Larry, too?"

I said that I guessed so.

"Christ, this case stinks," said Shea. "I've never had a case that smells as bad as this from so far away. What have we got—first-degree murder? Rape. Pimping. Extortion. Prostitution. Incest. Corruption of a Minor. Escape to Avoid Prosecution. Maybe someone did us a favour getting rid of a kid like that—ever think of that, David?"

"There are lots of kids like that in school, taking money from younger kids, and they don't get killed."

"They don't have sisters. And maybe they're not so greedy."

"Can I call my mother?"

"Be my guest. Tell her you're being held as a material witness to a first-degree murder. Tell her we can hold you here till you're eighteen and then transfer you to a penitentiary for life or the chair. Who knows, maybe this sister did it and you only helped. An accomplice before or after the fact, with a good lawyer—you might even beat it. Especially if you tell me everything."

"I didn't have anything to do with it."

Rick and Shea both snickered. "Kid, you've already got *something* to do with it. You led us to the body. If you left fingerprints up there, after all your denials, then we've got you—you're dead. We'll take your prints before you leave today, don't worry. If your handwriting checks, then the case is open and shut."

"I can prove where I've been every minute of every day," I suddenly claimed.

"You'll get a chance to prove it."

The telephone on Shea's desk rang; it was a relay mes- sage from the crime lab. A preliminary report: six days dead, strangulation and loss of blood as possible cause. Suicide note apparently in the handwriting of Laurel Zywotko, whose tests and notebooks were found in the room. None of Larry's discovered.

Thank God, at least I hadn't written the note. Rick slid my notebook back to me, and I remembered suddenly the margins of the pages were crammed with drawings of Laurel Zywotko. Shea handed back my pen and took one from Rick. It had helped to do some talking; if they'd intended to break me, they should never have let me engage in conversation. Interrogation was just a form of salesmanship; presenting the product, making claims, complimenting my taste and stating the price. Setting the hook and backing away. *He's taken the hook—let him* run! Only everything was reversed and the product was jail and maybe death and my taste was for sadistic butchery and the product was confession.

"Where do you think Laurel is?" Shea asked. His tone was conversational, at last.

"Laurel?"

"Yes. Laurel. She ever mention a place to you, friends, relatives, a place she came from? The school records say she and her brother came from Phoenix, Arizona—she ever mention Phoenix?"

"No." He looked so genuinely puzzled, I nearly told him— have you ever thought that she died, too? There *is* no Laurel? Or there is no Larry? But I couldn't tell him that without giving too much away. What we had done up there that day—*that*—I would never tell no matter where they put me. I was proud of my spontaneous misrepresentations. I was my father's son after all. He, too, could talk his way out of traffic tickets and customers' complaints. He did it by charm and subtle counterthreats; I did it by confessing my fears and weakness.

"This Laurel—was she, you know, stacked? Built? Sexy?"

"Everyone thought so."

"Think some boys were putting it to her and Larry was collecting from it? Or was it all just talk?"

I told him that was likely, not knowing exactly what he meant.

He flipped through his pocket notebook and read some facts to the stenographer. "Absences of Laurel Zywotko: fifty-three days in first semester. That's out of ninety school days. Absence of Larry Zywotko: fifty-eight. Not too healthy, were they?"

"I wonder who signed their school excuses," I said.

He wrote that down. "The next step is to check the school files anyway." He stood up, and pointed to my coat. "You can make that phone call now. Get your old man down here and tell him to bring lots of identification. I'm releasing you till all the results come in. Come out to the hall after you've made that call, and get fingerprinted. I'll see you upstairs."

By the time my father came, I'd been fingerprinted and taken to a carpeted second-floor reception area where all the people were white, some in business suits. My father came from

Seligman's in half an hour, an anxious, dark-suited man asking what the hell was up. Lieutenant Shea was properly reassuring to a well-dressed business man who invoked the names of several captains. "We're in the preliminary stages of a murder investigation in your son's school. He's been very helpful, and we've got his name and address in case we need him again, but I don't think"—and here he put a big-brotherly arm over my shoulder "—it'll be necessary, will it, sport? A fine boy you've got, sir, and a good day to you."

On the drive I mentioned why I'd been called and what I had seen.

"Did you vomit?" he wanted to know, after I'd described the scene in some detail. My father, an avid man for details, was the best person to be with. I described the smell, the sight, what little bit I knew of the boy. My father didn't seemed shocked or disgusted, nor did he ask the obvious question: how come I, the most innocent and uninvolved thirteen-year-old in Palestra, happened to be fingerprinted and called to make the identification?

"I vomited the first time, too," he said. "I've never told your mother this, so don't ever mention it."

He then began a story of a time and place and circumstance that I'd never associated with him. And he told it with relish, double-parking frequently just to give himself the time to finish it. Even that—the change from reticence to a kind of eager confession—was a kind of gift to me, no matter what the story itself was about. The year was 1926; my father was twenty-one. The place was New England, the back roads between Montreal and Waterbury, Connecticut. Until that day I'd not known a thing of my father prior to his thirty-fourth year, the year before I was born, when he strode into my mother's life. She had invented him for me. Her stories were all I had known.

Being a tough kid, "good with his dukes," he'd been hired by the bootleggers operating out of Montreal during Prohibition. He wasn't a driver; he "rode shotgun" and handled the money for payoffs along the route. There was a roadhouse in North Adams, Massachusetts, that the gang—three trucks—always stopped in. They pulled in at two in the morning. There was a waitress that my father—no, I should say Louis-Noël Boisvert—liked. He'd give her a bottle or two every week and promised to take her up to Montreal for a good time.

"She was a French girl," he said now. "We were all French. The only English we saw were when we loaded it in Montreal and when we dumped it in Waterbury."

"The Watch City of America," I said. "Waterbury."

But on this particular night in 1926 there were other men inside the roadhouse. "Wops. Soon's we got in, I could smell it. They were after our liquor. We had rules, you know—don't let anyone muscle in. The cops'll look the other way." The cops only wanted a clear winner. What they didn't want was indecisive warfare that would interfere with the steady payoffs and also bring in the higher authorities.

So that night (it was winter, he remembered, old snow against the buildings) out in the parking lot, the Wop gang hit. They had five more guys waiting in a car. They had guns. Two of the French drivers got hit right away. But what the Wops didn't know was that each of the Montreal trucks had armed guards inside ("like Brinks," I said), and they came out firing. Pretty soon the Wops were taking big losses.

"I had one of them up against the fender," my father said, and even now, nearly thirty years later, his fists were shaking as he struck the steering wheel, "and I was working him over like I never could in the ring, you know? Referee would have broken it up. But this son of a bitch tried to kill me. Every time I landed a punch, I got madder. You understand me?"

"Sure." He had pulled over, double-parked, and his face was red from the remembering, teeth clenched, his fists flying in the air, and my own adrenaline was flowing. *Give it to him, give it to him, Dad*! But if anyone had looked inside (thank God the windows were steamed), they might have thought that an aging man was trying to kill a boy.

"Sometimes when I lose my temper, I see his face again and I feel like I'm back there. I would have killed him with my bare hands, I know it. It wasn't anything to do with right or wrong. We were all doing something illegal, but they were *more* illegal—"

"Right."

But then one of his guards very calmly stepped up to Boisvert and tapped him on the shoulder and invited him to step aside. The Wop was half-draped on the fender, trying to stand. The guard just put the shotgun to the Wop's forehead and blew it off. Literally. There was blood on the fender, the windows, the roof, and all over all of them.

"*Abattoir*," he said. "You know what that means? A slaughterhouse."

And my father remembered the look of complete nonbelief and then complete understanding when the Wop stared into the muzzle of that gun. His face just got small, as though the gun barrel had pulled it to a point, like a drawstring.

"That's when I started vomiting," he said. "I thought I was a pretty tough kid, and I'd seen a lot of blood in the ring. But *Christ sanglant*, this was a . . . ("*Abattoir*," I said, and he nodded). "*C'était un abattoir*, like Custer's Last Stand. All I could see was bodies: our guys, their guys. And my clothes were muddy—that's what I thought—muddy. Then I reached down and the mud turned out to be . . ."

"The Wop," I said.

They took handfuls of the old snow and washed off all they could. But blood is oily; the snow didn't do anything but smear it around. They made up a story about hitting a deer and smashed the fenders a couple of times to make it look authentic. They only had five of their nine left, and the seven Italians were dead. One of the Canucks had gone around and made sure of it.

"I vomited all night. That's when I learned I didn't have it. All the others, you should have heard them singing. They even opened up some of the bottles."

They'd gotten a big bonus in Waterbury, and fewer guys to share it with. Boisvert went to New York and got a room in a flophouse. The North Adams Massacre was in all the papers for a week, and he followed the story in ten different papers, comparing the leads, trying to guess how close the cops were to solving it, and when they would put out a bulletin on him. The published accounts had it all wrong, but the police were on the payroll, so maybe they were only doing their job. Sometimes, he added, they put out false leads just to trick the guilty.

"They do?"

Boisvert dreamed of turning himself in. But at twenty-one, *quoi bon*? A life in prison in order to clear his conscience? He already had a clear conscience. It was self-defence, one gang of lawbreakers against an even worse gang. It wasn't conscience that was bothering him, it was just the gut reaction to the blood and killings and seeing the guy who'd been his friend walking around the parking lot and executing the Wops. One of them only had a leg wound and had been trying to crawl away. He'd almost made it. He kept begging for mercy.

My father relived it all, there in the parked car: the sweats, the fists, the French curses, and little details about the roads and villages he still remembered. I was thankful for that; as soon as I got home, I would take out my full collection of road maps and trace his route: Austerlitz, Copake Falls, North Adams, Troy . . . another blank part of America filled with story. I would never read of Waterbury or North Adams or Great Barrington without seeing a convoy of 1926 trucks (whatever *they* looked like), and imagining a pretty French waitress who might have been my mother—who knows—if those Italians had not shown up one night. It had been the longest talk of his life to me.

"What did you do, finally?"

He was taken by surprise, I think, by my wanting to extend the story. The motive for the story had been my vomiting at the sight of blood; that was the only connection between us. The memory of himself shaking in a flophouse in New York—that didn't relate to me nor to him now. My mother would have drawn it out and brought it back to where it belonged, not with a parking lot in North Adams or a flophouse in New York, but back to the twenty-one-year-old not-so-tough Boisvert. How did he become Lou Greenwood, Furniture Buyer of Seligman's, in this town, at this time, with this boy beside him?

"Me? Finally? What do you mean?"

He'd seen an ad for a car salesman in Newark. He liked to drive, but he'd never sold anything in his life. The dealer's name was D'Alessandro—an Italian-American. Which worried him, because Boisvert felt he was marked forever in Italian-America. Sooner or later all Italians got together and compared notes. Vendettas were their way of settling things.

He'd decided on a name ("Greenwood!" I cried triumphantly, but no): Irish Jimmy Mulcahy, the name of the only boxer who'd beaten him in Golden Gloves. But *this* Jimmy Mulcahy, since he didn't have any identification and spoke with an accent, would have to have just come off the boat. All his selling experience was in Ireland (Boisvert had even looked up maps, deciding to be from Cork, deciding that he'd fought in "The Troubles," lost two brothers to the Black and Tans). He had a large family waiting for him to make good in America. D'Alessandro took him in.

"Only he took me in too good," my father laughed. It was good to see him laugh. He turned out to be a very good salesman, and D'Alessandro had ambitions for him to move in with the family. The old man had a daughter and no sons and the Model T's were just coming in and everyone had money. They were taking orders for months in advance. And D'Alessandro's daughter—

"Pretty?" I asked. "Stacked?"

He snickered. "I didn't think you noticed those things." She was dark-eyed and pretty with very pale skin like he'd never seen before, and yes, solidly constructed. Her name was Alicia D'Alessandro.

I was still visualizing the whole scene, creating my own Alicia D'Alessandro and had fallen a couple of sentences behind in the story. Then I heard a word I knew—

"*J'étais coincé.*"

One of his favourite words: trapped. "Cornered," I said. "How?"

"She came to me and said she was . . . you know . . . in a family way."

"What does that mean?"

"She wanted to get married."

"Just like that?" Don't *you* ask *them*? I wanted to ask.

"Well, she said she was pregnant."

It's a wonder I didn't say *but you weren't married*? To cover my ignorance, I assumed an unearned sophistication.

"How'd she guess you were the father?"

My father seemed shocked. "Well . . . son," he laughed nervously. *Of course* she knew—what kind of girl did I think she was, living there in her father's house, and him a greenhorn Wop? She was scared to death—literally—of what her father would do. Probably shoot them both unless they got married that night. She had it planned. They'd get married in New York. She wanted a honeymoon in the Adirondacks and then a quick trip up to . . .

"Montreal!" I said.

"Montreal. A big honeymoon trip in one of her father's new cars to Montreal and around to Niagara and back to Newark and I'd be the manager of a second lot he was starting. *Sacrement!*"

He didn't have any papers and he was illegally in the country and *he was a wanted man* (and maybe he still was). She wanted to write to his mother in Cork. She wanted to meet a brother he'd invented in Boston. That's what he meant, *coincé*.

So he told her he'd marry her. He'd go down to the Western Union office and send a cable to his brother and another one to his mother. She should pack, but wait to tell her father till they were in New York. Or better, till they were in the Adirondacks.

"I put on my jacket, son, and I kissed her goodbye, and Christ—I took a bus to New York and I roamed around all night and the next morning I got a train back to Montreal. And did I pray."

"Prayed for what?"

"My life. Christ. I was a *kid*, twenty-one years old. I had that girl and her father after me and I had the police—I was on the wrong side of Italians, and that's something you don't live to tell about, especially if it has anything to do with their daughters. That's a piece of advice I hope you never forget." He pounded his finger into my chest. "That body you identified—was he Italian?"

"Polish I think."

"That's okay then. Poles have a temper but they cool off quick. Italians have a temper and it just keeps building. D'Alessandro in Newark if he's still alive is probably the biggest car dealer in the East. He'd be—Christ—eighty now. And he's probably still on the lookout for someone named Jimmy Mulcahy. I may even have signed a death warrant for the real Jimmy Mulcahy. *Don't ever mention that name, even as a joke,* I'm telling you. Someone hears it and a little light goes off somewhere. Old D'Alessandro had killed guys in Italy before he came over and he used to tell me stories about how his friends operated in New York. Jesus Christ, it turns your blood to water. Those guys aren't human."

We were driving now, up on the Ridge near our house. My head was buzzing not with gangsters and bodies but with the incidental revelation that somewhere out there—all these years—there was a brother or a sister! It *had* been true all along. If only my parents could talk together, they could have filled the world with stories. It was the longest talk my father and I ever had, or ever would. What it had been was my father's confession to me, and the admission, I think, that I was old enough to join the world of men and sudden death. This is "the little talk" father and sons were supposed to have, the "birds and the bees" that I kept reading about and waiting for him to initiate.

"Wash your hands off before you talk to your mother," he said, pointing to my inky fingertips. "That's a dead giveaway. And if the cops come around, let me handle it. I don't want her upset. Don't tell her a thing."

BIZARRE MURDER OF
LOCAL TEEN

read the morning's headline, complete with a blurred front-page photo of Larry Zywotko, cropped from a class shot. The left-hand column read PORTRAIT OF A TORMENTED TEEN and a middle box under the photo read POLICE PUZZLED BY FURTHER MYSTERY. The right-hand column picked up the lead and gave the sensational details.

Investigating repeated absences, Palestra Police yesterday discovered the partially decomposed body of a Daley Ridge Junior High School student, Larry Zywotko, tied to a chair and strangled to death in the Patience Street apartment where he and his fourteen-year-old sister, Laurel, were living. The girl is a material witness and is still missing. Not only had the boy been strangled with a leather thong, police theorize, but had also been brutally slashed with a knife in a sadistic sexual attack. He apparently had been dead for several days.

"We're on the trail of a sadistic sex-murderer," said Lt. Frederick T. Shea of the Juvenile Branch, who is heading the investigation. Lt. Shea said that one suspect had been taken into custody and then released, and that suspicion now rested with the missing sister, Laurel. A note discovered at the scene, and traced to the sister's handwriting, accuses her brother of sexual abuse and hints at retribution.

Police speculate that Larry was murdered by more than one person, perhaps by a torture-gang from the neighbourhood, from the Palestra underworld, or perhaps even from the school. "We can't guess the kinds of things that are going on even in good schools," said Lt. Shea. "Whoever did this had to know a great deal about the private life of the deceased. He kept his address secret. And right now we're trying to learn as much about his life as we can." Police feel that if they piece together the several mysterious strands of the boy's life, they will inevitably be led to the murderer, or murderers.

DOUBLE LIFE

The picture that emerges of Larry Zywotko grows more complicated as each new fact is learned. Larry and his sister were new to Palestra this year. When they registered at the Palestra School Board last August, they claimed an address on Ridge Boulevard, which *Star* reporters have traced to a service station. Files show one "Victor Young" signed the necessary forms and presented the normal transfer papers for both children from the Phoenix (Ariz.) school system. He also listed himself as legal guardian. *Star* sources have verified their authenticity; both a Larry and a Laurel Zywotko attended school in Phoenix last year. They do not, however, answer the description of the murdered Palestra teenager, or of his sister. In addition, the Zywotkos of Phoenix are twins and were in the same class; in the Palestra files, Larry is listed as fourteen and in the ninth grade, Laurel as fourteen (but ten months younger) and in eighth grade. And to add to the confusion, the Zywotko family left Phoenix last year following the divorce of the parents. A Mrs. Gladys Zywotko left an Oregon forwarding address and her ex-husband, Mr. Kasimir Zywotko, cannot be traced at present.

Police investigation has therefore been opened on at least four levels. The first involves the tracing of the alleged "guardian," Mr. Victor Young. The second, involving cooperation with authorities in Phoenix and elsewhere, is attempting to locate Mrs. Zywotko and determine her connection to the case, if any. The third is centred in Palestra, and is attempting to learn the identity of the killer or killers of Larry Zywotko. A fourth investigation is attempting to locate the missing sister.

"This may seem like four isolated investigations," said a police spokesman, "but they're all coordinated from the same office and they are proceeding simultaneously."

Under TORMENTED TEEN I read many of the things I already knew: the description of the apartment with its heaps of soiled clothes, the dresses, jeans, and undergarments. "Tests run on bed stains" to determine I knew not what, even incongruous details like the number of golf balls found in the apartment, which investigators felt was an important link to a more "adult and respectable" connection, perhaps to Victor

Young. Larry Zywotko was not known to have any interest in golf, but local country clubs and sports shops were given pictures of the boy and his sister. Neighbours, especially the proprietors of the *Polish-American News* in the same building, had no special recollection of the teenagers who apparently lived alone, possibly on terms of sexual intimacy.

Investigators were puzzled by a host of contradictions. In the first place, the victim's sister had totally vanished, leaving behind her sweaters, skirts, undergarments and cosmetics. It was highly unlikely that such a girl would deliberately desert them. The evidence was clear that no one but the two teenagers lived there, and the clutter indicated that they ate very little, and did practically no cleaning or schoolwork. Nothing relating to the school except two failing tests of Laurel's was discovered in the apartment, leading one officer to remark that Larry seemed to see school as a business, a place of work for extorting money and (it was rumoured) acting as a procurer for his sister.

On the other hand, the article went on, except for an undeniable physical likeness and the apparent fact that *somewhere* in America there is a Larry and a Laurel Zywotko who once attended school together, no hard evidence exists that links *this* Laurel with *this* Larry. They may not, in fact, have been brother and sister at all, but have chosen to pose as such to disguise their underage cohabitation. A check of the various "Victor Young" signatures on over one hundred absence excuses shows that all were forged by Laurel Zywotko. Refuse in the apartment indicated they lived an unhealthy life, sharing only hamburgers and prepared sandwiches purchased in the neighbourhood. They drank only cola drinks and black coffee. There were two coffee mugs, but one contained only Larry's prints, while the other contained a great many "partials," most of them presumably Laurel's. In a macabre twist, one cup of week-old coffee was still on the kitchen table: apparently the victim had just brewed it when his attackers entered. It is of course possible that he knew his murderers and that the coffee had been made for them.

And so the details pile up: golf balls, but no clubs!

A BOY IN TROUBLE

Larry Zywotko is not remembered fondly at Ridge Junior High. "A punk," "a smart-aleck," "a bully," say three different teachers. One remembers being threatened by him, but "not taking it that seriously." "He could be charming, absolutely charming," recalled Mrs. Wilma Hatcher, an English teacher. "One could see he was a troubled boy. It showed in his attendance, in the hostility of his questions. But he wrote occasional poetry," Mrs. Hatcher went on, "which was very beautiful. At first I was suspicious, I thought he'd cribbed them from some lesser-known poet. But the longer I got to know him, the more I thought he was capable of such things. I suggested that he let me publish them for him in the school magazine but he practically tore them out of my hands and never showed me anything else. And then he said something very strange. He said, 'Where I'll end up I'll have lots of time for writing poetry.'"

And though his grades were uniformly "D" or below (and his sister's are a practically unheard of straight "F"), his record did show one surprising "A" grade in beginning French. French instructor Mr. Steven Wilcox told our reporters that Larry had an undeniable gift for the language. Despite rare attendance, he scored near-perfect results on three multiple-choice exams.

Other students recall him as a bully, a boy who openly extorted lunch money from younger boys and openly procured from older ones. "He had a reputation for being mean and carrying a knife," said one seventh-grade boy, "so even though he wasn't that big, people usually wouldn't fight him."

But speculation in Juvenile Branch is turning on more fundamental questions, namely: who is Larry Zywotko, where did he come from, and where has his sister gone?

The school forms list his place of birth as "Too-son" (sic) Arizona. A telephone call to the Tucson City Hall showed no entries for a Zywotko birth any time in the late 1930s up to 1949. The same is true of Phoenix. Police are now proceeding on the assumption that "Larry Zywotko" and his "sister" Laurel are runaway lovers who failed to secure parents' permission to marry and that during the year they had been living together as brother and sister the relationship had deteriorated into a financial exploitation of Laurel by Larry. Police theorize the strong possibility that Larry, in entering the world of pimping, was treading on the territory of organized crime in Palestra. The almost ritual savagery of the murder could point to a single deranged killer as well as to a "coded" killing—one in which a "message" is being sent by a very crude but effective device. It is also possible that the same underworld figures have kidnapped the girl and sold her into white slavery.

"It's a powerful message to get out on the streets," said a police spokesman, "if you want to discourage amateur pimping and prostitution. Just tell your amateur he'll get a dose of what Larry Zywotko got."

So many terrible things happened about then. It was a week of revelation in which the papers were obsessed by the brutality of the murder, and seemed to be closing in on the truth, only to veer away from it to pursue some insanity like the golf balls.

I read the stories till I memorized them, and I wanted to say, "warm, warmer, you're getting hot . . ." or "cold, freezing." I had a dream that puberty would bring to me not the appurtenances of manhood but a swelling of the breasts and melting of penis, that I had now entered the cocoon and would emerge a woman. That all women had once been boys, all men one time been girls, and that as the butterfly does not remember the caterpillar he'd been, so are we blessed with the same forgetfulness, except for a few. I remembered the grub I had been; I would never forget the years of crawling as a maggot, as a boy. But in my dream, wrapped in the silk threads of my cocoon, I was ambulatory. I had walked down the seven hundred and eighty-three steps to Patience Street like Boris Karloff in *The Mummy's Curse*, and, attracted to a fellow mummy, fellow cocoon, I had murdered him.

Then I woke up.

Papers would say the sister was a suspect; her disappearance, especially for a sick girl with a heart condition (she'd had a doctor's excuse from physical education because of it) was suspicious. The doctor's excuse was produced from school files. The cardiac expert in Phoenix was questioned. The doctor admitted that he had written a letter for Miss Laurel Zywotko in Phoenix, and that she was indeed the victim of a congenital deformity of the valve system of the heart Then, in a major development, a death certificate for "Laurel Zywotko" turned up in St. Louis. Kasimir Zywotko, a new resident of St. Louis (the last name in the city phone-book) was called; yes, it had been his fourteen-year-old daughter, visiting him from Oregon, who'd died in St. Louis last summer. Yes, he had a son named Larry, Laurel's twin, but he was in Oregon with his mother. This was confirmed.

WHO IS LAUREL ZYWOTKO? asked the papers.

I sat like a god, sifting the stories, aching to call the papers or the police to tip them off. What good was it, having the answers, if I couldn't get credit for it?

Further contact with Phoenix proved fruitless. Two days later, another lead opened up. Cleveland Police announced that a juvenile named Paul Lachance, reported missing nearly two years earlier and never discovered, fitted the general description of the mystery victim. A Mrs. Berthe Lachance was traced from Cleveland to Pittsburgh then to Hartford, where she worked as a seamstress, when she worked. She'd heard nothing from her son—a troublemaker from the day he was born, she said—in the two years since his disappearance. He was crazy. If he was dead, she said on radio, it wouldn't surprise her. *Tant pis*, she said, which meant too bad. She was described as Canada-born, herself with a prison record, alcoholic, on welfare and a onetime prostitute. The story got seamier. She'd had a common-law husband named Stubby Tobin, or at least that was the name he was using. He was a gambler and a sometime musician, but dope had gotten to him. Afterward he wasn't good for much. When asked where her son might have gone, Mrs. Lachance suggested California. She said the one thing he wanted to do was act. That's probably where he went. She was sent Larry Zywotko's picture; it could be him, she said, but she didn't remember what he looked like too good.

Where was Stubby Tobin?

She didn't know. Dead, she hoped. All he did was beat her.

What about the girl, Laurel?

Thank God I only had the one, the boy.

And for the week that followed, I read the papers and was tortured by my omniscience, and hurt by the fact that even without my help the police had turned up a partial truth. *How dare they*? I yearned for recognition, like a murderer who reveals himself by being too helpful, or an arsonist who happens to be at too many fires. I dreamed of donning another frayed mask of innocence, as I had for Blackthorne, for being the stumbler, the outsider, who really held all the keys.

One murder had branched into several. Was Laurel guilty, they wondered, or had she also been killed? Or had she been a witness to the killing of her lover/pimp/brother and simply fled? There were no fingerprints for Paul Lachance. Other boys volunteered their experience with Laurel Zywotko: how they'd asked her for dates, been accepted, only to be threatened by her brother the next day. There were rumours that she had, however, bestowed "certain sexual favours" on some boys in the senior high, for money. I gloated, knowing someone else was down in Juvenile Hall sweating out his confession. How far had he gotten with Laurel Zywotko? What were "sexual favours"?

Four or five days after the murder was discovered, the police issued a position paper: Facts and Suppositions. *Facts*: The murder victim was *not* named Larry Zywotko. He did *not* have a sister named Laurel. He was a procurer. He had *no* "uncle" by the name of Victor Young. *Suppositions*: He was probably the missing Clevelander, Paul Lachance. Laurel was probably another runaway, and one or the other had met, either in Phoenix, Oregon, or St. Louis, the real and now-deceased Laurel Zywotko. The theft of the gym excuse was the only "real" piece of identification she had, which in turn dictated the entire facade of identity for "Larry." And "Victor Young" may have been Stubby Tobin; a bulletin had gone out for him. And the murder may have been committed by the Palestra underworld, where Tobin was "known."

On Friday of the same week, a special school assembly was called. I was still an usher and sat in front as usual. This was a solemn, even frightening assembly, for we were addressed by my old friend, Lieutenant Frederick T. Shea, head of the Juvenile Branch of the Palestra Police, and his message to all of us was the classic message of science-fiction movies and closed-room murder mysteries:

One of you kids out there is not what he pretends to be. We know for sure that one of you is a murderer. Or else he, or she, has aided and abetted the crime of murder.

There were gasps in the audience, outraged shouts of "No!" and unless I gauge things wrongly, a glow of recognition and complicity. They were trying to flush something out, to divide us, to get the concerned and responsible ones among us to turn over every gossip, rumour, and suspicion about the bad ones to the police. They let it be known that in the course of only four days of "discreet" investigations in the school they had uncovered evidence of alcohol abuse, theft, and a serious vice problem. The chief was speaking now not as a law officer but as a father and citizen. "We've always looked up to the Ridge. Me, I couldn't afford to live here, but I always hoped my kids could. Now I don't know. Maybe every place is like this if you start to look under the surface of things . . . one rotten apple can ruin a barrel, or maybe there's something worse going on. We hear a lot about a conspiracy out there to attack the morals of the young. If the morals go, the whole tree just falls right in without firing a shot."

He'd found that most of the leads he'd been following had led him to some pretty strange places in Daley Ridge and around town, places that he didn't have the authority to close down, though he wanted to. None of the "suspicious-seeming" students he'd been questioning were on any team sports, not one gave the reference of any local pastor, priest or rabbi. There was a soft underbelly and a cancerous growth at work in Ridge Junior High, corrupting the healthy and red-blooded among us, and he wouldn't rest until all the rottenness was surgically cut away. And finding the murderer of Larry Zywotko, or whatever his real name was, was just the tip of the iceberg. He was only the smoke. The real fire was still building, and he asked for our help before it broke out and consumed us all.

Mr. Wilson closed the session, and it seemed to me that I was the one he stared at as he promised the full cooperation of his office. "We will find out the ones among you," he said.

"We have records and we have turned all the records and all the profiles over to the police. There are times to protect confidentiality; there are other times in which immoral and unscrupulous persons attempt to hide behind the banner of this protection. We have stripped away the Fifth Amendment, that's all. I say to you, boys and girls, the innocent have nothing to fear. But let the guilty beware."

The papers on Saturday carried the inner headline: CANCER EATING WAY THROUGH RIDGE JUNIOR HIGH DECLARES JUVENILE BRANCH HEAD and the quotes made it all so probable that I was terrified. It was all so convincing to me: "Victor Young" or Stubby Tobin or whoever he was fit the profile of any agent on *I Led Three Lives*. I pictured him an avuncular figure, the kind who hangs out in bookstores and asks kids what they like to read. But his real mission lay in picking up violent boys like Paul Lachance from the underbelly of quasi-criminal America, training them and then releasing them in "good" neighbourhoods like human Dutch elm fungi to destroy everything they touched. Lieutenant Shea didn't quite spell it out but he'd used all the codewords like "master-plan," "foreigners and aliens," "un-American" and "smooth-talking, respectable-looking adults from nowhere." For the first time I doubted my omniscience; maybe there *was* more to it than I'd guessed. Maybe I'd been used, nicked in the neck by one of the vampires and become one of them. Maybe it was already in me, something that Laurel had planted like a fuse, something that was giving off a signal so *they'd* always know where to find me. And when they wanted me all they had to do was press a button somewhere and I'd be helpless.

I decided to give the police a week; then I would tell them all.

Sunday's paper saved me. MAJOR BREAK IN TEEN KILLING came the headline. "Victor Young" had finally been located. Six months earlier, a body had been discovered in Baltimore, savagely beaten, knifed and strangled, partially burned and badly decomposed. No identification had been made, since the fingers had been deliberately mutilated, gangland style. But dental records, which police had not thought fruitful at the time, had turned up the fact that the corpse was Stubby Tobin's. Born in California, time in Phoenix and Tucson, St. Louis, Cleveland, Pittsburgh and Hartford. Among his aliases: George Tobin, George Victor, Gerald Toupin, Victor George. Among his crimes: trafficking in drugs, possession of drugs, impersonation, forgery, pimping, assorted sex offenses. His old mug shot was identified by the Palestra School Board as being "Victor Young," the guardian of Larry and Laurel Zywotko. He was identified by Berthe Lachance as her "Stubby."

Who killed Stubby Tobin?

Larry and Laurel had both been absent the Friday and the Monday surrounding the weekend of Stubby Tobin's probable murder (the exact date could not be established). Baltimore was 150 miles away. Tobin was definitely placed in Palestra the week before—police investigators traced a bank account that had been cleaned out in the middle of the week.

Paul Lachance (by now the Zywotko alias was less frequently used) or at least a boy answering his description, was placed in Baltimore that same weekend. He was acknowledged by certain gamblers to be Stubby's "friend," not son or stepson. (The quotation marks carried the implication even down to my level of innocence; in many ways I understood quotation marks better than I understood the words they were bracketing.)

And so now there was an hypothesis. Everything had changed. Paul Lachance, raised in French-speaking American ghettos by a drunken whore of a mother, had developed both an acting ambition and a homosexual orientation doubtless due to the unsavoury influences of the various men and halfmen in his mother's irregular life. Doubtless he'd been beaten, abused and "used" by them and had finally been lured away by the last of them, Stubby Tobin, who had probably learned his homosexuality in the prisons of California and Arizona. A con artist and forger, he probably befriended doctors in order to steal prescription blanks to support his drug habit. Probably the Tobin-Lachance duo, travelling as father and son, got as far west as St. Louis or maybe even Phoenix, where Tobin had old contacts, and in one of those cities a chance encounter with the Zywotkos led to the elaborate construction of a new identity.

But then Stubby Tobin, a ten-time loser who lived in the shadows and under disguises, pimping off the weak-willed and weak-minded, met his match. He set up his young protegé in a cheap room, but the young thug double-crossed him, finding a runaway girl of his own. He furnished her with a new identity, including the all-important gym excuse, which was really the only "hard" evidence police had of *anyone's* existence. He tried to use her in the way he'd been used, but perhaps a touch of tenderness betrayed him after all. He couldn't allow her—or allow himself—to go through with full-time prostitution. That explained his last-minute intervention into the various "dates" he'd originally set up. The fifteen-year-old would-be Vice Lord of Daley Ridge Junior High got cold feet! But Stubby Tobin, perhaps smelling the opportunity for bigger earnings through the girl, as well as the continued satisfaction of his own perverted desires, forced Paul into continuing their unnatural relationship, coupled with pimping, at a time when Paul's own natural long-buried heterosexual feelings were beginning to emerge.

Reading it, memorizing it, I found it convincing. I wanted to believe it.

He rebelled and the rebellion took a predictably violent form. He accompanied Stubby Tobin to Baltimore, where Stubby had intended to run his recently withdrawn savings into a larger bankroll through gambling. Paul watched him lose $300, and, knowing the ways that Stubby intended for him and Laurel to gain it back, he murdered Stubby and returned to Palestra with the remaining $400. Psychiatrists working with the police on this case emphasized the "good husband" gesture of Paul Lachance; with $400 he might have been expected to go to a new location and "blow" it all on a good time. Tragically for everyone, however, he returned, paid $240 for another six months' rent and returned to the charade-existence of schoolboy.

Someone else, by then, had taken Stubby's place, or was trying to. Having no further need for Paul Lachance, sexually or financially, and perhaps feeling that Paul's "cover" as a schoolboy was in fact dangerous to their operation, they had him brutally murdered after forcing Laurel to write a murder note. Then they kidnapped her, or murdered her, but in any event, effectively wiped her off the face of the earth.

And so, before I decided to intervene, the police were searching for the kidnapped "Laurel" and were scouring runaway reports to establish her true identity. Paul Lachance was the likely murder victim of a local vice-ring that had been no doubt attracted to the earning potential in white slavery of an unknown, untraceable and by all accounts, beautiful girl like Laurel. The only hope of local police was to work backward from Stubby Tobin's known contacts in Baltimore, to possible contacts in the Palestra underworld, to find the missing link.

Because, said Lieutenant Shea in a long interview carried two weeks after the discovery of the body, the case still "smells." "There's something we don't have a grip on yet," he said. "There's a link missing somewhere. We've had to stretch the facts. We're dealing with a group of highly abnormal people here, and your normal rules just don't always apply. But the answer is somewhere in the facts that we've uncovered, I'm sure of it. The cards have all been dealt, and it's just a matter of arranging them in a way that gives us the best answer."

It's not easy to express yourself without a typewriter or handwriting—both too easily traced, I knew—using only words cut from a stack of magazines and newspapers, the way I'd read that kidnappers communicate with parents.

I was willing to sacrifice any personal recognition. The world would not yet know that David Greenwood all by himself ("Saviour Greenwood") had solved Palestra's crime of the century. My dream of becoming a masked "Avenger" and having police calls flashed in the sky was admittedly not practical. It took an entire weekend, and all the papers and magazines I'd been able to find, to cut out all the words I thought I'd need. And the necessary brevity, the missing nuances—like the subtlety one sacrifices in a telegram—changed completely what I'd intended to say.

I'd intended to tell Lieutenant Shea all that I and one other person knew about Larry Zywotko (he was still Larry to me). I wanted the world to learn about pure craziness. Maybe even Larry's killer had failed to understand; maybe it was the secret that Larry had gone to his grave to protect. But as I began composing my message, clipping out dozens of words that struck me as potentially useful, I found myself driven to express a far different message. Unless I, David Greenwood, or my alter ego "The Avenger," got full credit, it would be no fun, and I couldn't take full credit unless I submitted to more publicity than I wished. I could tell them what the thong and golf balls were for, but unless I confessed having seen them in use, my suggestion would be dismissed like the dozens of other "tips" the papers were complaining about.

The dozens of clipped-out words, some small as newsprint, others as bold as advertising capitals, confronted me like a jigsaw, a huge anagram to be recomposed. The contrast of so many print-faces was inevitably funny; there was no way that the condemning message I wanted to deliver—a sermon—could be glued to a page from the detergent ads, sports pages and the discount promotions that got stuffed through our door every day. The clearest message I came up with was the most frightening. "I" had disappeared. I had become Laurel. It said: *There are stranger things at work in the world than you think. I am Laurel. I am man and I am woman. I had to die in order to be born. The golf balls and the strap made me a woman. Laurel.*

As I cut the message down to fit the words that I had, I felt closer and closer to Larry Zywotko. I thought of him alone in that room stuffing golf balls in a black satin bra, applying the thick, careful lipstick and putting on the earrings, and I thought of the pain he'd gone through for his strange compulsion. Such loneliness was more profound than any isolation or any loneliness I had ever experienced. It was on the other side of loneliness, like the unknown side of the moon. And I thought I was as far from understanding him as I was from understanding Irving's math or Duivylbuis' science. Or understanding my father. I saw myself in my room, surrounded by mounds of papers and magazines, all of them slashed open, as lost as Larry Zywotko.

I read my message over and over again. And I was confronted by a crisis. Nature made mistakes, that's all: two-headed snakes, Siamese twins, boys who wanted to be girls. That's all. And it was a problem for nature, no one else. Either Lieutenant Shea was a genius who commanded my help, or Larry was a wilderness that must be preserved. Who did I want to help? Whose side was I on, anyway?

And if I answered truthfully, I knew I was on the side of fear, nightmare and of all unanswered things. I was on the side of the caterpillars and not the butterflies, the whippoorwills and not the eagles. In dreaming of "The Avenger" and being omniscient, I'd forgotten that. I saw there was another kind of omniscience, and that was watching the police and the papers make fools of themselves, laughing at all their mistakes and learning to keep it to myself.

In the end, I cut the message down to two sentences: *I am Laurel. Golf balls and a leather thong made me.* I pasted Shea's name and address on the envelope and took a trolley to one of the remoter parts of Palestra. When the sidewalk was completely empty and the mailbox was hours from being cleared again, I dropped the message in. For all I know, the message was read and dismissed like all the others. In a few weeks, Lieutenant Shea announced that the case would probably never be properly solved. It was too strange, too aberrational for conventional police methods.

A delicious Saturday in spring, early in my fourteenth year.
School was still on but after the opening day of baseball, its
season had passed. School couldn't touch me. And fourteen
was a *real* age; thirteen had been only a winding-up, most of it
wasted on still being a child. I was still fifteen pounds lighter
than I had been and on Saturdays I ventured out in dungarees.
And despite appearances I had begun to grow. Not like my
classmates, but an inch since Christmas—my pants had been
let down. I imagined myself returning to the ninth grade,
stooping under doors. "Who's that new kid?" the coaches
would ask. Give me an inch, I took a mile.

My winter Saturday rituals were unchanging and persisted
into spring. First I would count my week's lunch-savings, then
collect my allowance. With the usual $6, sometimes a little more,
I would plan my weekly stamp purchases at King Gordon's office
on Temperance Street. I'd planned on buying a single high-value
stamp that particular Saturday—£1 denomination—to complete
a recent Antigua issue. It would be my first value stamp, and
that would complete a page. Only a collector can understand
the passion for completeness. It's not tidiness; maybe it's the
opposite of tidiness. It's an unfocused possessiveness.

I'd discovered A. King Gordon's name in the Yellow Pages after having exhausted the stamp section of Mohrbacher's, Palestra's biggest department store. Stamps in a department store are a basic contradiction, bound to disappoint. What can you expect when stamps are found in the "Hobbies" section, with the model planes and railways? Collectors and dealers should approach each other like chess players, shuffling possible purchases like gambits accepted or declined. They each possess a perfect memory of their holdings, or agonizing awareness of their gaps. Mohrbacher's stamps were under glass and the salesmen were young and ignorant, bumptious recruits from the toy and clothing sections. Anyway, Mohrbacher's was Seligman's big competitor, the vampire that had drained us, and now the ghoul that was consuming the corpse. A year later, when Seligman's had no reserves and fight left, Mohrbacher's purchased the building and gutted it for a parking garage. They did not understand about stamps and stamp collectors.

But A. King Gordon did. His office was in a dingy brick building whose mirrored and mahogany-panelled elevator held only two passengers and the surly old operator with the overdeveloped left arm and shoulder. The hallways were lit with yellowed globes dark with the bodies of spent inquisitive bugs. The hall toilets had no outside doors, the doctors', accountants' and patent attorneys' offices all radiated the same sense as A. King Gordon's: there were not enough people in Palestra suffering the obscure ailments or requiring the exact tax advice or offering the precise innovation to comfortably support the specialist within. On the other hand, there were just enough clients to justify the office in the first place, provided one did not keep pretty young secretaries and install air conditioning, fluorescent lights or new typewriters. All the doors were usually open as I walked down the long corridor those Saturday mornings; it was a corridor I loved. The typewriters and the telephones and the men in suspenders with their jackets hung up, ties loosened and sleeves rolled back all belonged in some thirties movie.

As did A. King Gordon. He was a large, slow man, wheezing with each breath (the word "emphysema" had not yet entered the common vocabulary), always dressed in checkered pants with wide suspenders and a white shirt with various-coloured inkblots in the breast pocket. He favoured fountain pens but often forgot to replace the top. He'd been red-haired, then blond, and latterly white, but traces of all three were still present, especially in the moustache, much darkened by cigarette smoke. He was never without one, and the insides of his fingers were orange. His teeth were discoloured, his eyes reddened, his skin blotchy, but his voice was deep, young and mellow. When he spoke he didn't wheeze, but he rarely spoke.

I'd been going to him almost weekly for nearly a year. 213 When I entered he would take down his British-American albums without my asking, but otherwise we didn't talk. Very rarely would there be another customer; if so, he'd be a mute, older man and if there was conversation it would be highly technical and depressing to me: auctions attended, trades offered, collections rumoured to be breaking up. A. King Gordon would ignore me for a couple of hours (*he's taken the bait, let him run with it*); it was a form of respect, like a librarian fetching a book and trusting you with it. Like any natural collector, I would have resented his help. To collect is to yearn after an abstract wholeness; it cares very little for what the "real" world of dealers and auctions can possibly provide. An hour each Saturday was spent consoling myself over what King Gordon didn't have and couldn't get; gaps in the universe were more immediate to me than blanks on my page.

He kept his stock mounted in albums—some of them old, battered and suede-bound—just as he had purchased them. Some came out of the safe, but my selections were from the penny-ante stuff that he kept on the shelves: good adolescent collections from a generation earlier, when George V had reigned. Before so much. Maybe King Gordon had been in that office even then—every office in the building seemed to have a lifetime lease—maybe King Gordon had even known the boy who'd started that collection, and then had bought it from him when he grew up and left Palestra. A boy in knickers and greased hair who would skip down those unchanging halls, riding up with the same misshapen operator, passing the same open offices. It wasn't stamps, deep down, that I wanted. It was continuity I craved, the purchase on *time* promised by stamps.

I had $9. Enough for the £1 Antigua, with something left over. Or, enough for a new "short set" from Dominica, up to the 24-cent. (I never forgave those Caribbean dependencies for shifting away from the classic British coinage.) I'd narrowed my choice to those two when King Gordon, in his deep young voice, asked me, "Would you be takin' some advice?" He went to the safe and took out a small album bound in suede. "You've got nine dollars there, don't you? You're a reg'lar customer. To collect you've got to be reg'lar." He put the small, ledger-sized book before me and drew up a chair. His orange fingers opened the book. *They were there*, stamps that were only catalogue pictures. Queen Victoria. Edward VII. All the old dull stamps, all the old guys! "There's nothin' in this book that sells for nine dollars. I'm sorry to say it, but stamp collectin's a rich man's hobby. But listen to me. Nothin' here can ever—ever—lose its value. Every day it's warth a little more. I can sell you somethin' from here for twenty dollars—"

"But I—"

"—I know. I know. Who ever heard of a lad with twenty dollars to spend on a stamp, eh? Believe me, if you came in here with twenty dollars I'd call your parents—No, that's crazy. But." He held an orange finger up. "But—every Saturday you come in here, debate with yourself this set or that set and I take your money and off you go. But look—collectin' stamps, that's not wallpaperin', is it? You follow me? You're not just pastin' pretty colours over an empty white sheet, are you?" I denied that I was.

He wriggled a fat finger over a dull olive issue, a stamp no larger than his fingernail. A stamp that I thought I would never see. Queen Victoria as a young woman. 1853. My album had virginal pages of Victoria stamps, endless poses, colours, values, all beyond me, as remote from my collecting as the books Irving continually suggested that I start reading. PRINCE EDWARD ISLAND, Four Pence.

"This is my suggestion. You take this now. Give me what you were goin' to pay today for that modern junk. (*That's what it is, lad, sorry to say. That's wallpaperin' and you could do it better at Mohrbacher's than with me.*) Anyway, I'll take the nine dollars today and five next Saturday. Five the next Saturday and five the Saturday after that. Twenty-four dollars. This stamp is warth tharty, maybe more. Unused with perfect gum. Just think of the odds on a stamp surviving a hundred years with its gum still fresh? Why, it's like the mammoth they found in Siberia. And this stamp's just as extinct. Prince Edward Island doesn't even issue stamps anymore."

"Prince Edward Island," I marvelled.

"That's Canada," he said.

"I know." Then suddenly I lied. "I'm Canadian."

"Are you, now? From whereabouts?"

"Montreal."

"That so? You know, this was *my* first album. I collected all this myself. I used to go around to houses in Halifax and Saint John and even way-the-by-God-out to Corner Brook and places like Come by Chance and L'Anse-aux-Meadows on that great bleedin' windswept God-forsaken island of Newfoundland, and I'd beg people to let me into their attics. Seems like we're countrymen, you and me. Only I'm a Maritimer. Saint John, that poisonous place. But Lord God, a letter-writin', letter-savin' people the likes o' which we'll never see again. A feast for me it was. Old ladies taggin' along with me up to their attics 'fraid to God I'd sneak a look at a great-aunt's love letters when all I'm wonderin' about is how to get rid o' the stuffin's and keep the ruddy fine envelopes, y'know? And it wasn't always Canadian stamps I was gettin'. It was mainly letters from Jamaica and Barbados from all those rascals the families kicked out for raisin' hell in Halifax. Thank God for gentility—it built my collection in no time! You know," and he bent over closer, as though someone might be listening, "I was pursuin' a connection between a family in Halifax and one in British Guiana that I was sure would lead me to the prize o' prizes—you know the stamp I'm talkin' about, eh?—absolutely sure. Then the ruddy bastard's forgiven, all's forgiven, and before he can write that one last letter from Georgetown, the bugger's on a boat back to Dartmouth to marry the sweetheart who'd kicked him out. Ah, it broke me heart. And the old dame in Halifax is tellin' me the story—it was her grandfather, see—'bout what a happy story it is. How they settled down in Nova Scotia and never left. Oooh—made me want to retch, it did. Anyhow—I filled this album in about two years. Never thought it'd provide for me in my old age. It was a *hobby*, and my God, man, hobbies are *sacred*. You wouldn't break up your collection any more'n you'd sell your children into slavery, would you?"

He coughed, and I nodded.

"Well, that'll come later. First"—he pronounced it "farst"—"you've got to build. Build a *collection*, don't just fill in the blanks. Forget the easy stuff, leave it to Mohrbacher's. Otherwise you'll have a very impressive-*looking* collection with hundreds of stamps warth about half of what you paid for them even at my self-sacrificin' prices."

It was a handsome offer, but I felt for a moment like a child who had expected a bicycle for Christmas and been given a bathrobe instead. So old, so dull, and so adult! And only one stamp instead of ten. And I would have to come three more weeks just to deliver money, not adding anything to my book. But the other stamps in the same set carried prices like $200 and $600. I was being invited to cross over the threshold, sacrifice visible flash for dull intrinsic worth. I was becoming serious and I'd earned a bit of respect from an old-fashioned professional. I agreed to buy it.

Then he showed me an album of his most serious pieces; even the book was a collector's item. Nothing in it worth less than $500: mainly in excise stamps and postage dues—stamps like dull headaches. Yet, I now had to admit, not without "a sartin functional elegance." He showed me his masterpiece, a Guiana issue that Scott catalogued at $12,000. Only four known copies in the world, and he'd picked up his for practically nothing. "Followin' the auctions," he said, "and suspectin' that a sartin elderly British gentleman who'd been a solicitor in the London Sugar Exchange just might have had dealin's in the part o' the world I'm interested in." Otherwise, an undistinguished and disorganized collection; the whole thing had come to him for $500. "So it's not all luck and it's not all money, lad. There's a *touch* to it. Educated guesswork is what some people call it. But it's more, it's intuition, it's a feelin.' And it gets easier the more you trust it."

He related the stories behind his best discoveries; how he'd charmed the suspicious sods who'd doubted his sincerity—"Why, they thought I was a detective trackin' down lost heirs. That's all they live for out there, y'know, to learn they're the lost heir to some Scottish lands. Or they thought I was out to steal the old letters, when all I wanted was the stamps. They'd never heard of such a daft pursuit. Saint John, New Brunswick. A pile of rotting wood pressed against the sea, and every single attic is crammed with letters tied in pink ribbons. Trouble with Saint John is that they're all too close to the real thing. They don't know they're sittin' on a bloody fortune if they'll just open up their trunks. Oh, no, they're too afraid the darty bastards'll learn a deep dark family secret from readin' those ancient letters and maybe get a jump on them and invade their blessed privacy. They think the world's got as little to do as they have.

"I used to love those envelopes with their graceful hand-writin' in that old black ink that turned to olive after about fifty years. You could just look at it and imagine the young rascal down there in Barbados sittin' at his desk in a bunga-low overlookin' the beach, wieldin' that mighty goose-quill and thinkin' up insincere commiserations for the old folks on Ca'Breton and the harsh winter they were havin'. So now he'd been dead a hundred years or more, and his folks'd been dead even longer, and still these poor ignorant buggers wouldn't release the envelopes to me, for fear . . . for *fear*, mind you! Always fear. Can you imagine such superstitious people in this day and age?"

I told him that I could. And probably that's why they hadn't thrown out the letters in the first place.

He agreed and called me a clever lad. "Then maybe it's all for the best, eh, us comin' from such a place? Gives us a feelin' for things that the Yanks don't give two hoots about, eh?"

He picked up my hundred-year-old purchase with the blunt stamp-tongs and dropped it into a glassine envelope. It beat in my breast pocket like a second heart.

How far I have to go, I thought, walking slowly down my favourite corridor. It wasn't a pleasant feeling, though I was more in touch with history now than I'd ever been. All those bright new stamps, all my pages so nearly filled: worthless. I had only one that counted, and thousands more to go. And even that one was *bought*, not really collected. When would that *feeling* come, that thing beyond luck or money, that ability to collect and not merely gather? That's all I'd ever done—*gath-ered* things ("all this stuff he knows, he doesn't really control it. It controls him." What was it they called it—wise-idiocy?).

I'd intended to spend the morning with stamps and the after-noon at the first baseball game of the spring—activities that defined my passions at the age of fourteen years, one month. Each winter I would tell myself through the long, baseball-less months when I didn't think once of the game, "Great, that's it. Think of all those baseball hours you'll save. You're finally cured." But each April I'd start getting curious about who our "major league affiliate" was bringing up or sending down to us. The Braves this year were going to have the fastest team in the league, maybe the fastest team since the raiding of the Negro leagues. Of course, no one had ever seen the Negro leagues, but their universal speed was safely assumed. So, I would give them another chance. Which meant by the time I boarded the number 63 trolley outside King Gordon's office, I was already in my mindless baseball mood. Stamps were a thousand miles away.

I scuttled down the alleyway from the trolley stop to the 219 Home of the Braves, past the "kolbassi" stands where the husband-and-wife teams were already out, grilling their fat white Polish sausages on hot, oily rollers, and I emerged in the near-empty parking lot in front of the bleacher-ticket window. I had my quarter ready, but I found myself walking more and more slowly to the window. Syracuse was playing, a team even less well-stocked than Palestra. And I stood there in front of the bleacher window, questioning for the first time something that I'd accepted as naturally as Duivylbuis accepted God . . . *Do I really want to?* It was as though the stamp in my pocket— a new focus in my chest, like a third nipple—had begun to dictate. *Don't waste your time,* said Queen Victoria, who had kept her gum for a hundred years and who now trusted me to keep her intact for a hundred more.

Well. There *were* clouds in the sky. Rain *could* prove inglorious for my Queen. There'll be other games. I'll wait for Montreal.

I strolled across the main parking lot to the library and museum. I'd been given a summer's reading program, thanks to Irving. He felt I was salvageable *if* I began reading a book a day and didn't stop till I was about twenty-five. Every week he was putting five or six more classics between us, and soon we'd have no basis for conversation. And so, he'd given me a list of Great Books for Week One. Fiction: Stephen Crane, George Orwell, and Mark Twain (but only *The Mysterious Stranger*). The Russian writers would have to wait, at least till the end of summer. For history, *Ten Days that Shook the World*. It was to be read first, since it was the tool for analyzing everything else. He'd read it first when he was nine, so he figured most of it would be simple enough for me. Economics: *Das Kapital*, but *The Wealth of Nations* was a permissible substitute. Philosophy: *The Republic*, of course. I loved self-improvement courses, especially if they were guaranteed to work, like diets.

Ten Days, however, was the key to it all. I was looking forward to it—it sounded like science fiction. *Ten Days That Shook the World* was listed in the card catalogue, but it was stored in a special collection. *For research only. Librarian's permission and academic supervisor's authorization required.* I was curious about what dirty and obviously graphic things *Russians* could have been doing during those ten earthshaking days. And if I couldn't read that first, what was the point of reading anything else?

And so I headed down the dark, fragrant corridor toward the Dinosaur Hall. The museum brought out the best in me. Not my best performances, but my greatest confidence. I was fourteen and not as fat as I had been. I had an outside chance for high honours. If I could just keep growing, keep reading, and keep saving money enough to buy good stamps. The glassine crinkled as I walked. Life was all downhill from here. Just roll with it, wait to see what it kept turning up. For someone who hadn't read John Reed and didn't have the analytic tools, I was doing pretty well. At least I felt so, that day.

It was too nice a day for school kids to be inside. The Dinosaur Hall was empty, and the cases of stuffed animals stood flat in the distance, like luminous paintings. Old friends by now: the musk-oxen still fending off the wolf pack; the peaceful congregation of natural enemies at the waterhole on the veldt, and my old favourite, the *Nubian Lion, Attacking Bedouin and Camel.* I still liked it. I liked it more than I had last summer. And what a sense of confidence I had: I could have given a talk on it, just like a museum guide. "*And here we have Hannes Fischer's celebrated masterpiece of 1883. Of course the* tableau vivant *is not a very high art form. And Palestra is a little provincial for featuring so many. This has something to do with German Romanticism. I forget what.*" In fact, the *tableau vivant* was a pretty grisly art form: who killed all those lion cubs feeding on the zebra? The immature musk-oxen that the herd was trying to protect: obviously, all in vain. The wolves were not the enemy. Yes. If anyone had quizzed me and asked what I thought, I could have been pretty damned impressive.

And suddenly, 1883 wasn't so long ago. My new stamp was thirty years older.

I even knew what "J.A." meant, thanks to Irving. If that girl and her group of friends showed up again, they couldn't hold the initials over me like a code. *Junior Archaeologists.* And since this day was like a dream of perfection, it wasn't long before the Cretaceous Hall began to fill with a few tall and a few dumpy and bespectacled teenagers, standing in a group by the invisible door in the dinosaur's painted claw. Nervous boys with long, uncombed hair, in white shirts and stiff new dungarees worn with brown leather belts. Even I, that Saturday, was wearing faded blue jeans without a belt.

Well, good luck to them. What was it Irving had said about archaeology—overrated? *Arrowheads of illiterate people can't teach me a thing.*

"Kitsch."

I didn't have to look, but I almost threw my arms out to greet her. *Wait*, I caught myself, *don't show a thing.* She seemed even shorter than last year, but I remembered the accommodation to her face that I'd already made; this time I liked it from the beginning. Her dimples were where I remembered them. And she didn't seem to remember me. I'd been through a lot. I'd changed.

"I wouldn't say *kitsch*. German Romantic, maybe, but it's very well done."

"The details maybe, hmm, yes." I was afraid she was toying with me, about to say, *Come on. You didn't know what German Romanticism was last year, and you sure don't know any more about it this time.* I looked in her eyes for recognition and found none. Blessed anonymity.

"I can't help finding German Romanticism *kitschisch*, sorry," she said. "The lion should be shown in his natural habitat, attacking his normal prey. *Bedouin and Camel*, I mean, no wonder they became extinct if they had to wait for a Bedouin with a jammed rifle every time they got hungry. It's a misrepresentation. Also, it's a kind of libel against the species. What do you think?"

I gave it great thought. "Not necessarily. All the other stuffed animals are in their natural habitat. You've got the veldt, the tundra, the swamps..."

"And what's this supposed to be, then?"

"Well, without a mural behind it or sand underneath it, it's—"

"Precisely. It's a Hollywood stage. Tarzan wrestling a toothless lion with potted palms around to make it look authentic."

"No. Now let me finish. It's not a landscape. *Where* it's happening doesn't matter."

"Well, I'm sorry if it doesn't matter to you. But it's supposed to be an educational display in a public museum. So it matters to me. Why else bother with '*authentic flintlock and Berber clothing of the eighteenth century*'? That's classic obscurantism, isn't it? Throw in a bit of extraneous authenticity in the middle of a massive lie. If you show a lion attacking a human—especially an extinct breed—you're immediately demanding an emotional identification with the man. So any child who sees this is going to go away in sympathy with the brave Arab who's obviously going to get killed. But one thing is wrong. The world is full of Arabs today, and there aren't any more Nubian lions—that's my point. What do you think?"

I got her point and it was fierce. It was too clear to argue with. *Don't argue with her, she'll clobber you*, came the message from Queen Victoria. And I didn't want to get clobbered. I wanted to know her better, and, above all, I wanted her to respect me. A person doesn't usually get a second chance like I was getting. "Look—" I started, and then quickly changed the tone of my voice. "Oh, by the way, what's your name?"

"Judy."

"Judy. . . ?"

"Judith Freisilber."

"Well, Judy . . ." (a name I liked: Judy Garland, such a bright, golden colour of a name) ". . . my name's David Greenwood, by the way. Judy, I agree with everything you say. Everything. But I still *like* this display better than any of the others."

"Greenwood? Any relation to the Grunwalds on Good Works?" (guh-DWERKS)

"I said Greenwood, not Grunwald."

"Sure, sure. And I'm Freesilver. Look, no Green in Palestra is ever a simple *green*. Unless he's a Negro. You know that. Don't hide from me, okay?"

"Okay," I guessed.

"You go to temple?"

"No."

"Good. Where do you come from?"

"Where do I come from?" For the second time that morning, I stood ready to invoke that city I'd never seen; the second time added a certain dignity, even texture, to the lie. "Well, it's a complicated question."

"Isn't it always? You're . . . ah, German, right?"

"My mother is. She was born in London, but all the others were from Germany. But my father's from Montreal. They met in Montreal. I'm from Montreal."

"Montreal!—hey! My favourite city! I went to a camp in . . . what is it? Saint Something. Sainte Agathe?"

"Yeah, right."

"I have relatives in Montreal. You know the Berkowitzes?"

"No. My father changed his name to Greenwood. He was a Boisvert."

She frowned. "I know Braver*man*, no Braver." She was grinning widely, plump cheeks bulging, eyes nearly crinkled shut, dimples breaking out everywhere. Respect had come so quickly I was frightened by it. She took a step nearer and she seemed happy enough to give me a hug. If I had thought it was possible to touch a girl without causing disaster, I would have put my arms around her. She was as short as Irving's mother. I'd never felt thinner or taller in my life. But I didn't reach; I took a step back, toward the display and laid my finger on the glass.

"Now, back to this, Judy." (Judy, Judy. *Love, Judy*?) "I know why I like it and it doesn't have anything to do with loving lions or Arabs." My hands were sweating again, like the summer before. "It's a nightmare, Judy. Look, imagine, this Arab out on his camel in the desert with absolutely nothing around him. Then out of nowhere he sees this lion, at first a long way off. Like you said, lions never attack humans, so he thinks he's safe. But the lion senses something. He's a special lion. Let's say he knows that gun is jammed." Judy frowned, and I knew I'd spilled a bit of her respect. "It's a *nightmare*, Judy. You know how in a nightmare, if you're dressed in a suit of armour that has only one little hole in it, some arrow or something is going to find it, right?"

"I have never been dressed in armour in a nightmare."

"But you know what I mean. Something improbable just begins to chase you. It's usually something you're confident you can beat. That's why you let it get closer and closer. Maybe twenty impossible things had to go wrong for something like this to happen and he's thinking about every one of them. And so am I. Everything else in here is a picture of the normal way things happen, right? But this thing—sure, it's corny—but look at my hands!"

"Let me see." She touched them with her fingertips and smiled. "Wet, you poor thing."

It was spontaneous. She took my hand inside hers; the smallest hand I had ever seen, and warmer than a kitten. She took out a Kleenex and dried my hand. It must have looked at a distance as though I had been crying and balling up Kleenex sheets in my hand. I didn't mind.

"Whenever I look up at this, I can imagine all kinds of things that could sneak up on me. Look at his face—all pinched together as though a drawstring pulled it. He knows he's going to die. It's like the look on the zebra's face when he knows the lion has caught him. He underestimated it—that's what's frightening. And he let it get too close because he was confident till the last minute. Then—"

"Auschwitz," she said.

She said it distractedly, in a tranced voice. It wasn't a word I knew, and I assumed it was one of the German words we used in chess like *zugswand*.

"Right," I said.

She smiled, but on a different level that didn't involve her dimples. "Okay, you win. You're a bigger Romantic than Hannes Fischer even."

The word "Romantic" scared me.

"Are you here for J.A.'s?"

"What's that—Junior Archaeologists or something? Nah, I'm not a member."

"I can take you in."

"I don't think I'm too crazy about archaeology, really. I mean, what can a few arrowheads from a bunch of illiterate

Indians teach me, anyway?" I smiled, giving the profundity time to sink in. Her face went from a pale benign blankness to crimson.

"Ooo. Ohhh. You stupid *bastard*. You stupid smug conceited chauvinist ethnocentric *bastard*. Okay, don't come. Thank *God* you're not coming." Her face looked suddenly forty years old, stern as a principal's.

"Hold on, Judy. I didn't say I wouldn't."

"Well, *I* did. Get someone else to take you in. You sound just like an awful cousin of mine who thinks he's so damn smart. Ohhh, disgusting."

"I just meant it's no . . . you know, *Ten Days that Shook the World*, is it? I mean, for things it can teach you . . ."

She looked at me with a pretended, gawking stupidity. "It's no *what*? No, I daresay it's no *Ten Days that Shook the World*. And maybe you can tell me what *that* kiddies' classic has to do with archaeology? My father used to read me chapters of it before I went to sleep. Then I put away childish things. One 'arrowhead,' as you call it, is worth a thousand John Reeds, Mr. Grunbaum."

"Grunwald," I said. "Okay, okay, *please*—I don't know it all." She had turned and was walking away, and I followed, desperately reaching for her arm, but then deciding to pull away before we touched. "Judy, I'm sorry. I'm sorry for insulting archaeology. It was stupid. Actually I'm interested in archaeology. Egyptian stuff and really old things. I don't know why I said that. I know all the geologic eras in order. I can name all the dinosaurs in this hall. Judy—I've read *Kon-Tiki*."

She stopped and turned. Her face again was blank and pale, and I was breathless.

"It's just that the Indian stuff around here never really got to me, you know?"

"*No*, I don't know. How should the Indians behave so they can 'get to you'? They don't read *Ten Days*, you know. I'll bet they never even read *Kon-Tiki*—can you forgive them? God! If you'd take the time to learn instead of going to movies maybe they would get to you. And Potomwa-Nine happens to be one of the most advanced pre-Columbian woods-Indian cultures ever discovered in the eastern United States."

"Potomwa-*Nine*?"

"Yes, Potomwa-*Nine*. There you go again. Why do bright boys think they're being cute when they're really acting stupid? It's *okay* not to have heard of them. But it's not okay to make fun of them. If you're serious about learning, I'll teach you all about Potomwa-Nine. Keep your mouth shut and your eyes open and I'll show you things that are right at your feet that you never knew existed." She wanted me to meet the curator who was the head of the Potomwa project. She wanted me to tell *him* it was stupid, and she wanted him to kick David Grunwald through the wall. "And if I ever hear you calling archaeology stupid again, *I'll* kick you from here to Marble Arch, David Grunwald. That's a promise."

But she took my moist hand in her small warm one and hauled me away from the displays, into the Cretaceous Hall where the hidden door was still opened to let us in.

It was like being invited behind stage. The door opened onto a corridor from which several offices and storerooms branched: long, hyphenated and unpronounceable names were painted on the stippled glass. Curator of Man. Curator of Native Artifacts. Assistant Curators of Glass. Coins. Brass. Pots. At the end of the corridor we came upon a workshop where wide, cluttered tables and stools had been haphazardly arranged. A bearded old man in a blue smock worked in the corner on a stuffed leopard. An assistant lacquered bones. The windows were high and opaque; it could have been winter outside for the quality of grey, frosted light that entered. Most of the tables were piled with crates and cardboard boxes. It was like the confirmation of a dream for me: there were doors in every wall and behind every door there were mysterious societies hard at work on something bizarre. With the proper key, every wall would reveal such doors, and every door would hide such colonies.

Most of the boys were already seated, or at least slouching over their crates and boxes and were rummaging through them, not bothering to look our way. A wiry, crew-cut, grey-haired man—short and tanned, with a silver and turquoise tie-clasp sealing his flannel shirt—held up what appeared to be a shard of clay. "Judith," he called, "look!"

Forgetting me, she laid her purse down and skipped almost girlishly to him. I followed, holding back.

Within seconds, dipping into the same crate, he had assembled the lip of a clay pot from the parings of a dozen separate pieces. Most of the pieces didn't even look man-made—I surely would have thrown them away—until they were fitted together. "This is from *your* sample, Judith. I couldn't resist getting it started." He rubbed his hands together and sucked in his breath. "I think you're going to have fun today."

Her face was transformed. It was a flexible face, flat and sober only in contemplation. Now it was round and luminous, as though the box of dirt and rubble were a source of gentle light. Her eyes were wide, her mouth pursed with concentration. She was almost . . . cute. "Wow, and I thought I didn't have anything."

The man was my height, though powerfully built. He rolled up the sleeves of his flannel shirt and unbuttoned his collar, loosening the string tie with its silver and turquoise clasp. His arms and neck were thick, his face deeply tanned and weathered. "Hi," he said, "Phil Ottaway," looking me over with an air of discovery. "And you're—?"

"He's David Grunwald," said Judy, not bothering to look up from her boxful of rocks and broken clay. "He thinks what we're doing here is"—she looked at me slyly—"well . . ."

"A waste of time, that it?" he winked. He patted me on the shoulder. "Congratulations—it's a sure sign you're in the right place. There's not a person here—except maybe Jude—who doesn't think that all the time, I'm sure. It comes along with the calluses."

I'd never seen an older man like Phil Ottaway. He was the curator, but he was also a child. He bounced around the workroom like a monkey, taking the shortest distances, vaulting over benches, scissoring between tables, leapfrogging over stools rather than removing them. He spoke so rapidly that his breathing would fall behind, saliva would build up, and he'd have to suddenly stop to swallow and to catch his breath. He addressed the entire group from a squatting position on top of the table (hoisting himself on those thick arms and the wide, callused hands), and he spoke like a combination athletic coach and college professor. Listening to him, one could imagine that enthusiasm was an alternate form of intelligence. Maybe he knew that the J.A.'s needed praise and encouragement more than they needed a learned lecture. That all of us, imprisoned as we were in passions, attitudes and above all faces and bodies that had resisted anything remotely suburban and "adjusted" still yearned to be addressed by our own kind of coach who called us "Killer," or "Sport" or even, in Judy's case, "Sweetheart." Going out on digs was their summer camp and tennis lesson; piecing together pot fragments once they returned was a form of double-dating.

All of them—or should I say "all of us"—had passions outside of archaeology—music, chess, pure science, mathematics (and my inferior attachments to baseball and stamp collecting which I dared not admit)—what we didn't have was a place, like the classic soda fountain, where it was safe to be ourselves. But the sand-kickers out there couldn't follow us behind the dinosaur's claw. And we were sand-kickers ourselves out on Potomwa Ridge a few miles north of Palestra, at

"Level Nine" of the excavation where the mysterious civilization called Potomwa IX had passed a generation or two, a thousand years before.

Since we were all shy, we became uninhibited in the workshop. Boys began to smoke. We asked girls, especially Judy (who knew), what sex was about. We came to expect honesty in every response.

(I would be five long years in high-school society afraid to ask any girl for a date, but in the workshop that next winter, and for a few months afterward until she left for college in Israel, Judy Freisilber represented to me all the sex I was capable of understanding. I remember a Saturday when Judy and I were left to clean up. I was fourteen years, eleven months. She was talking about her "so-called boyfriend." These discussions always depressed me, though I wasn't honest enough to tell her. Her boyfriend was eighteen, a freshman in college. She wished he were a little more like me. "All he does is grab for my tits. I swear to God I haven't had a minute's peace since I got them."

I, of course, had respectfully noticed her breasts, immense and formless even at fourteen, and I said to her as I could not have said or even thought outside of that room: "I've never seen a naked girl. I've never touched a real breast." And she answered, "Well, God, David, be my guest." And that was how, in the Palestra Museum at fourteen years eleven months I touched, quite greedily, the warm, silken heaviness of Judy Freisilber's breast. She unbuttoned two shirt buttons and pulled down one bra strap for me, an act of supreme tact and gentleness that I was unworthy and unappreciative of until much later. At the same time she unbuttoned two of my shirt buttons and rubbed her hand on my chest. It was innocent.

I have seen Judith Freisilber's picture many times since then. Once in *Time*, as head of an Israeli archaeological survey. She, of course, looks older than her years in her army fatigues, squinting into the sun. No mention that she was once a Palestra girl—the question of her having been American simply didn't arise—the author at thirteen of a pamphlet on a local Indian culture called "Potomwa IX." Instead, she was praised for her "unaccented English," her fearlessness in leading a dig while mortar shells were going off overhead. "This is just a different front of the same war," she was quoted. "If I die, others will take my place too."

I see those pictures, and a kind of well-being comes back over me. Not just the old arrogance, that I know something that *Time* magazine doesn't. A larger satisfaction, that out of all the ones I knew, so intelligent and so blessed, at least one survived. I wrote to her, signing myself David Grunwald, but never got a response. Nor, I suppose, should I.)

The workshop was our only society; perhaps that's what kept it so pure. None of us attended the same high school, and we all lived in different parts of that cut-up city. We didn't try to see each other during the week (once in high school I competed against a workshop friend in a chess meet; we pretended not even to know each other's name), and if we ran across each other at concerts, the planetarium (a related obsession; antiquities unending), galleries, department stores, or even in the corridors of the museum and library, we'd barely acknowledge each other. Only in the workshop, as we brushed impacted clay from bones, flints and bits of pottery, and as we spent our hours working "on the books" entering every find with an elaborately coded set of details would we also talk, with that expectation of perfect frankness.

Phil Ottaway drove six of us out to the Potomwa excavation the next day, Sunday, ten miles north of Palestra along back roads. There was urgency in the work since the area was being developed and the museum had no way of reserving it. The only hope was in getting the state to declare it a historical monument, but, as Judy reminded us, there was no monument, and the site was prehistoric. I sat next to Phil because

Judy wanted him to work on me, to convince me of the importance, the *scientific* precision of archaeology. Actually she misunderstood me; I wasn't a scientist and I was already converted. She'd given me a pamphlet the night before, an offprint from *The Bulletin of the Daley-Palestra Natural History Museum*, with a volume number so long with Roman numerals that it taxed my ingenuity. "Notes on the Potomwa IX Excavation and Hypotheses Concerning Burial and Food-Gathering Practices in the Upper Potomwa Valley" by Philip Ottaway, Ph.D., Curator of Native Artifacts, and Judith Freisilber, Assistant.

"Judy's a brilliant girl," said Phil on the drive. "She could direct this whole operation without me." Judy was on my right, looking out the window, oblivious. She puffed on her cigarette meditatively, like an old European. I'd been amazed reading that pamphlet, at the speculations that could be drawn from chips on flint, the shape of a pot, the condition of an animal bone.

But what had impressed me even more, the day before, had been Phil's own talent for glancing into a box of debris and coming up with two or three pieces that suddenly fit. The patterns that emerged, the eye—like a microscope—that he possessed! The appeal to me that day was all through art, not science, the ability to pluck significance from chaos and relate it back to a single source. Back, in fact, to a single object. I tried to put as much of my admiration into words, and Phil dismissed it as "experience in the field, only experience. There's a pattern to everything; it's all connected. Fortunately these are the patterns I know. Pre-Columbian, Ohio Valley. But plop me down in Mexico or someplace and I'm just a tourist."

"Phil's getting mystical," said Judy. "Ignore him."

"She denies all mysticism, David. She keeps me honest. But it all comes back to the kind of mind you have. Why are we all here doing *this*? But I know we all basically think the same way. Say you're stripping off old wallpaper and you find a ten-year-old newspaper underneath it. It's junk. You tear it off. But if it's twenty years old—well, most people would still tear it off. But you'd probably take the time to stop and read it, right?"

I agreed that I would.

"Not if it was the *Star*, I hope," said Judy.

"She's hard, I warned you. But say it was *fifty* years old Now you'd drop everything and *pore* over it, right? It would be like a gift, something coming to you unbroken from the past. Even if it's a page of ads, even if it's a letter to the editor—"

"Or a stamp," I said.

"Right, of course. But the stamp has extrinsic value now. I'm talking about the cheapest words possible. No ideas, no beauty. And so on. Any junk—a cracked egg cup, an old razor blade that's a hundred years old—that's an antique! And something two or three hundred years old, I don't care what it is, it's art. And when *we* dig, we look for pieces of pots the Indians turned out by the dozen every week. Probably used them for target practice. But find one intact and it's priceless."

233

"'Thou still unravish'd pot of quietness . . . '"

"Listen to her."

"No, no. Seriously, Phil," said Judy. "I'm moved in my way. And it beats going out to old barns to hunt antiques." She turned to us and smiled, her slowest, warmest smile. "Honestly."

"Everything is priceless," he said. "Sticks that the kids played with. Bones that they threw to their dogs. Everything is precious. Everything."

"Do you believe that, David?" asked Judy.

"Yes, I believe that."

"I believe that," she said.

"So do I," said a boy from the backseat.

It was, in fact, the essence of all I had been believing, in my inarticulate and impure way, for the past fourteen years. I wanted to embrace them all.

PART 3

Thumb hitched in the pocket of my new "D" jacket, I could
spread my fingers to the jaws of the gothic letter and hide the
symbol of my sport—a pawn—imposed upon us chess players
by the more traditional athletes of Daley Ridge High School.
I was a tenacious, defensive chess player, whose competitive
function was to earn draws against fifth-board opposition.
Sometimes, however, on dark winter afternoons in the chessroom after school, I would practise against our celebrated
first-boarder, Irving Melnick, and be able to slip a queen or
rook into his blocked eighth row for a lightning checkmate.
Something about the quality of my play—its lack of elegance,
fire or dark romance—drove him to boredom, the only mental condition he couldn't handle. Boredom was my element.
Anyway, at a distance in my brown and grey "D" jacket, thumb
hitched and fingers cunningly fanned, no one would guess
(despite my stout officious body) that I was not at least the
manager of some more manly undertaking. After high school
it wouldn't matter. I'd be graduating in a few months and going
on to a university where I intended to lift the pawn with a razor
blade and project the image of an erstwhile defensive tackle
who'd given up the sport to concentrate on serious study.

The summer was laid out for me in a bolt of eighty-five days at my parents' furniture store. Evenings would be my own, since the store was open till ten, six nights a week. But the fattest sales were closed after the main lights were out and the front door was locked, when my father could turn on the pressure and the customers be made to feel guilty and rushed. By the time they did the books and stopped by a restaurant for a bite to eat, it would be past midnight before my parents got home.

The store broke even from the start, as it had to, since we'd opened it without a month's reserve of cash. It was a creation of the banks and of my father's vision, but this time my mother had insisted on a lawyer *before* the final papers were signed. We'd lost stores in the past through half a dozen loopholes; the first venture in Florida had been seized by creditors the moment the bank balance fell below $1,000. In my father's mind, lawyers were last-ditch operators, like brain surgeons, to be called in after everything else had failed. His universe, like mine, resembled those perpetual-motion gadgets concocted by autodidacts: breezily indifferent to invisible principles like entropy or pollution or even gravity, that eventually wear them down. Money spent on prevention was down the drain; eventualities were invisible and might never happen. If they did—who could stop them? He believed in luck, hard work, and the alchemy of the times, traffic and the feel of a product or a person. The rest would look after itself.

For my mother, invisible and malignant forces were always at work, and their results were everywhere. People are irrational and fate is capricious. It is not enough to dream and aspire; one must also leave a margin for fire, flood and other calamity. One must budget for depreciation. *Don't rent here, Lou*, she said of the empty restaurant we finally took over, *you can't see the entrance from the highway. People will overshoot us; they won't back up. Men hate to admit a mistake.* But the times were ripe, the traffic steady, and the old smorgasbord restaurant *felt* just right. So my father borrowed an extra $5,000 for a spectacular neon sign designed personally by Joe Whitehouse of Whitehouse Neon. Flashing lights and a throbbing arrow: *Greenwood Interiors*. Our name in lights. For a long time it seemed to me that my father had won that particular argument.

(How aptly named is the "nuclear" family! Bound like a hydrogen atom, the nucleus an impacted web of balanced forces, while a single electron rides its solitary orbit. I was that electron. The forces inside are still the most powerful on earth. Look what happens when it's split. I calculate its half-life at twenty years.)

"If I'm not a genius, then my life isn't worth living," Irving declared one afternoon in the chessroom as we debated the merits of various universities. He'd decided on St. John's, with a fall-back to Chicago, then Brandeis and finally Berkeley. He was the only one of my friends not to choose the great technical schools or the Ivy League. The purpose of higher education was to fulfill genius, obviously, which was not possible if professional training was the goal. Nor if women were around. At Brandeis they'd be Jewish, which qualified as a disincentive. After graduation from St. John's, he calculated that he'd know everything worth knowing, be sexually unreachable, and thoroughly unemployable. Such total social and technical dysfunction, in the year after Sputnik, had to be counted as a triumph of the will. I agreed with him to a point. I couldn't see myself fitting into any career or "stepping into" ("like a dog-dropping," he sneered) a profession. The only thing I seemed qualified for was to be a game-show contestant or a baseball historian. Better to hide and wait. Somewhere a new world was stirring itself for us, if we could only stay uncommitted and thoroughly unprepared.

Coward that I was, however, I had applied to the usual technical schools plus the Ivy League and its satellites. And I'd chosen (as we were instructed), a safety net: Halliwell College, a picturesque little campus in the hills of Kentucky, strong on scenery, sociability and basketball. It matched a dream of college life that I'd picked up from the movies. I didn't mention it to anyone.

Wesley Duivylbuis was our valedictorian, first out of five hundred in an intensely competitive class. All that officially separated him from the next ten places was the fact that his grades were unblemished and theirs, somewhere in four years, showed at least one minor flaw. The salutatorian, a hard-working non-genius, had lost his chance with a "B" in one semester of tenth-grade gym. But Wesley had gotten nothing but "A's" in everything: shop, gym, languages and English. And so modest about it! "They must have confused me with someone else," he'd say after each report card. His acne had healed and he was a wonder to us, a kind of eugenic breakthrough; a balanced mind in a healthy body, a noble outlook and a humble disposition. Eagle Scout and student minister. He'd decided on Cal Tech, whose local alumni had begun offering him scholarships and exemptions from English when he was still in the tenth grade. "If I manage to graduate, of course," he'd say. "And I have to pass my college boards."

I was fiftieth in my class, betrayed by "C's" in gym, "B's" in geometry and algebra, "C's" in shop. The rest were "A's," but soft ones. There was a message there, had I been able to read it. For Duivylbuis, Irving and a few of the others who stood well ahead of me, "A's" were an approximation; to be precise, their grades should have been extended like shoe-widths into doubles, triples and even quadruples. But my "A's" fitted snugly; they belonged on the same scale that graded the four hundred and fifty below me.

Everything I can say about adolescence is still lodged in the nucleus of that family atom. Since my parents provided for me the forms if not the content of knowledge—the umbrella as well as the storm—I'll add only this: in my studies I was still the child, the boy, and not even the adolescent. I'd never have Wesley's sense of mission. "Engineer" defined his essence, even more than "brilliant." He'd always assumed that energy and intelligence must be applied to some larger force whose ultimate judgments were not open to question. Such questions were "invalid" and "inefficient," his two most cruelly dismissive adjectives. The achievement of such trust struck me at the time as a marvel, a kind of admirable schizophrenia. Once in a senior physics class, our ambitious young teacher asked him, "Wesley, answer this off the top of your head. Does ice float?" And Wesley—who had no top to his head—paused several seconds while the rest of us snickered. Finally, smiling faintly, he asked, "In what?"

Exactly, cried the teacher, clapping his hands: *Exactly.* And those of us who'd been making "duh-h-h" noises suddenly shut up. *No unwarranted assumptions, you see?* Scientific skepticism, scientific openness. But Wesley left school early on Tuesdays and Thursdays to assist at church services, and when I once asked him, "Do you believe in all that?" he answered simply, "No, I don't believe. I have faith."

Nor did I have Irving's barbed and playful detachment from discourse itself, or any pretense to communication. In a boys' health class in our senior year the coach who taught us asked, "Should a baby be left out of doors in direct sunlight?" Hands shot up. "Melnick?" he asked, whose hand never did. "Should a baby be left in the direct sunlight?" Irving pondered the question long enough to cause the coach to gloat, the rest of us to fidget. "Well?" he demanded, now gleeful over the humiliation of a special tormentor. And just as the coach prepared his triumphant retort, Irving asked, "A baby what?" People are incapable of intelligent speech, Irving once said—*language* is incapable of intelligent speech, for that matter—and to believe their most ardent confessions, to show them the tenderest mercies is, in the harshest word he could muster, romantic.

I retained only a residual expertise in the areas where I'd once exercised unfocused passion. Geography, of course, then archaeology and anthropology, especially what I'd learned of pre-Columbian upper Ohio Indians from field trips with Judy Freisilber. I'd read a few more novels than my friends, but literary interests, in our circle, were treated as a personality disorder. I had no great books in my life as Irving did; no great principles as Wesley had. By seventeen, Duivylbuis already owned a patent for his work on a supersensitive carbon paper; Irving, under the inspired pseudonym of I. K. Meln'yk, was earning $50 a week selling chess problems to aspiring masters all over the world. Amazing, the power of the apostrophe; it made his middle initial suddenly belong, and the aberrational "Kenneth" could be dropped forever. Judy Freisilber still published regular archaeological articles in the museum *Bulletin*. But for me there was only the embarrassment of watching each interest slowly die. I'd start out on the broad superhighway of knowledge: *National Geographics* and encyclopedias at home, then the available books from open shelves of the library, but there'd come a day a few weeks or months into my journey when a helpful librarian would go to the Bound Periodical Room and provide me with a stack of journals whose pages were crammed with charts and numbers, heavy with Greek. That was my warning: *Bridge Out*. At the first signs of encroaching mathematics, like suburbs before a city, I learned to jump: abandon the discipline before the formulas took over entirely.

What I realize is this: I never understood any discipline; what attracted me was, to use the word as Irving might, its romance. Or its narrative. I sought cosmologies on every scale, but when the Omar Khayyámish names of stars yielded to their Greek and Latin equivalents, I would lose the thread. And I would take up something new.

As a consequence, perhaps, I would not be going to Cal Tech, Chicago, Princeton or MIT like most of the boys ahead of me. College Boards had done me in; they'd been fair and easy, I'd thought, but when the results came in, letters of rejection followed, and with them, confirmation of my mother's vision. I was merely competent; anything else ("Astronomer Greenwood . . .") was sheer pretension. *I'd never be great*, and the fundamental assumption of us all—Electromagnetist Duivylbuis and Omniscientist Meln'yk and Superficialist Greenwood—was that our disparate achievements would someday lead us all to Stockholm. The engineering schools didn't want me, the Ivy League rejected me, and the junior Ivy League put me on a waiting list. But Halliwell College accepted me immediately. I smiled bravely and didn't mention it to anyone. But secretly I was relieved.

Late in the spring my father and I drove down to the campus for a second, contractual visit. The visit confirmed that I was doing something foolish but necessary. My stroll on "the Quad" (how I loved that word!) in my starched hand-me-down Arrow Darts and charcoal suit, my shined black shoes, slicked-down hair and seal-shaped body, confirmed another unpleasant fact that four years of high school had helped obscure: namely, I was as alien to my time and place as I had been as a child. The boys at Halliwell were tall and lean, blond and polite. They wore blue or white Oxford cloth shirts with buttoned-down collars, Madras jackets, knit black ties and shiny khakis worn with paisley belts. Scuffed white bucks or shined cordovans. My father, attracted as always to uniforms, loved the place; he'd not abandoned his lifelong dream of joining a country club. He already pictured a daughter-in-law, one of those peroxided beauties from Louisville or Lexington. He advised me against Newport and Covington, or anyone from there. On fraternities, he suggested a rejection of any first offer. And when it comes to getting serious about a girl, he added with a wink, it never hurts to do a little investigating. It doesn't cost any more to marry a rich girl than a poor one.

Plans for the rest of high school and the summer called for learning about girls. Summer was to be a period of grace before rebirth; to go off to Halliwell as fat as I would graduate, or dressed as I had visited, or without the slightest social grace (I'd never had a date, and except for Judy Freisilber—who would sometimes stroll with me in the museum halls or sit at the same library table as we worked our way through back issues of archaeological journals—I'd never spent two minutes in the company of any girl) would be a disaster. All of that, starting in September, would have to change.

The only girl I knew in Palestra was Judy, not of Daley Ridge, but of an earlier version of Daley Ridge that had ceased to be a suburb and become merely undistinguished. It too occupied a ridge top overlooking the river; if there'd been bridges attaching Walnut Heights to Daley Ridge, I could have walked to her apartment. But such was the charm and inconvenience of Palestra; neighbouring hilltops could have been in different states or even different decades. Daley Ridge bad caught up to mid-century notions of gracious plumbing, but in Walnut Heights it was still 1933 with no relief in sight. Most of the white people in Walnut Heights were like the Freisilbers: survivors more than immigrants, bearded old fathers with incongruously lively second families, who'd come to America after the death camps and established themselves in the ancestral professions they'd once abandoned: tailors, jewellers, bakers and chocolate makers, all living above, behind, or under their tiny businesses.

Back in the tenth and eleventh grades, on weekends when Judy and I were working for Phil Ottaway at the museum, cataloguing, cleaning, assembling and occasionally lecturing to packs of Cub Scouts and Brownies, we would exchange little stories about ourselves. I told her what the South had been like for me—a Cretaceous forest where the dragonflies and amphibians of my memory ranked with all the reconstructions in the Dinosaur Hall, where the dank, numbing greenness obliterated the sky and sounds assaulted you from every level of nature. She didn't believe that alligators screamed like women, and she couldn't believe that I'd actually seen them swimming and sunning themselves on the shore. Nature for her was the mantle she must tear off, the incidental skin that separated today from a comprehensible human yesterday. And despite my impeccably English name and florid English complexion, I, too, was an immigrant's child, and my sense of place had an immigrant's feel for terror, accident and wonder. Yet I remained for her a Grunwald, never a Boisvert, and since she had Grunwald cousins in what she termed "The Argentine," I seemed to her placeable and familiar in my foreignness.

I was always stranger to myself than I was to her. And I tried to tell her of the Montreal my parents had left, the wedge it had driven between me and America ever since an offhand remark of my mother's a few years earlier: *of course* *you're a Canadian too,* she'd said (I was accompanying her to her annual alien reporting in January) *if you want to be. You'll have to decide that for yourself, later.* The idea had thrilled me, like learning that I'd been adopted or had a sister somewhere. And the fact that I was something unplaceable, *Canadian,* and not something more easily identifiable had appealed powerfully to me. No one knew what it meant. Something very close but still different; the essence of mystery. I felt like a spy, a shadow, someone with a secret identity.

But that had only become an occasion for Judy to tell me her life story, before which mine curled up in shame and blew away. Born in Germany, raised in Uruguay, she still counted in Spanish (Spanish! And to me she had looked like an Eskimo). And to my fantasy of an unmet sister she contributed a picture of ten brothers and sisters, all unmet, posed smiling on a lawn with two dogs and a governess, a plump, smiling mother holding a baby in her lap, and a stern, uniformed father with his hand on his youngest son's shoulder. "Misha, he's the oldest. He'd be . . . oh, fifty now. Pavel, Tanya, Bora, Freyda. . ." Dead, all dead. The eldest dead in the Russian Army, the rest in death camps. The mother gassed, and the baby. The picture had been taken in Dresden in 1936—my mother's beautiful Dresden, the city of trams and beautiful china, where she'd once read tea leaves and begun to hear strange voices, where she'd turned vegetarian and known only Jews. She'd told me stories of friends who hadn't gotten out and of those whom she'd met years later in London and Montreal. Their letters would reach us in central Florida or in Palestra at Christmastime, the undying scraps of Europe in her life, renewed now only once a year.

My mother might have met Judy's mother, or her sisters.

And I thought of the Bedouin with his jammed rifle, his leg raked by the lion's claw, the camel's anguished neck twisted in a way that would never straighten, and I knew again why that undead assemblage (Hannes Fischer, 1883) had moved me to tears that first day. Not for the camel or for the Bedouin, but for us all: Hannes Fischer and my mother and the Freisilbers and my father and the lions and finally, always, for me. All of us caught smiling and innocent and confident under a blue Hapsburg sky on broad lawns behind high fences, while out there on the street raged madness and final destruction. When Cub Scouts stood before that glass case exclaiming, "Hey, cool!" I wanted to slap them; even when Judy had upbraided me for responding to *kitsch*, I'd defended myself with unaccustomed passion. That *tableau vivant* of Bedouin, camel and lion stands for me even now as a picture of my adolescent mind as binding as that first one of my father, his broken rod and the alligator had been at five.

And there had been a second time with Judy when it all came together, an interlude of less than a minute in the workshop when I'd touched her. This time, at my insistence. We'd been sorting through mounds of pebbles and shards of flint, lifting out the suspected artifacts from the random richness of decaying nature, when we'd suddenly been aware of silence, absolute silence. We could have been the last couple on earth. The light was weak, hanging like grey sheets from the high rectangular windows. We needed the lights to continue our work, but somehow we didn't turn them on. We found ourselves standing at the same workspace, our hands working through the same unsorted mass of gravel and there was—what? Chemistry? Opportunity? Chance? It was the first (and still the most powerful) occasion of oneness in my life, of being absolutely lost to time and body and mind; lost in another's presence and in her body. Even the two of us could dance like mating swans; she was beautiful at that moment and possessable (I, who had no idea of what "possession" entailed) and for her I may have seemed masterful, the foreshadowing of whatever bizarre combination that would someday win her.

We didn't hug or kiss. I opened her blouse and she slipped down one bra strap and suddenly I was holding a breast, so soft and smooth my fingertips trembled and my arm arched as though I were curling weights. She lowered the other strap and her breasts filled my hands, they were immense, her entire upper torso. Her wrinkled, rubbery nipples and the tender pink infield around them were as wide as my wrist, forcing recalculation of all the knowledge I'd so stealthily gained from *National Geographic*, *Playboy* and *Confidential*, as well as giving the final proof, thank God, that however soft and pink and swollen my own were, they were decidedly within the bounds of masculinity. My fingertips froze as they traced the border between the pink and white parts of her breast and her eyes were closed and I couldn't tell if I were giving pain, or pleasure. Then she looked down at my hands with a kind of pride (or so it seemed to me) as though I'd just performed some intricate and brilliant reconstruction. If anyone had come across us at that moment it would have been catastrophic, but I like to think it is the nature of such moments to be inviolable, happening on a different plane, immune from interference.

It was not a moment to be sustained. And it couldn't be exploited; it was an act in itself. Signs of the quotidian were beginning to gather, like a traffic light that betrays in a flicker its intention to change. Judy blinked. A horn outside sounded and in an office someone coughed and in two swift gestures she lifted her bra straps and buttoned up her blouse. Then she turned and walked away. I cleaned up the workspace.

Two years later those ten seconds in the workshop of the Department of Man, Palestra-Daley Museum, still counted as my only proper sexual experience. So long as I could claim to have touched a breast, I wasn't *that* far behind the rest of my class. And I was well ahead of all of my friends.

But Judith Freisilber, I learned from calling the only Freisilber in the phone book, wasn't in Palestra anymore. She was taking her senior year in Israel, and she'd be excavating in the Holy Land that summer and attending Hebrew University in the fall. I looked upon it as a betrayal—my suddenly declared passions, my readiness for her, surely counted for more than the spurious claims of biblical antiquity.

There was only one other source for the knowledge I sought— "Schuman's," the old burlesque house on Charity Street. It wasn't far from the offices of my old stamp dealer; a dark, foul-smelling cave-in-the-wall, flanked by a woman's shoe store and by a dress shop that specialized in "hard to fit" sizes, whose wondrously large and often-nude mannequins could stop me in my tracks. The ticket cost a dollar and a half, announced on a grubby cardboard with hand-lettered numbers that also warned, "*Twenty-one and over. Strickly inforced.*" The admission fee included a mimeographed playbill detailing the names and most recent engagements of the "artistes"—meaning the three girls and two comic acts.

Everything about that theatre—its setting, its misspelled sign, the middle-aged lady (a former stripper?) who sold the tickets—meant SEX. Thursday meant sex. The number 47 trolley was a sexual trolley. The shows changed every Thursday, and in the spring semester of my senior year, by running from my final class and catching the 47 trolley, I could be there at three-thirty, half an hour before the second show. I dreamed of the summer when I could be there at one o'clock for the Grand Opening of the Week, when, in the interests of publicity, things were allowed to go further and the coloured lights were held to a minimum.

The treat that I came early for was a candid vision of the stars. Schuman's was an informal old theatre with seats that rattled and tilted forward, and there seemed to be no rear exit or entrance. And so the girls would enter as we had, singly or in a group, carrying their shopping bags, dressed in slacks and loose sweaters, and they'd joke with the ticket taker in the back and walk down the aisle waving at the whistles, responding to the regulars who called out, "Hiya Thelma, honey, how was Baltimore?" and they'd climb on stage, pull on the curtain—all of them used the curtain in their acts— then disappear into their various dressing rooms. And that was my treat—the assurance that I'd soon be seeing *normal* women out there undressing for my pleasure; not too pretty, not too young, and not too coarsened by their trade. Women like any on a trolley or in a store, like our customers, like our teachers.

The sexiest scene imaginable to me at seventeen would have been the casual exposure without the sleazy dance and fetishistic props of any probable-looking woman trudging onto the stage, wearily taking off her raincoat, letting down her mousy hair, pulling off the nubby sweater and finally stepping out of the slacks. No need for purple lights, elbow-length gloves, evening dresses and a curtain of gauze. Above all, no blond shoulder-length wigs. But that's what we got: bored-looking women under heavy makeup sweating and breathing hard (I sat close enough to hear them) doing heavy-footed impressions on a dusty floor of Rita Hayworth and Cyd Charisse. The dance, I wondered, was it there to excite or distract us?

I felt superior to anyone taken in by pretense, the moist-lipped teasing, the props of high society being debased. But I wasn't excited by the conventionally cute and dimpled; the fresh-looking beauties of *Playboy* only emphasized the impossible distance between us. I searched for older, heftier models—not the slatterns of the *Police Gazette*—for faces that showed some of the effort and a little of the shame of pleasing me. Breasts that flowed soft and shapeless as Judy Freisilber's had in my hands. If any of those plain women had taken the stage before getting in costume and makeup and announced that she was going to relax and cool off first, and then put down her shopping bags and undressed without coquettishness, I wonder how many of us would have stampeded the stage in a blind helpless rush of hands, to touch, to maul her.

Or would it have been only me?

And there were the six nights a week my parents weren't home. Friends—never Wesley and rarely Irving—would bring their tape recorders over and we'd tape and edit our own ads, our own news reports and presidential speeches. Tape recorders were new, and nearly any lucky juxtaposition of Elvis and Ike seemed hilarious. We made a modern and local "War of the Worlds." New scandals from scraps of old movies, soap operas and the news. We placed phone calls to a community-minded radio show whose aggressive flow of cheerfulness had been an aggravation to us over the years. One friend with a gloriously rich and convincing voice (undecided, at the time, between a career in radio or a calling to the ministry) was adept at compelling immediate trust. Hence, at initiating mass panic.

"As I sit here in my book-lined study," he'd begin, "a volume of Latin verse lying folded on my lap, enjoying the company of a fine cigar, music and an after-dinner port—and of course, my favourite radio show—I began wondering if the

Perseid meteor shower had not begun. Has anyone else this evening noticed the dazzling display of Nature's Sprightly Demons on the southern horizon?" Indeed, quite a few of us had; we were lined up on the extension phone to file our reports. Soon the meteor shower became a strange glow and the glow decayed to multicoloured lights and the lights to something eerie and throbbing, low in the sky. By then other gangs of like-minded high-schoolers picked it up, calling from other gamerooms of other empty houses to pinpoint the lights to their own suburbs and then to back yards on their own streets. It would take an hour or two before the fire department broke in, pleading with citizens not to converge on the so-called "landing site" and for the pranksters to please cut it out. By that time five hundred cars had jammed a church parking lot or the front lawn of a high-school principal.

And we kept up with the advertisements in the back of *Popular Mechanics*, requesting piano lessons for our gifted friends, filling out forms for cooking schools and dumping flour and egg yolks in the envelope as a pledge of earnestness. We signed up the class stutterer for speech therapy and sent memory aids and spelling lessons to Coach Church, our Boys' Health teacher. To the Galactic Order of Levitation we confessed our suspicions that we, too—like Isaac Newton and a few old pharaohs—were blessed with superhuman powers. We reported making people feel uneasy when we stared at the backs of their necks; we upset them noticeably when we gazed at them cross-eyed and stuck out our tongues. The powers were getting stronger as we exercised them and we were now afraid of what we'd accidentally do next. We'd started by rolling chalk off teachers' desks but now, as the enclosed photo demonstrated, we'd levitated a city streetcar.

From a taxidermy college we requested immediate instructions for the tasteful mounting of a pet lobster. They were prompt, and we asked about stuffing a trophy lion. Again they

251

responded. Finally we requested something functional but dignified for dear Ahmed, the faithful beater who'd flushed the beast in the first place. They didn't respond.

Under various Martian names we corresponded with the full spectrum of apocalypse cults, the most imaginative of which foresaw the waterspouts of Judgment Day coming to suspend the earth's oceans in a watery canopy, thus exposing for veneration the original Garden of Eden, the lost continent of Atlantis and the New Jerusalem. During the final semester of my senior year, as Father Chazarai of the First Church of Christ Solipsist, or as Sol Lipsist of Temple Chazarai, I was sending and receiving about twenty letters a day. A stuffed mailbox rewarded my return from school each day; television and a form of innocent fraud filled my nights.

Then one day I returned from school and was stopped by a man who'd been waiting for me, parked out front. He carried the day's stack of letters, all opened, and fanned through them as he spoke.

"Is this the residence of Mr. Kloop Gleep?"

Gleep was our Martian, accepted only too easily by the occultists and saucer spotters, with whom he shared as much of his rather intricate life story as I'd gotten around to inventing. Until my involvement with The Beyond, I'd not suspected the number of Martians already resident in the United States. But if this small man in the brown suit knew of Kloop Gleep, he must be "Brother Celestius," U.S.N. (Ret.), a saucer buff who'd written of intention to pay a visit.

". . . Alias Eugene Feustinger College of Forensic Rhetoric alias Masoch and de Sade Custom Furniture alias Crevette Brothers Haberdashers for Tiny People alias John Reed World Tours alias The First Church of Christ Solipsist?—" The list went on and on.

"Well . . ."

He was not Brother Celestius. He was government issue, and suddenly my mind fogged over.

"What exactly do you think you're doing?"

"Nothing."

"*Are* you a rabbi?"

"No."

"A professor."

I shook my head.

"You are already implicated in twenty-seven registered cases of mail fraud. Now twenty-nine. Do you have a deceased African individual named Ahmed mounted inside?"

"*No!*"

"Have you secured the proper exit and entry permits for the lion you state is currently in your freezer?"

"No—I mean, there isn't any lion. It's all a—"

"—a big mistake, is that it? Suddenly it's a big joke—is that what you're going to tell me?"

I denied that I was.

"We've had complaints from the Levi . . . the Levita—"

"From San Diego," I said. "The Levitators."

"From their secretary, Mr. Cecil Pohl."

"We call him Cess," I said. "You know, Cess Pohl?" Our eyes caught at that moment, and suddenly I burst out giggling. It wasn't the humour; it was release from three months of mounting anxiety over the utterly mad world I'd discovered out there ("Not *me*, fool—*them!*" I wanted to shout), and my immediate acceptance into it. Suddenly I knew it was wrong to seek out that world and to humour it along and it was terribly, terribly wrong to have mixed it up with our world, the one in which real stutterers could have seen only the cruelty and not the humour in the brochures we had sent. I would have accepted a five-year sentence on the spot had he offered it to me. But I was still giggling and I didn't look remorseful, and it *was* funny to picture the mounted lion-and-beater I'd described in a letter to Colossus Taxidermy College. He must have believed it *all*: levitating streetcars and supposedly sane people talking about their lives on other planets before beaming down to earth. It's a wonder he'd come alone, that he wasn't armed and that he hadn't ordered a raid by a team of agents ("Gleep, we know you're in there. Come out with your hands up. All of them.") from the FBI. I had to prop myself against the door to keep from collapsing with shame and laughter.

"This organization has sworn out a statement that you've extorted instructions for the training of certain alleged powers and that you have ignored repeated requests for payment."

"For levitating *streetcars*?"

"False presentation is an offense."

By then I had stopped laughing. Of course they'd billed us, but we'd ignored things like that. Most correspondence schools were willing to hint at the contents of their first two lessons if you sounded interested and asked the right questions. I'd saved all the correspondence, copies of my letters above various names and signatures (all now terribly illegal, I suddenly realized) plus all the letters, cryptic and illiterate, from a dozen occult groups. At twenty letters a day, a hundred a week, an enormous file mounts up fast, and it was the file that I offered to show the inspector. I was proud of my letters, the mimicry of each persona: the Great White Hunter, the wealthy widow attempting to communicate at any cost with her husband, the religious zealot, and Kloop Gleep, Ultimate Alien. Over a thousand pages in four thick binders: a picture of my mind at age seventeen.

"Let me consult my records," I said.

I invited him into the empty house. Nothing strange here; not what he'd expected. He refused to follow me upstairs, so I brought down my four volumes of "files" (as I called them)— *my book*, as I thought of it. He took my name and age and issued me a receipt in the name of "Sol Lipsist, Temple Chazarai" for four binders of letters. My parents and the school would be notified when charges were brought, or dismissed, should the chief inspector so decide.

And the files went with him, never to return. The final semester was an agony of dread and expectation. I didn't know if I'd be in Halliwell come September, or the federal pen in Leavenworth. What was the penalty for impersonating a Martian? Our mailbox was empty; all those people who could address a Mr. Kloop Gleep with a straight face, all the schoolteachers who believed in the waterspouts and the Kingdom of Atlantis, the secretaries who shared with Father Chazarai the bracing experience of levitation—they were still out there, still writing to *someone*. It was an anxiety that lasted for years, that at some moment in the remote future when on the brink of a major discovery, the agents of some vast absurdity would burst in upon me, shackle me and throw me for life into a prison for false presentation.

One Thursday in the spring, I missed the three-thirty show at Schuman's Burlesque, and so at five-thirty was threading my way down the crowded sidewalk, past the Outsize Shop and ladies' shoe stores that had such special significance for me because it was Thursday and I was in the neighbourhood of naked women. My fist was already closed on the dollar and a half. The second show was just letting out: a few old men hitting the sidewalk in full practised stride—I did that myself, easing anonymously from the theatre and tearing into the pedestrian flow like a car pulling out from a curb—when I found myself suddenly five feet behind a familiar back, retreating quickly. I was about to call out, "Wesley—" and stopped myself just in time.

By lagging a few steps behind, then jogging when he turned a corner, I was able to keep Wesley Duivylbuis in view. I didn't regret missing the new show; suddenly I was on to something even more exciting. He'd obviously just stepped from the theatre with the practised gait of an old-timer (Thursdays he'd always claimed early dismissal for stand-ing church commitments) and he obviously had even more urgent business downtown, for he kept checking his watch as he darted across intersections, and he walked in the gutters, rather than stroll behind window shoppers. What could he be up to at five-thirty, staying downtown? He bumped pedestrians without apologies, left a string of outraged women shaking their fists at his disappearing back. I was breathless, but not from the chase. It was the imminence of discovery, my private discovery. The thought that Wesley Duivylbuis was capable of any kind of deceit was a revelation of almost religious magnitude. If Wesley went to strip shows, then all things were possible. If he bumped old people on the street without apologies, he was capable of anything.

He entered one of the old Flatiron buildings on Temperance Street; a nineteenth-century office building with elegant carved scrollwork over the doors and lower windows and deep grooves cut into the rest of the facing blocks. I waited five minutes and went in: the single elevator had not yet come down. The lobby directory listed nothing remotely scientific, scoutly, religious or youthful. Some brokers, some doctors, some insurance underwriters. When the elevator came down I asked the operator, a black woman in a blue smock and torn, white cotton gloves, if she'd just taken a friend of mine upstairs.

"Oh, yes. Such a nice boy. You must be referring to David Greenwood."

My faith in Wesley Duivylbuis was so secure that for a moment I doubted my own right to be David Greenwood. Either I had gone up on the elevator or else I was an imposter.

"He . . . ah . . . David, went up the twelfth floor, didn't he? The Pharmacists' Insurance Group?"

"No, sir, he did not. Not young David. He goes up to nine. That's the Volunteers in Charity." She seemed to smile just from thinking of Wesley, or perhaps the volunteers.

"Can you take me up, too?"

The Volunteers in Charity occupied a small office between the toilets, utility closets and stairwells. They consisted of a matronly looking secretary and a young man with pre-softened Christian features, filing papers. I knocked and asked for "Wes." They hadn't heard of him.

And so, young Hardy Boy, I was left in a ninth-floor corridor with a prickly feeling in my neck. Somewhere in the building was a genius of a boy who had used my name. With no apparent reason to. It was a fourteen-storey building and I started casing it, floor by floor. Most of the offices were closed—it was nearly six—and it wasn't till I got down to the fifth floor that I found a light on. A doctor's office.

Dr. Richard P. Davidson
by appointment

I touched the door and it opened, revealing a panelled outer office and an unoccupied desk. Wesley's jacket was folded on a chair. Behind the desk stood a potted tree—the first I'd ever seen in an office, under a fluorescent light. There was a carpeted inner office with its door slightly ajar. I'd never seen a carpeted doctor's office. Voices came from it, but none discernible. I'd never seen a doctor's door without a specialty announced. That seemed sinister, as though Wesley had found a door in the universe through which he alone communicated. That was a favourite device in the science fiction we read: the communicating door, the space-time warp, the notion that in some parallel universe he just might be David Greenwood. And tomorrow, if I returned, the building would be a parking lot.

I silently closed the outer door, and as I did, a bell went off inside and I took off at top speed down the corridor, ducking into the stairwell and taking the stairs five at a time—I would not have felt the pain even if I'd broken an ankle—till I was sure I was three floors down and running by the time Dr. Davidson went out to check. And that left me, as I caught my breath in the now-deserted lobby, uncertain over what I had seen or heard. *Was* that really Wesley? I'd seen only his back. *Had* there been a woman here who called him by my name? *Was* I really David Greenwood?

There was a B & G Coffee Shop across the street and I lingered there over a Coke, watching the building I'd just left. I couldn't say for sure that Wesley had been in Schuman's Burlesque—it suddenly seemed absurd, heretical, to think such a thing. And what if Wesley were really sick; I could picture him, an ersatz David Greenwood, receiving a death sentence from some kind of expensive specialist in the Disorders of Genius, whose field was so grave that he dared not even advertise. I went to the pay phone and consulted the directory. Davison, Dr. Richard P. was listed. I was suddenly consumed with curiosity; what was wrong with Wesley? How was he dying?

This is Dr. Davison's Answering Service. Dr. Davison is in session. At the signal please leave your name and telephone number.

I looked him up in the Yellow Pages. I finally found him, and my fingers ran cold.

PSYCHOANALYST

Wesley's a psycho, came a voice that almost whispered. A psycho using my name. A split personality trying to take me over, thinking he was me! As I watched, he came out; no mistaking him. He stood at curbside, taller than the parked cars and visible through the breaks in the traffic. Wesley Duivylbuis, Wesley Duivylbuis lighting a cigarette, turning and walking quickly away.

My parents had not impinged on me for nearly four years. I always insisted that we "shared lodgings," and I thought of the room I slept in as "my apartment." But I was being as precise as I could be; we enjoyed a curiously formal relationship. Unlike my friends I was free of family, free to ingest the larger things: baseball, burlesque and British-American stamps. My mother would leave $5 on the dining table every day as she left for the store; with it, I'd go down to Kroger's after school and buy half a pound of hamburger, a can of popcorn and a quarter pound of butter. Later I'd pop up a giant bowl of popcorn soaked in butter and sit in my father's easy chair in front of the television—"Father Knows Best" and "I Led Three Lives" defined the poles of my receptiveness—licking even the film of butteriness off the bowl, cracking every unpopped kernel and often (watching the Anderson family with their adolescent boy and his two sisters, a father who called out "I'm home!" while hanging up his suit coat and exchanging it for a tweed jacket) I would fight back tears and masturbate into the popcorn bowl. If any ghoulish or extraterrestrial movies were playing, Irving and I would go out to them. Friends came over to make tapes. I sent my witless letters to occults and correspondence schools.

What I'm saying is it was paradise for a kid like me, responsible but secretive, lightly rooted in reality. My parents and the store were the only reality principles in my life.

Then, deep in the winter and early spring of my senior year, my parents staged a comeback in my life. I'd bounced them too early, before I was ready to stand alone. At fourteen, chastened by that precocious misadventure with Laurel Zywotko, I could have moved out and passed as a priggish but responsible little man. Or they could have sent me to a modest boarding school where I would have prospered like a model English schoolboy. But that would have kept me from the store and the streets and the school and without them what would my education, my life, have been?

By seventeen, things were going wrong. A gap was widening as college approached. If I didn't belong *up there* where I'd always assumed a berth, then what was I to do *down there* with the other nine-tenths? They were dating, marrying, holding jobs—talents as specialized as Irving's in chess and Wesley's in everything else. Thank God for Judy Freisilber's breast and Schuman's Burlesque; thanks to them I had *touched* and *seen* more than my friends and thanks to the store I could say that on weekends, summers and after school I, too, worked; I had a job. Three serene high-school years, then, had been passed in the eye of a storm, and now the winds were shifting again and I was about to be kicked out of childhood altogether. The store had a lot to do with it. The store was my final education.

The erstwhile "Greenwood's Interiors" had been a suburban mead-hall, a druidical hangar of dark wood and tawny plaster, ribbed with blackened beams and abutted by a disused fireplace capable of consuming a Christmas tree any way you'd care to wedge it in. The fireplace always reminded me of some Hollywood version of a primitive altar, something for Jon Hall to snatch Maria Montez from, but, cold and sooty it simply killed the floor, a dormant reminder of some past potency we'd not been capable of keeping up. Maybe a traditional fire burning brightly would have made it seem less unappeasable to me, less demanding of a new and appropriate sacrifice from us.

We'd never eaten there in its restaurant days, but when I thought of its likely clientele I pictured greasy-lipped Vikings tearing into platters of roast goose, suckling pig and shoulders of beef, staining their blond beards with flagons of red wine and warm beer served in pitchers of ground elkhorn. I imagined slave-girls serving sullenly, Rhonda Flemings in billowy tunics, others chained in the basement whimpering for release. And the fireplace was always the blackened socket, a skull. A few minutes on the main floor and my eyes would water and so would my mother's from the residue of sooty ceilings and the locked-in juices of thirty years' gorging, ten thousand nights of log fires and maybe a million meals served.

The vast, cold, dark interior limited the kind of furniture that could hold its own against it. Oak and maple, dark and heavy, with a lot of vertical thrust: bunk beds, breakfronts, ranch-house dressers with cathedral mirrors. We never possessed the store, but were rather like poachers in a gloomy Scandinavian forest. Only the former bar and checkroom in the entrance were bright enough for rugs and a few low, colourful, modern chairs and sofas. There was nowhere to sit and talk comfortably. We huddled in display sofas on the open floor, bundled against drafts, cringing under beams that pushed down like groaning boughs.

Our success was due entirely to my mother's patience in playing the customers and my father's skill in landing them with a *borax* gaffe. He put his office in the former ladies' room. The panelled toilet-stall remained, but its outer walls were papered with tacked-up delivery notices, bills and ads, and never do I remember the door to the toilet ever being opened. I don't think he even knew what lay behind the panelling. And for the three years he occupied the office, a full Kotex dispenser remained on the wall just above his head and I'm sure I'm the only one who ever noticed it. Customers and owners used the old men's-room facilities; the men's room became my own small enclosure in the store.

What I'm saying, I suppose, is that we were each in our way alien presences in that building, and feeling alien was not exactly an unpleasant or unfamiliar feeling. The curious scale of the building, the Aryan-revival style of the place, its weird inappropriateness as a furniture store—all *that* stamped the store as undeniably *mine*, something deformed and impossible that I could, at times, imagine inheriting. What I'm saying is that growing up as "son of the store," the putative heir, is an irreducible reality lesson. From the store I learned the final lessons in sex and money and life and death. I learned politics and I learned sheer terror.

In the first few weeks of remodelling when I pried off the boards of the putrid old meat locker, I found sheets of newspaper insulation underneath. Instead of stripping the papers away, I spent a weekend reading every word of a 1936 Palestra *Star*. Editorials congratulating a local *Bund* for blocking, "by force if necessary," the circulation of an anti-Nazi petition on the streets of Palestra: "*Known subversives, such as the group of alien ragamuffins who congregated on Good Works Avenue yesterday, are only begging for good American citizens to teach them a lesson. The lesson is: keep dirty European politics away from these shores.*" 1936! Don't listen to them! In the front-page photo, they were gaunt and bearded, backing away before a larger group of "concerned German-Americans." The same prickly feeling that used to affect me as a child gripped me by the back of the neck again: *farm family enjoying rural electrification ... modern Los Angeles ...* turn back, turn back! These people are going to lose their families, back in Europe, under a greying post-Hapsburg sky. The paper was moist but powdery; it lasted long enough for a thorough reading, then disintegrated.

We sealed the meat locker with a case of embalming fluid and then repainted. My mother made it into a small kitchen where she installed a card table and two folding chairs, a lamp and a hot plate, and there she would brew her tea, warm up soup, and try a few recipes with eggs—things that wouldn't smell up the floor. It became, in a sense, her office. She could tell when customers entered; only then would she leave her office to greet them. The locker was warm and enclosed and nothing in it was for sale or display. The only time I ever snuck into the store from the rear through the small warehouse and refinishing area, I caught a glimpse of my mother, arms nestled on the tabletop, head buried in them. I thought she was sleeping and I waited by the door an extra few seconds afraid to wake her. Then I saw her groping blindly for her tea mug and I saw her shoulders heaving and I could hear, muffled but plain, the low, deep moans of a woman sobbing from deep inside her. Thereafter I was always careful to enter noisily from the front and to find an excuse for standing out there until she came to greet me. My father stayed in his office; like a maître d' he held himself aloof from mundane chores, though he was always available for writing up a complicated sale.

There was a substantial area in the rear of the store where food and liquor had been cached in the old restaurant days. It served us as a repair and reception area. It was the pleasantest place in the whole store, removed from customers and the scrutiny of my father. I could happily spend a Saturday back there uncrating and assembling the furniture for display or delivery. And I would sit and talk with Franz the refinisher, our first eight-to-four employee, a man my father had plucked from the icy seas after Seligman's had gone under.

His full name was Franz Krysch. He'd come from one of those mountainous triangles of central Europe where a day's skiing brought him over more than borders; he'd grown up skiing into languages and into different religions and racial memories (still the kind of thing that could excite me at seventeen): Hungarian, Turk, Rumanian, Romany, Serbian. He was a Slav with a German name and Rumanian papers but he seemed to me an indentured labourer, a cause of infinite guilt because of what we paid him and how the world had mistreated him.

In those years Europe was still a cherished part of my personal mythology; for him it was a dead whore. He'd survived the war making skis for various occupying armies—his village had fallen eight times—and each set of victors had posted its list of villagers for execution, commendation, enlistment or transfer. By the end of the war hardly a hundred men out of an original three thousand remained. He'd lost brothers, his father and an older son. Mother and sisters had been carried away, raped or butchered. His only distinction lay in having survived it. And he survived because he possessed a skill. He liked to shock me; his favourite army had been the German. He generally agreed with their lists of executions. They paid for their skis at least—the partisans only took. The Nazis treated him fairly well (no one's perfect), everything considered. What did I know of it—comic books, war movies? They could have wiped out the whole village and no one would have known, or cared. And they didn't. They were selective and Franz was thankful for small favours. No, the only unforgivable sin, the American sin and the one I continually committed in his presence, was naïveté. Every time I opened my mouth I raised his blood pressure. He could have lived with the Germans. Or with nearly anyone else, except the Russians. They were the new element in the region, the slaughterers. Especially the slaughterers of cabinetmakers. He believed he would lose his fingers to the Russians. They'd chop them off and ship him to Murmansk, to pack fish like a woman.

At this Franz would hold out his remarkable fingers and I had to agree: they were a living toolchest. As adapted to sawing, sanding, rubbing and polishing as any power instrument we could have bought. He stropped his penknife on the flat, cement-hard heel of his hand. Then he'd test the blade by shearing off the cap of a callus or by carving the stony amber overhang of his fingernails. His fingers were squat and wide and he could extract enough strength from them to tighten clamps that my father—even with a hammer—couldn't loosen. He let molten sticks of plastic wood drip into the palm of his hand before working the paste into nicks and depressions, and when the scratch was in mahogany or cherry he'd dispense with paints and plastics altogether. For that he'd pass his wicked blade over the ball of veins at the base of his thumb and blood would seep like dark red caulking from a narrow spout and for some reason it would keep oozing till he'd rubbed enough of it into the scratch to make it disappear. Wood had a way of drinking blood. No wonder the palms of his hands were a thousand small black scratches where paints and dyes and oils had entered: tattoos of an Old World cabinetmaker, a man without naïveté who arrived for work at eight o'clock in his battered black Hudson carrying his own wooden cabinet of sticks, knives, paints, emery cloths, burners and fuel, and who left just as promptly at the stroke of four. He was not available for uncrating, for moving, or for delivery. Only Franz could touch his cabinet; only I could move the furniture. For tea to drink with the sandwiches he brought, he would shout from the back, "Missus! Tea!" and even if my mother were with a customer she would run to the kitchen and turn on the hot plate. A furniture store, my father often said, is only as good as its refinisher. And refinishers, because they were artists (in effect as well as temperament), were allowed freedom within the furniture world that would have been suicidal for anyone else, even the son of the store to try.

The placid period ended on the day of Joe Whitehouse's second visit. Three years earlier, when we'd opened, Joe Whitehouse of Whitehouse Neon had brought down a wreath of
flowers and thrown the switch on our flashing bank of red and
green, and it had felt like the day we could challenge the world,
we'd take our place with Mohrbacher's downtown and Little
Brothers down the road: *capitalists*. And then came a Saturday during the Christmas vacation when Joe Whitehouse and
a companion came back, strangely tanned and sinister, and, it
being Saturday, it was up to me to let them in. I said, "Hi, Mr.
Whitehouse, what can I do for you?" friendly and eager, son-
of-store to supplier and benefactor and he'd waited for me to
open the back door before he and his confederate pushed me
inside. A shove, nothing gentle.

Whitehouse was a plump greying man, with the barrel
chest and sloping shoulders of a Caruso. His companion was
tall and grave, also strangely tanned. It was rare to see winter
suntans in Palestra—I liked to think we were wise enough to
avoid Miami Beach—but both of them were nearly orange
and these were the days before bottled tans. They wore identical dark overcoats and white silk scarves. Same as my father,

over his Arrow Darts; they reminded me of my father and his salesmen friends, and I wondered if Whitehouse also wore nothing but black silk socks.

"How d'you guess my name, kid?"

"I met you when we opened the store."

What's a little push between friends? They were always punching each other; they thought of me as one of the boys.

A long cigarette smouldered in his fingers and on two of them he wore diamond rings. King-sized cigarettes were a little exotic in those days. His dark eyes were unexpressive, looking beyond me as though to assess if I had any help. I used to know how to handle salesmen, so I tried again.

"It's a great neon," I said. "Come over here and I'll turn it on."

I went through the morning rituals efficiently: heat, lights, hitting the right banks of switches for the dozens of floor and table lamps. The displays out on the main floor looked beautiful for a moment in that heavy grey morning light through the small leaded windows; a city turning on. The furniture was never brighter than against that orifice of a fireplace, the black hole at the far end of the store that acted like jeweller's velvet.

Whitehouse and his companion went through the floor displays as though it had been a used-car lot. Flipping sales tickets, they lifted lamps and slammed them back, tapped table legs like they'd been soft tires. If they'd been children it would have been time to firmly remove them, take away their toys and gently scold them for marring the finish. Whitehouse was up to something; he was trying to provoke me into acting first. A tactic of schoolyard bullies. The partner went out to the front, the old checkroom, now our "Rug Bar," and a second later I heard a distant buzzing from the rear of the store, Franz's workshop. It was the first time I'd ever heard it.

"Knock it off, Sal," Whitehouse muttered. Sal could not have heard it.

"Hey, Joe, guess what—" Sal shouted from the front.

"Come here."

"Joe, remember that buzzer—" he was closer now. I didn't like the idea of Sal taking over my store, the place I'd crawled over inch by inch.

"So what? So it's working." Whitehouse jerked his head as he talked and Sal seemed to understand the motions. He lined himself up a little behind me.

"What was the buzzer?" I asked. Still cheerful, but wary.

"Dintja ever know what this place used to be?"

I told him I didn't.

"That there buzzer Sal just rung used to be in the check-room when this was a restaurant, see? The hat-check girl used to have to ring it. It's attached to the back."

"And?"

"My father installed it. He was in the buzzer business, you might say."

"I see."

"I guess you'd have to know what they had going in the back room to appreciate why they had a buzzer out front."

He punctuated his explanation with long drags on that inexhaustible cigarette. "My father and his associates had some equipment in the back room, too, you might say."

"I see."

The initials on his larger ring and on his cufflinks said "GC," which bothered me. It bothered me because Joe Whitehouse hadn't seemed this way three years earlier. I remembered a friendly guy who'd taken off his suit coat to climb on the ladder and install the wiring. I remembered his wife, a thin lady with turquoise jewellery, who'd spoken to my mother about Acapulco. The cufflinks, like his company stationery, had a White House logo.

It must have turned eight o'clock: I could hear Franz entering the back. Whitehouse lit another cigarette off the first. I didn't like the way he'd been shouting in our store; no one but my father had the owner's right to shout.

"What was in the back room was gaming tables," he said.

"Interesting," I said. It really was; my brain was aflame.

"What I'm saying is, our company has a long-standing interest in this building. Where's your old man?"

"Coming later."

"What was that noise I heard?"

"The refinisher. He comes in at eight."

"When's your old man get here?"

"Nine-thirty, about."

"Call him. Tell him to come down here now."

"He's not awake yet," I laughed. "Saturdays he doesn't wake up till nine. Saturdays I open up alone."

"Call him now. Lots can happen in an hour and a half."

"Sorry." I tried one of my mother's smiles, a let's-be-friends-anyway smile. He nodded to Sal and Sal took a step closer. I had trouble catching my breath.

"You know, kid, all a sign is is a buncha light bulbs. Like this," he said, unscrewing a bulb from the nearest lamp and holding it up. "Light bulbs don't last too long, you know? They go pop—" And here he dropped it at my feet. When the explosion came, it showered my shoes in shards of broken glass. "Now you see what happens. That down there—what's that called?"

Suddenly I knew that whatever I said would be wrong and would get me in deeper.

"Glass. Broken glass."

"Naw, that ain't just glass, kid." Sal handed him another bulb, like a parody magic act. This time he popped the bulb in his hand with the top flying in every direction, leaving him holding the base and now brandishing the jagged edge and the insides very close to my face.

He was smiling. "What's this, kid?"

Glass.

"Kid, this is your future. And this is your old man's store. Now, I got an interest in this store. I don't want nothing to happen to it, understand? You've seen what can happen to glass. And lookit this—look how glass can just"—he bent over, holding the jagged bulb up high, like a magician, before suddenly plunging it down, and across a tabletop—"can just cut a table to shit. And look what it does to leather," another swipe and a cushion was laid open, like a German's cheek in a duelling match.

"Now what's that, kid?"

I couldn't answer.

"That's your derbis, kid."

Derbis? Another furniture word? I thought I'd known the whole lexicon of *borax*.

"Derbis. Tell your old man his sign might suddenly develop a disease, just like this table and like this-here sofa. It might suddenly turn to derbis. It needs repair."

"No—it's perfect."

I saw a slight nod of his head before I felt it; a blow just below my ribs in the back that landed me on my face and it seemed to me, in the sudden pain and shock that for the first time in my life I had actually seen my own face, seen my mouth wide open and making a perfect black "Ohhhh" sound, my mouth as big as the cold black fireplace behind me. I was on the floor amidst the shards of glass and I couldn't breathe, the whole breathing apparatus was temporarily paralyzed.

Whitehouse took a step closer and placed his cool, polished black shoe under my chin. One kick and he could tear my head off and still I couldn't move. A long way down the main aisle I saw Franz standing by the kitchen and watching. In the movies this would be the time. The cynic, the worldly wise Bogart figure would finally stir himself. Take out his knife and carve the villains up. But even as I watched, Franz went into the kitchen carrying his tea mug, and he didn't come out.

Whitehouse bounced my head a couple of times on the tip of polished shoes. I could breathe again. "Tell your old man he doesn't repair the sign, and the store here's a pile of derbis." *Derbis*? Derbis, and the pain and the shoe-tip fused a sudden meaning: he means *debris*. I was about to say it, the ever-helpful, ever-naïve me, except that my voice had not returned.

"You might give your old man a message. Tell him Joe Whitehouse stopped by on a friendly business call. No—a maintenance call. We like to follow up on all our signs and tell him I checked it out personal and it looked like it needed some repairs. It's my professional opinion his neon sign might burn out any minute. And the connections are old and they could take the store with them when they go."

He lifted my head as far back as it would go. My eyes were looking straight up into his. I felt like a puppy. "Got that?"

I closed my eyes.

"Tell him I figure we can handle the repairs for ten thousand dollars."

I tried to nod.

He lowered my chin again to the floor. "And tell him one more thing. Tell him the name isn't Whitehouse for him. For special customers on special insurance policies the name is Casabianca. Giuseppe Casabianca. Got it?"

I slowly got up to all fours, then rolled over to a sitting position. I could feel the cuts in my hands, in my thighs. It was the first time I'd really been touched. I didn't lead a charmed life, not anymore. I didn't dare stand until Whitehouse and Sal put on their gloves and carefully refolded their white silk scarves.

Franz was sipping tea when I got to the back. He didn't look up, but I noticed that he had uncrated some boxes from the day before; he had actually moved some furniture nearer his workbench. I took a broom and swept up and then I carried back the coffee table with the long gouge. I put the cushion on my father's desk in his office.

Franz said he could repair the table. He didn't ask how it had happened, but by not asking he obviously knew. "Peoples play rough," he said later. He'd been in America a dozen years working always in furniture and he'd seen it before. In America we didn't have to worry about invasions, so we had to have something else.

I called my father. I said to him first that Joe Whitehouse and a friend had dropped in to see him. And I said that Whitehouse wasn't his name. He'd wanted us to know his name was Casabianca.

"Oh my God," my father groaned.

And that they'd gouged a table with a broken light bulb and then cut open a leather cushion.

He was silent for many seconds, but I could hear him trying to catch his breath. Finally be asked, "How much did they want?"

I told him $10,000.

He didn't respond. He kept muttering, "Oh my God, oh my God," each time his voice rising as though to cry. I didn't mention that they'd knocked me down, marked my chin with their shoes. I didn't want him to be ashamed of me. Ten thousand dollars was all we had earned in that third year, our first real profit. I cradled the phone, vaguely aware that we'd entered a new phase in the store. We were big enough to attract sharks and we were no longer working for ourselves or to support our help.

Franz, Franz, I wanted to cry: *help me!* I sat in the back watching him work. I wanted a relationship; I wanted him to tell me more of Europe and how to survive. If Europe was a dead whore, I wanted him at least to paint a compensating picture of America. But he'd never lived in America either. He'd chosen a valley near Palestra that most resembled his native Wallachia where even the neighbours were immigrants from the same region. They butchered their own hogs, made their own sausage in the traditional ways and grew enough vegetables to be able to sell them in Palestra in the fall. He had arrived in

America with nothing but his knife and a razor strap, and now, a dozen years later, he owned a house and land, two cars and a truck, had two sons in college, a daughter in high school and a boy born in America who was blond, bright and a star athlete. They all held jobs, they all played music, and they obeyed their father with a fanatical respect borne out of terror. Even to the point of studying medicine and law in order to please him. His wife sold baked goods, lace and petit point; Franz had two businesses in the evening—toy repair and piano tuning. The two college boys ran an engine-overhaul shop in Franz's garage and the high-school girl baby-sat, cooked and sewed, and gave piano lessons. Franz seemed to me that morning the only American I'd ever met. Everything else was a lie, or on television like "Father Knows Best." Greenwood's Interiors was a small financial blister on the great round surface of the Krysch family's joint income; nothing more than a reference point as he took his financial bearings.

And it was that chapter of innocence that was closed to me now. When my father came in that Saturday morning, he went directly to his office, and when he saw the cushion, he flew into a rage, running back to me and throwing it at my face. I remembered suddenly his terror of Italians; I hadn't meant anything threatening by having added to the note on my father's desk: "Whitehouse equals Casabianca." I'd meant, I'm fairly certain, that he's another one of *us*, the name-changers who glide through America without anyone suspecting. Franz sipped tea; I pushed a few tables nearer to him, including the gouged one from that morning. My father leaned against the back door, head nestled in his arms, and one arm pounded the wall keeping time to his exclamations, "Damn it to hell. God damnit to hell! Bloodsuckers. Bonecrushers. They want everything, everything, everything. . . ." And soon his arm waved less frantically and his voice grew indistinct and finally only the heaving of his shoulders betrayed that there was any life in him at all. I was proud of myself for not having mentioned that they'd struck me, that I'd grovelled at their feet in the broken glass. And that something else in me—a new lack of naïveté perhaps—had stopped me short of calling the police or of suggesting the same to my father.

"Jesus God!" he suddenly screamed, louder than anything I'd ever heard. He kicked the door and the small panels of glass slowly dropped, crashing in a pile at his feet. He took a dining-room chair that had been waiting for small repairs and threw it against the wall, loosening a leg which he then wrenched free. And with that, like a machete, he cut his way back to the office toppling lamps and whacking the dust from every sofa along the way. Franz silently raised his hand, scarred palm toward me, then pumped it slightly as though putting on the brakes. "Don't go to him now," he said, in the first adult tone he'd ever used with me.

We were not quite so lucky with the rest of the help. Over the three years of our existence we went through more drivers and delivery men than Seligman's had in twenty-five. Our first driver was an ex-Teamster named Whitey—for his hair, eyebrows and eyelashes—a slow-witted, strong and maniacal father of eight—given to bursts of energy that could clean a week's deliveries out on a single staggering Saturday afternoon. But other weeks would find him limping through the day under less physical power than I normally commanded. On his bad days, he'd misplace invoices, lose his way in traffic, forget to collect checks or signatures, drop furniture, insult housewives, or in some cases terrify them with his glassy eyes, stumbles and mumbled curses. On those days it was my job to humour him with sports talk. We got rid of him when he finally scraped up the truck, necessitating a new paint job. Then my father hired a semipro pitcher, a young man of twenty who got me thrown in—catcher's mitt and all—to catch twenty minutes of his fastballs, curves and knucklers every lunch-hour.

I learned to dread those spinning, dipping, wobbling things; each time he wound up, I felt I was standing in the front seat of a roller coaster as it made its descent. Each pitch was an agony and most of all, to a slow glove like mine, dangerous. Finally we were all able to save face when Palestra (now with an expansion major league club) signed him to its farm in the Florida State League. It was the same team I had followed as a child in the swamps. I kept reading *The Sporting News* for the next few years, certain that I would someday boast of having caught the next Herb Score, but Ron Terlewsky never showed.

And then came the third delivery man, Paul Gaylord, and a new form of son-abuse. I'd known him before; he'd been two years ahead of me at Ridge High. In those years he'd been a school thug, a strong but scrawny basketball player when not disqualified for grades or other infractions. He'd already graduated or at least dropped out by the time I'd entered the high school. But I remembered him. I remembered the day in seventh grade when I'd stood on the stage and Paul Gaylord had supposedly received a message from Laurel Zywotko, via the medium-ship of Blackthorne the Magician. And I remembered a few months later mentioning Paul Gaylord's name to the police as a suspect in her murder. Nothing had come of it, but deep down I always thought of Paul Gaylord as Larry Zywotko's likely killer.

By the time he applied for work at our store he had filled out—in another five years he'd be a tall, fat man—those bean-pole bodies didn't know where to store it. He came to us one Saturday in November of my senior year, a few days after Ron had quit. I don't know why my father hired him, for Paul Gaylord did nothing to ingratiate himself during the interview. He loomed over my father, an unlit cigarette dangling from his thick lips, jerking his head in response to my father's questions, dressed only in a summer-thin T-shirt and jeans slung low over his thickening belly, secured with a thin plastic belt. On the inside of his forearm he'd been tattooed: a long dagger from which blood was dripping. And high on the bicep of his other arm he'd had a careful replica of a zipper tattooed, a zipper that ran from just under the shoulder to nearly the elbow. Somehow the tattoos confirmed to me that Paul Gaylord was the killer. Tattoos stood for something that race or class or accent never could—some absolute distinction from me and my kind and actions I could conceivably perform. I assumed that my father would see this, that he would, in fact, throw Paul Gaylord out of the office. I was there to make sure that he did. I wanted us to have a black driver, a "coloured man" in the argot of the day, because we'd been victimized for too long by men whose sole claim to the job was their lack of colour. The blacks who applied were inevitably well-dressed, soft-spoken, experienced and reliable; it's just that my father felt that our clientele wouldn't welcome a coloured man into their houses on days that he'd have to deliver without me. Or so he said.

And then Paul Gaylord turned to me and said, "Davey— haven't seen you since high school! How's it going, boy?"

No one had ever called me "Davey," and the effect was electrifying. "You know my boy?" my father stammered, a big grin breaking out on his face. Paul was the first young man claiming to be a friend of mine who at least looked capable of carrying a maple breakfront up three flights of stairs.

"Sure I know him. Don't I, Davey? We're old buddies."

There might have been a time back in the eighth grade when Paul Gaylord had stolen money or pencils from me. I looked quickly at my father and he was standing now and grinning, and even Paul gave me a friendly slap on the shoulder.

"Davey here was one of the brains of the high school. Sorry to say I never was. But I sure admired Davey and his friends."

"He does very well," said my father.

"Isn't that marvellous," said Paul Gaylord.

"How've you been keeping, Paul?" I said.

Once we were outside, our new driver said to me, "I used to see you and your friends waddling down the halls and I'd say to myself, *must be an asshole convention.* What was that freak's name with all the pimples, the real brain—"

"Wesley Duivylbuis."

"Yeah, Wesley Duivylbuis." He said it in a way totally without awe, a tone I'd never heard.

"His pimples are gone now," I said.

Because I made the nervous mistake of starting our first day's conversation off on our only mutual point of contact, Laurel Zywotko, Paul Gaylord and I never really got off the topic of sex, just as Ron Terlewski and I had never gotten off the topic of baseball and Whitey and I off his headaches and his awful wife and the buzzing in his ears. But without Paul Gaylord in my life, where would I have picked it up, that essential dirty knowledge that sex is central and everywhere? I would have been left like Irving, who referred to sex as "genital interaction" and to breasts as "mammary appendages" and to love as "narcissistic transference."

Laurel, Paul Gaylord would say on those Saturday deliveries. *Laurel.* "Laurel was all right."

I of course would agree.

"She liked you, you know. After that day onstage, she was impressed."

"Come on."

"Naw; no shit. She dug you. She dug that freakish friend of yours. She was stupid, but she still thought she was better than guys like me."

I denied all knowledge.

"Didn't you know that friend of yours used to see her? Can you imagine someone visiting Laurel Zywotko in an Eagle Scout uniform? That's the same guy, right?"

"Must be," I said.

"Makes you wonder," he said.

Gaylord had a habit when he drove of rolling an unlit cigarette to all corners of his mouth. His lips were prehensile; even as he talked, that cigarette kept moving, up and down, side to side. He may have had other dimensions—sports, politics, cars, money—but all that was ever mentioned in my presence was sex. Maybe I brought it out in him, a chance to be the unchallenged stud, the corrupter of innocence, the bringer of forbidden knowledge. Or perhaps he saw in me—or *sensed* in me for certainly nothing was visible—a competitor. I could match him thrust for thrust, my world against his, if he'd only known. But of course I played the innocent—I was the innocent, after all—and that drove him to feats of desperate insolence. As I set up bedframes he would drape himself in doorways, forcing the housewife to squeeze past him whenever she wanted to inspect the work. "Give it seven inches clearance there, Davey," he'd call out to me, then leer at the lady, "Seven inches is about all you can take, right?" He thought of himself, alternately, as Brando, Dean or Elvis Presley, and despite the lack of any resemblance he managed many of the same effects. I delivered furniture with him every Saturday in my senior year and every day after the summer vacation started, and there was not a day when he did not succeed with at least one of our customers—one memorable Saturday afternoon, with three. That's why he'd become a delivery man; life for him was stag film come true. All females between fifteen and forty-five were primary targets; even women my mother had talked to for hours about art and Europe and finer things before selling them something tasteful—even they yielded panties or hair ribbons or earrings to Paul Gaylord's collection. The entry was simple: he'd leave something behind. A pencil, a ruler, wrench or screwdriver. "Always give the lady a second chance," he'd tell me as I parked the truck under a tree and took out something to read. Oh, it was a curious perspective to the business life, one that extended the boundaries of the erotic into realms little dreamed of.

I would do the driving after one of Paul's heavy deliveries. He'd nap, hands cupped on his lap. We'd talk of Laurel more often than not; the other ladies were never as real.

"Fucking bitch, she got it good, though."

What do you mean? *Could* he know?

"After her brother got killed she took off to California. She was always talking about how she was going to make it big in the movies. What a load of crap that was! Anyway, about a month after he's killed, I start getting these letters. She's the one that knocked him off, see—"

I said very carefully, very innocently, "I didn't know for sure she killed him. I thought the papers said—"

"Fuck the papers, man, what do they know? I'm telling it to you the way it really happened, only I don't want you shooting your mouth off, see."

"I can assure you. I'm very discreet."

"They never proved she did it, but they *know* she did. They just never found her, that's all."

"But she wrote you—"

"Sure. From Hollywood, how about that? She finally made it. Changed her name of course. And you know what?'

What?

"I seen her last week."

Where? I dropped my disinterest and I had to fight to get it back: *like hell you did*. "Here?" I asked.

He rolled that cigarette around one full revolution before answering, "Nope. In a movie some guys got aholt of."

Where's it playing?

"God, Greenwood, you are such an asshole I can't believe it. *Where's it playing*? It was playing in my apartment for about three hours till I had to give it back to this guy who rents them out for three bucks an hour. You want to know her name now?"

"Vaginia. No, not Virginia, stupid. Vaginia. She must have got screwed two dozen times and I mean with things she never even dreamed of. My God—you had to feel a little proud, seeing it all."

Why, I asked, for old Daley Ridge High?

"Why? Why! Shit, man, because I was the first guy that ever stuck it to her. *Me*. Paul Gaylord."

To Laurel Zywotko now named Vaginia?

"Right. 'Mah name, suh, is Vaginia because everybody says ah have a real rich mound.'"

Ho-Ho. And we knew her when she was just a nobody.

"But shit, was I scared when her brother got it. If they'd ever caught her I'm sure she would have told the cops how I smashed him up a couple of times. That son of a bitch tried to collect money—can you imagine? Shit, I wasn't even into her yet and he's coming on about 'the rent.'" Paul did a small Presleyan shuffle there in the driver's seat. "But she was some kind of piece, huh? I mean for eighth grade—shit!"

"Real tight pussy," I put in, a punch line to a burlesque routine that I hadn't quite understood, though it had gotten a big laugh from the regulars.

"*Right*," Paul agreed, a trifle surprised, "real tight. Then, anyway. Not anymore though, judging from the movie. Hell, they got a stubby little Mexican, least he looks Mexican and there isn't any sound anyway, must have a prick—I'm not exaggerating—about as long as, I don't know—your thumb, maybe."

What a relief that was! I didn't know much about comparative endowment but I knew I exceeded thumb-length, so I felt secure sneering, "That's not so much."

"No shit. This guy's a real two-by-four, though. Only he's maybe a five-by-twelve. He's a freak. What he doesn't have in length could choke a horse. And in this movie he just wanders in and out of this apartment building—he's a sign-painter or a repairman or something—and all he's trying to do is take a comfortable piss. But he has to take his overalls off first, see, cause his fly isn't wide enough—"

"I understand."

"And so some broad is always coming out just as he gets unbuttoned and *slam-bam* she's dragged him back inside and pulled him on top of her."

"And one of those girls was Laurel Zywotko?"

"Right. You really catch on fast."

"How do you know? I mean, that was four years ago. A lot of things can change."

"No, Davey, some things *don't* change. Maybe someday you'll learn. It's her tits, man. Remember those firm pointed little tits? Well, they're a little rounder now but they are still outstanding tits and they could only belong to her."

I told him I still doubted it; tits weren't fingerprints, and furthermore, I suspected that Laurel Zywotko was also dead.

In all the foul-mouthed joking and in all the insults we traded, that was the only time that I saw Paul Gaylord actually angry. He grabbed my collar and lifted me from the seat. The truck swerved slightly and he pushed me against the door. "Something else," he said. "and don't you ever repeat it. I maybe acted like a big man back in ninth grade, but some of that was just a front. I told you I was her first lay, right? And that's true. And I'll tell you something else. She was my first one, too, and a man doesn't forget *anything* about his first fuck. Maybe someday if you're lucky you'll get laid and you'll know what I mean."

Long before I read *Zorba the Greek*, I'd encountered in Paul Gaylord a man who could wring his hands over the numbers of women alone on the streets, needing (as he thought) a man: himself. No good telling him they were probably married; they were alone *as we passed them* on the street, *as he saw them* in the stores and in their houses. Minute by minute they were alone and wanting him, and he was powerless to help them all simultaneously and that was the only depression he knew. Against that ocean of need his achievements were merely a puddle, and he grieved. And I wondered briefly, watching him during that winter of my senior year and into the summer when I was with him every day—my strange interval between the company of Irving and Wesley and whatever Halliwell College was to hold for me in September—if my father had hired Paul Gaylord because he'd seen himself in Paul: an undereducated, untrained brawler. I lived in fear of a customer's complaint, of a rape charge being entered— but were those crimes my father would have acted on? Or were they crimes he somehow respected, had perhaps even committed? I knew so little about my father and most of my suspicions about him had been picked up as reflections off his more flamboyant salesmen-friends. They were the ones who flirted with waitresses and went on about their conquests in every city on their routes. My father listened and smiled but never joined in—because I was there? Because he never did it? Or because he was the acknowledged king? I couldn't blow the whistle on Paul Gaylord because it would make me seem even flabbier in my father's eyes, and worse, intolerant in my own. But I couldn't shake the suspicion that Paul Gaylord was a plausible son for my father, tattoos and all; that if the Italian girl in New Jersey that he'd once told me about had borne him a son, my half-brother, this is the type of boy he would have been. Only now he'd be the age of Joe Whitehouse.

The hundreds of hours of company at least convinced me that he'd had nothing to do with the murder of Larry Zywotko. I'd caught him in his lies and his fantasies, but I knew too much (and too little) to press the advantage. And I believed him when he told me she'd been attracted to Wesley and even to me. That was too weird, too weird even to Gaylord, to have been imagined. And one night in a dream I saw Wesley walking down Patience Street in his Eagle Scout uniform, his cheeks pocked with acne as they had been that year, climbing up those stairs and finding Laurel on the couch under her coat and blankets, as I had. And through Wesley's eyes I watched her dance, watched her undress him and watched him reach for her and find the leather thong; in my nightmare I relived the moment when Laurel Zywotko dropped her bra and when her penis stood straight out and spurted—I awoke at that moment, spurting myself—and then fully awake in a cold, wet bed I relived the murder as it must have been: Wesley Duivylbuis a bit stronger than me and more twisted in his virtue and less capable of absorbing ambiguity. He overpowered poor Larry (having caught him in his male phase) and tied him to the kitchen chair and made him write that note and then butchered him. I wondered if his psychoanalyst knew him as Wesley Duivylbuis—or as David Greenwood. But it was summertime when I finally pieced it together to my satisfaction and Wesley was already out in Pasadena working in a lab as part of his scholarship. He'd be entering Cal Tech with junior standing and an exemption from English. It was as Irving had once said: no matter how hard you compete against Wesley Duivylbuis, you'll never beat him. And I'd be going to Halliwell, a place no one had heard of, where I expected to find the girl of my dreams and marry her and live happily ever after, like the Andersons on "Father Knows Best."

At the other end of the scale from required courses like Boys' Health stood a few others, experimental in nature, which were Daley Ridge's investment in daring innovation. Students in the top tenth were permitted to take "college level" courses taught by professors-on-loan from the local university. Most of the offerings were in science and math, but I saw one that interested me, especially since I had a bulging file of letters at home that I was dying to show to an appreciative teacher. So I signed up for creative writing.

I was the only boy among eight girls. The "poet-professor" was Virginia Pritchett, a woman of forty who radiated a troubled complexity as well as a mysterious attraction. I didn't yet understand academic irony; her reference to her own writing as meagre and untraceable, her attempts to discourage us from any form of writing except perhaps business letters, her tantalizing references to countries visited only to dismiss them as diseased, overpriced and disappointing. Her attractiveness (to me, at least)—though her hair was greying and her body stout—was her face, the most mobile I had ever seen, able to shed twenty years in a smile. Like my mother, she told stories well, though never to entertain. They would begin without pretense or introduction.

"A woman opens her door. Pay attention. Visualize this. She is forty-one years of age. How does the reader know this without her wearing a little tag? Think of details that add up to 'forty-one.' I see her carrying a grocery sack. Does she live alone, or with a family? If so, how much does she buy at one time? What kind of door? Heavy oak, apartment tin? How does she open it? Is she a lady of identifiable ethnic origin? Indicate that as well. She lives alone. She is suffering from some sort of anxiety. How would you indicate all this in a single sentence or perhaps two, about a woman opening a door? Does she have the key drawn in her hand even though she's carrying groceries, or must she set them down to dig for it in her purse? What sorts of things now peak out of the top of the bag—celery tops? Bran flakes? No, not soup cans—they'd be packed at the bottom. You see, '*she carries a grocery sack*' doesn't mean a thing: *how* she carries it, how *big* it is and *what's inside—they* tell us everything, if you're subtle enough, that we need to know. Ice cream perhaps. She's a little self-indulgent. A carton of cigarettes? What sort of woman living alone buys cartons at a time instead of a pack? What kind of cigarettes, by the way? *Of course it's important*! What does a forty-one-year-old woman living alone eat, drink and smoke? Why is she alone—did she walk out, was she deserted, or has she always been this way? Is she expecting someone: a man, a woman, her children from an earlier marriage—what? How does this relate to the key in her hand? Ah—a key ring? And other keys on the ring: a car, an office, safety-deposit box? What are the things that such a woman has keys to?

All right, then, so much for your first sentence.

"What shall we call her? 'I'? 'She'? 'Anne'? 'Natasha'? The last name's important. Italian, Jewish, Irish, English—what? Miss Jones? Mrs. Jones? Mrs. Forrest Jones, lately divorced, widowed, separated? Still married?"

By then, some of the girls had gotten the point and were developing marvellous sentences of their own; they were natural writers, naturally in command of a social reality. It was a talent I didn't have. Even Irving, who hadn't taken the course, wrote short stories, though usually it was to prove some perverse sociological point. A modern Othello, concerned with the anxieties of ethnic minorities in a position of political power. Applicable to Disraeli. Also to Hitler and to Stalin. A parody of *Paradise Lost* in which angels openly debated the charms of downward mobility.

The only reading sanctioned by my group of friends was science fiction. After that, *Mad* magazine and a few record albums: Lenny Bruce and Nichols and May. My first story owed everything to science fiction. It earned some favour, but for all the wrong reasons. I'd written of dinosaurs, a world of dinosaurs all placidly flying overhead or tearing into the flesh of their kin. But it was also a modern world: airplanes, skyscrapers, highways. My aim had been as narrow as my inspiration: to write a science-fiction story that my friends would admire. The point was clear to me: we see what we are trained to see. We have no concept of living dinosaurs; therefore, even though they are flying overhead today, though they are crashing through our hedges and over our lawns, we ignore them. We also ignore the footprints, calling them by other names. But plane crashes and UFOs and car crashes and incidents of people going mad—they were all there to tell us that dinosaurs exist, and that our worlds, deny it or not, impinge.

Miss Pritchett chose a different interpretation, one that earned me a certain notoriety with the girls in my class, which, had I been a bolder sort of fellow, could have gained me a lot of mileage. "Obviously," she said, "we're not to see David's dinosaurs as real dinosaurs. You people amaze me," she said. "This is actually very subtle. And very adventurous. What are the dinosaurs? No one seems to know, despite the fact that sometimes they fly, sometimes attack and most of the time just float around in swamps, placidly." Ah: dinosaurs were the collective unconscious, or they were the suppressed libido on the individual level, a contiguous world of monstrous forms. Rarely had she read a story so richly interpretable on a Freudian level. Freud was right: seventeen was a holy age. Evidence of sexual awareness (and frustration) lay scattered about the surface of all our stories, like nuggets; no wonder Freud had made such headway after inventing the tools to detect them properly. She asked me, then, if in the second story I'd write something a little closer to home.

Irving had once written a story set in the world of his favourite book of the time, *Ten Days that Shook the World*. A witness to the revolution (not the title, though it could have been), one of the many hundreds of common folk quoted by Reed for a line or two, then dropped, was picked up by Irving and allowed a few more minutes on the stage of history. The purpose of fiction was simple indeed for Irving: to force history through a very fine nozzle, the consciousness of a normal worker. The purpose of history was to erase the individual consciousness altogether. The details of what was in the grocery sack or what keys were on the ring (when I related classroom discussions to him) was, "Romantic. *Feh*."

And I could only ask myself a different question. Studying her as closely as I studied the strippers down at Schuman's, why had no man claimed her? Was she still a miss or had she been a missus? It was as inexplicable to me as the opposite fact: that so many of the prime battleaxes, fat and warted ("the universal fungus conspiracy" we called them, collectively), had married. There was always that touch of perversity in my attractions—it meant that if I had found her attractive there was a flaw in her, deep down, and it was the flaw, more buried the better, that kept my passion pure.

She demanded ten pages of "creative" work every week. She encouraged us to keep diaries which could then be mined or turned in straight. I didn't bother with the diary since I was writing half a dozen letters a day to various occults and correspondence schools—when my files reached a thousand pages, I intended to turn them in for a monster credit. A couple of months later, I had to surrender my files to the postal inspector, before she saw them.

I wondered, for the first time, if it were possible to improve one's looks with age. A teenaged Virginia Pritchett must have been an eyesore: the rough cheeks of forty must have been raw at seventeen. Her black hair merely greasy. Youth can suggest only perfect features, only age can support eccentricities of which she had many. And perfect features on a woman of forty looked freakish, pinched, as though reflecting a similarly shrunken intellect, a life led in retreat. Well, Miss Pritchett had a jaw and a fine wide mouth and thick dark eyebrows and even the hint of down on her cheeks and upper lip. Her hair was greying rapidly; she was suited to that indeterminable age that framed her perfectly. I was becoming more like Paul Gaylord every day; profoundly democratic in my tastes.

I remember an afternoon in April; the snows were long gone and spring rains were coming down hard. The air was still cold and the windows were fogged. Outside it was nearly dark; our writing sessions often went on till five-thirty. I'd done one story already (the dinosaurs) and had turned in the second; I was dying for her to reach into her briefcase and begin reading it. I had written a personal story as she requested, one that I could verify from my own life, and it had surprised me. I imagined that anything that still had the power to surprise me would have an even greater effect on the reader.

All that I had over my classmates, I thought, was the part of central Florida I'd once lived in. I had never lost the smell of mud and mildew, the feel of Florida heat, and I'd never surrendered a particle of resentment for the Yankee tourists who knew only Miami Beach or Fort Lauderdale and thought they knew Florida. And so I wanted Miss Pritchett and my classmates to know the real Florida that even then was disappearing; the tenant farmers who'd lived down near the lake, the creatures, a mudfish I'd once discovered while digging in the mud, the snapping turtles, snakes and gators, even the pumas that still stalked the woods and left their prints under the windows of our cottage. What I wrote was not exactly of myself, but of two boys, brothers from a clan of moss-pickers out in a frogboat, fishing. One of them is cruel and aggressive; the other, placid, content to trail his fingers in the water. The sun is setting and a full moon is high. And suddenly the water erupts and the air seems to fill with alligator; the older brother is knocked off the poling-ledge and is carried under as his younger brother helplessly watches. In my telling, the younger brother whose placidness is marked by an exceptionally low but intuitive intelligence, gently eases himself into the water to swim for the brother's lost pole. He doesn't expect to make it, and the story ends.

And it was on that cold wet April Friday that Miss Pritchett read my story, breaking now and then to compliment a phrase, or to apologize for a bad rendering of colloquial speech.

"Whatever made you think of writing this, David?" she asked.

"A Florida tourist poster of Miami Beach."

"But surely you've never seen such people?"

I caught a tone of suspicion. I mentioned that I'd spent my first ten years among them. I knew them well. She asked if I'd read *The Yearling*, Erskine Caldwell, or Faulkner; except for the Rawlings novel, I'd never heard of the others. "You're sure you didn't read anyone else's story?"

"No, why?'

"It's punishable," she said.

She asked me to stay on.

We had a talk about life and art. Art, she said, is more nuanced than life. If a teacher is lecturing and looking out of smudged windows, smeared with greasy obscenities (sure enough, ours were) it doesn't mean anything, in life, except that the cleaning crews are lazy. But in a story, if a professor is lecturing and the windows are smudged, we're obliged to think his words are similarly . . . untranscendent, right? I agreed. Or if I find my coat and boots are spreading a puddle of water in the corner—that doesn't mean anything either, in life, does it? There was, indeed, a puddle. "*The teacher talked about art and life. Water dripped off her raincoat enlarging the puddles under her boots.* Mocking, isn't it? Gently perhaps, but Chekhovian, no?"

One of the great problems with artists, she said, is they don't keep nuance and nature distinct. Import raw nature into a story or a poem and you've only ruined a story. Import nuance into life and you'll go mad. There'll suddenly be too much significance everywhere, a message in everything. Hamlet's disease.

She was beginning to lose me.

It was dark outside. An exciting time, always, when the school is empty but alight like a cruise ship. Schools were like ships for me anyway; on a voyage and self-contained, and I was a passenger who longed to be crew. Miss Pritchett astonished me by lighting a cigarette, a Chesterfield, something that wasn't supposed to happen outside of those densely empurpled teachers' rooms.

"Look at you."

I smiled.

"Do you mean you just thought that story up?'

It had happened to me, I explained. My father was fishing and an alligator attacked. The rest of it was made up.

"You made up those characters? You knew when to describe the trees and the water and the sky? You knew to put a moon up there?"

Yes, I did.

"Tell me more about this place."

And for the next half hour I talked about the schools I'd gone to where my left-handedness had gotten me into trouble, where teenage morons had sat among the first-graders, the jungle in flood, the moss-pickers who would come down to central Florida every summer. I told her about worms in my stomach and my childhood absorption into maps and atlases. I sketched in worlds for her, the first person who had ever listened, it seemed.

"You can see the puddles have dried," she said.

"I talked too much."

"On the contrary. I'm being educated."

She sat at the desk, smiling passively. I was in a front desk afraid to draw any closer. I'd never been alone with a teacher and it felt like that moment in the museum with Judy Freisilber; I expected something strange and terrifying to occur. As though all contact between students and teachers had to be group contact, because something violent would inevitably occur, like between prisoners and guards, if they ever found themselves alone. As though she would take off a teacher's mask, just peel it off and the revelation of what lay beneath would be deeply terrifying. For what can a teacher do, once he or she stops teaching? He can only become something else, and transformation of any sort I identified with madness.

"David," she asked, "why did you take this course?"

I told her I'd been afraid of doing badly in the advanced science courses, with my friends. And writing was something that came very easily.

"Has it disappointed you?"

I told her it hadn't.

"I want to do something for you. It's ridiculously early to say this, but I think I must: You might become a writer. I want to do something to help it along—think of something, please."

I'm sure she knew I was lovesick for her, that she saw in me someone with outrageous tastes. I think, if my lips had found the words and I had said, "feel your breasts" or "see you naked" (the extent of my erotic imagination) she might have smiled and promised them to me, lightly.

"Would you like to read some of my writing?" She took a small book of poems from her purse. *The Baking Poems*, by Virginia McQuade. I read the two shortest ones, the first poems I'd ever read outside of an English textbook.

"Read it aloud. Go ahead."

It was called "Apollo." She frowned as I read, eyes closed, tapping a finger. She must have seen that I was not a poetry reader; the words lay glued to the page, a strain even to read. I'd be lying if I claimed any kind of understanding of her poetry. I was embarrassed. The vision of her, a woman I was prepared to love as I understood it, cupping her buttocks in the sand and begging a man was mortifying.

"The girl is on a honeymoon," she explained. "At a resort, a beach, right? *They promised sand to mold/ and not constrain these mad effusions.* . She has two husbands—the man and the god, the husband in law—*in licensed passion*—and the divine rapist. I'm not shocking you, am I? I want to tell you what I am so that I can reach you, David. She begs her husband to bake her, to transform her in his heat. She is 'batter' on the beach. But he fails her. Only a spirit can bring her to life, only Apollo can 'invade her blood.' *Dear Apollo, peel my skin away/ gown my blood in blisters/ clothe my bones in your phosphorescent blood . . .* you understand? Sun gods are notorious. They can do that, they really can. But they're shallow and fickle. That's why, later on, she turns to the moon, her long day's journey into night. I think you do too—isn't that so?"

Agreement seemed to be called for, and so I nodded. Being a sun god, however, was an attractive notion, a long night's journey into day seemed a better idea. Paul Gaylord was a sun god, if I understood.

"Let me read this one, it's called 'Lunar Attractions.'"

It was better; no gods or references. A bride and her husband were both naked in their hotel room, watching the naked waitresses bathing at midnight on the beach. Chambermaids and waitresses, black and white, dancing, hugging, kissing, under a full moon. The bride wants to join them just to clean herself of "*. . . honeymoon juices. . .*"; the groom wouldn't mind a swim himself. But Miss Pritchett's description of a bride was shocking and maybe I couldn't hide it: "*A bride is a woman/ with nothing quite connected/ everything sprung, sprockets loose/ Half sunk in come.*"

It was the last poem of "The Honeymoon Suite."

"What do you want to ask?"

Nothing.

"You know what it means?"

She doesn't like her husband. She envies the waitresses.

"And '*genius of flesh*'? And being clean, the emphasis on being clean? And the moon goddess?"

I don't know.

"What is the poem saying to you, David?"

She doesn't like being married. She wishes she hadn't come.

"You understand that line . . . '*A bride is a woman . . . Half sunk in come*'? Do you know what *come* is?"

"I . . . think so."

"I don't think you do. It got the book banned ten years ago. But never mind. David, what am I saying in that poem?"

"Maybe you're saying why the name on the book is McQuade but your name is Pritchett."

"It was a short marriage—you're right there. A long time ago. And David—there won't be any other marriages for me— do you understand?"

I told her that I thought I did. I tried to match the slight smile she flashed me. In my Hollywood-saturated way, I assumed the husband had died young, and from grief she'd dedicated herself to teaching. Or that she'd discovered some horrible disease in herself and rather than contaminate a loved one, she'd taken a teaching vow.

A few weeks later, my files were confiscated; a thousand pages down the drain.

And so then, fired with a desire to write a story employing all I'd been shown about nuance, I wrote a murder mystery. All that I knew of the genre was that it had to be British and nineteenth century and there had to be an investigative duo, fat and thin, stupid and brilliant. There had to be fog, dogs, a manor house, maids and butlers and sooty train rides. Small boys were continually delivering telegrams, a process I never understood. In my story, Lord Farthingham lies murdered, wretched business with viscera scattered all over the parlour. The help is most distressed and suspicion attaches itself to Mathilde, the young French bride, barely a week in English society. She has utterly vanished after leaving a note accusing Lord Farthingham of having committed gross indecencies upon her tiny foreign person. The stableboy, Trevors-Upstart, is also under suspicion, having been seen with Lady Mathilde down by the mews. My Holmes-figure, Digby Strapp, is called in to investigate. After three days he informs the local constabulary that they can call off the search for Lady Mathilde. She is dead.

"'Ghastly business, that. The stableboy, I suppose. Mad fit of passion and all that. Murdered, you say?'

"'Indeed she was.'

"'But at the same time as his lordship?'

"'I should judge at precisely the same time.'

"'And where, sir?'

"'At precisely the same place.'

"'In the parlour? But surely we would have found traces—'

"'In the parlour. On the very rug where you found his lordship.'

"'You mean, sir, they were engaged in . . . ah . . . I'm afraid you're way off base, sir. We have searched the grounds. There was only one body.'

"'I didn't say anything about her body. The primary rule of deduction is to eliminate false conclusions. After that, the truth is staring you in the face.'

"'But, sir. To assume death without a body—*that* is certainly an unjustified conclusion.'

"'Don't exasperate me, my good man. I didn't say there wasn't a body, did I? A body,' he said, emphasizing the indefinite article just slightly.'"

And slowly it dawns upon Digby Strapp's weak-minded companion, Dr. Alastair Numbly, what the horrendous truth must be. A perfect crime was committed. "The Perfect Crime" was also the title. Lord Farthingham was murdered, and his beneficiary, Lady Mathilde, will never be captured. Strapp knows that Trevors-Upstart did it, and he knows why—jealousy. Everything, you see, had been cozy in the manor before Lady Mathilde appeared. Then suddenly she became the centre of social life, pitching her poor husband into a suicidal gloom. No one ever saw them together, in fact. The case was left "unsolved" though it was clear, even to Dr. Numbly, what had happened. Lady Mathilde had appeared suddenly from Lord Farthingham's own tortured subconscious. The stable-boy, deeply corrupted by his lordship's attentions ever since they'd slipped off to the woods together as children, turned to blind jealous rage upon his benefactor.

Normally, our stories were read aloud and discussed by Miss Pritchett. I wondered how she would handle the accents in mine, but she didn't bother. We sat through two weeks of readings, then she handed mine back. It had a brief comment on the back. "The parody of the detective convention is sometimes clever. But the central idea is sophomoric and unbelievable, not worthy of your abilities. It is preposterous, and, I might add, personally painful in its obvious attacks on me. I see I was wrong to have trusted you. Because the betrayal of your talent is more serious than even plagiarism, I'm giving you a D for this story. And since admission to this class is totally a matter of instructor's discretion, I am hereby withdrawing my permission for you to attend. I have already recorded a grade of B for you in the course, but I do not wish to discuss anything with you, or to see you again."

Paul Gaylord summed up his side of the story very well: when you're *really* hungry the last thing in the world you want is a fancy dinner, right? Fuck the snails and fuck the wine and the starched tablecloths, right? What you really want is to plop down at a counter somewhere with a hamburger and a Coke and a side order of fries. And you want it *now*: gulp it down and get the hell out, right? You want something plain and fast and you want something you're sure of, and even a bad hamburger isn't that different from a great one. Right? Well, that's how it is when you're really horny, like he was, always. Take your average little lady, a little bony or a little fat, skin bad, hair stringy, maybe grey, older, smelly, dumpy—so what (gobble, gobble)? They were all five-minute confections to him, each one as memorable and satisfying as, say, a Lifesaver. The only frustration he knew was in taking rain checks. I used to pray as I parked the delivery truck and waited for Paul's return that he'd be gone at least twenty minutes. Dry runs were as hard on me as they were on him; a betrayed Apollo was a lousy partner. *Lady says come back next week*, he'd snarl, stomping back to the truck and slamming the door. I'd have to drive—he might hit someone out of pure meanness. I never knew if his occasional failures were the result of flat rejections or counterthreats (I hoped at least some of them were) or if they were what he said they were, the two most hated words in the English language: *my period.*

"How come she flashed me the sign, then?" he'd mutter. He felt an honest betrayal; how can people be so cruel, so insensitive? And to Paul, every gesture was "a sign"! I always looked for *a sign* and never caught it. He called it a scent, something only the heavy scorers picked up, men who'd dedicated themselves to women, men who'd earned a woman's trust.

The rejection would put him in such a foul and uncooperative mood for the rest of the afternoon that I finally applied myself to a solution. "Next time she tells you she's got a period," I told him (not really knowing what it was and how it affected performance, but assuming it to be nothing more than last-ditch coquetry), "you tell her that's okay—you've got an exclamation point." He liked it; he said he'd use it.

And what was I, deep-down: cheeseburger-addict or patient, exigent gourmand? Creature of slovenly habit or of exquisite refinement? *Morbid monogamy,* Irving had once pointed out, like the quest for reciprocal adoration (à la Hollywood) was an Oedipal fantasy, a pathological projection of the infant's longings onto an unsuitable adult companion. For who, but one's mother (or so he'd heard) is ever quite perfect and attentive enough? Even Irving intended to scratch his name in the sexual annals of his time, once his intellectual grooming was complete. And he'd do it like Paul Gaylord, without Romance. I seemed to be facing precisely the wrong way, seeking chastity where there was only smut; imagining love where there was only mockery. *Borax* should have trained me better (or perhaps not so well); it wasn't just shabby furniture that had a coded ticket on the back, it wasn't just sofas that had two prices. My mother knew that, I knew it, and both of us had problems dealing with the knowledge. I created fantasies: no codes, no tickets. My mother only stayed in her converted office and occasionally, I knew, she wept.

How much of this was apparent to me then, I'll never know. Sometimes I think I knew from the age of five, that first intervention. I only know that seventeen was a period of passion: unacted, murdered passion in my life when the school, the store, the houses, the streets were teeming with bodies, all of them (if I squinted just right or put on my magic Paul Gaylord glasses and forgot what I knew or thought I knew about decent human behaviour) writhing with desire, all of them hot and uncomfortable in their clothes, all of them willing for a price, for a wink, for a crook of the finger, to take it off, take it all-l-ll off.

Our store's third anniversary fell in August, and my father wanted to celebrate it big. Drawings and door prizes, hostesses, balloons and magic acts, refreshments, ads in the papers, the radio and twice on television (what is it about car salesmen and furniture dealers that makes them want to do their own commercials?). We hired a DJ to originate his show all day from "the magical showrooms of Greenwood's Interiors" (although every time I overheard him it had come out "Greenberg's" and I could see that the paper cups of iced tea he was sipping were only for show; he had bourbon in his coffee cup). It was an extravaganza timed to coincide not only with the anniversary but with my father's greatest moment in furniture: the opening of a second store.

"Little Brothers" had been our biggest competitor in South Palestra. Bloodsuckers, my father called them. He so hated Little Brothers that he could only spit the name out, along with the inside dope that The Brothers were really Moe and Harry Klein, *borax* personified, who'd been trailing my father like hyenas through half a dozen ventures all the way from Florida to Palestra. Now the brothers had had a falling-out, after twenty years of dyspeptic partnership. They'd tried to sell to anyone but us: their hatred of my father was equally resplendent. Finally they'd passed the word, through the bank, that they were throwing it in. My father was delirious; if one act can be said to vindicate a life, this might have been it for my father.

Until I'd gotten too well-known, I'd been dispatched to Little Brothers every couple of weeks to do my code-breaking and comparison-shopping and at least once a day I'd manage to drive past their low, modern store to count the cars out front and gloat—or panic. When we all gathered in the bank to sign the various papers, Moe Klein grumbled that we'd sucked them dry, us and our discounting, our foreign help, our cheap immigrant ways, hiring family and paying nothing, living like . . . well, *he'd* driven past our duplex and seen it and he knew our car was three years old . . . living like coolies. Well, he and his wife couldn't take it anymore. If that's the way we wanted to play, then life wasn't worth it, it was too short. We were jackals ("Not you, missus, you're a refined lady, I can see that"—but *him*, my father, he wasn't human, he didn't know no mercy, no kindness). It was a revelation to me, that other people didn't work as hard as my parents, didn't live or expect to live curled like worms around a core of absence and denial, that people expected more to life than eggs on a hot plate and mugs of instant coffee.

And it was the greatest revelation that we'd won. They hadn't been sucking us dry—we'd done it first! The bank commended us for never missing a payment, for being admirable risks despite a certain . . . well . . . initial doubt they'd had over earlier failures, age, and an unpromising location.

There was nothing unpromising about Little Brothers'. Low, long and modern in the plate-glass-and-cinder-block style of the distant suburbs, it was bright and air-conditioned and on each of my visits I'd felt shame for our store and merchandise (*no wonder they're murdering us*, I'd thought: *they're better than we are*). Like my father, Moe and Harry had always stayed in the office (a proper office, not a ladies' room with a desk) and actual clerks had come over to me in a minute or two: a sibilant young man with polished manners, or an attractive older woman (wife of a Klein, I'd always assumed), slightly overdressed and overmade-up for the setting, more like a Mexican hostess than a saleslady, with large black eyes and dramatic green eye shadow, gold hoop earrings and sequined glasses hanging from a chain, whose voice, figure, clothes and swaying walk had made me think of a single word: *showgirl*. She'd always been the best part of my espionage; it didn't take much to set me off. I wondered now, if like chattel, we took over the clerks, too; if she were to serve us in her Rhonda Fleming blouse and tight skirt. It was exciting to think, that bright blue August morning in the bank as the keys and papers were turned over to us, that like a conquering army we'd taken possession of everything: air conditioners (a place to go when hay fever struck), office, inventory and showgirl—if she were not a wife. But when the Kleins got in their black sedans. I saw two old, coiffed blond women with rings on most fingers already inside, and not the showgirl. And I realized we had made a very complete and unconditional conquest.

The plan was that my mother would continue to operate the old Greenwood Interiors by herself. Franz would be transferred and Gaylord would drive for both stores, at his own request. We would retain Little Brothers' employees with the young man being transferred to help my mother. Hence the extravaganza: Greenwood's was here to stay, prospering and getting bigger. Outside of the downtown stores we would soon be the largest retailer in all of Palestra. My father talked of building a house out in the hills, once I left for college. He talked of turning over the store and taking his first vacation—up to Montreal to look up the friends and relatives who'd always doubted him—or maybe down to Florida for a month. Arthur Godfrey's Florida, the unreal Florida that had always eluded us. Or Acapulco, I suggested. A brave day, then, dreaming like that. August before hay fever, before college, the high, ripe summer of our success. *Enjoy it.* I thought, and even my mother seemed happy. I allowed myself to think the pollen might spare me that summer, for once.

This time I knew we'd get a crowd. They started coming at nine o'clock, thinned out at lunch, bulged again in the afternoon and then descended in a crush after supper. I stayed as long as I could in the back with Franz, whom nothing could distract. People wandered in; Franz shouted them out. Occasionally I'd go out to the main floor. For the first time, the fireplace was entirely hidden by people. Blackthorne had cleared a space near the Rug Bar where balloon-toting children had gathered to watch a few shabby tricks with silk scarves and ping-pong balls. Not up to his standard. He acted as though he didn't remember me, and I avoided service as a volunteer. My mother stayed in her office, pleading a headache. It was as loud as a basketball court out there; the DJ's music on loudspeakers, a bingo-caller, announcements of door-prize winners every hour: my father loved it. Our new clerks weren't bashful—they even managed to write up some sales.

Sheila Roberts—the showgirl—was especially active. She posed with my father for the publicity shots, and when she bent over to demonstrate the convertible sofas—and held the pose, head up and laughing with the blouse falling loose—I could feel the electricity, among the men. And of course in myself. And when she smiled for the camera it was as though I'd already seen the final glossy—she had a show-biz way of projecting a pose, eyes sparkling, lips moist, smile warm and natural, the moment the shutter fell. She seemed to know most of the salesmen and buyers who stopped in during the day for a drink and a handshake; she'd been married to a furniture man who'd died. No matter where she stood on that crowded floor, she seemed to stand out, as though over the blare of music and a hundred people loudly babbling, I could hear the tinkle of her bracelets.

She even came back to the back, where Franz and I were talking. She was holding a paper cup of punch and she seemed just a little flushed. I didn't quite know the etiquette of dealing with her: she was help, after all, and I'd seen enough of her in the first week to consider her crude and vulgar. And, of course, exciting, like a stripper. "And whose little boy are you?" she asked, or demanded. Her voice was slurred and the tone cutting.

"David Greenwood."

"Da-vid. Green-wood. You don't say."

I smiled.

"And who's that over there who doesn't even stop working when a lady enters the room?" Franz looked up and went back to his work.

"God damnit, I'm talking to you. What's your name?"

I told her it was Franz. She'd never get a name out of him.

"What's the matter? You his manager or something?"

Franz looked up. "I speak."

"Oh, good—I'm honoured. You also hear?"

"*Ja.* I hear very good."

"And you—you hear good, too?"

I told her I did.

"Good. That's very good. Because I only say things once." Her fingers strayed over her blouse, touching her turquoise jewellery, then finally resting on her bosom. "I was working—no, I was *schlepping*—five years for Harry Klein. I gave him five good years. Hard years, but I didn't complain. And Harry Klein sure didn't, either."

I watched. My eyes were on her fingers, their enamelled red nails, as they fluttered idly on her bosom. Franz had gone back to work; I wished I'd had a way of showing my indifference. "Five of my best years—" and her voice had a whine in it, something close to tears. I looked up and her eyes were moist, but hard. "Then his brother pulls out. Wasn't his brother, really. It was Harry's wife made him pull out."

"Why's that?"

"Shut up. Little . . . fat . . . queer."

"What do you mean calling me that?"

"Just to show you where you stand. You're not a tenth the man your father is. Would you tell that bastard to quit working?"

Franz slowed down and looked up. "Why must I stop?"

"I said to."

"You don't give orders to me."

"I give orders to you *and to you*," she said. "Lou just gave me the authority. And not only do I tell you two where to get off—I also tell *her*, too."

"*Her*?"

"You want me to spell it out?"

It was too monstrous to believe. This *creature*, giving orders to my mother. I stood, my hands tight little fists.

"You give orders to me?" Franz demanded. "You give orders to Missus Greenwood?"

"That's the size of it. Check with Lou if you don't believe me."

At this Franz began a familiar daily ritual: stacking his bottles of stain in the cabinet, then the knives and the burner and the sticks of finish. He didn't say goodbye to anyone, but simply carried his cabinet out to the Hudson and drove away.

"Good riddance," she said, standing by the door, the very place my father had stood and cried after Joe Whitehouse's visit. We were alone in the back, and even the main floor sounded strangely quiet. My brain was filled with cotton. I couldn't think; I didn't want to think. I felt suddenly at ease with her, free to try anything I wanted.

I'd meant to warn her, merely test her seriousness. But it came out differently. "You give any orders to my mother and I'll break your neck," I said, in a burst of glorious lust and hatred. It was all I could do to stay put, not to advance like Frankenstein's monster, hands out, fingers ready to close around her. My warning didn't surprise her.

"I already told her we wouldn't be needing her anymore. Tommy's a good salesman—he can handle this place alone."

I must have snickered. "I know he's good," she said. "I raised him myself. I told you, we waited five years for that goddamn store to fall in our laps. Then we lost it. I'm not losing this one."

"What in the hell do you *mean*—not losing it? What makes you think you've got it?"

I was standing close to her now, five steps away, and my breath was short, arms trembling, hands still clenched.

"One thing," she said.

"What?"

"Want me to show you?"

I didn't answer. Perhaps I expected a gun, something she could hold and point and threaten me with. But of course that wasn't it. The bracelets tinkled violently even before I saw her move, and in an instant I was confronting a lady with her skirt held high and nothing on underneath, and as in a dream I was advancing, my hands open and ice cold, advancing not for the throat but on that vision: oh, I knew so suddenly *everything*, how the parts and the passions fitted and I swear it was a moment of love—unashamed and inviolate and heedless of consequence. Then my own small pistol went off in a loud report, doubling me over as she dropped her skirt the moment my fingers touched her there and she was gone and the music came back louder than ever and I found myself clutching the same door frame for support until the spasms passed and then I ran far from the parked cars to lie in the grass under the sun and to wait for the god to invade my blood.

Clark Blaise (1940–), Canadian and American, is the author of 20 books of fiction and nonfiction. A longtime advocate for the literary arts in North America, Blaise has taught writing and literature at Emory, Skidmore, Columbia, NYU, Sir George Williams, UC-Berkeley, SUNY-Stony Brook, and the David Thompson University Centre. In 1968, he founded the postgraduate Creative Writing Program at Concordia University; he after went on to serve as the Director of the International Writing Program at Iowa (1990–1998), and as President of the Society for the Study of the Short Story (2002–present). Internationally recognized for his contributions to the field, Blaise has received an Arts and Letters Award for Literature from the American Academy (2003), and in 2010 was made an Officer of the Order of Canada. Blaise now divides his time between New York and San Francisco, where he lives with his wife, American novelist Bharati Mukherjee.